Purgatory

Down in the forward hold of the stricken Familyship there was less water sloshing around now, and the planking was flexing very little. A sheen of water still trickled down the boards, but there seemed to be no bad leaks.

Molele was there, looking considerably worse for wear. Her hair had escaped from the bandana that was supposed to be keeping it out of her eyes. Her skirt clung damply to her legs and her blouse was torn. She and a younger girl were in the process of moving a plank along the wall so that she could reach a spot that needed more caulking.

Cheynou helped lift the board into place. "Had a rough night?"

She leaned on it, her body sagging. "Pretty bad. It's just so damned frustrating! We get it all caulked, and then a big wave hits and water starts coming in somewhere. We fix that, and it comes in somewhere else. I don't know what to do!"

"You might consider stopping."

"I can't. As long as we keep the caulking in we don't have to pump, and everybody's so tired. We just have to keep going."

He took her by the shoulders and turned her away from her work. "No, you don't. The shipwrights have to finish repairing that rib. Then they can support the weaker planks so that they'll stop flexing and spitting your caulking out."

"Oh. That's good, because I'm…just…so…tired."

To his dismay, she burst into sobs, standing there with her hands limp at her sides, the tears running down her already-wet cheeks.

He glanced helplessly at the craftsman, who frowned and made a 'go to her' gesture with his head. Rolling his eyes, Cheynou did so, putting his arms around the girl and holding her head to his chest. The carpenter grinned, clouted his gawking assistant on the shoulder and went to work.

As the girl's sobs slowly calmed, he released her until he was standing with one hand on her shoulder and the other behind her head. When she looked up at him, he shook her slightly. "Did you work all night?"

"I had to."

"Molele, there are two or three hundred people on this ship. Some of them presumably know how to do caulking."

"Well, yes, but they were all so tired."

"And you aren't?"

"I am now, I guess."

"Well, your mother has had a good sleep and is looking very chipper this morning. You, on the other hand, would be a disgrace to be seen on deck. Scurry off and clean yourself up, and report to the bridge deck."

"Aye, sir."

"I like you when you're tired. You don't argue so much."

"Don't think of taking advantage of it."

"Me? Take advantage of a poor, tired girl I just rescued from a terrible death? Where do you find these awful ideas?"

Her head lifted. "Just keep your mind fixed on that 'terrible death.' It could be arranged."

She swung past him, a lift to her step, and he followed, shaking his head.

PATH OF WATER

PETRELLAN SAGA 3

Gordon A. Long

AIRBORN PRESS

Delta, B. C.

Path of Water

Gordon A. Long

Published by
AIRBORN PRESS
4958 10A Ave, Delta, B. C.
V4M 1X8
Canada

ISBN: 978-1-988898-21-6

Printed by Amazon

Cover Design by Mihaela Voicu

More from Gordon A. Long

"Factory 4-80" Freighty 1
"Outback Rebellion" Freighty 2
"Asimov's Laws" Freighty 3

"Ocean of Grass" Petrellan Saga 1
"Waves of Stone" Petrellan Saga 2
"Zoysana's Choice" Petrellan Saga 4
"The Innkeeper's Husband" Petrellan Saga 5
Coming in early 2021:
"Mercenary's Dream" Petrellan Saga 6

"Out of Mischief" World of Change Book 1
"Into Trouble" World of Change Book 2
"Mountains of Mischief" World of Change Book 3
"The Trouble with Tents" World of Change Book 4
"Queen of Mischief" World of Change Book 5

"A Sword Called...Kitten?" Romantic Comedy with an Edge
"The Cat with Many Claws" Sword Called Kitten Book 2
"Cloud Cat" Sword Called Kitten Book 3

"Why Are People So Stupid?" Social Humour with a Point

Look for Gordon's books, selected reviews, poetry and short
stories at <airbornpress.ca>
Gordon's opinions on humanity are at the
"Are People Stupid?" blog
Find his weekly reviews and his ideas on writing at
"Renaissance Writer"

CONTENTS

Thanks

To Cas Peace for her ever-vigilant editing.

1. ENTERTAINMENT ON THE ROAD

Cheynou shifted in the saddle, contemplating the long voyage ahead of him, then twisted to look back at the carriages following. It was a pleasant spring day. The road was smooth, the sun wasn't too hot and they were making good time.

Yet he couldn't shake the idea that was running around his head. He turned to his companion. "Kendra, I have to ask you something."

She tossed her head, indicating her small passenger. "Something important?"

Cheynou grinned and glanced over his shoulder at the dark little head behind his own saddle. "They seem to be occupied."

The twins were busily taking advantage of being on horseback instead of in their mother's carriage. Every insect, every new tree or building, every blade of grass seemed fuel for their active, five-year-old imaginations. Fortunately, they spent most of their energy communicating these ideas to each other, so their transports could have a conversation of their own.

"So?"

He made his face serious. "Do you find me amusing?"

"Constantly."

He sighed. "All right. Wrong question. Let me start from the beginning."

"We have all day."

"Not that far back." He took a moment to organize his thoughts. "This is a 'spider webs in the hair,' problem, Kendra. I might be making a mistake."

She immediately dropped her smile. "Of course. What is it?"

"I was talking to Miranra this morning. Just chatting, you know, as we rode along. Out of the blue, she laughed at something I said. I must have looked at her strangely because she stopped, laughed again in a different way and said, 'Oh, Cheynou, you are so entertaining.' The problem was, I wasn't trying to be entertaining. I thought we were having a perfectly normal conversation."

"Which, with you, can be highly entertaining."

"It can?"

"Well, sometimes you have the strangest ideas."

"I do?"

"Of course you do. You are a completely original person and from a different culture as well. Many of the things you say are...different."

"So, you all laugh at me."

"At times, you really do say the funniest things."

"Oh."

They rode in silence for a while. "You aren't upset, are you?"

"I'm trying to decide whether I should be. If everyone is laughing at what I say, I suppose I am."

She reined her horse near to his and laid a hand on his arm. "Cheynou, don't you be silly, now. They all laugh, but they all love you. It's different."

"What?"

She took a moment to disengage her small passenger, who was trying to pull his brother out of his seat behind Cheynou's saddle.

"You heard what I said."

"That's not why I requested a repeat."

"Oh, Cheynou. Of course they love you. Don't you know that?"

"I assumed that they all liked me, liked both of us. That's pretty obvious, the way they treat us, but I wouldn't be tossing the word 'love' around so freely."

She sighed. "Cheychan, you are so dense sometimes."

He sighed louder. "Please enlighten me."

"Look at it this way. Cruzon and Cedenye are never going to have children, right?"

"I guess not."

"So they see you as the son they could have had. Would have liked to have had."

"They do?"

She grinned. "Oh, yes. It's very convenient for them. They never had to go through the 'crying all night' stage, or the 'I'm a real person, why don't you treat me as one?' stage. They have this already-mature, intelligent individual whom they can treat as their son, enjoy his company, worry about his progress, glory in his achievements."

He nodded, reaching back to rescue his passenger, who was determined to slide off the horse's rump. "All right. I can see Cruzon and Cedenye. What about Maksa and Miranra? They have no special reason to love a stranger." He ruffled Jode's hair. "And they certainly have enough of this to keep them busy."

She chuckled. "A barbarian from beyond the mountains you may be, but you are far from being a stranger to these people. Maksa and Miranra are in the middle of raising these two," she pointed a thumb over her shoulder, "and they look at all the young men of their acquaintance to see what their sons might turn out to be."

He shrugged. "Unless they think it would be a good idea to raise a son who goes off gallivanting around the world, far from home in untold dangers, possibly never to return, maybe they had better not look to me."

She froze, her hand raised, her face turned toward him, frowning. Finally, she spoke. "Is that what your parents think about our journey?"

He shrugged, uncomfortable. "I don't know what they think. It's a possibility."

She rode in silence for a long while, the frown still hovering. She reached back absent-mindedly and hitched Taden into a safer position, then turned to Cheynou. "I never thought about that. I didn't consider what my parents would be thinking. Not seriously."

He shrugged. "I guess it's the same for all parents when their children go away. They handle it the best they can. Some better, some worse. I always figured it must be sort of a relief, actually."

"A relief?"

3

"Certainly. Your child is gone, out of your control. Whatever problems he gets into," he grinned over at her, "or she gets into, well, you just can't do anything about it. So you can't really worry about it, can you?"

"Hah! That shows what you know about motherhood."

"I'm expected to know something about motherhood?"

"Mothers always worry about what they can't do anything about."

"They do? Well, they shouldn't. I worry about what I can do something about. If I can't do anything about it, what's the point?"

She shook her head. "I envy you."

"What for this time?"

She reined her horse closer again to clout him on the shoulder. Both passengers squealed in glee.

He ducked the main force of the blow with the ease of long practice, and they jogged on peacefully for a while.

"Do you think it's time to return these two to their rightful place?"

"Yes. I think they're getting bored." Cheynou looked back at his passenger. "They're starting to listen to what we're saying."

She glanced over her shoulder in mock horror. "That's one aspect of parenthood I'm not ready for."

"Along with a lot of other aspects."

They turned out of the road to wait for the carriage to catch up. Unloading the protesting pair into their mother's arms, they dusted their hands ostentatiously, mopped their brows and cantered their horses ahead.

"You didn't really answer my question."

"You didn't really ask it. Are you worried why they laugh at you?"

"Not worried, but I'd like to understand. It isn't very comfortable, you know, to realize that your friends, the people who apparently love you, are laughing at you."

"Cheynou, don't be upset."

4

"I don't think I'm upset. But I want understand."

She slumped in the saddle for a moment, thinking. "Let's look at it this way. Look from the point of view of Cruzon and Cedenye, dealing with Faranos."

"All right. They're trying to develop him into the kind of person who could take over from them and run the Rochana Home when they are old."

"Correct. How are they doing?"

"I don't know. Fine, I guess. He's young and he's got a lot to learn."

She actually giggled, something Kendra rarely did. "Listen to yourself, old man. He's only a year younger than you. Do you see what that means?"

He thought a moment. "I guess not."

She shook her head. "Cheychan, you are so smart, and so stupid."

He rolled his eyes. "If I knew the answer to this unspoken question, I wouldn't be asking you. If it makes you feel good, tell me. If you're not going to tell me, don't waste my time."

She shrugged. "If you want to follow your old teacher, Sarasha, you'd know that there's no point in telling you. You need to figure it out for yourself, or the answer is useless."

"It's not that important. I don't *need* to figure it out. I just want to. It would make me feel better." He glanced over and brushed a hand along the side of his head. "Unless there's a spider web in my hair, in which case it would be really kind of you to let me know before I make a fool of myself or worse."

"Exactly. If it was something that really might affect your future, I would tell you. And it won't."

He glanced at her a second time. *She either can't or won't tell me. Fair enough.*

He tossed her a shrug and a grin and gazed down the road again. Then a thought struck him. "What about you?"

"What about me?"

"You said they all love me. What about you?"

5

She shrugged, grinned. "Everybody is expected to like me. Was there ever any question?"

He stared at her long enough to show that he had not missed her evasion, then faced the front again. The topic was definitely closed.

He gazed along their little caravan. "I miss Cinders."

"Martan, too. But they're happier where they are."

"Yes, Cinders will be the mother of a long line of loyal and intelligent herding dogs."

"And Martan will end his life protecting the sheep in the mountains to the south. They have found what they came for."

"But we have not. So, on we go."

Kendra, too, faced forward, sitting straighter in the saddle. "On we go. Barbarians from the south about to assail the capital of the Kyabran Empire and bring them to their knees. We couldn't be better prepared."

"That is very true. We couldn't be any better prepared than we are, because that's how prepared we are." He shook his head. "Of course, we couldn't be worse prepared than we are, either."

2. APPROACH TO KYABRAEN

They rode along beside the Eastern Panjhali River for a few days while the road got wider and firmer, the farms and towns grew in size and ostentation and the inhabitants grew more numerous and prosperous. Twice they "dropped in" on people who treated Miranra as an old friend. People with large manor houses by any standard.

And life became more formal. The servants took better care of their clothes. Dressing for dinner became the normal procedure. And worst of all, the training with Maksa stopped. The officer no longer worked out with his men in the evenings, and Cheynou got the feeling that his own in-between status made them uncomfortable with him on the practice field here in civilized climes.

Then the road divided in the middle of a huge caravansary and market area, and they cut east to Kyabraen, the City of the Emperor.

Now the way was paved with flagstones and wide enough for two carriages the size of Miranra's to pass. It made for easy, if noisy, travelling with the carriage wheels setting up a constant rattle, backed by the clopping of the shod hooves of the horses.

"You certainly couldn't sneak up on anyone on this road."

Kendra regarded the sloping ditches. "And nowhere to set up an ambush. We must be in real civilization."

Cheynou nodded towards a troop of soldiers marching stolidly towards them. "Which doesn't necessarily mean we're safe."

"I suspect here the danger comes from within the hierarchy rather than from outsiders."

He grinned. "We're outsiders. Does that mean we're not dangerous?"

"You never know. We're going to have to watch what we say and who we talk to."

"Agreed." He slowed his mount and Miranra pulled alongside. She was riding today, on some sort of contraption that allowed her to sit with both legs on the same side of the horse. He wondered how she would stay on at a gallop.

She glanced at them. "Serious faces. What's up?"

Cheynou gestured towards the road ahead of them. "Just wondering what awaits. Who we might meet. What fate has in store for us."

Kendra grinned. "Also, what new dangers may arise, since there are no bandits, avalanches and wild animals to worry about."

The Kyabran woman nodded. "Very prudent. The Capital is full of danger of a political nature. If someone decides you're a threat, you have to take steps. There's no sense in waiting for an attack just to be polite."

"Do you have such enemies?"

She laughed. "No, we ducked a lot of that when we left for Velika. Out there, we're no threat to anyone in the capital." She mused a moment. "Of course, there are always my family's traditional enemies. I tend to forget them. They're a fact of life."

Kendra frowned. "Then we are targets as well. What can we do to protect ourselves?"

"It's not that kind of danger." Miranra waved a languid hand. "No ruffians will be lying in wait in dark alleys. At least, none we know...it's hard to explain. I'll talk to my father. He'll fill me in, and I'll tell you what you need to watch out for."

"How long before we get to Kyabraen?"

"One more day."

Cheynou nodded. "I thought the road was getting crowded."

"Wait until you get close to the capital." She laughed. "This is nothing. Kyabraen is the largest city in the world."

"That we know of."

She glanced at him. "A good point, but not one I would go spreading around. People with big empires tend to be touchy about their reputations. I can't think why."

He laughed as well. "Don't worry about us. I'm very good at playing the impressed yokel, because that's what I am. Kendra will fit in as if she was born here. That's her skill."

Miranra glanced at Kendra's skeptical face. "In spite of the language problem?"

He scoffed. "A minor inconvenience. It's how you act that counts."

"A good point." The Kyabran nodded. "I'm sure you're right, and I'll introduce you to some very nice people who will welcome you appropriately."

Cheynou nodded. "Do you think there will be opportunities for us here in the capital?"

Miranra gave an elegant shrug. "If you like, but we can do better than that."

"You can?"

"Of course. I told you back in Rochana Home. I have family in Port Tenet. Maksa has it already set up that we will be doing business in that area." She glanced behind and beckoned to her husband, who trotted his horse ahead.

"What is this little group plotting, out here in the open where no one can get close enough to hear you?"

She flicked her fingers as if to brush off a pest. "Planning our moves for the next little while. Do you wish to contribute?"

Maksa turned his attention to the two explorers. "As it happens, I have business elsewhere for the next month. I will be taking the boys to visit their grandparents. With our new trading in the Velikan area, there are possibilities I must discuss with my family. However," he included his wife in the conversation, "I wouldn't expect you to be interested in those boring financial details, my dear, when you could be visiting your cousins on the seashore," he smiled theatrically, "and incidentally perhaps exploring some shipping opportunities?"

She nodded. "I'll run these two out to Port Tenet, get them established there, introduce them around, do some business on the side, and then I can join you and the boys at Mandir, or you could bring them to us at Tenet."

Cheynou shook his head. This was going too fast for him. "Get us established?"

"Yes. Kendra and I have already talked about it. She needs a place of her own because you'll be aboard ship a lot. She doesn't want to stay in an inn alone, and we'll be travelling around too much."

"You already discussed it?" His eyes turned to Kendra.

"Yes. I'm looking for a place to stay for a while. I'm not like you. I don't mind travelling to get somewhere, but I don't enjoy traipsing up and down the country all the time. Cruzon has granted me an allowance if I act as his agent in that area, making contacts with merchants who are sending goods down the Kernegata River. I'm going to Port Tenet." She smiled sweetly at him. "What are you going to do?"

He shrugged. "When do I ever get to make a decision?"

"You want to make a decision, but what you need is a boat."

"Couldn't agree more. Let's go!" He spun his horse and trotted down the road, not looking back because he knew they were laughing at him. It didn't bother him at all.

3. THE LION'S DEN

Kyabraen, the City of the Emperor, was everything Cheynou expected it to be. Including being much larger, more beautiful and also uglier than he had predicted, which didn't surprise him a whole lot, either.

The Rimmon mansion stood in its own grounds, capping a hillside on the upwind slope of the bustling, crowded city. It was a low, rambling structure with several different styles of architecture, giving evidence to the long, slow ascendency of this powerful family. In general, it followed the usual pattern of Kyabran construction: thick walls painted in light colours to reflect the sunlight, which the travellers from the South found intimidating in its own right.

The interior was also ruled by the climate, with open passages, fountains and courtyards shaded by many types of trees, some resplendent in their spring blossoms. The dimmer inside rooms were cooled by errant breezes, and the beleaguered eye was soothed by dark wood and soft, pastel fabrics.

Even Kendra was awed. She buttonholed her travelling partner the first chance they got in private. "These people are seriously upper class, Cheynou."

"I had noticed." His hand swept around to indicate the high-ceilinged room. Its marble walls were hung with lush swags of light purple and green, the family colours.

"No, no, it's not the luxury or the money. It's power. Political clout."

He grinned. "You can smell it, can't you?"

She flicked his arm with her fingertips rather than the usual swat to the shoulder. "And we must act accordingly."

He shrugged. "I don't have to worry about that."

"You what?" She stared at him. "This is our big chance to be accepted in this society. You be polite to people."

"Kendra, in case it had escaped your notice, I am unfailingly polite to everyone." He tipped his head to one side. "It's really the only way to act when you have no idea who you're supposed to be polite to."

She sighed. "Yes, you're right. It's so easy for you. I have to learn everything so quickly, including the language, and you just bumble through and everyone accepts you. It's hardly fair, you know."

"That's what I brought you for. You or Miranra — or even Jode or Tad, for that matter — will always step in and cover up any little slips I make. I'll be fine."

"We'll be putting that to the test very soon, my young friend."

They both turned. Miranra herself stood there, her dress far more ornate than any they had seen in Velika, her hair piled high and intertwined with pearls.

Kendra stepped back in awe. "Are you going to a party?"

The noblewoman smiled. "No, just returning from an afternoon renewing old friendships. Profitably, as it happens."

Cheynou regarded her. "And this has something to do with my good manners?"

"As it also happens, yes. Would you like to meet the emperor?"

Her gracious smile turned to a grin. "Don't stand there gawping at me like a couple of yokels." She took the arm of each and led them into a small, comfortable sitting room. Her quick glance and nod sent a nearby serving woman dashing off.

"Now sit down, and I'll tell you all about it while we're waiting for our tea." She indicated their chairs and sank with what she probably considered an unladylike flop onto a silk-embroidered divan. From there, she leveled a stare at them.

"Don't think that this has a whole lot to do with your personal importance. As I'm sure you have already figured out, there was movement afoot in your direction before you came over the mountains. Some kind of contact between our peoples was inevitable. It just happened to be you."

"Lest we get feeling uppity and important."

She wrinkled her brow at him. "Oh, you're important all right. Especially to Cruzon and the Cheolean family and their allies. If things here go well for you, they go well for all of us."

Kendra nodded. "We understand. And what has this to do with the emperor?"

"Emperor Trahan IV is a wise and far-seeing man. He also appreciates the aid of his supporters. Of which my father is one of the strongest. By bringing you to Kyabraen, we have signalled a new stage in our development of Velika, spurred, of course, by our new knowledge of markets and sources beyond the mountains.

"So he will signal his approval of our projects by receiving the leader of the foreign expedition at a formal viewing." She smiled at Cheynou. "Don't worry too much about messing it up. You're only on display as a symbol of the new direction the Empire is looking."

"In case I got puffed up with my own importance."

She tapped his nose with her fan. "Not that I ever feared you would. Follow my lead, keep your head down and exude that earnest courtesy you do so well. It will be over before you know it."

Kendra frowned. "You make it sound like he's having a tooth pulled. Why keep his head down?"

"Because in a formal viewing no one is allowed to look at the emperor's face. That is important, Cheynou. I can guide you in everything except where your eyes point."

He shrugged. "I can follow the guidelines of a new society, no matter how weird they are."

"You consider our customs weird?"

He faced her. "Miranra, do you really believe that an empty gesture like looking at the floor makes any difference to the people who actually count?"

She gave her gentle smile. "Those gestures are meant for another group that counts."

"The general populace."

"Precisely."

"I see. Well, don't worry. I'll perform in your little charade…" he held up a finger to stop her "…your huge, ornate, and very important charade, and I'll do my best not to be seen snickering behind my hand."

She tapped his nose again, harder this time. "See that you do, young man. Snickering is definitely off limits in the emperor's court."

* * *

It was fifteen days before Cheynou and Miranra found themselves entering the Imperial Palace. According to her, that was no wait at all, and demonstrated the importance the emperor placed on their projects. Cheynou, who had spent the time being bombarded with instructions from a worried Kendra, merely nodded with appropriate sobriety. He was nervous enough that he didn't trust himself to handle their usual repartée.

As they moved on through the crowd and the ceremony, Cheynou compared it all to the Priest-Admiral's rites on the Flagship, and came to the early conclusion that there was little difference. A great many people found it important to be in a certain spot at a certain time to perform some arcane duty that forced everyone else to stop and wait until they were finished. Once that hurdle was passed, the visitor was allowed to go and stand in line for the next performance.

This gave Cheynou leisure to observe what was going on around him. The Palace was huge, with tall stone columns holding ornately carved arches. For Cheynou, whose only use for rock was ballast, ammunition for catapults or weighing down the bodies of the dead, all this stone seemed a bit overdone. It was impressive, though, and he assumed that this must be the effect that the builders desired.

The people around him were more interesting. Each had a distinctive costume, versions of the same basic pattern: loose pants covered by a flowing, belted robe with wide sleeves.

14

Women's robes were longer than men's but both sexes had braided hair, some in intricate patterns. He assumed most of them could tell what each small difference signified.

He had the growing impression that these people were only good for either holding visitors from progressing or observing them and making comments behind their backs. Probably with the purpose of impeding their progress in another way at another time.

It took them over one bell to get through the entrance hallways. Then they became attached to someone called a 'majordomo' whose duty was to lead them through the rituals but, it seemed to Cheynou, only served to make the ceremonies longer.

Finally, they could actually see the Reception Room. Miranra used the hand poised formally on Cheynou's arm to give him a reassuring squeeze. Then they were moving ahead.

They paused in the doorway, waiting for the majordomo person to motion them forward, and Cheynou was able to view the throne.

The emperor was old. This came as a surprise to Cheynou, but his next immediate thought was, *why should I be surprised?* It was just that no one had ever mentioned the emperor's age before. *I wonder if it isn't polite.*

He was so interested that he missed the signal, but at Miranra's nudge he moved into the room, trying to look around without gawking. It was lofty and bright, with soaring pillars and many windows with shutters thrown wide. Colourful hangings softened the stone of the walls, and exotic — at least to Cheynou's eyes — plants grew in a profusion of pots and planters.

The form of the Audience was much like a Conclave back on the Ship, with important people in their assigned places. He could almost tell from where they sat relative to the throne and the expressions on their faces who was important, who was on his way up, who was on his way out.

"So, Miranra. You have decided to grace us with your lovely presence again. It has been too long." The voice matched the emperor's age:, raspy but not weak.

"Thank you, your Majesty."

"How is life in the wilds of the south?"

"My sons thrive, your Majesty, and the Empire stands firm."

"Miranra, you are by far the cleverest manipulator of the Kyabran language I have had the pleasure to meet."

"Flattery from one such as yourself is high praise, your Majesty."

"You dare to accuse your emperor of flattery?"

"Only to emphasize the modest level of my abilities, your Majesty."

A gravelly chuckle. "I will allow you to redeem yourself. What is this present you have found for me in the wilderness?"

"Your Majesty, I beg leave to present to you Cheynou Chan, of the Navigator's Craft of the Familyship Sea Eagle, brought here under the sponsorship of the Rochana Family."

"A Navigator. Should I have heard of this Familyship, the Eagle?"

"No, your Majesty." Cheynou fought the urge to look up. "We sailed on the Great Southern Ocean, and our Ship was Beached two years ago."

"A Navigator without a ship."

"Yes, your Majesty. My people now live on the Great Prairie, south of what you call the Barrier Range."

"I see. And what brings you to our empire and our court?"

"Navigation, your Majesty. It is my desire to explore and map wherever I can, and when I discovered there was a whole new people living here, I came to find out about you."

Again the raspy chuckle. "So we are being investigated by an explorer from another society. That rather turns things around, doesn't it?"

"From your point of view it might, your Majesty."

"And I suppose you have many stories of your hardship and trials and the act of bravery in coming over the prairies and mountains to find us."

"I do not wish to disappoint you, your Majesty, but I had good planning, good companionship and, except for the condition of the trail, made a reasonably uneventful trip here."

"Hmm. Honesty, anyway. And if this jaunt is so easy, why haven't I sent my armies over the pass to claim that land for my Empire?"

"Two people on foot, one donkey and a dog, your Majesty."

"Ah. I see. Not the kind of trail for an army."

"And nothing at the end of it, your Majesty."

"Nothing?"

"A huge expanse of Prairie, fairly dry, with soil too poor to farm."

"I see. What do your people do to live on this arid steppe?"

"We herd, your Majesty. Cattle, sheep, goats, horses. We move frequently as the grazing dictates."

"Nomads."

"Yes, your Majesty. It suits us, having come from the ocean."

"Good enough."

"I'm sorry I have no great exploits with which to entertain you, your Majesty." He hoped the grammar was right on that sentence, but had nowhere to look for a reaction.

"I have little regard for great exploits, young man. I am not so interested in what you have done, except that your deeds tell me what kind of man you are. I am only interested in what you might do in the future, what good you might be to my Empire."

"Anything I can do that will profit your Empire and benefit my people, your Majesty."

"You qualify your desire to please me, young man."

"I must, if I am to speak honestly, your Majesty. What is the worth to you of loyalty that is easily thrown aside for a new master?"

"You, a barbarian, see fit to question me?"

"I apologize for my barbaric form of expression, your Majesty. Lady Miranra has been trying to drill me in the proper forms of respect."

The emperor snorted and tapped his long, wrinkled fingers on the arm of his throne.

"You speak reasonable Kyabran. How long have you lived with us?"

"Five months, your Majesty."

"But you spoke Kyabran before that."

"No, your Majesty, but your language is similar to the speech of the Western Continent, in which I was trained."

"The Western Continent?"

"Yes, your Majesty. Frasian is spoken by almost everyone else on this continent, and I assume that the Kyabrans must have come here from the Western Continent at some time in the far past. Your language has changed a great deal since."

The emperor did not respond, and Cheynou wondered if he had committed the unforgivable sin of boring him.

Finally, the emperor cleared his throat. It did not seem to change the rough tenor of his voice. "You may not know us well, young barbarian, but you have a better grasp of geography than many of my advisors. Tell me. How big do you think the world is?"

"How big, your Majesty? I...I...doubt if anyone has much of an idea. I would suggest, however, that it is probably twice as big as most of us think."

"Why exactly twice as big?"

"I would not like to bore your Majesty with mathematics, but I'm sure your wise men have noted that, as summer comes on, the sun rises higher and higher in the sky at noon. Then, as we turn to winter, its path is lower and lower in the sky."

"That is a well-known fact, here in the civilized world."

"You may guess, then, as we in the Southern Ocean have observed, that as you go farther and farther south, the winter sun rises lower and lower in the sky. We suppose that there must be a point where, at midwinter, the sun does not rise at all. No one has ever managed to reach this point, because by that time of the year, the sea is ice-covered."

"And what do you speculate might come after that?"

"We don't know, your Majesty, but our explorers found nothing past the coastline but ice and snow; the terrain is completely barren of life. So, as far as humans are concerned, the world ends there."

"As good a definition of the end of the world as many I have heard. You have not explained why this makes our world twice as big."

"To do that, your Majesty, we must now move north. It is equally possible to guess that there is some place in the world where, at midsummer, the sun rises directly to the east, follows its path to straight overhead, then sets directly in the west."

"This is more than possible. Our sailors have reached that point."

"They have?" His enthusiasm brought his eyes to the emperor's face. He looked down quickly. "May I ask what they found there?"

The emperor's voice seemed to smile. "Yes, you may ask, young searcher for knowledge. They found nothing. The ocean went on as before, to the horizon."

"That supports my theory, then, your Majesty. Due to the symmetry of nature, I suspect that there is an equal part of the world above that line, where the sun runs its path through the southern skies. I find that difficult to conceive, but I must allow the possibility. Whether that area contains land or anything useful to humans is yet to be discovered."

"But that same argument might apply in the opposite direction. Perhaps that means there is another part of the world, equally large, to the south. That could make the world four times as large. Perhaps there is a sunlit area like ours even farther south. Perhaps these zones repeat themselves, over and over, forever."

Cheynou thought furiously. Finally, he nodded. "Yes, your Majesty. I cannot escape my own logic. However…"

The emperor waited a moment. "However?"

"I do not wish to seem to disagree with your Majesty."

"Oh, please, my young friend. Disagree with me. It is such a rare pleasure."

He risked a quick glance; saw a cynical curl to the lip, but nothing more. "Such a formation would require another sun for each repetition. Our observations lead us to conclude that the sun is a very great distance away from the world. Surely, if there were another sun, an equal distance away, we would see it from here?"

The wrinkled hand on the arm of the chair flicked that idea off like a bothersome fly. "A specious argument. You argue the non-existence of something because of your inability to conceive of it being there."

"I cannot disagree with that, your Majesty."

"Of course you can't. Disagreeing with the emperor once is risky. Twice is stupidity."

Then one finger of that hand flicked towards him. "How about east and west?"

He tried not to pause too long to think. "The sun gives us no information, your Majesty. Our navigation tells us that if you go east or west on a line where the sun rises to a certain level, nothing changes, and the sun continues to follow its usual path, no matter how far anyone has gone in either direction."

"So, the world changes greatly to north and south, but stays the same to east and west."

"Yes, your Majesty. Except for the changing areas of land and water."

Again, there was silence, as the emperor mulled this over. Finally, he cleared his throat again. Cheynou glanced up and saw him register something off to the side, near the right-hand door. "I have little leisure for pleasant discussion of this sort, interesting though it may be. You have attained reasonable knowledge for your few years, and I think you truly seek wisdom. Visit me again when you have gained more of either."

Cheynou bowed and was about to turn away when the gravelly voice stopped him. "Don't wait too long." His startled glance flicked to the emperor's face, caught a glimpse of weary humour in those pale blue eyes.

He waited a moment, but the emperor spoke no more. He bowed again and followed the prescribed path to the door. Miranra made her own bow, then slid in beside him.

"Lady Miranra."

They both froze. She held him still with one hand and turned towards the emperor. "Your Majesty?"

"It is good to have you back, even for such a short time. As always, you bring novelty and grace to our court."

"Thank you, your Majesty."

Cheynou could not see what happened next, but her hand was in the formal position on his arm again, and they continued out between the bronzed columns and into the anterooms beyond.

There, her grasp turned into a friendly one, and they strolled together through the colonnaded gardens towards the city. Following her lead, he did not speak.

It was not until they had left the palace grounds and were walking on the public street that she spoke. "That was interesting."

"I would have to agree. Not necessarily pleasant, but interesting."

"Not pleasant?" She tugged at his arm, and he looked down at her.

"Not particularly. It is difficult to have a meeting of minds when there is such a gulf of protocol between two people that one cannot look the other in the face."

She shook his arm gently. "Ah, your barbarian notions of equality."

"No, Miranra, the Sea People have equally restrictive rites hedging their leaders about, keeping them from truly meeting anyone. It is only myself and my small group of friends who have these revolutionary thoughts."

"Are they truly revolutionary? Should we be speaking in hushed whispers behind thick doors?"

"No, they aren't really revolutionary at all. I believe that some people have to be leaders, and others have to follow. If a ship had no captain, there would be chaos. I have no problem with the emperor leading his Empire. It is the obvious manipulation of the protocol that I find onerous.

"For example. Why does there have to be that ridiculously high doorsill in the Audience Room? I know the answer. To make you look down as you enter. To make you show your respect. Don't they realize that it actually shows the opposite?"

"It does?"

"Of course. If people are looking down as they enter the emperor's presence, it's just so they don't trip. It doesn't show true respect, only the semblance. You want to find out if people really respect the emperor, you give them the option and then see what they do. If they feel respect they will show it. That is true respect, not forced or manipulated."

"I see what you mean."

"So my question is: who makes up all these rules? Whom do they benefit?"

She smiled up at him. "And may I assume you have an answer?"

"Well, I doubt if it's the emperor. Anybody who has the strength and intelligence to work his way up to that position has more confidence than to worry about doorsills."

She shook with silent laughter. "I am certain the emperor would be pleased to know that you find him suitable for his position."

Cheynou tilted his head up a fraction, firmly maintaining his serious mien. "It is of great advantage to anyone to obtain an opinion of himself from a truly impartial observer."

She glanced sideways at him. "Now come down off your pedestal and tell me the answer to the question."

He shrugged. "I haven't figured out exactly who benefits the most, but I would wager that we stood in front of a lot of them today."

Now she became serious. "But, Cheynou, think of the alternative."

"You mean, if all those active minds didn't have something to keep them occupied?" He took her silence as agreement and forged on. "If the flies are buzzing around, remove the bait."

It took her a moment, but then she shook her head. "And then the flies bite you."

"Not if you swat them first."

"If it was that easy, I'm sure the emperor would have already done something."

"Maybe not. If you want to solve a problem, you don't give the task to those who caused it. They are not motivated to solve it, and they don't have the right skills."

"I'm sure the emperor would be pleased to hear how well you understand."

"And will you be telling him?"

She threw up her hands. "Heavens, no. Don't get the idea that because he seemed so pleased to see me I'll be having tea with him on a regular basis."

She turned and flicked a signal to the coachman, who had been following behind them. "And speaking of tea, I think I have had enough of a walk. Shall we ride?"

He bowed in what he thought was the proper way and handed her into the carriage. As they drove, raised above the bustling crowds that thronged the pavement, he wondered whether their little walk outside the palace had been for exercise or privacy.

4.   A VISIT WITH THE EMPEROR

Three days later, Cheynou was studying some maps Maksa had found for him when he heard a knock at the archway to their suite. He looked up from his low desk to see one of the many servants that thronged the mansion. A familiar one, dressed with a certain amount of flair. Cheynou straightened.

"Come in."

The servant, butler or whatever he was called gave a dignified bow. "My Lord Maksa requests that you hold yourself in waiting, sir."

"I will gladly comply. What am I waiting for?"

"I do not know, sir." Then his pose relaxed slightly. "But a squad of soldiers in the emperor's colours, commanded by a Thousand-Prime I recognize as someone from his Majesty's personal guard, have presented themselves at our front door."

Cheynou regarded this knowledgeable man with new respect. "Do you have any advice for me?"

A ghost of a smile twitched the firm lips. "Well, sir, if they are coming to arrest you, I suppose you might wish to wear something sturdy but not valuable."

"And do you think they are coming to arrest me?"

"It would be presumptuous of me to predict the emperor's actions, sir."

Cheynou sighed. "And what is my other option?"

"If I might suggest, sir, the emperor sending a Thousand-Prime is usually a sign of respect, and you might dress a touch more formally." He gestured to an alcove nearby, hung with a scattering of Cheynou's clothing. "For example, that blue vest with the delicate embroidery has caused a certain amount of envy in the lower levels of the manor."

Cheynou shrugged. "As long as it doesn't look as if I'm trying to arouse envy in the emperor's court..." He took the vest down.

Somehow, it ended up in the hands of the servant, who slipped it over his shoulders, straightened it, and smoothed the collar. "Quite appropriate, sir."

"Well, if I pass muster, will you be so good as to lead me to wherever I am supposed to wait?"

"Of course, sir. Please follow me." He bowed and began to turn away.

"If you don't mind..."

"Yes, sir?"

"You have been good enough to ease my way through the unknown nature of this situation. What should I call you?"

"I am Rasreura, sir, and I am the Third Butler."

"And I am pleased to meet you, Rasreura. Please lead me to my doom."

"Or your fortune, sir. Right this way." With another faint smile, the butler led him towards the formal receiving area of the mansion.

They finally reached what Cheynou figured was probably called the Second Semi-Formal Receiving Room or some such appellation, where his guide paused and motioned him forward.

"Thank you, Third Butler Rasreura." He nodded formally and turned through the door.

He took it as a good sign that Maksa and the visitor in the beautifully sculpted bronze cuirass were sitting and seemed to be chatting. The soldier immediately shot to his feet and set himself at attention. He was a bulky figure, a full head taller than Cheynou and probably twice the weight. From the look of him, most of it was muscle.

Maksa rose in a more leisurely manner. "Ah, there you are, Cheynou. Allow me to present Thousand-Prime Terek of the Emperor's Guard."

Cheynou assumed the formal greeting pose of his people. "It is an honour to meet one who has attained such a position."

Terek saluted, crossing his forearms horizontally at his waist and clashing his bronze bracers together. "The honour is mine, sir, to meet someone who has accomplished such a lengthy trek." He then assumed a more relaxed position, his wide mouth taking on a smile that turned down at the corners.

"Thank you, Thousand-Prime. Do I assume this is not a social call?"

The Thousand-Prime drew himself to a formal pose again. "You are invited to accompany me to the Imperial Palace, sir."

Cheynou nodded thoughtfully. "Invited, you say. What if I choose to decline the invitation?"

The soldier's pose relaxed slightly, and he looked Cheynou over a second time. "I suppose many have thought of that question, sir, but you are the first that I have heard say it out loud."

"Is my audacity novel enough to deserve an answer?"

The Thousand-Prime nodded. "The emperor does not play with words, sir. I was told to invite you. If you choose to decline the invitation, I will return to the palace and make your wishes known."

"I see. So the invitation came from the emperor, did it?"

The officer's lips formed a stiff line.

Cheynou would get no more information with that trick. "Don't worry, Thousand-Prime. I'm coming with you. I just wondered."

"Well, now you know, sir. Shall we?"

"Certainly." Terek nodded formally to Maksa, then turned and strode to the door. A servant led them down the hall to the front entrance. There, the soldier retrieved a short, useful-looking sword and an ornate helmet and led the way into the courtyard, where his soldiers stood as rigidly as statues. He motioned Cheynou forward.

He grinned up at the big man as he passed. "Do I walk in the front with you, or in the centre to be protected?"

The firm mouth turned down slightly. "Anywhere you like is fine with me, sir."

"But..."

"What do you mean, sir?"

"I heard a wealth of reservation in that response. Where would you really like me to walk?"

"Beside me is best, sir. There have been no incidents lately, but I cannot completely guarantee the safety of the streets."

"Right. And no matter how remote the possibility, there is no chance you are going to lose the package you have been sent to fetch."

"Something like that, sir."

"That gives me a great deal of reassurance, Thousand-Prime. Since my safety is so much your concern, I can relax and enjoy the walk."

"No one can see to your safety as well as yourself, sir. In my experience, sir."

Cheynou sighed. "I suppose you're right. It was a forlorn hope." He slipped into the vacant spot the soldier had opened, and marched, not quite in step, off down the street towards the administrative centre of the city.

This time, they did not go through the formal gardens but took a much shorter route from a back lane straight into the palace itself. As they entered, their guards peeled off in another direction, and Cheynou and the officer strode on.

"Somewhat safer in here, is it?"

The soldier glanced down with that same twist to his lips. "Oh, no, sir. It's much more dangerous in here."

"Different kind of danger."

"Quite right, sir."

"Thank you for the warning. Another situation where one is one's own best guard." He looked up at the soldier. "Did I say that right?"

"It seemed correct to me, sir. It was very formal language, though. We don't usually say 'one' when we speak of ourselves. In the Senate chamber they talk like that."

"I should have said, 'I am my own best guard'?"

"That would sound more normal, sir."

"Thank you, Thousand-Prime. I'm trying my best to learn to speak Kyabran properly."

"You're just learning to speak Kyabran?"

Cheynou grinned up at the man. "That was a very smooth compliment, soldier. I imagine you don't get to run errands for the emperor unless you have a certain flair for diplomacy."

Once again, the downward smile. "My tact has been mentioned, sir."

"Now, that sounded formal."

"It was. That form is one of the standard responses to a compliment."

"I see. Thank you again. I will remember."

"The proper bow for that is slightly deeper, with a move of the hand...so."

"Like this?" Cheynou imitated the open-handed turn of the wrist.

"Quite correct, sir."

"Well, Thousand-Prime, I must thank you again, then. I will remember." This time he did the bow properly.

The soldier did not break a smile, merely inclined his head. "It is a pleasure to aid so apt a pupil."

Cheynou recognized another standard response and practised it a few times as they strode down the hallway. He noticed that he was now in step with the soldier and decided to continue that way.

They passed along three corridors and traversed a garden and a paved atrium before the officer stopped at a door guarded by two even larger men. They saluted, he responded in kind, and one of them turned smartly to rap on the door. It immediately opened, and a young man in a finely woven robe gestured Cheynou to enter.

Before he did so, Cheynou turned to face the officer squarely. "I do not know all of your customs, Thousand-Prime, but in my people, when someone has gone out of his way to turn a mere duty into a pleasure, it is considered polite to acknowledge it."

This time, the smile actually turned the right way up, just a fraction. "Thank you, sir. It truly was a pleasure."

They exchanged more formal nods, and then the soldier wheeled smartly away and Cheynou turned into the room.

It was a comfortable space, big enough to sit twenty people, although a group of just four men stood with the emperor now. As he approached, Cheynou had time to notice that they were all facing their ruler as they spoke to him. Then the man turned, and Cheynou allowed his gaze to drop.

The emperor laughed. "Welcome, Cheynou the Barbarian. This is not a public audience. It is permitted to look upon my august visage, as long as the brightness of my radiance does not overwhelm you."

Cheynou thought he detected a chuckle from the others. "I appreciate that, your Majesty. I did mention to Lady Miranra that it is difficult to have a meeting of minds when the two bodies are separated by a gulf of formality."

"You misunderstand the meaning of a public Audience. There was no intention of any meeting of minds."

"Would you instruct me on the intention of the Audience, then?"

"The Audience is to demonstrate certain points. In your case, it was to indicate something that interests the emperor. It is an effective way to make my concerns and wishes known."

"I see. I thank you, your Majesty." He made the appropriate gesture. "I will remember."

As he raised his head, he caught a meaningful glance from the emperor to an older man standing nearby. He had time to register short grey hair and a stern face before His Majesty spoke again. "And neither is this the place for a meeting of minds. It is more like a gathering of particulars. As I become interested in our southern border, I realize what a small gleaning of information we have about what lies beyond it."

"My exact reason for coming here. To see who your people are, what their lives are like, how you run things."

"There's only one way to run an empire. With an emperor."

Cheynou nodded. "Implied by the name, I suppose."

"Exactly. Remember that."

Cheynou regarded the old man. *Should I take the risk?* "And you're keeping an eye on me in case I bring some strange barbaric form of government to foment in your population."

"The thought had occurred to me."

"You don't have to worry. The only thing I can contribute is a warning."

The grizzled eyebrows peaked. "You dare to threaten the Emperor of Kyabra?"

"Only in a historical sense, your Majesty. The Priest-Admiral of the Southern Ocean ran an empire of a sort. But over the centuries it became bureaucratic, elitist and top-heavy. At this moment, his ship of state is in the process of turning turtle on him. My people's rebellion was only the trickle of ballast that started the shift."

"And do you predict rebellion in my empire?"

"I have no idea, your Majesty. I may view your government with fresh eyes, but they are too fresh. I have seen nothing to indicate such an outcome, but that could be due to seeing nothing at all."

The emperor nodded. "I would be happy to allow you your exploration of my territories on one condition."

"Of course, your Majesty."

"Visit me on your return and, should you come to any conclusions that might be useful to me, please do not be hesitant in stating them."

Cheynou nodded. "An impartial assessment by an outside observer."

"It might have value." The graceful hand waved towards the grey-haired man. "And at the moment, you could do me the favour of speaking to Sofades, my advisor for the South, about your people and the others who inhabit that area."

"Of course, your Majesty..." He paused.

"I note a reservation..."

"I made it very clear to my people when I left, and to Lord Rochana while I stayed with him in Velika, that I am not here to spy on anyone, nor am I here to sell information about my people to any who might become their enemies. Lord Rochana was satisfied as to my motives, and yet he was relieved when I decided to move deeper into your empire, so there could be no question whether he gave away information to a spy."

"Of course, there are other, more forceful, ways to obtain information."

A chill shuddered down Cheynou's spine, but he allowed no outward reaction. "Of course, your Majesty. And then you would have to sift through everything you learned to try to winnow the truth from the lies. Why resort to that, when there is a much easier solution?"

"And what is this easier solution?"

"Accept what is freely given, and have your people, who will soon be travelling regularly in that area, check the accuracy."

"Regularly travelling? Which of my people are these?"

"The Rochana and Cheolean families, your Majesty. They are opening a trade route as we speak."

The emperor nodded. "Of course." Then he smiled. "And a subtle reminder that you are not without friends."

"I'm sure your Majesty takes many facts into consideration without need of reminder from me."

"Tactfully said, young barbarian. Where did you learn such diplomacy?"

"It would be remiss, your Majesty, to think that other peoples do not have their set of formalities and diplomacies, even though they are different from your own. My people usually tend to settle differences with their swords, but they do have a very long tradition of formal diplomacy, as well."

"So your people are swordsmen, are they? What about yourself?"

"Not really, your Majesty." He held up his hand. "Too small."

The emperor shot him a quick, appraising glance. "But competent, nonetheless."

"Oh, yes, your Majesty. Competent by our standards."

"And by ours?"

"I don't know your standards that well, your Majesty."

"But you have been living and travelling with my people for several months."

"I do not wish to be evasive, your Majesty. By the standards of the frontier soldiers I have worked with, I am competent. More skilled, perhaps, but lacking in wrist and arm strength."

The emperor nodded, turned that wry smile towards his advisor. "There you have it, Sofades. Information to be found, if you are careful how you extract it."

He turned back to Cheynou. "So, my young barbarian friend. Indulge me and speak honestly to my people, while saying nothing that might do harm to your own. I repeat my invitation to visit me again when you have spent some time in my little demesne."

With a complete lack of ceremony, he turned away and left the room. Cheynou waited until the door had closed before turning to the others.

"I am at your service, gentlemen."

The elder statesman eyed him carefully. "The emperor has a certain confidence in you, sir."

"I am happy to hear that."

"Are you willing to answer some questions then?"

"My answer is the same, whether the emperor is here or not."

The grey head nodded. "Good. Come and sit. There is wine, and we can speak together comfortably."

Making a mental note not to be lulled by the drink, Cheynou sat in the proffered chair. The young man who had ushered him in took a seat at a low desk and busied himself with pens and ink. The other two men stood behind Sofades, but not in formal poses. Cheynou wondered at their function.

"Tell me about your people, Cheynou Chan." He motioned to a servant who poured a deep red wine into crystal goblets. "Who are they, and where do they come from?"

Cheynou launched into a brief description of the Sea People, their religious hierarchy and the rebellion that had led to his Ship's demise, the Beaching of her Families, and their subsequent trials.

When he had finished, the statesman nodded, thinking. "I do not hear, anywhere in your tale, the reasons which have sent you to us."

Cheynou thought for a moment. "From my reading of history, I believe that mine is not an unusual experience in a rebellion. The leaders of the uprising may have been unhappy with those in power, but they are still tied to the old ways. There is often another group, usually younger, who would like to take the new ideas farther."

"And you were one of these. Are one of these."

"Was. We had a leader who was able to reconcile our differences with the desires of the powers that led."

"But now...?"

"She died."

"I see."

"Without her diplomatic ability and personal strength, the situation polarized. Those who were unhappy left the camps and went to live with the native peoples of the area. The present leader was thus able to consolidate his power and gain further control over the Crews."

"You did not go to the native camps, but there was no place for you with your own people."

"Correct. Also, no one there had need of my skills. I am what your people call a Navigator. On the Southern Ocean, my trade has broader responsibilities, all the way from helming the ship to seeking new information about the people we meet ashore."

"I understand. Since you had no ship left to helm, you sought the other part of your duties."

"True. Now I seek to become an explorer and map-maker." He grinned. "And I have a desire to helm a ship on this other ocean."

The older man gave a wan smile of approval and glanced at the writer, who was scribbling furiously. "Tell me about this lady with whom you travel. She is not one of your people, I have been told."

"That is correct. There is a settlement of farming people near where we landed. They were the ones with whom we had the original conflict. She is one of their nobility."

"Nobility?"

"Yes."

"A lady of noble blood, travelling this far, with only one retainer?"

Cheynou gave the man a level stare for a moment. "Was that a question?"

The man shot him a quick, appraising glance. "I will be more specific. What are her reasons for being here?"

"Perhaps it would be better to ask her that question. She is a lady, and she follows what interests her. I do not presume to answer for her."

The statesman smiled lightly. "I do not have the leisure to speak with every visitor to the capital. Perhaps you would indulge me and save me the time."

"I don't know, sir. Perhaps you should find the time to speak with her. You might find the experience enlightening: at least enjoyable."

"You have a high opinion of her."

He grinned. "Of her entertainment value, at least."

The cool, grey eyes regarded him, and he wondered how much this man knew and what he surmised. As far as Cheynou could see, none of it mattered much to the empire or to his own people, so his answers to these questions were of little importance.

"Do you have any more questions about my people, Lord Sofades?"

The Kyabran took a moment, then apparently decided to allow him to control the conversation. "No, you have been very forthcoming on that topic."

Sofades leaned back, ticked points off on his fingers. "I see your people as no immediate threat. For the next few years, perhaps ten or even twenty, they will be completely concerned with learning to survive in their new surroundings. It remains to be seen whether their trading with the empire will eventually lead to a growing prosperity and military power that could threaten us in the years after that."

The grey-haired man smiled. "I can be forthcoming with you on that count. If the trading is of benefit to the local merchants, whatever long-term danger it poses will be ignored."

"Merchants seem to be quite influential in the Kyabran Empire."

"There are some very wealthy merchants, with influence in proportion to their wealth. Soldiers cost money, and an Empire needs a lot of soldiers."

"May I ask you a question, Lord Sofades?"

"That seems fair, since I have asked you so many."

"I am getting a picture of the spread of your empire. To the south, you have almost-impenetrable mountains, with no dangers beyond them. To the west, you have drier and drier land, becoming unpopulated desert. I don't know what is to the east, but I have heard nothing about powerful enemies there. To the north is the Inner Sea, which I gather your navy completely controls. Where is the need for all the soldiers? Are they required to control the populations within the empire?"

Sofades mused a bit. "That question has a more complicated answer than you might expect. We have little unrest within the empire at the moment. Some would say that is because of all the soldiers. The other part of your question deals with our borders. Unfortunately, we cannot ignore our borders, no matter how innocuous they may seem, nor our neighbours, no matter how weak. You seem to be a student of history. Surely you know that ignoring potential danger has been the downfall of many a kingdom."

"So you spend all that money on all those soldiers, just in case?"

"That is a fair assessment of the situation. Our system has worked quite well for a couple of hundred years. We see no reason to change it."

"I can see one."

The statesman's head came up. "What reason is that?"

"My leader said it the clearest. Grow or die."

"Grow or die?"

"Exactly. Nothing in nature or in humanity stays the same. Either you change or you are left behind."

"That sounds like the philosophy of a young revolutionary."

"She was a young leader in a time of change. Perhaps it seemed more important to us at that time but, so far, I have seen no evidence in the Kyabran Empire to change my opinion."

"You see us as old, rigid, and ripe for a fall."

"I have seen no evidence of that, either."

Again, the wan smile. "And what have you seen?"

Cheynou shrugged. "Too much and too little. You are a varied and complex people, and I have only experienced a small sector. Ask me in ten years."

"Do you see yourself here in ten years, so that I could ask you?"

Cheynou smiled. "I don't know where I'm going to be in ten days."

The statesman returned a shadow of the smile. "Given the emperor's interest, if I were you, I wouldn't be anywhere but here without advising someone."

"Does that mean I am not allowed to leave the capital without the emperor's permission?"

"Not at all. It means it would be polite to let him know if you have travel plans."

Cheynou sighed. "I suppose it is wise to be polite to emperors and people like that."

"It seems to be."

He was about to ask whom he should inform when he decided that Miranra would know, and he shouldn't be searching out ways to demonstrate his ignorance.

After a bit of small talk, the Thousand-Prime was summoned, and the two reversed their journey, picking up their guard outside the palace and marching briskly back to the Rimmon residence. The officer seemed to relax even more, probably reasoning that his charge, having survived his visit to the palace, must be in the good graces of the powers that be. So Cheynou was able to pump him about various aspects of Kyabran life and familiarize himself with the forms of speech and accent of the area to the east of Kyabra, where this soldier had been born.

So they parted, if not friends, at least as friendly acquaintances, and Cheynou entered the mansion.

He was sure it was no accident that his hostess was waiting casually in the small sitting room near the entry.

"So, you came back in one piece."

"Yes. I persuaded the emperor that I gave better information if I gave it freely."

"You bargained with the emperor over the information you would give him?"

He smiled. "It never hurts to let people know where you stand."

Miranra shot him a glance. "Many people have found it terminally painful to take a stand with the emperor."

Cheynou shrugged. "I suppose he was in a charitable mood. I did remind him of my powerful friends."

"Did you, now?"

"I merely mentioned names in passing. He was the one that inferred a reminder."

Again the look. "I would have loved to be asleep in the sun outside the window while that conversation took place. What did he actually want?"

"He is interested in my people and their possibilities as trading partners or enemies. The emperor did not stay long, but left me to speak with Lord Sofades."

She nodded. "A wise move. I have had occasion to drop a word or two in his ear myself."

"Is he on our side, then?"

She smiled gently. "He is on the emperor's side. If we can persuade him that our enterprises are to the empire's benefit, then he will aid us. He is a good administrator. He does his duty and will not be swayed."

"You mean he can't be bribed."

"He is too rich and too proud of his name to be bribed. He has the ear of the emperor, so he cannot be swayed by promises of power. That makes a good administrator."

"Unless he takes a dislike to you."

"Sofades is not one to dislike an individual for random reasons. If you rouse his ire, you probably deserve it. Your best chance is to get him to like you. He is not swayed easily in that way, either, but it can't hurt."

"We discussed my plans for the near future. Do I have any plans?"

She laughed. "You mean other than ones the emperor may have for you?"

"I got the impression that I was free to leave, but I'd better check before I actually put an oar in the water."

"Yes, that would be mannerly. He has no reason, and I think no desire, to keep you here."

"Good. That was how I read it, but I wasn't completely sure I had all the nuances of the conversation. Not that it matters."

"Which means...?"

"Well, I'm not going anywhere, am I?"

"We discussed visiting my family in the Inner Provinces. I have done all I need in the capital. I believe you have as well. I am sure that Kendra would be happy to take a break in a land where she speaks the language fluently."

He grinned. "I thought she was having a good time here."

"I am sure she is. Nonetheless, I know the feeling, living in a place where every conversation is a struggle." She frowned slightly. "Do you not feel the same way?"

"Oh, at first. There were times when my head was so full of words of different languages that I would stumble over my own native speech. I find if I concentrate on the new language, that part soon passes."

She made a wry smile. "The definition of 'soon' differs with different people."

"I suppose it does. However, as you say, I have accomplished a great deal here, and would be happy to move anywhere that is closer to the Sea."

"Maksa and the children will be returning from their grandparents' home and they will follow us at their leisure. We can leave for Tenet as soon as we are organized."

"Fine. Whenever you're ready."

"As long as it doesn't take more than two days. I can see we'll have to overtake you, swimming to get there."

"We go by water?"

"Yes, there's a harbour at the mouth of the Panjhali River. Port Riel is not much of a city, but many ships stop there. We'll take the weekly packet boat to Tenet."

"Fine. Wonderful!"

"Calm yourself. I expect to leave in about six days. Plenty of time if you have new friends to say goodbye to."

"I should probably make mention to the emperor."

Miranra laughed aloud. "You consider him a friend, do you?"

"He seems concerned with my welfare." A thought struck him. "Does Kendra know about this?"

"Yes. We had only waited for word from the emperor before we told you."

"You knew he would send for me?"

"It was a possibility."

He looked at her with renewed respect. "No wonder he remembers you, in spite of your being away so long."

She flicked her fingers at him, brushing his compliment aside, but a smile quirked her lip. "Do not stand on ceremony, Cheynou. I'm sure you have things to discuss with Kendra. She's in the garden. Off you go."

Grinning like a child dismissed from school, he strode through the mansion. Despite his excitement, he couldn't help but appreciate the beauty of the building, now that he was leaving it. He wondered if the kind of eye that allowed the shipwrights to lay out the sinuous curve of a new hull could turn itself to envision the proportions of this hallway: wide but not too wide, inviting in the perfect height of its warm stone walls.

Kendra seemed to be appreciating the intricate structures of the garden in the same way, and he slowed as he approached her still form. She was gazing over the fountain, her fingers trailing idly in the water, her mind on something else. She came back slowly, her eyes changing focus, then centering on him.

"So, did you have a nice chat with the emperor?"

"A brief one. I'll tell you about it when we have time."

"Are we in a hurry at the moment?"

"Certainly. Only six days to pack our worldly belongings…"

She laughed. "That usually takes about half a glass."

"…and say goodbye to all our new friends."

"We don't have any."

"We don't? You met plenty of people."

"And so did you."

"But mine were all business. We talked trails and transport, maps and mountains."

"As were mine. We talked fashions and frills, men and marriages."

"I thought some of them were quite friendly to you."

"They were friendly enough. But you don't break into a society like this in such a short time. They already have their circles, set before they were born. I am a mere foreigner, an interesting item to fill their gossip." She waved a hand to negate his indignant frown. "I don't mind. One of them would be treated in similar fashion at home."

"You never expected to make any friends."

"I am always open to the chance to make a friend."

"Or a conquest?"

She waved that away. "The men are the same. Anyone of the status that I might marry has been promised since his birth." She levelled a stare at him. "And don't even ask about a romantic fling. That would put me in a quite different status with the young ladies and their mothers."

"I can see that."

"Ah, Cheynou the Diplomat understands these things, does he?"

He shrugged. "The emperor seems to think I'm worth talking to."

Then her head came up. "So now we move on."

He grinned. "To a place where they speak like you."

"I won't deny that will be a rest." She looked up at him, her face serious. "And there's an ocean, and ships."

"What will you do?"

She thought a moment. "We never discussed this, did we? You've always said you wanted to Helm one of their ships. We never looked that far ahead."

They stood thinking similar thoughts. If he were to get a position on a ship, it would be for a long time.

"Do they allow women on their ships?"

He shrugged. "I don't know. Maybe wives and children. Not as sailors."

"I see." Her back straightened. "That's fine. I speak the language. I have friends. Cruzen will support me. I'll make myself worthy of his friendship."

"It's good of him. He never offered me anything like that."

"Of course not."

"I suppose he wouldn't."

"He has more faith in you than that." She flicked his arm with her fingertips.

"So we will have to separate, at least for a while."

"Is that what's bothering you?" She stepped closer and ran her palm down the side of his face. "Don't let it. We're still on our great voyage together. Maybe our exploration has changed, but we're both still pushing ahead. Maybe we'll find what we're looking for in Tenet. Maybe we won't, and we'll have to go farther."

Her enthusiasm was beginning to get through to him. "That's right, I suppose. We'll just have to see what happens. We have a new land to explore first."

"That's the spirit!" She tugged on his hand. "Let's go pack. We only have six days."

5. SUTA

The society of Tenet was much smaller and friendlier than that of the capital. Miranra was able to introduce them to a great number of people, because she seemed to know everyone. It was also a somewhat slow season for novelties, so they were immediately invited to several parties, teas and other affairs.

Kendra took to the social swirl as if it was her chosen milieu, and Cheynou found a way to fit in while he looked around for a ship. He had taken rooms in the *Bosun's Bunk*, an inn just far enough from the harbour front to be respectable, and he spent his time checking out the boats that tied up, chatting with the sailors and any officers who would give him their time, creating a picture of the way the Kyabran mercantile system worked.

This was exactly what a Navigator was meant to do whenever he was ashore, and he threw himself into it with joy. However, he didn't seem to be making any progress in getting work.

He also missed the Weaponless training he had been taking with Maksa. Once again, he was stymied by the rigidity of the Kyabran social system. Weaponless was for nobility; he was a foreigner. End of story.

Kendra didn't get it. "Cheynou, you're a diplomat. You solve everything with your logic. Why do you have to practise all these violent things?"

He shrugged. "Two reasons, I suppose. In the first place, I can't shake my Raider upbringing. Anything I can do to increase my fighting skills is worthwhile." Then he grinned. "Also, I'm smaller than everyone else, in case you didn't notice."

"But you never let that bother you."

"That's right. Because I know I can handle most men half again my size. Because of all this violence I practise."

"Your logic is impeccable, if your social view is a bit skewed. However, I suppose you could ask our hostess what to do. She seems to know everybody."

When he broached the topic with her, Miranra shrugged her shoulders. "For once, I am at a loss. Maksa might know someone you could practise with, but I don't have that kind of contacts. Wait till he gets here, and we'll see what we can do."

He glanced at her. "I suppose it's not a big problem. I could just spend more evenings down at the harbour. There's enough fighting in the taprooms to keep me in shape."

She gave him her usual serene smile. "Well, with a threat like that hanging over our heads, we are duty bound to come up with a solution, aren't we?"

The solution showed up a few days later. As Cheynou approached Kendra's little house, three large and beautifully groomed horses honoured the driveway with their presence. One was especially impressive: a bay mare of about sixteen hands with a black mane and tail. As he walked past, he noted a symbol tattooed on her near hip: a circle with two wavy lines crossing it vertically.

When he entered, Kendra jumped up from her conversation. "Here we are, Suta. This is the barbarian warrior I've been telling you about."

Two men rose from their chairs and stood forward: by their posture, military types. "Cheynou, this is Suta Pankal. He's going to teach you Weaponless."

The taller of the two bowed formally, and Cheynou returned the gesture. The man was about thirty and well built, with a handsome, craggy face and laugh lines around his eyes.

He immediately turned to Kendra and held out his hands, palms forward. "Now, my Lady, that's not exactly what I said."

She just gave her "whatever you say" smile.

His attention returned to Cheynou. "I'm pleased to meet you, Mr. Chan. A student of the Arts of War such as myself is always interested in meeting a practitioner from another school." He gestured to his friend. "And this is Sergeant Sabino, a frequent training partner."

The other soldier also bowed with a friendly smile. "And the beautiful lady who graces us with her presence is my wife, Teveria, who is no mean practitioner, herself."

Cheynou had been around this area long enough to know how to bow to a lady. "I'm pleased to see someone close to my own size in the group, ma'am."

She acknowledged the situation with a wry glance up at her husband and his friend. "Overconfidence. It gets them every time."

Cheynou flashed her a smile and turned to Kendra. "And now that you're finished embarrassing me by telling all sorts of stories exaggerating my skills, shall we sit down and be sociable?"

She smiled again and brought him a cup of wine.

He sat and regarded Suta. "Now, Kendra's enthusiasm aside, what have you really promised? It is clear that as a foreigner I am closed off from the secrets of the Kyabran Weaponless."

The big man nodded. "In essence, that is true. When I practise with my fellow Masters, we follow traditions many years in the making, and we guard their sanctity." Then he grinned. "But I am also a soldier. When it comes to staying alive and keeping the men in my regiment in the same state, I am not so strict. As we often say, the move you learn today may be the one that saves your life. So, we are willing to learn anything from anyone. And we teach the same way."

Cheynou nodded. "I wholeheartedly agree. My people also have many strictures and rules in their training. However, as Kendra may have remembered to tell you, I was a Navigator and Helmsman, not a Raider. I learned a less restrictive method. A mercenary I know says that the most effective weapon is the one that's in your hand. I take that one step farther. I fight with anything I can pick up."

"And if you can't find anything, you use the nearest part of your body available."

"Hmm. That's a good rule, too. Where did it come from?"

Suta's chest swelled. "I am not just any soldier. I am a graduate of the Kantoon School of Warfare." He grinned. "I'm sure you've never heard of it." Tossing back the loose sleeves of his shirt, he revealed a circular tattoo on each forearm. "This one is for Honour and this one is Open Hand. I specialized in that because of my Kyabran Weaponless training."

Cheynou grinned. "If that's Honour and Open Hand, what does the one on your horse's rump mean? Beauty?"

Both soldiers shouted with laughter. Cheynou looked around, wondering what was so funny. Teveria was smiling, and Kendra had covered her face with one hand.

"Oh, Cheynou, you've done it again."

"What? How?"

"Because that's what it does mean. Suta's mare is named Beauty."

He shrugged. "A lucky guess."

Suta put on a ferocious frown. "But nobody ever connected the name of the symbol to its place on the horse." He shrugged. "But that's tradition for you. The identifying mark always goes in that position, never anywhere else."

"Could we change the topic to something less likely to get me laughed at? What part of the army are you with?"

"I am a mere captain, commanding, as you might guess from the quality of our mounts, a troop of cavalry. Sergeant Sabino leads my number one patrol and takes care of most of our regiment's training."

Cheynou thought Teveria might be feeling left out. "And you, my Lady? What position do you hold that requires a horse of similar quality?"

She glanced sideways. "A position where I must remind the upper-class ladies — of which I am not one — that owning and training a beautiful horse is not an exclusive privilege."

Sabino made a shushing motion with his hand. "My wife is a renowned horse trainer and riding instructor. She's the one responsible for the quality and ability of our horses."

She frowned. "If I have to send my husband off to fight, at least he will have the best horse possible to get him through the battle." Then her face cleared. "I assume you ride, Cheynou, despite your upbringing?"

He shrugged. "I hate to admit it in this company, but I am an indifferent rider. Not in the sense of being indifferent to my mount, you understand. I am very careful to know what my horse is doing and thinking at any given moment. That way, I have a chance to predict what he might do at the next moment, a skill I am still working on."

Kendra leaned forward. "You must realize that until two years ago, Cheynou had never been on a horse's back."

The other three looked at him with surprise tinged, he was sure, with pity, which they immediately tried to hide with weak smiles.

"I know exactly how you feel. I'm sure I have the same look when I hear about someone who gets seasick."

The evening went on and, as the conversation ranged to different topics, Cheynou began to feel rather uncomfortable. At first he couldn't think why, but then it came to him.

He emptied his cup and put it down. "Well, I have other things that must be done this evening, so I bid you a fond good night."

They persuaded him to stay for another cupful, but then he managed to tear himself away, taking along a copy of Suta's training schedule and an assurance of a warm welcome any time he showed up.

He assured the big soldier that he would be at the next practice and stepped out into the night, headed for his room down by the quay.

As he walked, he analyzed the evening and decided there was no doubt about it. In any group of three men and two women, there was bound to be a certain pairing off in couples, leaving an odd man out. This evening, Cheynou got the distinct impression that he was the extra.

6. LOVE AGAIN

"I have an invitation."

Cheynou looked up from the scroll he was reading. They were sitting in Kendra's garden on the sunny side of her little house. "Another one?"

"And you're included."

"I am grateful. You are performing your function admirably."

"Of course I am. But this one is special."

"Because..."

"Because this time you are going to meet some people who have expressed interest in you."

He shrugged. "Everyone is interested in me. Except a captain who needs a navigator."

"Don't worry. That will come. These are ladies."

"Hmm. Lining me up with one of your friends?"

"Hardly. But I think you will find them interesting."

"I can hardly wait."

She frowned at him. "Cheynou, this is a different stage of our adventure. We are no longer travelling. We have settled, at least for a while."

He swung a hand to indicate the cottage and the garden. "At least, you have."

"That's right. And so should you. Especially since you don't have a ship. You need to have a social life."

"I thought I had one."

She pushed his shoulder. "Not that kind of social life. You know what I mean."

He sighed. "Yes, I know what you mean. I will come to this party, and you may parade a bevy of beautiful women past me, and I will do my best not to embarrass you."

She gave him a sideways glance. "That's a rather halfhearted approval."

"No, no, you're right. We may be in Tenet for a long time. I've been here long enough to realize that their sailing life is not what I'm used to. These people are tied to the land, and sailing is their occupation. They do not live on their ships. They stay on them when they are working, but their homes are ashore. I need to be settled, even if I'm sailing most of the year."

"Right. And the people I have met here do not have the strictures of those at the capital. They are Frasians, not Kyabrans, and their attitudes are different. You could find a girl here to spend time with. It will be good for you."

"And you're going to find me one?"

"No, I'm going to give you opportunities to find one for yourself."

So, he went to the party, or reception, or tea, or whatever they called it. It was in the formal garden of a very pleasant and stately home, too small to be termed a mansion, but lush nonetheless. Unlike similar occasions in Kyabra, the social groups seemed to include men and women of various ages standing and talking to each other.

After they had circulated for a candle or so, Cheynou and Kendra found themselves standing, wine glasses in hand, in a small, private arbour.

He glanced around the party, noting the people they had talked to. "These folk are very...accepting, I think would be the word."

"Yes. It's as I said. And you haven't called yourself 'barbarian' once."

"Didn't seem necessary."

"Meet anyone you like?"

He shrugged. "I like them all." He grinned at her. "Haven't fallen head over heels, but I'm working on it."

She raised her nose. "I'm not expecting miracles."

"That's good, because..." He stopped, alerted by feet brushing the grass at his side.

"Why, Lady Kendra. Who is this handsome gentleman?" The voice was soft and low.

Cheynou turned and readjusted his vision. The young lady who confronted him was short — the crown of her head just reached his nose — and she was...rounded in an alluring way accentuated by the tight corset and uplifting bodice she wore. Her skin was as dark as most Frasians', and her hair was jet black, flashing with small gems artfully inserted in its folds.

He glanced at Kendra for a hint.

The temperature in the garden had dropped considerably. "Good afternoon, Lady Popinea. I didn't expect to see you here."

The girl waved a languid hand, dismissing Kendra's reaction. "Oh, I know it's a bit early for my usual style." She glanced up at Cheynou, her eyelashes fluttering. "But there was a rumour going around. It seems you have been holding out on us?"

Kendra, too, glanced at him. "If you mean my travelling companion, I have no hold over him. He usually has too much serious business to waste his time with such affairs." Her dismissive gesture mimicked the other woman's action.

Lady Popinea's eyes widened. "Aha! A businessman as well as..." her eyes scanned him top to toe "...everything else."

Mindful of etiquette and rather enjoying this interchange, Cheynou kept his mouth shut.

Kendra sighed. "I suppose there's no avoiding it. Lady Popinea Chieti, this is my companion and navigator, Cheynou Chan, formerly of the Familyship Sea Eagle. Cheynou, may I present Lady Popinea Chieti..." She paused as if unsure of how to label the newcomer.

Cheynou came to her rescue as she had expected. "I am enchanted to meet someone of my Lady's grace and accomplishments." He gently took the dainty fingers she extended and ever so subtly pulled her forward as he leaned in. "Also to finally meet someone approaching my own stature."

She removed her hand from his grasp, regarding her fingers as if to check for damage. "Sailors are such rough people." Her eyes flashed up to meet his briefly.

"Quite the contrary, my Lady." He wiggled his fingers. "The helming of even the largest ship requires the gentlest touch."

Again the wide eyes. "Ooh. I see." Her hand fell, barely touching the side of her close-fitting dress as it moved down her body.

Cheynou felt the ice radiating from his travelling partner.

Popinea looked up at him through dark eyelashes. "So you are the dashing barbarian that has all the young ladies in a flutter."

He grinned. "Except for Lady Popinea, who would not stoop to anything so undignified."

She snapped her fan open in front of her face and stared at him from its trembling protection. "The right person might induce a minor quiver."

"And what kind of person might induce a quiver in the heart of the wonderful Lady Popinea Chieti?"

"Popinea is my given name, my friend, but far too complicated for everyday use. You..." she poked a lacquered fingernail into his chest "...can call me Poppy."

"Poppy...?"

"Yes. It's a flower that grows in this area. A rather beautiful one, in my opinion."

"Oh, it must be, in order to lend its name to a person of your rare qualities."

She spun away, lowering her head to look up at him through her long eyelashes. "My, you are a flatterer, aren't you?"

He shrugged. "No, as it happens, I'm not. I meant it."

She rolled her eyes. "Oh, how blunt you are. How forceful."

"How honest. I'm sorry, I don't know how to play these games. Why would anyone have trouble telling you that you are beautiful?"

She frowned — ever so slightly — and tilted her head to one side. "Cheynou Chan, I am going to have to be very careful with you. A girl's head could be turned."

"Oh, I wouldn't worry if I were you. I have a feeling your head turns exactly as far as you want it to, and no further."

"Do I detect a note of censure?"

"Of course not, my Lady. Admiration, perhaps."

She tapped his arm with her fan then snapped it open again to peek over it. "I am not sure about you, Mister Chan. I think perhaps your barbarian ways will tempt me into paths I should not dare to tread."

There was no good response, so he simply smiled and waited.

She paused, looked sideways at him, then away, inviting an answer.

He tacitly refused the opportunity.

She frowned and glared at him. A very pretty little frown, and the glare of a kitten. "What, no defence? No protestations of innocence?"

He grinned. "Honesty, remember? Perhaps I am not as innocent as you would like me to be."

"Well, then I think my best move would be a strategic retreat." She spun and stalked away, every line of her body suggesting that she knew he was watching.

Which he was.

There was a chuckle at his elbow. "So, what do you think?" Kendra fluttered her fan in front of her face. "Isn't she a work of art?"

He grinned. "I think she's cute."

"Well, of course you do. That's the whole point."

"Perhaps not the whole point, but most of it." He looked his friend up and down. "She's shorter than me."

"A great recommendation, I'm sure."

"Kendra, you've told me enough about people of this class to understand she's the product of her society. Her objective in life is to gain a mate. Her skills and her training have all been aimed in that direction since she was a child. I'd have to say she learned her lessons admirably."

"What? You mean you like all that kittenish fluff?"

"Of course I do. Why wouldn't I?" He glanced at her with a frown. "She's one of the best in her society at what she does. The fact that she chooses to practise her skills on me is flattering, to say the least. I have no illusions about my chances at any meaningful relationship. She is too young and I am too...inappropriate, I suppose. But that doesn't mean I can't enjoy it."

"Hmph! Do I hear your voice coming from somewhere below your belt?"

"Great. Now you're mad at me too. Are you going to flounce off, swinging your hips like she did?"

"Not likely. In the first place, I wouldn't know how, and in the second, the heels of my shoes are too flat."

"Oh. Is that how she does it? Interesting..."

"Not too interesting, I hope. I have a higher opinion of you than that."

He looked once again across the garden. Poppy was talking in animated fashion with two other girls, but every once in a while she checked over her shoulder to make sure he was still watching.

He sighed. "You know, Kendra, I will be very happy to find a ship and just sail away from all this." He glanced at her. "Why are you smiling?"

She jabbed a knuckle into his ribs. "Because that's the old Cheynou we know and love. I'm glad to see you're still you."

"Oh, I'm still me, all right. No precious flower is going to change that."

"You just make sure she doesn't."

* * *

Suta, on the other hand, changed Kendra. No, to be more accurate, he changed her relationship with Cheynou.

And when he thought about it, that wasn't true, either. They still had the same old friendship: close, but not too close. He hated to admit it, but this must be what brothers and sisters shared.

And with Suta it was the same.

Often, when Cheynou showed up at Kendra's cottage, the mare called Beauty would be standing at the door, and he knew he would be welcomed in like one of the family. When he went to training sessions, he was treated equally to all the other students. Maybe even better, if being pushed harder, thrown farther and hit more was any indication.

So Cheynou worked hard, trained hard, and took every advantage he could in this new society to fit in, to become accepted, to make progress. But he kept looking for a ship, and his motivation increased as the month went by.

Because all the signals were plain to read. He could show up much earlier in the day, now, and Suta would be at the cottage. Like as not Beauty would be stabled in the small barn at the far edge of the back yard.

Unwilling to interfere with something he could do little to affect, he stayed away. And, having nothing else to do in the evenings, it was easy to slip into the habit of accepting the invitations Poppy arranged for him.

A fact that Kendra soon noticed and commented on.

Cheynou smiled lightly. "Oh, come on, Kendra. Don't you think she's cute?"

"Hmph. About as cute as a cat playing with a mouse."

"Don't you think cats are cute when they're playing?"

"A cat playing with a mouse looks cute until you think about what it's doing."

He thought about that for a moment. "You haven't cast me as the mouse, have you?"

Kendra glanced at him. "I don't know. Have you?"

He waved a negating hand at her. "Come on, Kendra. When have you ever seen anyone get the better of me?"

She lowered her head, raised her eyebrows knowingly. "I recall hearing Sarasha say that love made smart people just as stupid as the rest of us."

"I'm not exactly in love, Kendra. Not yet, anyway."

"She also said that's the first symptom."

"I just can't make you happy, can I? You've been after me for weeks to find a girl. Now that I've found one, she's not good enough."

She touched his bottom lip. "Well, my pouty friend. I thought you had better taste, that's all."

He brushed her hand away. "Look, you've got Suta. You can't keep both of us. Let me figure out my own life for once." He seized her hand and held it, forcing her full attention. "He's important to you, isn't he? Different from all the rest."

Her brow wrinkled. "What do you mean by different?"

"He doesn't order you around. He treats you like...I don't know, like I do. As an equal."

She nodded. "I've watched him with his men. He's the perfect officer. He doesn't shout orders. He lays out the plan and then informs his men when it's time to do what they all agreed they would do."

"So when he drops his sabre forward and yells, 'Charge,' he's not telling them what to do?"

"No. Everyone agrees already that they're going to charge. He's just telling them, 'Now is the best time to charge.' And they all do. Every time. Willingly, because they think they had a part in the decision."

"And he treats you the same way."

"Exactly."

"And that's what you've been looking for. A man who doesn't try to dominate you."

She grinned. "And a bunch of other qualities, as we have discussed."

"Hmm. Father of your children?"

"Well, maybe not quite that. But close."

* * *

Poppy, on the other hand, was quick to assess his relationship with his travelling companion. After the third social occasion they had both attended, she invited him to her family home for a "private tea," whatever that was. He soon realized that it was an opportunity for her to set things straight.

He didn't mind, especially. He gazed along the settee to where she sat, her teacup in her fingertips, sipping gracefully while she regarded him. He reminded himself to thank Kendra. This was certainly a pleasant change from the bars on the seafront.

Poppy set down her teacup, dropped her hands in her lap and looked up at him. "You're in love with her, aren't you?"

He closed his eyes, took a deep breath, and let it out slowly, forcing his shoulders to relax. Then he raised his hands, inspecting them. Looked at his arms, his body, finally his legs. "What is it?"

"Pardon?"

"What is it about me that this keeps happening? Do I invite this sort of thing? Sarasha was always telling me I was in love with the big, wide world. Kendra is always telling me I was in love with Sarasha. Now it's you!" He shook his head. "It's getting so I'm afraid to talk to another girl. She'll tell me I'm in love with you!"

He slowly turned and stared at her, thoughtfully, "Of course, it stands to reason that one of you, sooner or later, is going to be right. Maybe I really will be in love with some lucky damsel." He gave a Sarasha-like snort. "Of course, I'll have to ask some other girl before I find out."

"Who is Sarasha?"

"Hmm. We do get to the point quickly, don't we? It's too hard to explain."

She wiggled herself (in a pleasant way, he couldn't help but notice) into a more comfortable position on the sofa. "I have time."

He shook his head. "It would take a lifetime."

"Why, Cheynou Chan, you romantic boy! Are you proposing to me?"

"Sorry, girl. I've been teased by the best. You're going to have to do better than that to get a rise out of me."

"Oho! A challenge."

He grinned. "Right. You just keep working at it. I'll let you know how you're doing."

"So, who was Sarasha?"

He shook his head and sighed, as if to himself. Then he turned back to the girl. "She's dead, so it doesn't matter. And I wasn't in love with her, so it doesn't involve you at all."

She didn't quite pout, but he could see that she was disappointed. Too bad. He would not let Sarasha become a subject for lovers' banter. However, he took pity on her. Seizing her hand, he pulled her to her feet. "Come on. Let's take a walk around your beautiful garden and you can tell me all about how I'm in love with somebody else."

She tugged, but not quite hard enough to get away. "I don't want to talk about that!"

He pulled back just enough that she overbalanced, then took his advantage to spin her in beside him, her hand tucked under his arm, both of them strolling gracefully towards the garden doors. He was gratified by a small gasp of surprise, and glanced down at her. It was nice to have someone looking up at him for a change. Especially through such long, dark lashes.

He was really beginning to enjoy himself.

7. Bar Meeting

The day Suta invited him out for a drink after Weaponless practice, Cheynou knew something was up. He shrugged his shoulders. "I'd love to find out where the cavalrymen hang out. I was getting rather tired of the same old sailors' taverns down on the docks."

The big rider grinned. "Well, it's time you hit another part of town. Get your coat and let's go."

"Not over at Kendra's this evening?"

"I told her I had business."

He stopped and looked up at the bigger man. "Is this business?"

"Oh, no...no, not at all."

"I see." Cheynou didn't see, and laid a bit of sarcasm into his comment. Suta did not take the bait.

The tavern turned out to be little different from what he was used to. Same weathered building, same scarred furniture and straw-covered floor. Similar clientele, although the footwear differed, and there were more uniforms in evidence. Of course, instead of a dock crowded with ships across the road there was a huge stable, corrals and a farrier's shop.

Suta shouldered through the door, tossing brief salutes to the bartender and a couple of patrons, and led the way to a small table near a window looking out to another stable yard in the back.

"I like to sit here." He gestured towards the window. "A never-ending source of entertainment."

"I imagine."

"Oh, I don't think you do. We had a horse stick a hind foot through the glass last year. Didn't like his rider's hair colour or something. What do you want to drink?"

"Whatever you recommend. If the ale kicks like the entertainment, I'll have to be careful."

Suta laughed. "You are a sharp one, aren't you?"

He chuckled. "Not everyone notices."

The cavalryman signalled to the server, and soon a tray with two mugs appeared.

Cheynou sipped. "A cut above what I'm used to."

"That's good, because it's the best in the house. Nothing too good for my barbarian friend."

Cheynou took another sip and put his mug down. "Suta, you don't have to grease my throat or break the ice or anything diplomatic. You're a friend. Why don't you just ask me?"

"Ask you what?"

"Whatever it is you want to know about Kendra, of course."

Suta covered his confusion by taking a large swig of ale. Then he, too, set his drink down. "You really are sharp, aren't you?"

"You're not asking yet."

The man sighed. "No, because I'm not sure what I want to know."

"How about 'Why is she here, and what is she really looking for?' Would that do?"

"It would be a start."

Cheynou collected his thoughts. "I don't think she knows, herself. It's no secret that she left the society she was brought up in because she couldn't fit in with the requirements."

"She has mentioned that."

"Right. And she appreciates that you don't impose those requirements on her."

"I don't, or my society doesn't?"

He grinned. "That's for you to figure out."

There was silence as they watched a particularly fine bay horse being led across the yard outside.

"Don't you want to ask the 'marriage and children' question?"

"Maybe I don't want that answer, either."

"And I'm not sure I have it. With Kendra, there's the answer she has at the moment, the real answer, and the one she gives you because she thinks you will understand it. And I suppose the one she gave me, because she knows I understand."

"And what answer did she give you?"

"The one I can't tell you."

"Because it was given in confidence."

"No, because I'm not sure you would understand it."

"Thanks, Cheynou." Suta reached out a heavy hand and clouted his shoulder. "I have the only answer I needed."

"That's good, because I didn't think I was telling you much."

"No, you told me what I should have known already. If I want answers, I know who I have to ask."

"There you go. Wise words, and you came up with them yourself."

"Did you do that on purpose?"

Cheynou grinned. "This is the point where I smile and look mysterious, and you go away thinking how wise I am. In actuality, it was your own wisdom."

Suta nodded and took another long drink. "Another ale? It's getting busy in here, and later it will be difficult to catch the bartender's eye."

"No, I'm fine."

As they talked, the taproom had been filling up and getting noisy. They drank in silence for a while, watching the crowd. A group of men in rougher riding clothes than the rest pushed their way through and took over the table next to theirs. They all glanced over as they sat. The largest man, a young fellow with a florid face in need of a shave, turned his chair sideways to stare at Cheynou, who afforded him one glance, then returned to his drink.

"Hey, little foreigner. I ain't seen you before. What are you doin' in a Riders' taproom?"

Cheynou glanced at the man, looked pointedly at his own mug, then raised his eyebrows.

"What's wrong, kid? Can't talk?"

Cheynou rose, drink in hand, and slid near his opponent, just enough behind him to make it necessary for the man to turn his head to keep a possible threat in sight. "You don't want to mess with me, Rider."

"Oh, I don't? And I suppose you got a good reason why not?"

"Of course. Because you can't win."

That brought a roar of laughter from the table.

The rider rose to his full height and turned to stare down. "And what gives you that idea?"

Cheynou gestured to indicate the man's stature. "Look at you."

"Whattaya mean, look at me?" The stubbled face twisted in a suspicious frown.

"You're twice my size. Think it through. What happens if you and I get into a fight?"

The man laughed. "I squash you like a bug."

"Exactly. And then you look like a bully and a coward. And what if I don't squash so easily?"

"Huh?"

"I mean, what if you're wrong, and I'm tougher than I look? What if I win? Then you lose the fight and you look like a complete idiot. I tell you, friend, it's not worth it."

For a moment, the rider stood, uncertain. Then he gestured to Suta. "You just talk big because of your fancy officer friend, there."

Cheynou sent a warning glance to Suta. "I didn't even mention my friend and all his mates up at the bar, there. If you wanted to pick a fight with him, why didn't you have the nerve to stand up and say so? That's pretty sneaky, sliding around to come at me and make it look like it's his fault." Cheynou slid half a pace closer.

"I tell you what. If you really want to work out whatever's eating you, come over to our table and tell us straight out. Prove you're worth the effort. If you're just looking for entertainment, you've had it, and you got off light. I'm going to sit down and finish my ale with my friend, and I'd be happy if you did the same. When you've had some time to think about it, you come over and let me know."

He turned away and sat with his back to the other table. He could tell from the movement of Suta's eyes that the rider stood, undecided, then also sat. Soon a shout for more ale arose.

Cheynou grinned and winked at Suta, who shook his head. "That was instructive."

He shrugged. "For him, anyway."

"No, for me. I would never have thought to handle him like that."

"You're twice my size and fighting ability. You're in uniform with twenty friends in the crowd. Why would you worry about handling him?"

"Because I'm an officer and I pride myself on my ability to deal with men."

"Then you probably would have dealt with him in an equally impressive manner."

"I'd like to think so."

"Besides, we don't know whether this is over yet. I did give him the option of coming back."

Suta looked up. "You're about to get your answer."

The bartender finished with the next table and turned to theirs, dropping fresh, full mugs in front of them. When Suta reached for his pouch, the man shook his head, nodding to the table behind Cheynou. "Don't know what happened there, sir, but thanks for keeping a lid on it."

Suta grinned. "No credit to me, Jonas. It was my young friend, here."

The barkeep looked down at Cheynou. "Want a job, son? Times I could use that kind of diplomacy."

Cheynou laughed. "Thank you, but I'm looking for a ship to sail on. Us sailors like our visits to bars short and entertaining."

The bartender chuckled. "Well, you keep this corner of the house quiet for a while longer, and the next one is on the house."

"Sorry to disappoint you, but this is my limit. After two ales, I get grouchy."

With a laugh, the bartender returned to his post.

The noise at the next table increased, with scraping chairs and jingling harness. Cheynou raised his head without turning it too far, confirming that their neighbours were leaving. Soon, a heavy hand descended on his shoulder.

"See you, little sailor. Thanks for an entertaining evening."

Cheynou looked up. "Thanks for the ale."

"Oh, it was worth it for the story I got." The man shook his head. "I never seen the like."

Laughing, he followed his friends out the door.

Suta grinned. "There's your answer. You won."

Cheynou shook his head. "I was lucky. He wasn't really nasty, just young and looking for some fun. I provided it." He gestured around the bar. "He was also out of his element and smart enough to be aware of it."

"You've never been here before. How did you know that?"

Cheynou shrugged. "I watch people. The way they walked when they came in, the way they gathered tight at the table. The way his friends kept an eye on the crowd while we were talking. And then he told me."

"He told you?"

"He was the one that mentioned you. It was on his mind all the time."

Suta shrugged. "You make it all sound so simple. But it adds up to good leadership."

"Leadership? Me? You know the total of my experience. Two people, one dog and one donkey."

"But Kendra was one of the people. I won't malign the dog, but I know about donkeys."

"I admit it was good training."

They both laughed and finished their drinks. Suta raised his eyebrows, and Cheynou nodded. "I guess we're done. I'm sorry I couldn't give you what you wanted."

The big cavalryman leaned back. "And what did I want?"

"My permission to woo Kendra."

"Is that what I wanted?"

Cheynou raised a hand, palm down, and wavered it. "Not really, but that's what it amounts to. Kyabrans are a formal people, and your relationship with her is quite devoid of formality. Thus it is open to all manner of interpretation, which has its positive and negative sides. I can only tell you one thing. I don't think Kendra dislikes formality. She just didn't like the forms her people wanted her to follow. Does that help?"

Suta shrugged. "Anything helps. I don't know what to ask, because I don't know what I want." He shook his head. "She baffles me without even trying."

Cheynou laughed. "She's been baffling everyone all her life. She doesn't do it on purpose." He raised a hand to stop the other man from speaking. "And don't even bother to ask whether I love her or not. Everyone loves her. I'm one of the few people who can manage to live with her. You're one of the few people she might manage to live with." He shrugged. "There. Those are facts. Deal with them as you choose."

Suta rose, dropping coins on the table. "Can't argue with that. I asked, you answered the best you could."

Cheynou followed him out the door, then hurried to walk alongside. He glanced up and caught the other's eye.

All he got in return was a crooked smile and a tilt of the head.

They walked down the hill towards the harbour in silence.

8. ENDING

Cheynou strolled up the gravel drive to Poppy's mansion. It was not large compared to other residences nearby, but it was beautifully designed, nestled into the hillside above the street. A light marble portico extended across the whole front, twined with greenery and shading the tall, ground-floor windows. It supported a balcony guarded by a wrought-iron railing, accessed from the second-floor rooms.

Poppy reclined gracefully against the railing, her white dress highlighted against the dark metal. She was staring off into the afternoon sun on the water far below.

Ah. I'm being put in my place today. I wonder what reason she has invented this time. He fingered the gilt-edged note in his pocket. *Definitely more formal than usual.*

Reaching a position directly below her, he took a "rest easy" pose and waited. He was good at waiting.

Finally, she looked down. "Oh, there you are."

"I am." He smiled up at her and waited again.

After another long gaze out over the sea, she sighed. "I suppose you might as well come in."

He held his pose until she looked down at him. "If you'd rather I didn't..."

She straightened. "No, if this must be done, let's do it now." She turned and strode into the house, her back straight. Soon, the front door opened, and there she was, posing prettily.

He grinned. "I don't know what's going on, but this is quite entertaining. May I come in, my Lady?" He leaned closer to regard her face. "Although I'm not sure my reception will be as warm as the fine summer day outside."

A flash of what might have been honest emotion surfaced, and then she pouted. "Don't make this harder than it already is, Cheynou. I want to talk to you seriously."

"Oh. All right. It's a good idea for friends to have a serious chat once in a while. Keeps things straight."

She turned and walked — at a normal pace, he couldn't help but notice — through the house and out to the cosy bower where they often sat. She perched on the edge of the wrought-iron bench and nodded him to a spot at the other end.

Taking his cue from her posture, he sat upright. "Now, what is this all about?"

"I have talked to Kendra."

"Oh. And I don't have to ask what about."

"No, you don't." She looked up at him seriously. "You really are in love with her, aren't you?" She reached out and pushed down his hands as they rose into his line of vision. "No, Cheynou. I don't want a joking answer this time. If you are in love with someone else, then I have to do some serious thinking."

"Oh."

"I'm not saying I might not put up a fight for you. I just have to decide whether it's worth it."

"Oh, I'm worth it, all right."

"I don't have any doubt of that, Cheynou. That's not the problem. It's the risk of losing that bothers me. So answer the question."

He shrugged. "Am I in love with her? You know, I've been thinking about that for months, and I can't really give you a straight answer. She was the first stranger I met after we came ashore from the Southern Ocean that didn't treat me like an enemy. We have been travelling for months, alone with each other for much of that time. If you get along with a person, you can't help but form a strong feeling for them in that sort of situation.

"Now I'm living in a foreign land, and she is the only one who speaks like I do, the only one who knows my people, the only one who really knows me. There can't be any doubt that there is love there, Poppy. What kind of love is the question."

"Do you want to bed her?"

He raised his eyebrows. It wasn't the kind of question one would expect from a well-bred Kyabran girl.

"The first answer is yes, of course. The second answer is maybe not. Then I think of the reality, and the answer is probably not."

"Why is it so complicated?"

"Well, we talked about it when we started the trip. We both decided it wouldn't be a good idea. You could fall into the habit of treating someone like you were in love when you really weren't. For all the reasons I just mentioned."

He turned to her. "I have to be careful I don't think I'm falling in love with you, for a bunch of similar reasons."

"Such as?"

"Such as, you're beautiful and exotic and different."

"How can you make such a wonderful compliment sound so negative?"

He shrugged, grinned. "It's a talent I have. Does it work?"

"Not on me!"

"Oh, good. I'll have to keep it in reserve, then."

Her smile faded. "Cheynou, thank you for being so honest with me."

"I didn't really answer your question, did I?"

"No, but as you say, there isn't an easy answer, as I might have known. It helps to know how you are thinking. You see, I'm at that stage where I have to make a decision. I find you handsome and exotic and different, but I know that's not enough to call it love."

He smiled. "Well done."

"Thank you." The dimple appeared briefly, then was gone. "But I have to decide whether to leave it at that, or let it develop to something more."

"With the full knowledge that you could be hurt."

She nodded. "I know love is like that. There's always the risk." Her head came up a fraction. "But I'd like to think I have some choice in the matter."

"If you believe you do, then maybe you do."

"So, I have to decide. That's why I need to know how you feel."

He sat down, rubbing his hand across his forehead. "Well, Poppy, then I'm going to give you some advice." He shook his head. "I am just so stupid, but I am going to tell you. Leave it."

"Why does that make you stupid?"

"Because I believe you. If you decide to let it go, then you will. And I like you. A lot. I find you…"

"I know, beautiful, exotic, different. We went through that."

"Right. It will be hard on me if we stop seeing each other. Even if I know it's the right thing to do."

"Are you sure?"

"Not completely. But there's another part of this that we haven't discussed. I'm a barbarian and a Navigator. I know that makes me exotic and different, if the other stuff doesn't quite apply…"

"It does!"

"Thank you. But it also means that I really am different. Some day, hopefully soon, I am going to get a position on a ship, and away I will go. I will be gone for a long time. At least a year. There is a small possibility I will not come back."

"And a possibility that you would come back, but not wanting to, because what was out there was so interesting?"

"You have been talking to Kendra."

She smiled slightly. "Get to know the competition, I thought. I never realized until I talked to her that the competition," she swung her hand to the sea, "was so powerful."

He looked at her quizzically. "I'd like to have been behind a bush when that conversation took place. What did Kendra tell you?"

Now, she really smiled. "A whole lot of the things you just told me. Of course, I didn't listen that closely, considering who was saying them. I could tell she knew it because she paused, and looked at me and smiled. And then, out of nowhere, she said, 'Go for him. I would.' I must admit, I was stunned for a moment."

"She said that?"

"Those exact words. So, I asked her why she hadn't gone for you. She grinned and answered, 'I said that I would if I were you. I'm not you. I'm me, and that's a completely different set of choices.' I can see what she meant, sort of."

"Aye. She's got that kind of a mind."

"Convoluted?"

"And honest."

"Strange combination. Do you trust her?"

"Absolutely." He thought a moment. "No, that's not quite true. I think she'd lie to me if she felt it was important. But she would be sure that she was doing the right thing for me."

"So even if she was lying to you, you would still trust her?"

"See what I mean? Convoluted."

She sighed and rose to stand beside him. "I don't consider it very romantic, talking about another girl."

He grinned. "That's why I didn't tell you about Sarasha."

"Hmm. That's fine. Kendra did." She turned to him. "She was really a wonderful person, wasn't she?"

"No doubt about that. She was also an unholy terror. For example, she would have you in tears immediately."

"Me! Why?"

"Because of all those little games you play." He raised a hand. "I'm not complaining. I like them. Some of them are cute, and some of them are downright seductive, as you well know. The rest are harmless. Don't stop them, please."

"You've done it again."

"I know."

"So why would she have me in tears?"

"Because she saw through every game, and called it, out loud, the moment one showed up. Far stronger people than you have found themselves stumbling away spluttering in embarrassment because they thought they could match wits with her."

"And here we are, talking about other women again."

He sighed. "I suppose, since you have decided we aren't going to be romantic, it doesn't matter anymore."

She spun, slapped his arm lightly. "Don't you put this all on me, Cheynou Chan. I was acting on the best advice."

"Hmph. Mine. Hardly impartial."

"Don't worry, Cheynou." She took the same arm, hugged it. "You'll find another girl who is just as beautiful and exotic as I am, just a little less smart."

"Or a little more smart."

"You can think of it that way, if you like."

"Is this the part where we talk about staying friends?"

"If you like. Is it a custom with your people?"

He shrugged. "I don't know. I never had a girl back with my people. I'm figuring this out as I go along."

"Well, you're doing a fine job, Cheynou."

"I am? And what does a fine job look like?"

She frowned. "Well, you've got rid of me with a minimum of fuss, no tears at all, at least not yet, and even made it seem like my idea."

"Well, wasn't it?"

"We just went through that."

"Oh, yes."

"And maybe, if I could give a small hint?"

"Certainly."

"If you want to keep it from being messy, now would be a good time to leave."

"All right." He turned towards the garden wall, and they walked to the gate in silence, her arm still wrapped around his. At the gate, he stepped through alone, then turned. She reached up, touched his face lightly.

"Goodbye, Cheynou. I'm really sorry, you know. We would have made such beautiful babies."

He stood a brief moment, staring at her. Then he grinned and bowed slightly. "Very well done. You almost had me for a moment."

She grinned back. "Teased by the best, were you?"

"All my life."

He bent over, kissed her gently on the lips, then retreated slowly, turned and strode away. He did not look back, because she would be watching, and he wanted to send no false messages.

His pace slowed as he came down into the town and he realized that he had no place to go. When he reached the turning that would take him up to Kendra's cottage, he hesitated. Perhaps it would be disrespectful to Poppy, going to see another woman so quickly.

He stood there a moment, feeling the emptiness inside him. He really did like her. A lot. And now she was gone, and he was alone again. His shoulders slumped, and he turned up the hill.

Kendra was home, directing the gardener with the planting of a garden she was creating. Arguing with him, to be more accurate. His knowledge of local plants and weather was coming into conflict with her wider understanding and the unusual varieties she wanted. Cheynou stood at the gate, smiling at her insistence. Finally, the old man gave in, and she turned away. He saw a satisfied smile, suddenly widening in astonishment.

"Cheychan! What brings you here?"

He didn't have an answer.

She strode up to him, looking him levelly in the eye. "What's the matter with you?"

"Nothing special."

"In other words, something important. Poppy playing hard to get? No, let me guess. Poppy playing easy to get. It's one or the other. Sometimes both, I wouldn't be surprised."

He sighed. "No, Kendra, she isn't playing any games at all. Not with me, anyway."

"Oh?" She pulled him around in front of the cottage and pushed him down on the bench in the shade. "Tell Old Auntie all about it."

He shot her a glance. In spite of the gardening clothes and the mess of her hair, she wasn't looking much like anybody's old auntie.

"Come on. The medicine was obviously sour. Spit it out."

"No, Kendra, the medicine was the right one, and the right dose. I'll just have to suffer through it."

72

"Having a tiff, are we?"

"No such luck. We just had a serious conversation."

She pulled at his shoulder, frowning at him. "A serious conversation. Oh, Cheynou, you are so stupid."

He found himself grinning sheepishly. "I said that, too."

"And you told her you were not the right one for her, because soon you would be off and away, and maybe never coming back."

"Something like that. There was more."

"Oh, I'm sure there was. But the end result is that she fell for it, and gave you the big heave-ho, as you sailors put it."

"Something like that."

"Cheychan, when you say, 'Something like that,' I know I'm right on the path."

"Aye. She did. She gave me the heave-ho."

"So why are you here? Why aren't you down in the pub with the other sailors, drowning your sorrows or celebrating your freedom?"

He sighed again. "Because I don't need that. I need a friend, and I don't have too many of those."

"Oh. Are we going to get drunk, then? That might be fun. I've never seen you drunk."

"Whatever you say."

"Well, don't sound so enthused!"

"I'm not here to give you an excuse for a party, you know."

"Why, Cheynou, my dear, that sounded downright grumpy. Look at me and tell me you don't feel just the tiniest bit relieved."

He turned to her. "I don't feel the tiniest bit relieved."

"You mean that, don't you?"

"I ever lie to you?"

"Probably not. Does that mean you are in love with her?"

He leaned his weight heavily on his elbows where they rested on his knees, staring at the ground. "No, probably not. Not yet. But I was getting very comfortable with her."

"Comfortable? With all those games? 'Come here, I want you! Oops no, I guess I don't.' How could you stand it?"

He straightened. "Kendra, I don't expect you to understand, but I liked that. It was fun."

"It was?"

"Of course. It was only games. I knew that, she knew that. When she wanted to speak to me straight, there were no games." Kendra still looked skeptical, so he went on. "Tell me, Kendra, when she came to you, to ask about me. Why did you tell her?"

Kendra thought a moment. "I see what you mean. I wasn't really sure, you know, whether she was playing some sort of deeper game."

"Typical female suspicion."

"No, Cheynou, don't ever fall for that. Feigned honesty is one of the hardest games to beat."

"But you decided…?"

"I decided that if she was being honest, she deserved the truth."

He nodded slowly. "And if she was playing games, the best way to beat her…"

"…was to tell her the truth."

They grinned at each other. Then Cheynou sobered. "Thank you for that, Kendra. Whatever the outcome, good or bad, I know she was acting on the truth."

"You don't know what I told her."

"Yes, I do."

"You do?"

"Perfectly. You told her the truth, just like you said."

"How do you know that for sure?"

"Because I can only think of two reasons in your head. The first one, the pleasant one, was that you were thinking of my best interests, and that would mean you would tell her what I would want to tell her, which was the truth."

She nodded. "I'm not sure I'm going to be so happy about reason two."

74

"Probably not, but it's much more interesting. If you were really interested in keeping me for yourself, you would have told her things that would make it seem that I was a bad risk. In other words, the truth."

She laughed out loud, short and sharp. "Cheychan, I think you need a drink. Nobody can be that convoluted when they're sober."

"All right. Bring the wine."

While she was gone, he raised his eyes to the sea before him. *If I had to live on land, this would be a good place. From here, I could see all the vagaries of the water, watch the tempests come and go, and yet be removed from the danger.* He snorted softly to himself. *Some day, when I'm too old to stand on a deck. If that ever happens.*

"What's funny?"

He grinned up at her as he accepted the glass. "I was just thinking that this would be a good place to live out my last days, when I am too old to sail."

She frowned. "Can you imagine being that old?"

"That's what I found funny."

She sat down, took an appreciative sip of her wine. "I've often thought the same."

"You have?"

"Yes. Lord Rochana was very generous. I could have had many homes with more status than this one."

She turned with an evil grin. "But we're getting off the topic. I was about to find out how Cheychan, Barbarian Lover, got his comeuppance."

His momentary lift disappeared. "That's not funny, Kendra."

"No, I suppose it isn't. But you have to realize, Cheynou, that to us ordinary mortals, it's quite interesting to see that people like you have problems, too."

He sat a moment, trying to understand. "Kendra, what kind of nonsense are you talking?"

To his surprise, she slammed her glass onto the table beside her, so hard that wine splashed. "Cheynou, there is something you had

75

better get through that thick skull of yours. You are not the same as all the rest of us."

"What?"

"You. Are. Not. The. Same!"

He sat back, not sure how to react. "Are you saying that I'm some kind of freak?"

"No, no, no. I'm saying you're someone special."

"I don't know what you're talking about."

She sighed. "All right. Let me put it this way. How do you picture Sarasha? How do you think of her? How did everybody think of her?" She placed a hand on his arm. "No, don't try to answer out loud. Just think of how you would answer. Do you have it?"

"I suppose."

"All right. Now apply that to yourself."

"Nonsense."

"That was too quick, Cheynou."

"What?"

"You didn't take your usual time to think about that. You rejected the idea out of hand. That means that it is either too unpleasant to think about, or you have already considered it and rejected it. Probably some of both."

"I think you're exaggerating, Kendra."

"Am I? Five languages — pardon me, now six — unless you count the new version of TradeSpeak they use here: seven. How old are you, Cheynou?"

"Seventeen. You know that."

"So why are all these men, these experienced captains, listening to a seventeen-year-old? Are they stupid or something?"

"They are interested in new ideas."

"New and useful, plausible ideas. Not the ravings of a young dreamer." She leaned forward and refilled his glass. "No, Cheynou, you have to admit, you're a bit ahead of yourself."

"Ah. It's because I'm a stranger. Once they get to know me, their interest will fade. Do you see any of them hiring me on his ship?"

"That will come."

"I wish I had your confidence."

"You don't need it. You stay your own, modest self and let the rest of us sweat and scrape for what we get."

A note in her voice brought his head around. "Kendra, what's wrong?"

"What's wrong with me? Nothing. This is about you, remember? Your heart is broken, and you're going to get drunk to forget about it. Finish that glass. You're behind."

"I'm behind? Why are you drinking so fast?"

"You might say I'm celebrating, too."

"Oh. What are you celebrating?"

"Nothing in particular, everything in general. You know."

"No, I don't. What do you mean?"

"Well, look at me. I have this cottage. I have powerful friends. I have a place in this society."

"You have a handsome lover, I would also mention."

"That too." She raised her glass in a toast, drank deeply.

"Is there something wrong with you and Suta?"

"No, no, not at all. He's off on duty somewhere, but he'll be back. He'll always be back."

"That's good."

"Yes, it is. He's a good man."

"I think so. Any talk of marriage?"

"I don't see him as that sort of man."

"That surprises me. He seems…would it be an exaggeration to call him loving? He's always so concerned about other people."

"Yes, that's his greatest asset. When he talks to you, you have all his attention. That he really cares about you. And I think he does."

"I agree. Then what's the problem? From my limited perspective, that sounds like a good man to marry."

"But he cares too much for others. He has no care for himself. He wants no responsibility." She shrugged. "A man of his talents could move upward through the ranks. But he refuses. He likes where he is. He enjoys his life, collecting people."

"Collecting people?"

"Do you notice what interesting friends he has? People of all walks of life; he doesn't care, as long as they are interesting."

"Yes, I see that."

"You're quite a trophy, you know."

"I'm getting used to that. Handsome barbarian and all that."

"Who has had an audience with the emperor. This is a fairly sophisticated group, but there are few in this city who have met the emperor face to face. And none of them young enough to be seen in our social circles." She grinned. "There's even a rumour that you had a private meeting with him."

He regarded her. "And what do you say when they ask you, as they always must?"

She lifted a shoulder. "I say that if it was a private meeting, then it was private. If the emperor wanted anyone to know, he would have told them."

"So, I'm a trophy for Suta, am I? And what about you?"

"Same thing. They are nice people around here. They call me 'the foreign princess' behind my back."

Cheynou shrugged. "Well, I don't mind being collected. He's a decent fellow, and I like him."

"Me, too."

"But if he asks…will you accept?"

"That depends."

"On what?"

"Oh, a lot of things. My opinion changes from day to day. I don't take that as a good sign."

"No, it probably isn't." He held out his glass for a refill.

"It definitely isn't. That's why it depends. I'm not going to make an important choice, like who is going to be the father of my children, when I'm likely to think something else the next day. Especially when I'm not sure he wants children."

"That's an interesting way to look at it."

"Why?"

"The father of your children. Not your husband. The father of your children."

She turned slowly to face him. "You have some learning to do, Cheynou, my boy."

"I suppose I do. Are you going to help me?"

"I don't know. I don't want to destroy your youthful romanticism."

"Oh, go on, spoil my romanticism. I'm in the mood."

"All right, young man, you asked for it. I am about to break a time-honoured trust, and all the young women of the world would scratch my eyes out if they thought I had revealed all to the enemy."

"The enemy? This sounds serious."

"It is. Once I tell you this, you will never look at a young lady the same way again."

He hitched forward, his hands cradling his half-empty glass. "This sounds interesting."

"Oh, it is, it is. Picture this, lad." She stretched her hand out, as if indicating a scene. "There he stands, Cheynou, Barbarian Lover." Her hand swept over. "There she stands, the demure and beautiful young daughter of the nobility. What are they thinking? I don't have to tell you what he's thinking. He's devouring her body with his eyes, as he will soon devour it with his hands, his whole body." She turned, fixed him with a glare. "But what is she thinking? Go on, tell me."

He grinned uncomfortably, shrugging his shoulders. "I suppose she's looking at his body, thinking how great he will be in bed."

"Right, and wrong!" She slapped her hand down on the table, to the continued danger of her wine glass. "She's looking at his muscles, but it has nothing to do with bed."

"It doesn't?"

"No. She's thinking of his muscles because she wants to know how well he will protect her children."

"Her children?"

"That's right. Her children. She's assessing whether he will be a good father. Is he smart enough to give them brains? Will their children be handsome enough to be successful? Will he be enough of a leader in the community to give them all the advantages they need to get ahead? Will he be a good enough hunter, fighter and warrior to protect and…wait a minute."

She got up and took the empty wine bottle inside. He sat there, thinking. It was an interesting perspective on the marriage game. He wasn't sure he believed her. Not completely. *Oh, it must have some effect. Now that I think of it, growing up as she did, with the certainty that she would be married off to whoever her father needed an alliance with… of course she would think differently.*

"Here. Have some more."

"Thanks. I've been thinking about what you said."

"You don't believe it."

"Not completely. I'm sure you do. I'm sure most girls take it into account a bit."

She smiled in triumph. "And you will never be able to look at another pretty young girl without wondering…"

He regarded her over the rim of his glass. "Are you being diabolical again?"

"Always." She toasted him again.

"All right. So let's say I believe you. So where does that put me? Parentally, so to speak?"

She placed her drink carefully on the table and turned to him deliberately, holding up one finger. "Absolutely the top. Number one."

"Now, that's real nonsense! Look at me. Smaller than everyone, footloose…"

She swept his arguments aside with a wave of her hand. "Top. No question. That Poppy is an idiot."

"What?"

"Idiot. Completely."

"That's not fair!"

"Fair? What has this got to do with fair? She let you go, didn't she?"

"Oh, right." Something was nagging at him but he couldn't quite bring it into focus.

"But you told her...told..."

"Told her the truth."

"That's what I said." He struggled to hold the logic.

"You did?"

"That's what I told her. I said you would tell the truth, because you knew that was what I wanted."

"That's very good, Cheychan. That's a very good reason."

"But if you think she's always playing games, why did you talk to her at all?"

She held her glass out, and he realized that the bottle stood at his feet. He poured and listened.

"Because she played the same game on me."

"What game is that?"

"The complete honesty game. The 'let's talk seriously' game."

"Why do you think it's a game?"

"They're all games, Cheychan. Even the one we're playing now."

"What game are we playing now?"

"Oh...all sorts of games."

"Gimme an example. What game are we playing?"

"All right. We are playing a game that you're upset because Poppy-Doppy gave you the heavey-hoey."

"But that's the truth!"

"I told you."

"I know. The truth is the deepest game."

She nodded seriously. "It can be, it can be."

"What other games are we playing?"

"Hmm, let me see. Oh, yes. We're playing that I'm your friend, and I sympathize."

"But you are! You do...don't you?"

"I tell you, Cheychan, the one thing you can count on is that I'm your friend. Don't you ever forget it."

"Of course not. I could never forget that."

"But as to the rest of it..."

"The rest of what?"

"The rest of it. All the rest of it." She swung her glass around, taking in the cottage, the garden, the town below them.

"Oh."

"That's right. The rest of it is all up for grabs. All the possibilities."

"Oh."

They sat for a moment, thinking about that. After a while, her head sagged onto his shoulder.

"It's very interesting, you know."

"What is?"

"You. Drunk."

"Is that interesting?"

"Yes." Her voice took on a dreamy tone. "It's always interesting to see people get drunk. They change, usually. You find out what they are really like when they forget to hide anything."

"And do I change?"

"Yes...no."

"That's really precise, Kendra."

"Well...yes, you change, but not really. You just get more Cheynou."

"I get more like me."

"Tha's right. More Cheychan than ever before."

"What does that mean?"

"It means that you're really you."

"Oh. Who else would I be?"

"That's what I mean. You're always just like you. You don't try to be somebody else."

"I see."

There was another pause.

"This is nice."

"Yes."

"I like it here."

"That's good."

"Are you going to stay?"

"Stay? Stay where?"

"Here. With me."

He slowly extracted himself, sat her upright. "What do you mean about staying here with you?"

She waved her hand, generally. "You know. Here. Kyabra."

"Oh. Yes. I think so. I have to go out, you understand, and do my Helming. But I'll be back."

"Good. That's good." She looked up at him from under the hair that fell over her face. Her voice became singsong. "That's not what you thought I meant."

"I didn't know what you meant."

"Yes, you did. You thought I meant tonight. Here. Stay with me."

He felt his face go red. "I didn't…"

She pushed his hand down. "Yes, you did. Admit it."

"The thought did cross my mind."

"And what did you think of that?"

"I don't know…"

"Yes, you do. Tell!"

"I thought I would be too drunk to make it worth much."

She laughed. "You lie, Cheychan, you lie."

"But it's a nice lie."

"Of course it is. You're just too polite to turn a lady down. You put it all on yourself. You are such a diplomat, Cheynou the

Barbarian. Such a diplomat." Again, her head leaned against his shoulder, and gradually it rested heavier. He set her gently upright, but she would not stay there. He slid his arm behind her shoulders and raised her up, but she would not stand. In the end, he slipped his other arm behind her knees and, with some difficulty, carried her into the cottage, taking great care not to bump her head on the doorjamb. He did find it necessary to lean there for a moment, half inside, half outside. Then he brought her in and straight to the back where her bedroom was. He laid her on the bed and stood, looking down at her.

To his blurred senses, she looked very thin and vulnerable, and he thought how cruel he had been to bring her all this way. Then he saw the look on her face. Satisfied, partly smiling. She was happy. He pulled a blanket over her and slipped out, closing the door gently behind him. The light was fading as he stumbled down the hill to the town, and he placed his feet carefully, aware of his condition.

9. CAPTAIN JATU

When he reached his rooms, there was a piece of paper pinned to his door. Since very few of his acquaintances here knew how to write, he took it down with eager care and read it.

Captain Nera Jatu requests the honour of your presence on the Courser at the fourth bell tomorrow morning.

He shook his head, desperately trying to think clearly. The *Courser*. What sort of ship was she? Small, or he would remember more. He sat on his bed, reading the note again. Captain Jatu. Had he heard anything? He couldn't remember.

Fourth bell. In the Kyabran time, that was earlier than back on the Eagle. Or was it later? He couldn't remember. He would just have to get up when he woke up and hope that he wasn't too late. He somehow got his shoes untied and fell onto the bed.

A loud banging on his door forced its way into his consciousness. He rolled over and was sorry. He wondered whether his stomach or his head would betray him the worst. The door thundered again, and he decided it would be his head. He eased his way erect, running into the bedpost as he did.

He made his way as quickly as he could across to the door. Anything to avoid that racket again. He slid the latch, pulled the door open a crack peered through.

A man in livery stood there, his fist ready to strike again. Seeing the door open, he stopped, waiting.

"Well..." Cheynou cleared his throat, which seemed completely clogged, yet dry at the same time. "What is it, man?"

"Lady Popinea requests the honour of your presence at the fourth hour."

There was something familiar about that, but he couldn't think what. "Of course. Tell the lady that I'll...no, wait a moment. Just wait there a moment."

He closed the door and returned to his room. Yes, there it was, the slip of paper. He read it again, then returned to the door, fumbling for the right words.

"Would you please inform Lady Popinea that an important engagement...prevents me from attending her at that time. I will come as soon as I can after that."

The servant nodded, saluted him and turned away. Cheynou mumbled the message again, aware that the ending was weak, but it was all he could think of.

Suddenly, a wave of fear washed over him. What time was it? Then he relaxed. It couldn't be near the fourth hour or bell, if Poppy expected him to be with her by that time. If the hours and bells were the same.

He shook his head, but his thinking wasn't working quite as well as it should. Remembering the amount of wine they had polished off last night, he wasn't surprised. Shaking his head hadn't been a good idea, and both the head and his stomach rebelled.

He had very little experience with hangovers, but he knew enough to listen to his throat. He was very thirsty. He went to the ewer on his dressing table and drank deeply. That seemed to satisfy his stomach. At least he didn't have to get dressed.

Then he looked down at his shirt, which looked as if someone had slept in it, and his pants, which seemed to have been in the way of several dribbles of wine.

Groaning, he peeled out of the soiled clothing, selected something dull and businesslike from the wardrobe and straightened it as best he could. Then he washed his face, patted his hair down, tugged out the messed laces so he could put on his shoes and staggered downstairs.

"Top of the mornin' to ya, sir."

He waved a hand in the innkeeper's direction, hoping a lack of voice would elicit a similar response. No such luck.

"Would you like a bite to eat, sir?"

"Yes. Just some bread, please, and light beer?"

The man grinned sympathetically. "Just the thing to settle the head and the stomach, sir."

"Is it that obvious?"

"To those of us with the proper experience, sir."

"Oh, what time is it, Loutra?"

"Just gone past the third hour."

"What bell is that?"

"The same, sir. Third bell."

"Oh. Good. Thanks, Loutra."

"I'll get the bread and beer, Mister Chan."

"Thank you." He rested his head on his hands as he waited.

"Here you are."

The bread was fresh, and the yeasty smell turned his stomach again, but he gamely chewed and swallowed. The beer at least helped it down.

"Dressed for business, sir?"

"Huh? Oh, yes. Do you know where the *Courser* is tied up?"

"A mere step away, Mister Chan. Over to the Merchants' Dock: the east side, I believe."

"What do you know about her, Loutra? Or Captain Jatu?"

The man nodded, sat as he was invited. "A good ship, from all accounts. Profitable. Long voyages, though. Some won't sign on 'cause they say some day she'll go too far and never find her way back."

Cheynou found a smile for that. "I'm a Navigator, Loutra."

The innkeeper grinned. "Then at least if you don't come back, you'll know who to blame."

"I haven't signed on, yet. Just got the message yesterday."

Of course the innkeeper would know about the message. "Yes. I spoke to the sailor that brought it. Close mouth."

Cheynou nodded in approval. No sailor should be spouting his Ship's business to an innkeeper.

"Does this mean you'll be leaving us, sir?"

"Could be, Loutra. I'm paid till the end of the month, in any case."

"That's good of you, sir."

Cheynou slid the empty platter across, shoved his unsteady way to his feet. "I suppose I should go and see what the man wants."

The innkeeper stood before him. "A moment, if you'll allow me the liberty, sir…" His hands were busy before he finished, tugging at Cheynou's collar, straightening, brushing, refastening. It didn't take a moment, and the man stood back, surveying his work with a satisfied smile. "Much better."

Cheynou tried to look down at himself. "That was very deft, Mister Loutra."

"Learned in the army. Batman to a colonel."

"Well, thank you, Loutra. I'm sure I look much better than I feel."

The man stood back. "Your good luck is my bad, sir, but I'll wish you good fortune anyway."

Cheynou grinned and, feeling more able to face the world, stepped outside.

The air was fresh and still cool, and his head cleared as he strolled along the dock. He was early, so he took time to observe the ship from a distance, taking her in as he approached. She looked very tidy: a three-masted brigantine with a good length of deck. The aft section seemed low, but he was continually adjusting his eye from the Familyships he was used to, with their huge, and he now knew ungainly, fore- and sterncastles. If the Eagle had taken off half the windage of her bow and stern fighting towers, she could have sailed so well that she never would have had to fight.

He clamped down on the pang of nostalgia that brought, and stepped forward more briskly, trying to erase his final image of his beloved ship, her back broken on the rocks.

An alert sailor whistled his approach, and the bosun was there to welcome him aboard. Looking around the deck, Cheynou was again impressed. Despite the usual dockside repairs and lading, the ship was still neat, and the gear looked well used but not severely worn.

The bosun noticed his glance. "You'll not be findin' a rope's end out of place, sir."

"She looks trim, Bosun, I'll say that for her. How does she sail?"

"Like a swan on the breast of the water, sir."

Cheynou took a moment to show appreciation for this flight of poesy. The man laughed. "I heard a lady say that once, and I sorta liked it."

"It's very pretty, Bosun. I doubt it'll get your drinks paid in a dockside tavern, though."

They shared a chuckle, and the sailor opened the door for him.

The captain's cabin was aft of the wheel and led straight off the deck from a sheltered alcove. Cheynou approved. The man in charge needed to be available to the helm at any time.

Then he was inside the cabin, all his concentration on the man before him.

Captain Jatu was a stoutish gentleman of about fifty, his face red under the dark tan of the sailor. Kyabran in heritage, probably. He had an open smile and seemed genuinely pleased to greet a visitor to his ship.

"Welcome aboard, Mister Chan. What do you think of our little vessel?"

"She looks very trim, sir."

"Aye, she is that."

"Smooth lines. Do most ships of this class have that much tumble-home?"

"Ah, you have an eye for design. No, most don't, but I like it. They say it makes it difficult to lade, and that's true, for our gangplanks are half a fathom longer than most. But in a beam sea she rides much more comfortably. When she heels far over, she still rides well. No wallowing."

"I have heard that said. I hope to observe it at first hand."

The captain laughed. "Well, perhaps you will, my boy. Perhaps you will. Come in and sit down, and let us have a chance to know each other."

Cheynou sat; the captain was observing him closely. He returned the gaze politely.

"I must admit, lad, that I'm a bit taken aback by your apparent youth. How old are you?"

"Seventeen, sir."

"Only seventeen, yet you have been voicing yourself around as a fully qualified Navigator."

"That's right, sir. I passed my apprenticeship three years ago, and have stood my share of the watches since."

"A journeyman at fourteen? Is that usual where you come from?"

"Not completely unusual, sir. We start training at six years."

"You have been training to navigate since you were six years old?"

"That is correct, sir. Every Navigator in the Fleet does."

"This is not a fleet I would know."

"No, sir. I trained on the Great Southern Ocean."

"So it really exists, does it? I have seen some maps, but they were very sketchy."

"Oh, aye, sir. I can witness it. Many's the night in the rigging, trying to get a star shot, I got more than enough of the Great Southern Ocean."

"You do star shots, do you?"

"I do, sir. I can navigate by sun, moon or stars, if you have the tables. I understand you have superior time-keeping as well."

The captain flicked a hand towards an ornate machine standing in a prominent place near the door. "It works quite well, although a really bad beam roll will slow it down."

"Even with the pendulum swinging fore-and-aft?"

"Seems to make extra friction. It doesn't stop, just slows down."

"Which is rather dangerous."

"Oh, aye, I'm surely aware of that."

"Are you a Navigator yourself, sir?"

"I can make the standard sightings, but my talents lie more in dead-reckoning."

"That's good, sir, because that is one area where a new Navigator on a ship is always deficient, and since I have never sailed on a schooner-rigged ship, I will take some time to become familiar with her, especially the degree of leeway."

Their conversation moved into the technicalities of sailing and navigation, and Cheynou was soon enjoying himself. Juta was knowledgeable enough to bridge the differences between the Kyabran systems and the methods that Cheynou understood.

The ship's bell rang six times, and both of them reacted in surprise. The captain chuckled. "That was a fine session, lad. I'll grant you good training. Do you see any problem in being an officer at your age?"

"The men usually understand me, sir."

"Understand you, do they?"

"Yes, sir. Once they understand that what I ask them to do is essential to their survival, they usually cooperate fully."

The captain laughed, loudly this time. "That's either the most naïve statement or the most insidious threat I have ever heard."

"I would prefer to think of it as realistic, sir."

"Well, perhaps I will get a chance to watch your system work. Are you available for a short voyage? A half-month only, just over to Kornat and back. Simple navigation."

Cheynou thought quickly, picturing the few charts he had been able to see. "Doesn't that take us past the Otok Reefs?"

"Aye, it does that, but the winds are usually offshore at this season, and we go upwind easily. In normal circumstances, we would pass there around noon of the second day."

"If circumstances were always normal, then any fool could be a Navigator, sir."

The captain's loud laugh rang again, and he rose, clapping Cheynou on the shoulder. "And any fool could be a captain as well. Come, lad, and we'll have a walk around the ship. You can bring your gear aboard tonight or tomorrow morning. We sail on the early afternoon tide the following day."

"That would be fine, sir. I'll come tonight. I could use the time to familiarize myself with your charts. That is, if you don't mind..."

He had discovered that some captains were as jealous of their charts as the Navigators on the Masterships. Some would not allow a stranger the chance to see his precious trading routes, with the opportunity to slip ashore afterwards with the information, never to return.

"Of course I don't mind. The more you know, the safer my ship will be. Do you need time to ask around, check me out?"

"I don't think so, sir. I enjoyed our conversation, and there are many things I can learn from you. A half-month trial would suit me."

The captain offered his hand, and Cheynou took it, realizing that this was probably the only formality they would observe.

"You'll get journeyman's rate for this trip, plus a small percentage of profits. Regular officers get shares in the enterprise as well, but we'll save that for later, if everything works out. Fair enough?"

"More than fair, sir."

They walked around the ship, once again lost in technical conversation, each enjoying the chance to discuss a ship with someone of different experience.

Suddenly, Cheynou slapped his head, as a thought intruded. "Captain, I completely forgot. I have an…a meeting that I promised to attend as soon as I was finished here."

The captain regarded him from under lowered brows. "And it would be best not to keep her waiting too long? Especially when you will soon be asea?"

Cheynou found himself blushing. "It…it's not quite like that, Captain, but you have the right idea."

"Well, don't stand around talking to an old man about boats, lad. Go and meet this lucky young lady and give her the bad news!"

"Thank you, sir. I'll see you before sundown."

"Good enough."

Cheynou saluted in the best Kyabran manner he could and jumped ashore, jogging down the dock. He couldn't really afford transport, yet he didn't want to arrive sweaty and breathless, so he dropped into his travel pace and strode up the hill to the Chieti manor.

When he arrived, he was shown into Poppy's receiving room by an older servant with a disapproving frown. Wondering what it was all about, he entered.

Poppy was sitting at the window, staring out, it seemed. When he entered, she turned, and he could see that she had been crying. He went to her immediately and knelt beside her.

"Poppy! What's wrong?"

She turned to him fully, took a deep breath, opened her mouth to speak, then suddenly burst into fresh tears, her face buried in her hands. "Oh, Cheynou, how could you? How could you have done this to me?"

"What? What did I do to you?" He patted her shoulder awkwardly, knowing he could take her in his arms, but fearing the consequences. *And I thought we were going to work this out logically...*

Gradually, her sobs settled and, finally, she raised her face.

"Now tell me what's wrong, Poppy."

"You really don't know?"

"No, I don't. When I left here, I thought we had done what was best for both of us. I still do, no matter how much it might have bothered me."

"Bothered you!" Her voice went up a pitch. "Bothered you? I hear you took care it wouldn't bother you for too long!"

He simply knelt there, unable to understand.

"Don't give me that innocent look, Cheynou. What did you do last night after you left here? Admit it!"

"What did I do?" A small idea began to form. "Do you mean going to see Kendra?"

"Yes, I mean going to see Kendra."

"I think I'm beginning to see. After leaving you, I went to visit Kendra. You think I shouldn't have done that."

"No, you shouldn't have done that."

"I'm sorry, Poppy. I'm very sorry if that bothered you, but I still don't see what the problem is. It's not as if I went to find another lover or something."

She took a deep breath, opened her mouth…and closed it again. She looked at him for a moment. "You really don't see the problem, do you?"

"No, I don't, Poppy. When I left you, I was certain we had done the right thing, but I wasn't happy about it. Truth be told, I was feeling pretty rotten and very lonely. I don't have very many friends here. In fact, I only have one. So I went to see her. I didn't have anyone else to go to. I went to Kendra and told her all about it, and how I felt, and she opened a bottle of wine and got me completely drunk, and I woke up this morning feeling so awful that I'm sure you couldn't think of any worse way to punish me for whatever blunder I have made."

As he made this speech, the fire seemed to go out of her. Finally, she shook her head. "For a smart man, you certainly are stupid, Cheynou. I try to blame it on the fact that you're a barbarian, but I doubt even your people treat each other like that."

"Well, if I'm so stupid, I guess you had better explain it to me carefully."

She sighed. "I would much rather be berating you for your unfeeling caddishness, you know. You have somehow twisted this around so that I get to do you a favour and feel good about it."

"If you would like to see it that way, I would prefer it. May I get up and sit in a chair for the lesson? My knee is getting quite sore, and it will affect my concentration."

She laughed at that and waved a hand towards a chair.

"All right. I'm ready to listen. Please tell me what heinous act I performed last night."

"Cheynou, I will only take a small amount of joking about this. I was truly hurt."

"And I am truly sorry. Explain, if you would."

"All right. I'll try to put it in terms that even a barbarian of limited mental ability can fathom." A tiny smile took the sting from her words.

"You say you lived on a ship. A big one, as far as ships go, but if you thought of it as a town, it would be very small."

"That's right. Only about four hundred people."

"Right. So you should know how everyone knows what everyone else is doing. Gossip, story, rumour, that sort of thing."

"Yes, I understand that. We Navigators stood apart from that, but I do understand. Did I create gossip about you?"

"Yes. Well, I'm not sure, but you could have. What does it look like, when you jilt me and then run to another woman?"

"But...but..."

She put a finger to his lips. "I know. You're going to say that it wasn't like that at all, and I have to agree with you. But that's not what it looks like, don't you see?" She leaned forward earnestly. "When you come and talk to me, then you go directly to her, and later word gets around that we are no longer...romantically connected..."

He sighed. "I see. It looks like I gave you the old heave-ho and ran immediately off to my real love, laughing all the while. Then they all can laugh at you, or look at you with sympathy, because you're such a fool. Oh, I'm sorry, Poppy, I didn't think of anything like that. Couldn't you spread it around that the barbarian is an idiot, and you chucked him, and he went running back to Mama?"

She sighed too, and sat with her hands in her lap, staring at him. "You are so difficult."

"I'm what?"

"You are just so difficult. You listen so well, and understand so fast and are so genuinely sorry that I can't hate you; I can't even be very angry at you."

He sat back. "Seriously, Poppy, that's a very dangerous state to be in."

"What do you mean?"

"Think about it. I don't want to seem arrogant, but there is one more choice, and it isn't the right one."

"Oh. You mean deciding that I like you more?"

"Yes. And I have some news that should help."

"News that will help me not like you any more?"

"I hadn't thought of it that way, but yes. I've found a ship."

"You have? That's good!"

"It's the *Courser,* with Captain Jatu. I'm only signed on for a short voyage: a half-month out to Kornat and back. But if things work out, I'll sign on for a longer voyage. Maybe as long as a year. Won't that help?"

"Help what? Oh, help me? Yes, I suppose it will. Don't worry about me, Cheynou. Once my mind is made up, even I can't change it sometimes. I think this is wonderful. You have a ship!"

"Thank you, Poppy. I'm so glad you aren't angry with me."

She shook her head. "I'm not angry. I was hurt, and I needed to be reassured. Now I am." She sat upright, in a pose she knew was pretty, and smiled at him.

"Now all you have to do is fix the eye shadow that is running down your cheek, and I'm sure you will be presentable to anyone, especially the next handsome young man who falls into your grasp."

Her eyes widened. Her lips tightened, and then she laughed. "Cheynou, I'm going to make an exception."

"Are you? I gather I am going to be this exception, and I am supposed to be greatly honoured?"

Her smile brightened. "Cheynou, you are such a gentleman. Yes, I don't usually find it a good idea to try to stay friends with an old lover. However, in this case, I think I will try."

"Since we were never lovers, that might help."

"Of course we weren't. Heavens, I've never had a real lover! It was just a turn of phrase. I thought it sounded better."

"It certainly sounded impressive, and I am overcome with gratitude."

"As you should be."

"And now, my friend, I have a problem."

"Do you?"

"Yes, and you can help me with it."

"For a friend, anything."

He smiled ruefully. "Maybe not this one. I have to go and tell Kendra now. You see?" He demonstrated with his hands, as if helpless to explain. "Here...to there...sort of directly."

She waved a hand airily. "Oh, of course you must tell her. She will want to know. She will be so proud of you!"

"Yes, I suppose she will be."

"If she's at home, of course."

He caught a note in her voice. "What do you mean?"

She smiled archly. "Only that while you were sleeping off your indiscretion this morning, the Fourteenth Lancers Troop rode in."

He felt a moment's pang, but tried to ignore it, to smile. "Then I'd better get over there in a hurry, because she won't be home for long."

He turned away from her searching gaze, rising as he did so. "So if you don't mind..."

She was on her feet before he remembered he was supposed to help her up. "Of course. I'll see you to the door."

There, she kissed him briskly on each cheek, as the Kyabrans did with their friends, and gave him a little push, speaking loudly. "Have a safe voyage and come and visit us when you get back!" Then, with a quick wink, she disappeared inside.

He grinned to himself. *That ought to take care of the gossip.*

He strode down the road, his feelings at war. He was so pleased to be able to tell Kendra that he had a ship, but if she was off somewhere with Suta.... He consoled himself that maybe the officer had duties that would keep him busy during the day.

He was doomed to be wrong on both counts. A sweated Beauty stood, hip-shot in weariness, outside Kendra's door. He slapped the damp, warm shoulder, appreciating the quality of the animal, and knocked at the door.

"Come on in!" The loud male voice sounded from somewhere in the interior. He took a deep breath and obeyed.

Suta and Kendra had been sitting on the sofa in front of the window, but both rose as he entered.

"Cheynou! How is my favourite barbarian today?" Suta greeted him with the one-armed hug, cheek-to-cheek, that the locals favoured.

He returned the hug firmly. "Quite well, thank you. More than quite well, actually."

The soldier pulled back in surprise, his glance going to Kendra. "That's good, Cheynou. Kendra led me to believe…"

He grinned. "No, that's over with. Even more so, now. I have a ship!"

"A ship!" Kendra threw her arms around him, spun him around, then let him go and plunked him down on a chair. "Tell us all about it."

With two interested faces confronting him, his feelings of unease evaporated, and he explained it all.

When he had finished, Suta nodded. "I know Juta. He brought a horse from Glendambo for me once. Takes long voyages. Takes risks." He grinned. "Makes money."

"Well, for the next half-month he's taken a risk that's going to pay off in the long run, because he's going to get himself a truly superior Navigator."

They both laughed. "That's the way, Cheynou!"

"Go get it, lad!"

Suta rose and tugged them both up, one with each hand. "This calls for celebration."

Cheynou pulled free gently. "Actually, Suta, I'd really like to, but…" his hand flapped between the two of them "…you just got back."

They both began to protest, but he shook his head. "I have to be on board before sundown, and I have a lot of things to take care of. You know how it is. You think you're ready to pick up and leave at a moment's notice. Then the moment comes, and a dozen things really need to be done."

"So this is it, then?" Kendra's face lost all its joy. "We won't be seeing you until you get back?"

"Fifteen days, more or less."

"Of course. Well, have a safe voyage." Her arms went around him, tightly this time, and she seemed not to want to let go. He looked over his shoulder at the soldier, who grinned slightly and rolled his eyes. Cheynou had to grin back.

Then she released him, making a big show of fixing her hair, but he saw her wipe her cheek. He turned to Suta for another sturdy hug, then left the two of them, each with an arm around the other's waist, standing in the cottage door like a comfortable, married couple. He firmly planted that image in his mind as he walked away. It was a good picture. She looked so happy. The more he believed that, the easier everything would be. He thought again of Poppy. Maybe, when he got back, he would check on the status of their friendship.

10. OFFICER

Being an officer turned out to be quite different from what he had expected. He was confident of his navigational skills, and he was right about that. Once he had the ship's upwind abilities figured out, he became accurate in his dead reckoning, and when the weather closed in, he got sunshots only his father would have made and, in all, he kept the ship on the shortest, safest course anyone could ask. It was the officer part that worried him.

He discovered that while it was very easy to watch officers work and note the mistakes they made, it was another matter to see why they were successful. *After all, when someone makes a mistake, it's obvious, and then you figure out what he did wrong. It's much more difficult to figure out why someone doesn't make mistakes. Which I am not doing. Not making mistakes, that is.*

He rolled over in his narrow bunk, hearing the ship's clock strike an hour when he should have been long asleep. *Which is why my mind is going around on stupid thoughts like that.*

He rolled over and banged his elbow on a ledge that wasn't there in his cabin on the Eagle. A deep sadness rolled over him as he thought of his little closet, about a third the size of the cabin he now owned, but far dearer to him.

What in the name of all the gods am I going to do about Noyes?

He rolled over again, and his mind rolled over as well.

* * *

"Captain Jatu, I have a problem."

The captain looked up from the ledger he was writing in. "What is it, lad?"

"Well, I find it difficult to put this, sir, but I am an officer on this ship, am I not?"

"Of course you are. The Navigator is technically the Second Officer: above the Bosun and below First Officer Toban."

"Are the men aware of that?"

The captain shot him a keen glance. "You are suggesting that they are not?"

"It's a difficult situation, sir. It was the same on our Familyships. As Navigator, I'm really outside their chain of command. I don't have to know a thing about working the ship in order to perform my duty. Therefore, it is not necessary that an order from me would have any validity."

"True, but you are an officer on this ship. If you give an order, it must be obeyed. If it is not, we have a problem."

"I know."

"Do you wish me to speak to the men?"

Cheynou shook his head slowly. "I don't think so, sir. Nothing you could say will increase my personal authority."

"If anyone refuses an order, he could be flogged."

"I don't think that would help much, sir. Not with the kind of problem I'm having. Nobody has actually refused an order yet."

"But you think they might."

"Unless I do something about it."

"Oh. And do you have something in mind?"

"Yes, I do, sir. I was just checking with you first, so I was sure of my position."

"What did you have in mind?"

"I'll just talk to a few of them, sir."

"Talk to them? These are sailors, lad. I doubt that talking will get you far."

Cheynou grinned wryly. "I think perhaps I talk different from most people, sir."

"That's true, Mister Chan. You do." The captain waved a dismissing hand. "You go talk to a few of them and let me know

101

how it goes. If it comes to a flogging, we must have very good reason."

"I have seen far too much flogging for bad reasons, sir. Thank you."

Cheynou picked his time and his man very carefully. Noyes was a good sailor, a bit older than most, and the definite ringleader if any mischief was up. The opportunity came after chow the next night when Cheynou was lugging the ship's astrolabe up the companionway. The Kyabran astrolabes were far bulkier than those of his people but they were more accurate, so he didn't complain. This one was a fine piece of equipment and it wasn't that heavy, but with its thick canvas cover it needed both his hands to carry on a pitching ship.

"Hold that door for me, will you, Noyes?"

The sailor looked at his predicament, grinning. "That thing too big for you?"

"No, Noyes, but it would be a whole lot easier if you held the door."

The man reached out slowly, pulled the door open, secured it, then stood back to watch his officer wrestle the astrolabe through.

Cheynou stopped, set the instrument down and beckoned. "I need a word with you, Noyes." He strolled to the rail, leaned against it. At his gesture, the sailor did the same.

"What do you think of this ship, Noyes?"

The man looked around, surprised. "I don't know. She's a trim ship."

"I would agree with that. When you're ashore and you walk down the dock towards her and you see her there with all the other ships, what do you think?"

"I think she's trimmer than most, sir."

"And why is that?"

"I dunno. We just keep her that way."

"And perhaps because the First Officer is pickier than average?"

The sailor frowned, glanced at him, then away. "I suppose so, sir."

"But even so, you're proud to be a sailor on her."

"That's true. I'm proud to sail on this ship."

"You know, where I learned my sailing, it was even more than that. The ship I sailed on was my Family's home. She was all we had. If the honour of our ship was threatened, the honour of our Family, our Crew and our whole people was threatened. Do you understand that?"

"You mean to say you lived on a ship all your life? And your whole family, women and kids and old folks and everyone?"

"That's right. Can you see how you would feel towards a ship that was your whole life?"

"I can see as the ship would be important to you."

"Right. So you can understand that I'm even prouder than you when I walk the docks and see our ship, standing out among the rest."

"I see, sir." By the puzzled look, Cheynou could tell that the sailor really had no idea where this was going.

"Right. But on the other hand, if I see something that makes me less proud of my ship, it bothers me. And because of my upbringing and because I'm an officer, and responsible, I'm even more bothered. I find myself...disappointed, I suppose is the word. Disappointed in the crew, disappointed in myself. Understand?"

"I think so."

"When I see a sailor who doesn't treat an officer with proper respect, for example."

There was a pause, and the sailor's eyes seemed fixed on the deck in front of him. "Oh."

"You can see that I might be quite disappointed in that crewman, because proper respect for the officers is part of the pride of the ship."

The eyes slid sideways to him, then back to the deck. "You gonna have me flogged, sir?"

Cheynou grinned. "For what? Not holding a door open quickly enough? No, I don't think that would be good for the ship, no matter how it might gratify me."

"Oh."

"You understand my problem, Noyes. If you get in the habit of answering slowly when I speak, you might think it was a fun little game to test out the new officer, but it could cause all sorts of trouble. If I need a course change because I know there's a reef, and I call it out and you react slowly, then where are we?"

"Up on a reef, sir."

"Not likely, of course, but it is possible. And one thing I know is that people don't suddenly get good at things just because there's an emergency. They get good at them because they practise them all the time. Even little things like showing proper respect to an officer."

"I see, sir."

"I think you understand."

"Oh, yes, sir. I understand that you wouldn't want to be…disappointed…in your ship."

"That's right, and I wouldn't want you to do anything that wouldn't make this a ship you are proud to sail on."

The man nodded, and they lounged against the rail for a while.

"So you're not gonna have me flogged, then, sir."

Cheynou leaned away from the rail to look at the sailor's face. "Do I sense a bit of disappointment there?"

"Disappointment? At not bein' flogged?"

"Yes. I think I do."

"That would be pretty strange, sir, if I was to be disappointed at not bein' flogged."

"Yes, but I wonder if it wouldn't be worth a short flogging just to get the upper hand on an officer in the men's eyes. I know it sounds backwards, but it is possible."

"I suppose."

"I think a person who was willing to go through that for the small advantage it would give him does not think, perhaps...as a normal person does."

"It does sound pretty strange, sir."

Cheynou nodded, thoughtfully. After a while, he nodded again to the sailor, pushed away from the rail, and went to work on his sightings, leaving the man still staring at the decking.

The First Officer caught him the next evening as he was putting his equipment away after his sunset calculations. "I've been meaning to talk to you, Mister Chan."

"Certainly, Mister Toban." He followed the other officer out onto the deck, and they stood together at the weather rail, gazing out at the darkening sky.

"I have noticed a problem, Mister Chan."

"With the men, sir?"

Toban turned to look at him. "Yes. You are aware of it, too, are you?"

"I gather it is not unusual for the Second Officer to have that problem. Since I was hired on primarily as Navigator and only as Second Officer by default, it is likely that it will be more difficult to establish myself. My age doesn't help."

"Exactly. You will have to assert yourself more firmly. This is something that does not seem to be in your nature, Mister Chan, and I find that disturbing."

"Disturbing, Mister Toban?"

"Yes. There is a potential for serious difficulty. Difficulty for an officer disturbs the smooth flow of the operation of the ship. That, I find disturbing."

"I can see how you would, sir." He waited a moment, but the other officer did not seem to have anything to offer.

"I have spoken to the captain about it, sir."

"Asked him for support, did you?"

"No, sir. I clarified my position and asked for his permission to take steps to deal with the problem."

The older man turned to him with more respect. "That was well done, Mister Chan. What steps will you take?"

"To start with, I had a chat with Noyes."

"A chat? Mister Chan, that is one man you will not get anywhere with by chatting. I suggest, since you have realized that he is the ringleader of any disturbance, that you take the first possible opportunity to have him flogged. The rest will fall in line."

Cheynou gazed out over the water for a while, thinking exactly how to put this. "Mister Toban, you need to realize that I am not like you."

"Of course I realize that."

"I do not have your age, your upbringing, or your training. Nor do I have your personality."

"I am fully aware of that, Mister Chan, and that is what worries me."

"However, I do have a background of my own. I have had a full lifetime of experience with how people act on ships. I have observed officers, good and bad, my entire life." He turned to the other officer.

"So you must allow me to solve this problem in my own way. I am confident that I will succeed. My only concern is that, because you and I are so different, there may be some...misunderstanding on the part of the crew. Because you are more direct, and I am more...shall we say...encouraging, they may think I am trying to curry favour with them, perhaps at your expense. I will do my best to ensure that does not happen, sir."

Toban shook his head. "I am not happy about this, Mister Chan. I have seen too many young officers who thought they could succeed by being friendly with the men. It always ends in failure."

Cheynou nodded. "I understand, sir. But it is my nature, and if I follow my own nature rather than trying to take on an aspect of yours, I will be more successful in the end. Do not think that I will be any more forgiving of error because of it. In fact, that is one way in which I will follow your lead. I notice that when you give discipline, it is almost always for some flaw in sailing performance, not in obedience. In that way, you are upbraiding the man for failing to perform his duties and thus putting the ship at risk. Otherwise, you would be challenging the man for his obedience to you, which puts it on a more personal level."

"I am pleased you understand that, Mister Chan."

Cheynou grinned. "I have a few sailing tricks up my sleeve as well, Mister Toban. I can keep the men on their toes."

"I hope you can."

Cheynou sobered. "So do I, sir."

The captain seemed to have taken some thought to Cheynou's problem, because he began to find opportunities for the Second Officer to take responsibility for supervising small parties of crew. Cheynou also took more care to observe the sailors at their work, learning the craft of seamanship as it was practised on Kyabran ships.

He was patient, taking care not to intrude unless he was absolutely sure.

"Jonis."

"Yes, sir?"

"I think you rather rushed that lashing."

"Oh, no, sir. I did it real careful."

Cheynou regarded the sailor with mild interest. "You misunderstand, Jonis. That is my polite, barbarian way of asking you to re-lash that spar. It looks messy, there are three loops hanging free which could catch on another piece of rigging, and," he shook the spar firmly, "any pounding we take in a head sea will shake it loose about that fast."

"We aren't in any kind of head-sea situation, sir."

"Jonis. Are you seriously suggesting to me that you consider this a good piece of work? The best you can do? The safest for the ship and all your crewmates?"

"Well...no, sir."

"So why are we standing here discussing this? At the beginning of this conversation I thought you had perhaps made an honest mistake. Now I'm not sure of your abilities."

"Oh."

"So, please reassure me, Sailor. Show me that you know how to do a proper lashing."

Jonis tore the offending line off and lashed it carefully and securely. When he had finished, he stood back with a 'find fault with that' attitude.

Cheynou ran a hand over the work, tugged here and there and nodded. Then to the sailor's surprise, he began to take it off again. "I'm going to show you something, Jonis. On the Great Southern Ocean when we are weathering a winter storm we sometimes need to be more certain that spare lumber doesn't come adrift about the deck. So when we do a square lashing, as you did..." he started the same way the sailor had "...we add an extra loop here, and pull it thus...do you see?"

The sailor's puzzled frown faded. "Oh. Yes, sir. That doubles the tension, sir."

"Exactly."

"Try it."

The sailor immediately repeated Cheynou's procedure.

"Well done, Jonis. However, you also realize that if you lash it that way, it takes an extra twist to undo it. If we were to leave it like that and one of the other sailors needed to get at that spar in the dark, he would have trouble because of the unfamiliar lashing."

The sailor nodded.

"So I think you should take the opportunity to teach the other crew members that trick. Then, when we need a really secure lashing, I will order it, and you will all know how to do it, and everyone will recognize it when it is done."

"Aye, sir." The sailor thought a moment. "Are you saying I need to take this off and do it again, the old way?"

"I think that would be best, Jonis."

The man shook his head. "By the Lady, sir, I think I would have been better off having done it right in the first place."

"Possibly, but now you have learned something, and the whole ship will be safer for it."

"True, sir."

"Carry on, Jonis."

"Aye, sir."

Cheynou turned away, making certain that the sailor knew he wasn't staying to see if the job was done properly. He had every reason to believe it would be.

11. Historian

The rest of the voyage was like a dream. He was doing everything he had pictured. His navigation was accurate, the crew responsive to his orders and the business went well enough that his small share of the profits made a comfortable bulge in the purse at his belt. But he didn't look back as he left the ship.

Dropping his duffle off at the *Bosun's Bunk*, he put on his best shirt and headed up the hill.

He was surprised, upon entering the cottage, to see the books. Books, scrolls, single parchments, packages.

"Sold the place to a library, have you?"

She greeted him with her usual lingering hug, laughing. "No, they're all borrowed."

He released her reluctantly and looked around again, impressed. "That's a lot of trust." No matter what the subject, the value of the knowledge in this room was incalculable.

"You're not the only good talker in this expedition."

"And what have you been talking about?"

"History."

"History?"

"Don't say it like that." The hand that slapped his shoulder continued its arc to indicate the piles in the room. "History is interesting."

"I'm sure."

"Now you're treating me like your half-wit cousin. I'm serious. Oh, not the kind of history where you just memorize what happened, then tell it to people."

"What other kind of history is there? Are you planning on making up a new one?"

"Exactly!"

"I was joking, Kendra. If you make up history, it isn't history, it's just a story."

"No, no, you're wrong. You started me on this yourself."

"I did?"

"Yes. With the languages."

"What do you mean?"

"You were telling me about the languages, and how they are similar in some places and different in others. And back up on the trail, when we found that ancient campsite, we could figure out who had been there, how many of them, how many animals and how long ago. That gave us all sorts of information that isn't written in any history books," she stopped for a breath, "or if it is, we can confirm it, because we have solid facts."

"Right. I see. So, what about the languages?"

She tugged his sleeve, bringing him to the kitchen table, which now had a map spread across it.

"Look at this. If SeaSpeak, as you call it, is spoken here, where I come from, and on the Southern Ocean, where you come from, and also in the Inner Provinces, away to the north, what does that mean?"

"I guess it means we all come from the same people."

"Right. And as far as anyone knows, there are only two ways to get from there to here."

"The trail we came on, and..."

Her finger traced along the coastline to the east, "...and through this strait here, between this continent and the next one."

"That map doesn't seem sure that passage exists."

"Not absolutely sure, because no Kyabran ship has ever recorded traversing it. Now our language analysis gives more evidence that it exists."

"You're saying that my language knowledge can help me learn history, which gives me information useful for my Navigating."

"Right!"

He tilted his head, made a downward smile. "I'm impressed. What are you doing with all these books?"

"I'm getting an idea of Kyabran history. Not recent history. The old stuff. I can apply this kind of thinking to it, put together a lot of what they think are unrelated facts, and firm up a lot of their ancient history."

He smiled. "And what do the local historians think of this revolutionary technique of doing their business?"

Her head came up. "There are some who call it the arrant nonsense of an ignorant girl."

"They did?"

"Well, one old fogey said words like that, apparently."

"I hope you put him in his place."

"Didn't get the chance. I've never met him, probably never will."

"What about the rest?"

Her hand swept the room. "What do you think?"

"I think they've given you enough rope to choke yourself about five times over."

"Cheynou, have faith!"

"Oh, I do. I just find it difficult to picture that they do."

She laughed. "A lot of them probably don't. That doesn't bother me. As long as they've loaned me all these precious books, they can think what they like. The ones who really are interested have given me more than books. They've told me some areas where I might be able to work: places where there are holes in the history texts. That's how I can tell whether they're serious about helping me."

"Well, it looks as if you've got a lot of help."

"I do."

She pulled him outside to sit on their usual bench, facing the sea. "There's another thing I have to thank you for. You kept telling me that the things I learned at home would be useful, and you were right."

"I'm usually right. It's nice to have it recognized once in a while."

"Aha! But you weren't right in that sense. You see, what I discovered was that when you observe the manners of a group of people from the outside and analyze them, you can apply some of the same history techniques!"

"You can?"

"Yes. Customs and habits work the same way as language. If you know that somebody makes his formal bows in a certain way, and you find somebody else that uses the same set of bows in the same situations, you have found a historical connection."

"I suppose so."

"Even cooking!"

"Wait a minute." He regarded her face keenly. "All right. You're not joking. That's worse."

"I am serious, Cheynou Chan. If two people, hundreds of leagues apart, cook the same meal the same way, then there is some connection."

"Wait a minute." He pretended to think. "This is really bad. I'm starting to follow you."

"Aha!"

"Yes. If they cook it the same way and call it by a similar name..."

"Right. That ties it all together."

"So you propose to travel around the Empire, sampling the food, learning their manners and comparing names for everything."

"What a good idea, Cheynou!"

"You never thought of that, I suppose."

"I hadn't. I was busy with the studying part. I must learn a great deal before I have anything to compare to. But once I have the basic history laid out, I could do that. I might even hire you to be my trusty native guide."

"And language expert."

"That, too. Unless I'm better at the languages than you by that time."

"You really are planning to study, aren't you?"

"You know, it's amazing how many of the most ancient history texts are in Frasian..."

"Which supports my theory about Kyabrans coming from somewhere else."

"Could be." She made a rueful smile. "I still have to learn to read Kyabran better than I speak it."

"It sounds like you are planning to take a long time at this."

"I'm not setting out next month." She glanced sideways at him. "But you might be?"

He seesawed his hand. "Captain Jatu was satisfied with my work. He's been talking about his next journey, and it sounds like a long one. The fact that he spoke of it in front of me is significant."

"And if he hires you, that means we'll be based here for some time."

"As long as I work with him."

"That's good."

"It is." He glanced at her. "But you mean something else, don't you?"

She looked away, then up at him. "Yes, it's good because I'm not going to be very good at travelling for a while."

"Not good at travelling? What does that mean?"

"It means awkward, heavy, difficult to move, and eventually burdened."

He shook his head. "I'm not getting this, Kendra. Please just come out and tell me."

She smiled up at him. "It means I'm pregnant, of course."

"Oh." The heartbeats ticked by, and his opportunity to say the right thing, whatever that was, disappeared.

"Don't just sit there gaping. Congratulate me."

"Oh, certainly." He held out his arms. "Congratulations. That's…wonderful…"

She laughed as she hugged him. "I caught the pause." She straightened. "It's hard to know how to react when a single woman is pregnant, but I'm happy about it."

"Then I'm happy about it."

They regarded each other for a moment.

"And I don't really have time to stay much longer. I only came to let you know we were in harbour, and now I have to go back and help with the unlading and the paperwork."

She gave a small smile. "Of course you do. Why don't you come to dinner tomorrow night? Suta will be glad to see you."

"Certainly." A thought struck him. "What does he say about it?"

"I haven't told him, yet."

"You haven't told him? Why not?"

"I wasn't really sure, and I wanted to do this exactly right."

"Of course you did. I'm sure he'll be ecstatic."

She tilted her head from side to side. "I'm not sure ecstatic is the right word. We'll see."

"Right." He jumped to his feet. "And now I really have to go."

She slipped up beside him, an arm around his waist, pulling him towards the door. "Back to work. Continue to be impressive. Get that Navigator position."

"Yes, I most certainly should." He gave her a quick hug outside then strode away, not quite fast enough to be considered running. The houses and shops passed by in a blur, while a phrase kept twisting through his head. *It means I'm pregnant.*

He rounded a corner and realized that he had passed his turning and was too far down the dock. Shaking his head, he returned to his proper course, resolving to pay attention. The

115

sight of the *Courser* sitting at the dock, a line of burdened longshoremen trooping down the gangplank, allowed him to break from his funk and think about his duties.

After one slow turn to look back up the hill, he dove into his work.

12. Parting

At supper the following night, the mood was light. Sabino and Teveria were there, and everyone was interested in his stories of the voyage. He watched Kendra and listened to her conversation, but it was certain that she had told no one about her condition.

As he was leaving, he tried to open the subject, but she put a finger across his lips. "On my own time, Cheychan. In my own way."

He forced a smile. "Well, just do it, and soon. It isn't fair." He leaned down to kiss her cheek, then straightened. "I won't be seeing much of you for a while. Jatu wants my opinion on some maps he has. He's gearing up for a big voyage."

"But that's wonderful. If he's talking maps, it means he's going to hire you."

"I hope so."

"Well, don't hang around here entertaining yourself. Get down to that boat and earn your keep!"

"Aye, ma'am." He looked at her. "I think you'd make a good captain."

She giggled. "I can just see that. At least I'd have a navigator to keep me from running ashore."

"Right. Well, until that unlikely day, I have a real captain to impress. I'll get back when I can."

"Don't you come up here unless you have good news."

"Right you are, Miss Tyrant of the Seas."

They laughed and hugged, and then he was off down the hill to the boat.

* * *

Two days later, he was at her door, his face hot and his breath coming in gasps.

She stood back to let him in. "Is the harbour burning up? I thought you were coming back with good news."

"It is. I'm leaving soon, Kendra. Captain Jatu offered me the place. Lead Navigator!"

"Oh."

He regarded her. "I...thought you'd be happy."

"When will you be back?"

"I don't know. A year, maybe more. Possibly not at all."

"Not at all!"

"Well, we're travelling west, checking out new trading possibilities. If we get far enough and discover, for example, a strait that leads into the Southern Ocean, I might just decide to continue my voyage and end up back in Ternata."

"But what about our journey? If you're continuing, you can't leave me here!"

"In case it slipped your mind, you're pregnant."

"So? I can still travel on a ship!"

"In case you also forgot, I'm not the father."

"So?"

"So, we aren't exactly 'we' anymore, are we? You have someone, and soon you'll have a family. This is a good place for you, Kendra. He's a good man. You can't keep on running."

"And you can?"

"I'm not running, Kendra. Searching, yes. Running, no. You've found what you were searching for. If you keep going, then you're running. You stay."

"But, Cheychan, what if I didn't find what I'm searching for?"

He regarded her and made his decision. "All right, put it another way. Whatever you have found, it doesn't include me. So I guess I'm running."

"I see."

"Do you?"

"I think so." They were quiet for a moment, looking out over the sea. She turned to him. "Promise me something?"

"If I can."

"Will you promise not to go away forever? Before you make the plan and actually keep going, will you come back and check on me?" She looked up, and he could see pain in her eyes. "Please?"

He shook his head, uncertain how to answer, but her obvious distress made him honest. "Jatu's backers are local, so sooner or later he always comes back to Port Tenet. The plan is for not more than a year. Of course, you know how these things go. You get a cargo, you deliver it, you find another cargo, it takes you somewhere else. As long as the captain is making money for himself and his partners, he keeps moving. Jatu has a reputation for moving farther."

"I see."

"And it's not very likely that we will end up in the strait to the Southern Ocean and meet another ship going the right direction that needs a Navigator. That was just me, dreaming dreams of glory."

"You will be back?"

He turned to her, trying to read her face. Finally, he gave up. "If I'm alive and able."

She smiled. "I'll take that."

"Good."

"What kind of ship is she?"

He sat down, relieved to be talking of something else. "Well, she's a three-masted barquentine. That means her sails are attached to the mast at the front, except for the foremast, where she has square sails like the Familyships. You've seen lots of those around here."

"Yes, yes, I know what type of ship she is. You told me that before you left last time. I meant, what kind of ship is she to sail on?"

"But I like that idea. She can actually sail upwind! If only Captain Tourne could see that." He shook his head. "Sail upwind."

"What is Captain Jatu like?"

Cheynou held out a hand, rocked it gently. "I like him…"

"…but?"

"Well, I don't exactly know. He's an older man, about fifty. He's well respected down on the docks here and at Kornat. You learn quite a lot about people in a two-week voyage. He runs a tight ship and I still like him."

"Then what's the problem?"

"Well, it's hard to say, but I get the impression that he's not that much of a seaman."

"Not a seaman? He's been a captain for all this time, and he's not a seaman?"

"That's what I mean. It's hard to figure, but having spent some time on the ship, I notice that he doesn't make that many decisions himself. He trusts his officers."

"That sounds good."

"If he has good officers."

"But if he doesn't know that much about sailing, why is he captain?"

Cheynou raised a finger and smiled. "Ah, but why are we sailing? To make money."

"I see."

"Right. And Captain Jatu is a very astute businessman."

"I see. He hires good people to run his ship and does what he does best, which is keep the money rolling."

"I knew you'd understand."

"Scratch any good farmer and you'll find a merchant."

"Exactly."

"It seems like a good ship, Cheynou. What is Jatu like as a person?"

"He's very friendly. Like a businessman, you know. Not much like the captains I'm used to."

"I suppose the important thing is that he will take you on."

"That's true. Not every captain recognizes the benefits of having Cheynou the Barbarian on his ship."

"And does he?"

Cheynou grinned. "I think I acquitted myself well on the voyage. He also tested my knowledge every day. Not obviously, but I could tell. I have to admit, for someone who doesn't know sailing like a captain should, he certainly knew what questions to ask a Navigator."

She smiled. "But why you? Surely there are plenty of experienced Navigators around here."

"That's the point. The Navigators around here have experience — around here. They know the area well, and that's all. Captain Jatu wants to take a risk. He wants to travel farther than the local Navigators have gone. Plus, there's the matter of cost."

"Cost?"

"Yes. A Navigator who has travelled a long distance costs a lot of money to hire. I'm rather inexpensive."

"Don't you sell yourself cheap, Cheynou Chan!" She jumped to her feet. "You're worth as much as any Navigator around here, maybe more!"

"All right, sit down. I happen to agree. But it's difficult to find a captain who thinks the same way. Captain Jatu does. At least enough to pay me a decent wage plus a rising percentage of the profits. Plus a chance to be the Lead Navigator on his ship. Of course, I'm Lead because I'm the only one. But that doesn't matter. I'm the Navigator!"

"And that means a lot to you?"

"It's my very first Ship, Kendra. Back on the Southern Ocean, I wouldn't have made Lead Navigator on a Ship until my father and my uncle died. But here I am, at seventeen years, with my own Ship!"

"Oh, Cheychan, I'm so proud!"

"You are?"

"Of course I am. I always believed in you. But I wasn't sure you did."

"What do you mean?"

"I watched you, Cheychan. I watched you calling yourself "The Barbarian" because that meant it was your name, not one someone gave you. I watched you worrying that you wouldn't get a chance to do what you want to do so badly. I worried too, Cheynou. But now you have your chance. I'm sure you'll do well."

His heart warmed and, for a moment, he could almost forget… "And when I come back, you'll be a mother."

There was a long silence.

"You'll be a good mother."

"Do you think so?"

"Of course. Whatever you want to do, you do well." He had a sudden thought. "Do you want to be a mother?"

"Of course! I mean…I didn't have it planned for…right now, but in general, yes, I want to be a mother."

He held out his hands, palms up. "Well, there you go. You'll be a good mother."

"I will certainly try my best."

He looked at her. "So you did it."

"I did what?"

"You succeeded in what you came for."

"I did?"

"Yes. I've been listening, you know. I have figured out why you came on this journey."

"Well, bringing you along was a good idea after all, because I've never been sure myself. Why did I come, and how do you know?"

"I just put it all together. The one thing that is most important to you, that your society would not allow."

"I can't wait."

"To choose the father of your children."

"That's it?"

"Of course. That's what you've been telling me, and I could see that you believed it."

"While you, of course, didn't."

"Doesn't matter what I believe. This is you. And that's what you wanted the most in your whole life. To make that choice. And now you have. You've done it, Kendra. You've achieved what you came for, and all this as well." His gesture took in the cottage, the books, ended with the beautiful view out the window.

"Then my quest is over."

"I suppose so. Congratulations."

"But yours is not."

"Not yet. But I'm working on it. I'm making progress."

She placed her hands on top of his. "And you'll come back and see...us?"

"If I'm alive and able. That's a promise, Kendra."

A sudden, radiant smile lit up her face. "Fine." She gripped his hands and shook them lightly. "This is good, Cheynou. You are getting what you wanted, and I think you're right. I may be getting what I wanted as well."

She stood up, started to pace. "Now, don't you worry about me. You just concentrate on getting settled on your boat and being the best Navigator they ever had. I'll take care of myself and the baby, and we'll see you when you get back. All right?"

He had risen when she did, and stood facing her, buoyed by her enthusiasm. "I suppose you're right. I'll do my best."

A thought struck him. "But tell Suta soon, Kendra. He'll want to know."

"You don't worry about that. I'll take care of all those details. You just concentrate on your work. That's what's most important."

She was moving away, and he had no choice but to follow. At the door, however, she seized his hand, stopping him. "When are you leaving?"

"Three or four days. Depends on the lading and the tides."

"I know you'll be very busy, but come and see me once before you go?"

"Of course. As soon as I have a definite time."

"Good." She threw her arms around his neck and held him tightly. He responded, amazed that the slim form in his arms would soon be burgeoning into motherhood. He smelled the scent of her hair, felt her lips against his ear, and then she pulled away, laughing.

"You know, Cheychan, I think everything is going to work out!"

His heart gave a pang as she slipped out of his arms, but he smiled, then turned and left her before she could see the sadness take over.

He looked back once as he walked away, and she was still there. She waved merrily to him, and he resumed his march down the hill. Down to the harbour and the waiting ship that would take him away from her.

The sailing business being what it was, he barely had time to see Kendra again. The next three days were filled from sunup to sundown with planning and supplying, and once the candles were lit, there was more planning to do. Some of the cargo was late, but once it came, the tide was rising and there was no stopping that.

Breathless, he pounded up the road and knocked desperately on the door of the small cottage.

"Cheynou! What's wrong?" She had been doing housework, her hair knotted at the nape of her neck and her apron smudged.

Now that he was here and she was at home, he could relax. "I'm sorry, little parlour maid. I came to speak to the lady of the house. Do you think you could find the manners to invite me in?"

She scoffed and slapped his arm. "Come in then, if only so I'm not seen chatting with errant sailors on the doorstep."

Once he was inside, she turned to him seriously. "But what's wrong, Cheynou? Why the hurry?"

"The tide's turning in two glasses and the ship's leaving, Kendra. I couldn't get away sooner. You know how it is."

She nodded. "I know. Can you sit down a moment?"

"Not long."

"Then come in." She took his hand and led him through the house to the bench that overlooked the sea.

They sat in silence, looking out at the ships, the water and the far horizon. She had placed herself very close beside him, and the warmth of her body seeped into him through her thin dress.

Then he felt her head on his shoulder. "Do you remember that day in the mountains, on top of the cliff?"

"I suppose."

"Do you remember what you said? About how wonderful the world was, and how you wanted to see it all?"

"I spouted off quite poetically, as I remember."

Her head left his shoulder, and she tugged him around to face her. "Well, you do that. You get out there and see the world. Enjoy it. Be a wonderful Navigator, Cheynou Chan, because you can and because you want to."

Taken aback, he smiled gently and looked down at her hands, clasping his tightly. "Thank you, Kendra, for your faith in me."

She released one hand, whisking it briskly away. "Oh, that's nothing. I know you're going to be successful. That's not what I'm talking about."

"It isn't?"

"No. It's about enjoying yourself. You love navigating, and I want you to go out there and be the best Navigator you can be, and be proud of it!"

She grasped his hands again, this time with more earnestness. "This is why you came here, Cheynou. This was the choice you made. We talked a lot about choices, but we never discussed what you do once you have made a choice."

"I thought that was…"

"Oh, no. You think it's enough to just make a choice and then see it through. That's not good enough, Cheychan. It may be good enough for others, but it's not good enough for you."

"And what is good enough for me?"

"You have to make a decision, and then you have to throw yourself into it and do the very best you can. And you think that's it. But it's still not good enough."

"It isn't?" He was truly puzzled now.

"No. You have to enjoy it. There's no sense going to all that effort and then being sorry. There's to be no second-guessing, Cheynou. No, 'If only I had…' You have to know that you have made the best choice, that what you're doing is the very best you could do, and you have to enjoy it. Can you do that?"

"Enjoy being a Navigator?" He smiled. "I think I can handle that."

"But no second thoughts. No sitting around saying, 'If only I had…' no wondering if Kendra had…or if I had…or if we had…you understand?"

"Oh. That."

"You understand?"

"I think so."

"Promise me?"

"Promise you what?"

"That you won't waste any time worrying about you and me, and how it might have been, could have been, should be, might be. None of that."

126

"That's a difficult promise, Kendra. You know how I…"

"Fine." She cut him off. "I'll take that as a promise. How soon do you have to go?"

"Very soon, now. I don't want them to wait for me."

"Then let's just sit here until then. We don't have to talk. Think of all those days on the trail where we would go for glasses without talking, just walking or riding, at peace with the world and each other."

He doubted that she had ever gone in silence for more than a glass, but it would be unwise to mention it at the moment.

"I know what you're thinking."

"Probably."

"So sit here, and I'll prove you wrong."

And she did just that. She clasped his arm, laid her head on his shoulder and sat, gazing out at the harbour and the ocean. She said nothing and, realizing her wisdom, he did the same. Everything had been said; more words would only make things more difficult.

He wrenched himself away from his reverie. "Kendra…"

She looked up. Tears beaded her lashes. "I know."

She rose, took his hand and led him to the door. Their embrace lasted a long time, but finally she wrenched away. After one look, one smile, he turned and strode down the lane, absently brushing her tears off the curve of his jaw.

The ship was bustling as he approached the wharf. The moment he was spotted, a shout went up, and lines began to snake aboard. He sprinted amid the laughter of the crew and leapt across a widening strip of water to the deck.

Good-natured jibes followed him up the companionway to the bridge, and he remained at the rail, setting in his mind the cottage, its doorway, and who stood there.

Then, remembering his promise, he strode into the Navigator's room and began to sort his charts.

13. MASTERSHIP

"Ship ho! Two points off the sta'b'd bow."

Cheynou reached for the viewing tube and searched the horizon. Sure enough, there was a sail. He twisted the lenses to bring the focus tighter. There was something familiar about that shape.

Suddenly, at a click in his brain, the fear hit him. He spun to the man at the wheel. "Helm alee. Tack her around."

"What...?" The sailor was confused by an order from an officer who was not on watch. His eyes shot to the First Officer.

"What's this, Mister Chan?"

"Unless you like the thought of slavery for the rest of your life, tack this ship around and hope they haven't noticed us."

That spurred them into action, and soon the little ship was racing away upwind. The commotion brought the captain on deck. "An unusual course change, Mister Toban."

"The Navigator, sir. That ship up to port, she's some kind of danger."

The captain turned to Cheynou. "What's the danger, lad? That ship doesn't look to be too much trouble at this distance."

"Do you know what a Mastership is, sir?"

"A Mastership? Can't say I do."

"Have you heard about the Sea Raiders of the Great Southern Ocean?"

The First Officer laughed. "The lad's been listening to the minstrels in the taverns, sir."

"You think the Masterships of the Priest-Admiral don't exist? That's reassuring, Mister Toban, to know that the tyrant that kept my Family and Crew in bondage for so many years is just a tavern story."

The captain frowned. "You have true knowledge of these Sea Raiders, these supposed pirates?"

"Sir, you know what some people call me. Cheynou the Barbarian. From the Prairies beyond the Barrier Mountains. Right?"

"I have heard this, yes."

"Do you think I learned my seamanship and navigating skills riding a horse?"

The captain smiled slightly. "Your logic seems impeccable, if your facts are accurate."

"Well, I have a fact for you, Captain Jatu. Train your lenses on that vessel over there and count the masts for me."

The captain stared for a long while through the tubes, finally shaking his head. "She's too low on the horizon. Toban, you're spry. Nip up on the ratlines for a better look."

The officer sprang to the rigging and stood, statue-still on the rolling ship, expertly training the tubes at the distant sails. Cheynou saw him lower the tubes, seem about to call down, then shake his head and go back to staring through the device again. Finally, he shook his head again and clambered down the ropes more slowly.

"Well, what is it, man? How many masts?"

"I couldn't be sure, sir, but I think...five."

"What? Five masts? Impossible. Nobody has ever built a ship that big. She'd break her back in the first storm."

The First Officer shook his head. "I think five, sir, with perhaps one full suit of sails above the topgallants."

"Two."

Both men turned to him. "Two?"

"Yes. The royals and the skysails above them."

The captain looked at Cheynou with new gravity. "And you say these people are notorious pirates? Are there many of them?"

"There are, in the Southern Ocean. The Priest-Admiral who rules the Fleet once commanded at least thirty Masterships like that one, and upwards of a hundred Familyships, threemasters like I was born on."

"Once? And now?"

Cheynou shrugged. "I don't know, sir. I came ashore with the Crews of eight Familyships who rebelled against the tyranny. When the Masterships came after us, we destroyed four of them and killed the Priest-Admiral. Then we moved north, inland, and haven't been back since."

"Well, you seem to know a lot about this, lad, what's your guess?"

"This might be a Mastership that has broken away from the Fleet. If so, we're in no danger, because making those big things go to windward is like driving a pig up an irrigation ditch.

"On the other hand, if it's part of a larger squadron of the Fleet, then every person on this Sea is in danger, on the water or on the shore. We need to warn someone."

"Hmm. So you say this Mastership doesn't go to windward well?"

"As you can see, she's square-rigged on all masts. Even carrying full staysails with her sheets in hard, she can't come more than two points above a beam reach, sir, and then she'd make so much leeway it wouldn't be worth it."

"Then we could close with her, as long as we keep a good weather gauge."

"It's always a risk, sir, but yes, I think we could."

"All right. I am intrigued by your story, and whether it is true — or shall I say whether it applies in the case of this ship — I would like to know more, as would the other merchants of Kyabra." He turned to the helmsman. "Tack her about again, man. Let's go look at this monster."

At the cry of, "Helm's alee," *Courser* swung back in the previous direction and bore off on a broad reach, running across the wind to the west.

"Sir, if I might suggest?"

"Of course, lad. We're going on your knowledge here."

"Extra lookouts, in case there are more of them."

"I was thinking of that myself."

"And if the wind begins to lighten, break off. They have very fast rowing gigs."

"Good advice, Mister Chan." He turned to give more orders.

They stood at the rail as their ship slowly closed the distance to the giant below her. Finally, the captain called aloft. "Any change in course?"

"No change, sir. And sir?"

"Yes?"

"She's not got five masts, sir. She's got four and a half. The mizzentop's gone at the hounds."

The captain grinned over at the First Officer. "There's your problem, Mister Toban. Your eyes aren't going bad, after all."

"Didn't think they were, sir."

Cheynou had taken a bearing on the ship the moment they tacked over again, and now he took another.

"She doesn't seem to be moving very fast, sir."

"No?"

"Hard to say at this angle. I'll take another reading in a while."

"All the better. Unless it's a trick."

"If they're trying a trick, sir, don't fall for it. That ship has three times the length of the *Courser*, and about twice the speed on a broad reach."

"I'll keep that in mind."

They watched in fascination as they passed half a league upwind of the behemoth.

"She's in trouble, sir."

"I can see she's moving slowly myself."

"She's low in the water, as well."

"That's low in the water? How tall does she stand normally?"

"About a fathom higher, I'd say. They are all designed identically, so I know the profile well."

Toban raised the sight tube again. "Plenty of action on the deck, but no panic. Looks like they're working on repairs." He peered closer. "What's that structure on the bow below the waterline?"

"A ram, sir. If she were trimmed properly, it would be just above water."

"A ram? On a sailing vessel?"

"Yes, sir. Rather impractical, you might say, but that's what it is. That's why the bowsprit points so much higher than on Kyabran ships. A broadside hit is very effective."

"I imagine it would be."

"But two boats crossing rams head on makes an incredible mess and usually takes the foremast out."

"So why do they have them?"

"Tradition, sir. The Priest-Admirals are big on tradition."

"You keep using that term. Is it some sort of religious rule?"

"That's right, sir. The Admiral is the Head Priest."

"And mutiny is also blasphemy. Hah!" The captain spat over the side. "I always said, you give a man that much braid on his sleeve, he thinks he's god. But I was joking."

"No joke, sir."

"I don't imagine. From what you say, I don't think these are the kind of people we want sailing around freely in our Sea. However, I cannot take the unsubstantiated story of a barbarian to the Kyabran Imperial Navy." His smile took the sting out of his words. "I think we must make contact."

"Be very careful, sir."

"I didn't get to be fifty years of age and a ship's captain by not being careful, Mister Chan." He turned to the bosun. "Catapult, if you please, Mister Freye."

"Aye, sir."

The sailors bustled around and set up a strange contraption on the aft deck. Cheynou was familiar with catapults, and this was a moderate-sized version, adapted to function on a heaving deck. The remarkable feature was the pocket, which seemed to be of metal, spoon-shaped, and blackened as if by fire.

At the captain's orders, the ship bore off the wind, down toward the sluggishly moving Mastership. As they came alongside, they hardened up the sails to run beside the larger ship.

"What language do they speak?"

"We call it SeaSpeak. It is similar to Frasian."

"Call to them, Mister Chan. Identify us and ask if they need assistance."

Cheynou jumped to the rail and, one hand on the ratlines, called the message across. He could see the response forming as the archers rose above the rail on the stern castle. He leapt down, calling a warning.

A volley of arrows skittered across the deck to stick in the planking. A sailor swore as one pierced his lower leg.

The captain remained cool. "Only essential crew on deck. Shield the helmsman. Catapult, load and light."

Now the meaning of the blackening became clear. A sailor came out of the cabin with a ball in a sling and lowered it gingerly into the spoon. Another man stepped up with a smoking torch, and the ball burst into flame.

"Fire when she's in range. Helm, bring her in."

The helmsman swung the wheel over, and they ran closer to the larger ship, bringing another hail of arrows. Then he swung back broadside again. As the ship turned, the catapult crew released. The ball, trailing smoke and flame, arched up against the sky. All eyes on both ships followed its arc until it struck the main lower topsail and slid, spraying fire and hot oil, to the deck.

The crew of the *Courser* cheered madly, but Cheynou tugged at the captain's sleeve. "They'll put that out. We need more weather gauge."

"Harden all sheets. Pinch her up, helmsman. Get us out of here."

Slowly, the smaller ship pulled forward and upwind of the stricken Mastership. They were too far away to see, but Cheynou could imagine the running crews, the buckets of sand, the flaming sail cut loose, no matter the cost to the mast'n. Sure enough, soon the smoke trailed away, and the Mastership slogged on.

"Well, that's enough for me, lad. I'm beginning to believe you for real now, and I have evidence to support it." He gestured to the arrows sticking in the cabin bulkhead. "I thought the phosphor would get them. Water just spreads it around."

"They have buckets of sand ready."

"Yes, they would."

"I have an estimate of her course, sir." Cheynou indicated the map on the chart table. "If they hold to it, they'll be in the Armorican Islands in two or three days."

The captain nodded. "We couldn't do much good trying to outrace them, since we don't know their intent once they get there. If they know the area at all, they might be thinking of hiding out in one of the back channels to make repairs."

"If they don't know the area, they'll grab somebody who does and press them into service."

"Pleasant people."

"As I keep saying."

The captain had made up his mind. "Maintain our course for Liore. We'll be there in two days. At the Imperial Naval Station they have the tonnage to take even a ship that size."

Satisfied, the *Courser* tacked over again and pushed off upwind.

Cheynou was surprised at their reception at Liore Naval Station. It seemed that the Imperial Kyabran Navy took their responsibilities seriously, and pirates were high priority. His history was heard in detail, first by a lieutenant, then by a board of several captains. The two days' voyage had given him time to think, and he laid out his ideas clearly.

"This ship is called the Springbok. The Western Fleet Masterships are all named for predators, so she must be of the Eastern Fleet. That means she probably came around from the east somehow. Alone, they will do serious damage to your shipping and your shoreside towns until you stop them. If they are harbingers of an invasion, you have a much greater danger to face, and I would look to the east."

"How accurate is your estimate of 130 ships?"

Cheynou faced the senior captain squarely. "At the time I left, it was very accurate. I could give you the names of every Mastership in the Western Fleet and most of the Familyships. However, as I say, the past three years have been rough on them, perhaps worse than I know. We were eight vessels that went ashore. In the ensuing battle, we killed or wounded near a thousand Raiders and sank or seriously damaged four Masterships and three Familyships. Plus one of our women killed the Priest-Admiral."

"A woman killed him?"

"Yes, sir. Her name was Leide. She stole on board the flagship, set the fuel storage on fire, locked herself in his cabin with him, and took the whole lot of them with her."

"A formidable woman."

"Yes, sir. She was seventeen."

There was silence around the table.

The admiral directed his attention to Captain Jatu. "It seems we must relieve you of your Navigator for a time."

"I understand. I can arrange to pick him up afterwards."

Cheynou felt a rush of gratitude, but the admiral had another interpretation. "Worth it, is he?"

"Yes, sir."

"Then we must be sure you get him back. If this Mastership turns out to be the problem he says, we might owe the two of you a great deal." He turned to Cheynou. "Move your belongings to my ship immediately. We have been preparing while we met, and the tide is fair for departure."

Once again, Cheynou was impressed at how smoothly this navy functioned. He doubted if a fleet of his people could have put to sea any faster.

Over the three days it took the Kyabran fleet to run downwind to the Armorican Islands, the naval captains grilled Cheynou several times, throwing tactics at him, asking how the Mastership would react. He did his best, at one time dropping his hands on the table in exasperation. "I was a Junior Navigator on a Familyship, gentlemen. I have never been belowdecks on a Mastership, and I have no idea whether the knee braces are integral, laminated, or made of the cook's leftover noodles."

A chuckle ran around the flagship's conference table. "I suppose you don't, lad. I guess we'll just have to take her intact and have a look."

"I noticed from your tactics that you hope to take her, not sink her."

The admiral nodded. "A five-master is unknown in this sea. Our shipwrights do not have the lore to create such a large vessel. We would dearly like to have them look her over."

"I suggest they look her over with a jaundiced eye, sir."

"And why is that?"

"The lore that goes into the design of those ships is a combination of the gleanings of centuries of skilled designers and the detritus of centuries of rigidly unchanging traditions. Half of their skill is used up making outmoded practices function."

"Witness the rams."

"They do have their uses, but they are very limited."

"Bordering on suicidal, I suggest."

"They will be less effective against a boat that can climb to windward. The reason our ships were declared heretic was because we shortened our bowsprits to take them out of the way of the ram. We also raked the foremast forward, which made the forestays more vertical and increased the lift of the flying jibs. We could go to windward at least one point above any other ship."

"And were thus a challenge to the supremacy of this Priest-Admiral."

"Right. And he could not change his ships, because he was tangled in his own rules."

"So they will try to ram, but we should be able to avoid them."

"Yes. If you can catch them among the islands, you will have a great advantage. Even if they have captured someone with local knowledge, they draw a lot of water."

"How much does she draw?"

"At least three fathoms, sir. She was low in the water when we saw her, but they will have solved that by now, I think."

"You said there might be more than a thousand people on board."

"Yes, sir. Four to five hundred will be able sailors and fighters."

"A formidable force."

"I have faced one in battle, sir. It was not a successful engagement."

"What happened?"

He recounted as much as he knew of the battle at Ternata. Once again the questions flew.

At the end of the session, when the other captains had returned to their ships, Cheynou sat for a while with the admiral.

"You have great knowledge for one of your age."

"I am not unusual in the Sea People, sir. I understand that your sailors live ashore and only go aboard when they are twelve to fourteen years or older. I was born on my Familyship. Until I was thirteen, I never spent a night ashore. My experience is woefully inadequate in much of the world, but on a ship, I am well-versed."

"Yes. Your credibility has risen through these sessions. We have yet to catch you in an inconsistency."

Cheynou grinned. "I did sometimes note the same question asked several different ways, sir. I charitably assumed it wasn't through lack of listening or memory."

The admiral laughed. "Well, Cheynou, if the tacticians on our enemy have minds as quick as yours, we're in for a fight, no matter how many bottoms we have, or how much tonnage we can throw into the battle."

"Fortunately, sir, you will not find that. Their tactics, as I have indicated, will have the same strengths and flaws as their ship design."

The admiral nodded. "Right. Finely developed tactics, hampered by the inability to change or improvise."

"And perhaps even some detrimental practices, followed out of pure conservatism."

"Well, let's hope we can outthink them, then. I'll be depending on your experience, Mister Chan."

"If she gains the open sea, how do you plan to take her, sir? If you don't want to sink her, you'll have to board. Even amidships, she sits much higher than your decks, and she'll have a mass of archers on the bow- and sterncastles."

"I agree. The difficulty will be in getting enough ships alongside amidships, attacking the lower deck all at once. Our only advantage is maneuverability."

"And her lack of upwind ability. But that's no use once we engage, because she'll work downwind and have speed and weight on her side."

The admiral steepled his fingers. "Is there any way of keeping her from turning downwind?"

"Short of grabbing her by the nose and pulling her upwind, I can't think of a way."

"Are you serious?"

"Pardon me?"

"Do you think we can grab her and tow her nose around upwind?"

"No, sir. I wasn't being serious...I don't think..."

"If you were serious, how would we go about it?"

They both sat and thought about it.

The admiral broke the silence. "She'd have a speed advantage on any ship that tried to cross her bow."

"You couldn't cross her bow. You'd have to be there already."

"How do you mean?"

"If she thought she could ram you from behind, but at the last moment, you reached back, hooked the bowsprit or the ram, and cut upwind..."

"But you can't tow anything upwind." Larone demonstrated with the model. "The drag pulls your stern downwind."

"Not if you have a long tow-rope. You can crab across the water sideways."

"You'd want a long tow-rope, anyway, in case she got her speed up and you were dragged."

"Wait, wait." Cheynou pulled another wooden ship model on the table towards him. "Here's the Mastership." He took another model. "She follows us, thinking to ram. We trawl for her ram, catch it, and scoot upwind on a long rope. Not too long, or they'll get it cut before we pull."

"When we hit the end of the tow line, we pull her nose up, and she slows." The admiral moved the ship so that both vessels pointed straight upwind. "But it slews our stern around, and we're both in irons."

Cheynou took a third model. "But if another ship grabs our bow..."

"...and pulls us back on course..."

"...temporarily, at least..."

"...that's all we need. That ought to drag her around, slowing her down until the rest of our ships can close with her."

They sat back.

"It's pretty complicated." Cheynou shook his head. "There are a lot of things that can go wrong."

"True. We could practise."

"What we need is something the Masterships aren't going to expect. Their lack of ability to improvise is our other advantage."

"What can we do that they can't? Go upwind..."

"Tack."

"Tack? Yes, of course. They have to wear around."

"Right. So if the ship that hooks the ram immediately tacks," Cheynou moved the models, "and sails in the opposite direction..." Here he slid the smaller model back towards the larger one. "The Mastership is much heavier. She won't stop, just slow down. The little one is going to get dragged backwards. Sooner or later, she'll be pulled right alongside, being towed stern first. I think I'd want a really long tow-rope."

The admiral shook his head, moving the smaller ship directly alongside. "Not at all. We're looking to board, remember?"

Cheynou gulped. He hoped he wasn't on that ship. If the rest of the fleet did not come to her aid, she would be overrun rapidly by the massed boarding parties of the Mastership. "Of course, she could cut the towline if it looked like the other ships weren't going to attack in time."

He had another thought. "If someone snagged the ram on my ship, I'd just send a crewman with an axe to chop it off."

The admiral smiled. "Your people don't have steel cable?"

"What's that?"

"Fine strands of steel, woven together like a rope."

"I saw a lady's necklace like that. Silver."

"I'm talking about a rope as thick as your thumb, made of nine strands of wire. As strong as five times its size in hemp rope. And very expensive."

"But we only need enough to go around the ram or the bowsprit."

"Exactly."

140

A bell rang, and the admiral got to his feet. "Enough thinking for the moment. We'll toss these ideas around with my officers at supper. They'll be sure to have objections."

Cheynou forced himself not to react. It came home to him that he had just spent the afternoon chatting with the admiral of a fleet. Not a big fleet, but a fleet nonetheless. And here the man was cheerfully expecting argument from his officers. The Mastership didn't have a chance.

Unfortunately, there was nobody available to tell the Raiders that.

14. Sea Battle

The next day, at the captains' meeting, one of the senior captains listened silently to the new ideas, then spoke up.

"Let me get this straight. You expect me to act as a decoy. I run in front of this huge ship, which is moving at almost twice my speed. He'll be trying to ram my stern. What would happen if he actually connected?"

Cheynou shook his head. "I've never seen a stern ramming, sir. I gather it doesn't usually do too much damage, because there is little speed difference. But it does throw the pursued ship off course, slowing her down more, and the pursuing captain can maneuver for a boarding whichever side he chooses."

"Unless he should happen to take out the rudder..."

"In which case his prey is helpless."

Satisfied nods around the table.

"You have to realize, sirs, that in any situation where a Mastership is chasing a smaller ship, the conclusion is pretty certain in any case."

"Unless she can tack away upwind."

Again, everyone nodded.

There was a moment of silence, and Cheynou decided it was time to introduce a topic that had been bothering him. "There is one other factor we have not discussed, gentlemen."

Their interest turned to him again.

"You understand, this is a Mastership, but it is also a Familyship."

"Which means?"

"*Family*ship, sir. All the people are on board. Sailors, officers, women, children, babies. Everyone."

There was silence as the captains absorbed this.

"If you board successfully, you have to be aware of this. Your men do too. What will one of your marines do when confronted with a woman carrying a baby? Do you realize that she will have been told, and will believe to her soul, that he is going to rape her and then kill her and her child? Your man must know that she will be trying to kill him. As far as she is concerned, both she and the baby are already dead. She will throw the baby in his face and put her dagger in his gut."

A longer silence.

"So it would be better if we could solve this without having to fight belowdecks?"

"That is probably true, sir. The families stay at their stations, mostly belowdecks, during a battle."

The admiral sighed. "Merely another complication. It seems we have to do this right, gentlemen, or we're going to be in a serious mess, no matter what superiority we have. These people are at the end of their rope. They are defending their only home, and they will all fight to the death. A situation faced more often by our colleagues in the Army, I gather. Now it's our turn."

In the end, it was much less difficult. They found the Springbok a day out of the Armorican Islands, wallowing towards the approaching fleet. The mizzenmast was full height now, but something seemed wrong.

"Why is she travelling so slowly? You said she could make twice our speed."

Cheynou was at a loss for words. He watched the mighty ship ploughing through the waves at a much slower rate than she should have. "I don't know, sir. There's obviously something wrong with her, but I don't know what."

"I'm not complaining."

"Her bottom's foul."

"It's what?"

The Second Officer gestured towards the other ship with his tube. "Watch when she rolls. There's seaweed and barnacles on her hull. She's badly fouled."

143

Cheynou stared. Sure enough, the usually sleek bottom of the Mastership was a mass of flowing greenery. "How did that happen?"

"What do you mean?"

"Well, of course a bottom gets fouled after a while. We always careen once a year. But she looks like she hasn't been cleaned for years."

The admiral laughed. "So, Mister Chan, we were all fooled by something not even you were aware of. Seaweed grows much faster in this warm water. We careen the Navy ships three times a year. Your friends over there obviously didn't realize it either."

The officer shook his head. "Why haven't they careened?"

Cheynou laughed. "I told you. They run on tradition. The third summer month is the month to careen. It's only the first summer month, so they won't careen for two more months."

"Even if it slows them down that much?"

Cheynou gestured to the Mastership. An answer was not needed.

"This is going to help."

"Will we still try to tempt her to ram?"

"I think so. After all, they don't know how fast our ships are, and they don't know how much they've been slowed. Signal the decoy alongside us. I want him to take it slower than usual."

The decoy ship ran close alongside, an impressive display of seamanship, and the admiral called out his ideas. The other captain saluted and veered his ship downwind into the course of the approaching enemy.

It was a tense time. The archers on the bowcastle of the Mastership, high above the little decoy, rained arrows on her deck, and catapults hurled rocks and metal bars at her rigging. In order to shorten the engagement, the captain slowed his ship even more. Then the davit in the stern swung aft, the loop of cable neatly lassoing the hooked beak of the Mastership. Immediately, the decoy hardened in her sails and pulled away upwind, leaving the Mastership to plough majestically past her, spitting arrows all the while. Kyabran sailors swung the davit away, leaving the line secured to the base of the mizzenmast.

For a long time, nothing seemed to happen. Then they could see the rope looping between the ships rise and straighten. With a snap, it rose from the water, bar-tight, and the smaller ship was brought to a sudden halt, her bow rising, masts tipping backward. The Mastership's massive weight reacted more slowly, but gradually she slewed to windward, her sails backing, and finally she stood there in irons, rigging slapping in the breeze. The smaller boat regained her wind first and pulled ahead again. Once more the rope came taut, and the Mastership's bow, which had started to fall away from the wind, was jerked again into irons.

It was enough. The fleet of smaller ships swarmed around, grappling hooks flying, boarding parties eager at the rails.

The Kyabran flagship, standing the tallest, had opted to attack the sterncastle despite Cheynou's doubt. As she pulled in, it became evident there was no chance to board. The Mastership's high walls towered over her, and any crewman climbing a rope would be cut down as he crossed the rail. A squad of archers leaned over that rail, peppering her deck with arrows. The captain gave the order to sheer off and steered instead to the opposite side of another Kyabran ship, already warped tight to the enemy's midsection.

The boarders poured across the other ship and joined the mêlée on the Mastership's main deck.

Cheynou drew his sabre. "Permission to board the enemy, sir?"

The admiral looked at him a moment. "I suppose you have reasons of your own."

"I do, sir."

The officer gestured. "Take care of yourself, lad."

Cheynou knew exactly where he was going. He had been aboard a Mastership a few times and knew where the Chartroom would be, directly forward of the wheel. He vaulted the rail and headed towards the bridge deck just forward of the sterncastle. The fighting was fierce there, and he was glad of his officer's uniform. He joined a rush of Kyabran marines up the outer companionway, hemmed in too tight to do anything but push forward.

As the attackers reached the open deck they separated, each assuming the man next to him would hold the line, and Cheynou was forced to stand his place among the heavier men. The marine beside him, a sergeant about twice his weight, glanced down. "Where are you headed, sir?"

He pointed ahead. "The Navigator's chartroom."

The marine shouted to his squad and pushed in that direction. Cheynou took up a position close on the man's left, guarding his low line so he could concentrate on the heads and shoulders of the Raiders confronting them. This combination worked well, and soon they found themselves in advance of their men.

"Hold position here, sergeant. We're going to be cut off."

A lanky Raider was circling behind them, using his superior reach to threaten the marine's back. Cheynou threw himself to his knees and deflected the cutlass, which swished over his head.

"I can't hold him off, soldier."

The marine glanced back and shouted to his companions, who threw themselves at the surrounding Raiders with renewed fury. Their tall opponent had to look to his own defense, and Cheynou regained his feet.

"You doing all right down there, sir?"

Cheynou slapped the man's heavy shoulder as he slipped towards the beckoning doorway. "Thanks for the ride, soldier."

Bursting through the door, he surprised an elderly man stuffing books into a sack. "I'll have that."

The Helmsman looked up, shocked to hear his own language. He made a protective gesture, but Cheynou had no time to parlay. Running him through, he grabbed the sack and scanned the chart table. It seemed the man had finished his job. Cheynou nodded grimly to himself and ducked back out the door.

By this time the bridge deck was secured, but the battle ebbed and flowed across the main deck. Cheynou pattered down the stairs and ducked through the mêlée, lending a hand where he could, but intent on getting his precious cargo to the admiral on the Flagship's deck.

"That was quick, lad. Too hot for you over there? I see blood on your sword."

"I wasn't after revenge, sir. I was after this." He held out the sack. "It may be worth more than the ship herself."

Light dawned on the admiral's brow. "Logs?"

"And maps, sir."

"You're giving them to me?"

"It's your victory, sir. I assume you divide the spoils as you see fit."

The admiral grinned. "And you're the only one who can read them."

"There is that."

"Good enough. It isn't my victory, yet. Stand by; I may need you."

"Aye, sir."

Some time later, Cheynou stood where he had never thought to stand, giving orders on the bridge deck of a Mastership. The Crews and Families were lined up in their proper places, and he took his place beside the admiral, explaining and pointing.

"Those are the shipwrights over there. Valuable men for your naval architects to talk to." An order was passed, and the indicated Raiders were hustled away.

Cheynou turned to the group of officers who stood, heads bowed. "Where is the Priest-Captain?"

A man stepped hesitantly forward. Cheynou used the point of his sword to push the man back.

"You aren't the Priest-Captain. Where is he?"

147

"What's wrong?"

"It's one of their tricks, sir. The Priest-Captain has ducked out somewhere and left his subordinates to take the punishment."

The admiral again gave orders, then turned his attention back to Cheynou. "I need you to talk to all of them. Tell them they will not be harmed or made slaves. Make them believe it. All they have to do is cooperate, and they will be turned loose to make what living they can in the Empire."

Cheynou grinned shortly. "I doubt if they'll believe it, but I'll tell them."

Stepping forward, he raised his voice, but he did not speak the admiral's words.

"I am Cheynou Chan, Navigator of the Eagle. I am the friend of Sarasha the Lame and Leide Tourne, who took your Priest-Admiral and your Masterships, the Wolverine and the Lion, with them to the Great Ocean in the Heavenly Skies. Two women, Two Masterships, one Priest-Admiral. They considered it a fair trade."

There was a muttering and shuffling in the Families.

"What was that about?"

"I told them who I was, sir. They know. They have heard of our battle. That is an interesting piece of information that you can be sure is true, no matter what stories they weave. Now that I have their attention, I will tell them who you are. Then I will give them your message."

"Proceed."

"This is Admiral Larone of the Kyabran Empire. Yes, Empire. The Kyabrans have a land-based Empire that covers the whole north part of the continent. They have as many ships as the Sea People's Fleet, and that is a small part of their power.

"You have ventured into seas far beyond your ken. You have no way of coping with these powers. You have no way of continuing your raiding.

"But these are not vindictive people. They do not have a history of raiding and pillaging to avenge. To this point, you have committed no serious crimes. All they want is peace within their territories so that their trade can move.

"You will not be harmed."

A subdued sigh ran through the Families.

"You will be Beached."

Heads bowed, sobs were choked off.

"You have the means to make a living. There are plenty of ships on this Sea. There will be sailing work for many. There is an Empire to feed. Fishing is good here. But there will be no raiding.

"So, if you would look to the future and think to survive in this new world, cooperate with the admiral and his men, and you will not be harmed."

He let that sink in for a while.

"Your way of life is over. You must already know that, or you wouldn't be here, so far from the Great Southern Ocean. Like the Crew of the Eagle and her allies, you must now find a new life."

He indicated Larone. "I have found friends here. You might, as well."

He stepped back, raising his eyebrows to the admiral.

"They seem more relaxed."

"People tend to be less tense when they realize they aren't going to die or be sold into slavery, sir."

"Hmm. I suppose so. Thank you, Mister Chan. I will need you when we talk to the officers."

"Certainly, sir. You will also want to talk to the Heads of Crafts and the Heads of Families."

"They aren't the same?"

"There's a lot of overlap."

"Take a squad of marines." He gestured to an armoured sergeant. "Bring the right people to me." The admiral was about to turn away, but a thought brought him back around. "You have given me good advice today, Cheynou Chan. I will give you some. Stay with your escort and keep your distance. There will be many who consider you both a traitor and the reason for their loss today."

"I'll be careful, sir."

Flanked by six large men with drawn sabres, he moved down onto the main deck, registering the positions of the groups, relating them to how his own ship would have stood to Crew Assembly.

He was in the middle of choosing a representative from the Ladingmen when a scuffle and a stifled squeal distracted him. Over by the rail, a shapely girl was hiding her head, a Kyabran sailor standing by with a smirk on his face. Cheynou looked up to the marine sergeant. "Did you catch that?"

"Yes, sir."

"How do your people deal with that sort of thing?"

"Very firmly, sir."

"Please take care of it."

"Yessir." The sergeant snapped his fingers, and two of his men closed in on the startled sailor. When the man was gone, Cheynou moved closer to the girl, spoke softly.

"What happened?"

Her hands gradually came down, revealing a tear-stained face. "He...he touched me, sir, and he said he'd see me later."

"Don't worry, girl. He won't be seeing anything but the inside of the brig for a while. I said you would be safe."

He turned to the worried-looking woman beside the girl. "And get word to the Priest-Captain that the same applies to him. Where does he think he's going to escape to, and why? It looks like you're all going to be turned free anyway."

He waited until understanding dawned on the woman's face, then went back to his duties. Ship's gossip as it was, he figured it would take a string of about four people to get his message delivered.

He returned to the bridge deck, knocked at the door of the captain's cabin and entered on command. "I have the Heads here, sir."

"Good. Have them wait, and come in, yourself."

Cheynou complied. "The Priest-Captain should be here soon, sir."

"How did you manage that?"

"I sent him the same message that the others got, but personally. You did mean it, sir? They'll all be turned loose?"

"Unless they have committed some atrocities within the Empire."

"Fair."

Larone raised his eyebrows. "Thank you, Mister Chan, for your approval."

"Sorry, sir. I have met several different peoples recently, and I am always interested in their beliefs and ideals."

"And you approve of ours?"

"So far, sir."

"I'll pass that along to the emperor. I'm sure he'll be relieved."

"Thank you, sir. He will be pleased that I have aided his empire as he requested."

The admiral stared at Cheynou. "He will?"

Cheynou grinned. "He gave me to understand that he would be interested in my progress, the last time we spoke."

The admiral sighed. "Having taken care of the more important details of state, let us return to the matter at hand."

He outlined how he wanted the Heads questioned. Cheynou was not to add anything of his own to the questions, but was to comment to the admiral on what he heard. A midshipman would record it all.

A tap on the door interrupted them. "Visitor, sir."

"Have him come in."

151

The door opened fully, and a man strode in, flanked immediately by two of Cheynou's marines. Before he could speak, Cheynou held up a warning hand. When he had the man's attention, he spoke a careful phrase. Startled, the man responded.

"He's the real Priest-Captain, sir."

"How did you work that?"

"It's a code, sir. Navigators must be able to identify Priest-Captains from other Ships, and vice versa. He responded correctly. Of course, he could be a Navigator, posing as a Priest-Captain, but that's an outside chance."

"I'll take him at face value. Ask him who he is and what his ship is doing in our waters, attacking our shipping."

The tale was long and rambling, and Cheynou listened to the end, then turned to his Admiral. "You don't need all the rationalization and religious cant. He brought the Springbok far around the eastern end of the continent and through to the Inner Sea because the Western Fleet has split. Following the death of the Priest-Admiral, there was a battle for supremacy. One faction won that battle, and the new Priest-Admiral was rapacious in demanding compensation. Instead of complying, many of the Masterships left. Some of them took their Familyships with them and formed a new Fleet. Others, like the Springbok, came alone.

"Why didn't his Familyships come?"

"He allied with the wrong faction, was cut off and had to run. And keep running. The rest is a tale of ineptitude, bad luck, and the usual problems of travelling in uncharted waters."

"Ask him why he fired on your ship."

Cheynou translated.

The Priest-Captain puffed his chest out. "We considered ourselves to be in a weakened condition in hostile territory and had a right to defended ourselves.

"From an offer of assistance."

"We didn't understand that."

"You're understanding me well enough now."

"You?"

"Yes. I was the one who shouted the offer of help, so the admiral knows exactly what I said."

He turned to Larone. "He's not being completely frank, sir. I'm sure he shot at us because that's what Masterships do to strangers."

The questioning continued. Finally, Cheynou began to notice a familiar note in the questions.

"Admiral Larone, do you have any new questions, or are you just trying to trip him up by asking the same things twice?"

The admiral smiled. "Was it that obvious?"

"I'm afraid so, sir. A man who worked his way up to Priest-Captain of a Mastership is a consummate politician and power broker. You will not catch him out. Do you wish new information?"

"Of course. What do you have in mind?"

"I'd like you to get an idea of how he really thinks."

The admiral waved a hand. "Go ahead. I'm interested to see your technique."

"Thank you, sir."

He turned to the Priest-Captain and continued, translating both questions and answers for the Kyabrans.

"Captain Begine, what do you know of the rebellion that brought down Admiral Ballajero two years ago?"

The Priest-Admiral's face took on a reddish tinge. "You will call me by my proper title, boy, if you know what's good for you. And you will do the same for the Honourable Priest-Admiral Ballajero if you value your soul."

"My soul, is it? Tell me, Captain, how you think my treatment of you, considering our relative positions at the moment, is going to affect my good fortune. How do you think my attitude towards a Priest-Admiral who was stupid enough to get himself and his flagship sunk by a sixteen-year-old girl is going to have anything to do with the future of my soul?"

The man's face contorted. "Those are lies! The Priest-Admiral went down in battle, bravely defending his ship against unholy magic."

"Like you bravely defended your ship by hiding while it was boarded and taken."

The angry man started forward, but the two Kyabran marines guarding him closed in, and he backed down.

"Let's say I'm a polite sort, and I'm willing to treat you with better manners than you ever treated your own people. Priest-Captain, what do you say to the charge that the people of your Familyships hate you and only obey you because of the power of your Mastership?"

"Nonsense. My people are loyal."

"What about the people of your own ship? They seemed quite happy to hand you over to us when you tried to hide."

"There are malcontents in every society. They will be dealt with."

Cheynou stepped forward. "You haven't figured it out yet, have you? You are finished. Your ship is finished. The tyrannical reign of the Priest-Admiral and his Masterships is finished. The Great Southern Ocean will finally be free to all."

The Priest-Captain drew himself up as if he was commanding his own quarterdeck again. "That's where you're wrong, boy. The power of the Masterships is unchallenged. When the Priest-Admiral has settled the malcontents in their places, he will follow where I have led. The Masterships are on my heels, and their tonnage will sweep this sea clean of all these flitting little boats."

He raised his head to look down his nose at Admiral Larone. "And when they come, they will raise me up again, and I will put my foot on the necks of these Kyabran landsloggers. Cower in your cabins, Kyabrans, for the Raiders of the Southern Ocean are coming, and there's nothing you can do about it."

He stood, his head high, his chest heaving. Cheynou's slow, calm translation took the wind from his sails, and his posture sagged.

When Cheynou had finished, the admiral smiled, shaking his head. "If I had any doubts that you were exaggerating, that tirade certainly settled them." He glanced at the marines. "He is a dangerous man. Keep him under strict guard at all times. When we reach Port Tenet, he will be taken to the capital for further questioning. The emperor needs to hear this."

He waved a casual hand and turned his back. "Take him away."

The marines were not gentle, and hauled the Priest-Captain off his Mastership and into the hold of the Kyabran flagship.

Once he was gone, Cheynou looked at the admiral. "Will you need me to go with him to translate?"

"No, I'm sure the emperor has people in his employ who know all the languages of the world."

Cheynou must have looked dubious, because the admiral grinned. "Slaves, perhaps. Do you think one of your people was never captured?"

"I suppose. Various members of our Crews spend time ashore, especially when they're young. Some don't return."

The admiral steepled his fingers. "Sit down, Cheynou. I have a question for you."

Cheynou took the chair nearest to the desk. "Will I join your Navy?"

Laronc shrugged. "That was the obvious one."

"And if I say no?"

"Just like that? No bargaining?"

Cheynou shrugged. "I have no desire to follow the Priest-Captain into captivity, but I have a responsibility to my ship, and she is short a navigator at the moment."

The admiral sighed and flipped a sheet of paper across the desk. "And she is at the moment making a provisioning run to Liore Naval Station."

Cheynou picked up the paper. "She is? I'm sorry to ask, sir, but how do you know?"

"Because it is very easy to keep a small merchant ship busy so she is available when you need her. On that paper you will find her schedule, and orders transferring you to Liore to meet her. You will also find a draft for a month's wages at a rating of Lieutenant, Junior Grade."

"Oh. Thank you, sir."

"And you will note that even if it takes you a week to get to Liore, you still owe me a week of enlistment. You will report to the Station Commanding Officer at Liore and tell him everything you know about Masterships and their tactics. Will you do that?"

"Gladly, sir. I work in the merchant ships now, and a Mastership is a threat to my business."

Larone stood and held out his hand in the Kyabran fashion. "Off you go, then. The *Panther* leaves for Liore on the next tide, and you have passage."

But when Cheynou grasped his hand, he did not release it. "And if that blowhard turns out to be telling the truth…"

Cheynou nodded. "You call, and I will come running, sir."

One firm shake, and the admiral was spinning him towards the door. "Off you go. The emperor thanks you for your service."

Cheynou grinned over his shoulder. "Will he ever know?"

"I suppose he might. I know better than to let the deeds of a person of your quality go unnoticed."

Cheynou paused in the door to salute in the Kyabran manner. "Thank you, sir. Until I see you again."

"I'm afraid you might."

The admiral turned to his papers, and Cheynou followed the ensign to the waiting longboat.

15. BATTLE ON THE DOCK

"There it sits, Cheynou!"

"Aye, Captain."

The *Courser* was anchored just off a small, out-of-the-way dock on the north side of Voges Island, far to the west of Port Tenet and the patrols of the Kyabran Imperial Navy.

"That cargo is worth the whole voyage so far. Deliver that to the Torrens, and we could go home happy."

"Right you are, sir. We'll run straight in and pick it up, then?"

The captain grinned. "That you will, lad. The cargo isn't too heavy. The big lighter with the bosun and six crew should handle it in two trips. Remember, the leather case comes with the first load. That case is worth half the cargo, so take special care."

The captain looked around at the heavily treed hillsides that surrounded the small bay. Nothing was moving. "I would prefer to bring the ship alongside, but I have been told that the water is too shallow. Less risk, anyway. Carry on, Mister Chan."

"Do we expect any trouble, sir?"

"No more than any time you go ashore in a strange place."

"I'll keep an eye out, sir."

"Do that. But get that cargo aboard."

"Aye, sir!" He turned to the rail, where the bosun was already seeing to the lowering of the biggest cargo carrier.

When it was in the water, Cheynou called to his crew. "I know this is stevedore work, men, but let's have a cutlass each, shall we?"

They nodded, glanced at each other and headed to the rack at the foot of the mainmast. Armed, they slipped down into the boat and prepared their oars. The bosun took his place at the tiller, and Cheynou swung down into the bow. The moment his foot touched the thwart, the bosun gave the order, and he was pleased with how effortlessly the boat pulled away.

"Very smoothly done, lads. This is an important cargo, and the captain will be rare pleased when it's safely stowed." He grinned to himself as he felt the extra surge of the boat as the oarsmen put a touch more enthusiasm into their task.

True to his word, he kept his eyes open as they approached the shore. He was glad there wasn't any real concern, because it was not a comfortable landing-place. The narrow dock, half-blocked by a pile of bales, led straight to a small field, just a clearing in the forest, and to a weathered building that looked part cottage, part warehouse. Probably for storing smaller cargoes of perishable goods. A man, presumably the watchman, sat by the door. There were rocks at the shoreline, tall trees and heavy underbrush pushing close. A whole army could be hidden nearby.

He stared around, but nothing moved; nothing was out of place as far as he could tell. He waved, and the watchman waved back but did not rise from his chair.

Then his attention was taken up with docking and mooring the lighter. Again, he was pleased at how skillfully the sailors performed their tasks, and the enthusiasm with which they moved.

He had just set up the transfer pattern and the first bale was moving towards the boat when the bosun froze.

Following his gaze, Cheynou spun around, his heart sinking.

They were already out of the woods and striding to the landward end of the dock. Ten of them, armed and helmeted, led by a stocky man in a sleeveless leather jerkin.

Cheynou turned to his crew. "Keep loading, men. Spring lines off, Bosun. Single hitches fore and aft." He spotted the brown leather case on the top of the pile. "Make sure this goes into the boat, underneath something."

Freye nodded and turned away, his body hiding the case. Cheynou faced the approaching party, now thudding down the dock, the unison of their stride shaking the structure. He could hear bits of gravel dropping into the water below.

"Jonis. Cargo net. Round behind." He spoke without turning his head, counting on the sailor hearing him.

"Stop that lading, you thieves!"

Cheynou frowned and stepped forward, raising his voice in the Trade language the man had used. "Thieves? This is legitimate cargo, sir!"

The leader continued his march until Cheynou was forced back a step. Then the man stopped, his guards a pace behind, hands on sword hilts.

"Legitimate cargo, true. But not belonging to you!"

Cheynou held up empty palms. "Someone must be misinformed, sir. Our captain has taken a legal contract for this cargo, and he intends to deliver it."

The swish of the sword past his face was too quick for him to react, so he didn't. "I said, stop that lading!"

Never taking his eyes off the man's face, Cheynou lifted a hand. The sounds behind him gradually stopped, and he could hear the shuffle of his men's feet as they moved to back him.

He raised his eyebrows. "You seem very sure of yourself, sir. Whose goods do you think these are?"

"That's none of your concern. Get that cargo back up on the dock."

Cheynou shook his head. "Oh, but it is my concern. If there is a misunderstanding, then surely it can be straightened out with little fuss. On the other hand, if my cargo is being stolen by brigands, I may decide to react differently."

The man's face took on a look of surprise, then a smile. "You may decide differently?"

"That's right. We are peaceful traders, but we are from Kyabra. The Kyabrans do not suffer thieves lightly."

The swordsman flexed his bare right arm, and the muscles slid smoothly under heavy tattoos; the sabre was more threatening, but the grin remained. "I don't see that you have much choice, little man."

Cheynou smiled as well, shaking his head affably as he stepped forward. Gently, with two fingers, he pushed the sword tip aside. "There are always many choices, my friend. Come, I do not like to deal with a stranger. I am Cheynou Chan, sometimes called the Barbarian, Second Officer of the Kyabran trader *Courser*. What is your name?"

The larger man paused, unsure. His enemy was inside his guard, but making no hostile move. His pride took over. "I am Ashmet Khrem, Personal Safety to Lord Giron of Voges."

Cheynou nodded. "I cannot suggest we are well met, Ashmet Khrem. But now that we know each other, perhaps the matter can be resolved to the satisfaction of all. I am interested in your decorations. 'Honour,' 'Open Hand.' Do I see 'Beauty?' That is an unusual sigil for a warrior."

Again, the pride exerted itself. "Those are the signs of my training, little barbarian. The Honour of my School of Warfare, the Kantoon. The rigorous training of the Open Hand. The Beauty of any movement, performed to perfection." The man created a fist, and his left hand slid through a pattern, ending in a slow punch that stopped just short of Cheynou's nose.

Cheynou nodded again. "I felt they must be important. And the graduates of your school become mercenaries and bodyguards? I certainly do not see them becoming bandits."

The proud smile faded, and the chest rose. "Graduates of the Kantoon School of Warfare are welcomed into the personal service of the powerful of many kingdoms."

Cheynou nodded. "So tell me, Ashmet Khrem, whose cargo do you think this is? May I assume the lord to whom you owe your personal allegiance has some interest in the matter?"

"Again, I say, that is no concern of yours."

Cheynou turned and sat, shoulders slumped, on a nearby bale. "I suppose you are right. It is no concern of mine," he looked up, "but there truly seems to be a misunderstanding here, and my captain will be concerned with discussing the problem with the person who has the authority to solve it."

He rose again, moved in on his adversary. "If you do not aid in this, I may rightfully suppose that you are merely brigands. In that case, I might decide to fight."

He was again inside Ashmet's guard, but the mercenary could not back up without losing face. Once more, he took refuge in laughter. "Why, little barbarian, I do not see you as being that stupid." He gestured. "Standing here, I could hold off your whole crew single-handed."

Cheynou nodded. "I'm sure you could, if you stayed here, between the cargo and the edge of the pier. And if we played fair."

"Played fair?" Then the man's eyes followed Cheynou's to the sailor who stood above him on the bales, heavy net at the ready.

"Yes. You see, your position, while holding great advantage if we were to attack, holds an equal drawback should you need assistance and your men could not get to you.

"You know," he continued thoughtfully, "I suspect the training you received at your famous Kantoon was excellent in individual fighting skills, but perhaps had less concentration on tactics and troop movement."

"Tactics? That is for the generals and those who stand behind the lines and give orders from safety."

"I beg to differ, Ashmet Khrem. Even in my barbarian society, all of our Raiders are given training in small-troop deployment and detached duty. Invaluable in a situation like this."

"Hmph. No matter how well you deploy your men, if we fight, you will all die."

"True. After you are dead, your men will probably still be able to beat us."

"After I am dead? But I already know about your net!"

Cheynou shifted around, gesturing. "Oh, that was only the part of the plan I showed you to give you time to think." As he moved, his hand brushed past his belt.

Then his marlinspike appeared, pressed sharply against the arm of his opponent. "What if this was poisoned?"

161

The man froze, looking down. Then he laughed, a bit shakily. "Poisoned? A marlinspike? Not likely."

Cheynou shook his head. "You have to be careful, Ashmet Khrem, when dealing with small people. What they lack in size and strength, they make up for in intelligence and guile."

He pushed a bit harder, then drew the point away, leaving a fine white scratch. He slid the marlinspike back into its sheath. "As it happens, it isn't poisoned."

He stepped backward again. "I suggest once more, Ashmet, that you tell us who we have a misunderstanding with and let my captain deal with him. We will leave the cargo here until they come to some agreement."

The big mercenary considered. "Fine. You put the cargo back on the dock, and I'll allow you to sail away with your neck in one piece."

Cheynou frowned, pretending to consider. "No, I think we'll take just a bit, to make sure that my captain has one small chip to bet when the bargaining starts."

"Little barbarian, I fail to see where you have any decisions to make. You are heavily outmanned and you have revealed to me all your little tricks. I think you should put those bales back on the dock."

Cheynou frowned in amazement. "How many gifts must I give you to persuade you that there are more in my hand?"

"More?"

Cheynou shrugged. "It would seem foolish to tell your enemy everything, wouldn't it?"

Ashmet shook his head and grinned. "Little barbarian..."

"And that's another point, Ashmet Khrem. Do you think people like me enjoy having our size thrown in our faces?"

The man's eyebrows went up. "I fail to see why I should care."

Cheynou matched his expression. "So, at your famous Kantoon, they teach you to go around making enemies for no reason, especially those of the crafty and subtle variety?"

Once again, the loud laugh rolled across the water. "No, Cheynou Chan, I apologize. You are doing your best to get your men out of a difficult situation, and I have to grant you that. Take your crew away, Cheynou the Barbarian, and tell your captain that if he wishes to deal on this cargo, he must go to Lord Giron in Voges City."

The sailors were already moving with grateful speed towards the lighter. Cheynou bowed to his opponent, then turned and dropped to his position in the bow. "Smartly now, lads!"

The bosun gave the order, and the boat pulled smoothly away from the dock. The sailors were beginning to strain at the oars, but a soft word from Cheynou relaxed them. "Gently there, boys. We aren't running."

Freye's face split into a relieved grin. "Oh, yes we are." But he did not counter the order.

The captain was pacing the deck anxiously as they pulled alongside. Cheynou was first over the rail. "What was that about? Why is the cargo still there?"

Cheynou bowed his head. "I'm sorry, sir. I did not take proper precautions against an ambush. If we had been prepared, we might have held them off at the end of the dock while we loaded more of the cargo. But we were unprepared, and I wasn't able to fulfill my duty, sir."

The captain frowned. "But who were they?"

"I believe they were personal retainers of Lord Giron of Voges, sir. They said the cargo was his."

"Well, it isn't. The cargo is ours. We paid full price for it."

Cheynou shrugged miserably. "I thought that too, sir. I considered fighting for it."

"We should have, sir. I could have taken the leader. He looked tough, with all those tattoos, but I still..."

"Bosun."

The man's voice tapered off.

"You couldn't have taken him." Cheynou turned to the captain. "Sir, do you know of a School of Warfare called Kantoon?"

Jatu frowned. "Turns out bodyguards, that sort of thing. A lot of tattoos or that kind of silliness, I believe."

"That's it, sir. The leader was one of the Kantoon."

The captain shook his head. "You don't want to tangle with one of those, Bosun."

"We still could have had him, sir. Several of us at once."

"I think he's right, Captain. I actually could have killed him myself at one point in the negotiations. But I kept thinking that maybe there really was a mix-up, and they still outnumbered and outarmed us, and what if I got a lot of people killed because of an error?"

He straightened his back, facing the captain. "You may call me a coward, sir, but we are here, we are alive, and the cargo still sits on the dock. It has not escaped us."

The bosun let out a single epithet. "I wouldn't call him a coward, Captain. When he stepped ahead and pushed that guy's sword aside with his fingertip, I was like to crap myself."

The captain could not hide his disappointment, but he nodded reluctantly. "I could still wish you had found a way..."

"I'm sorry I let you down, sir. And the whole ship. We only got a few bales."

They turned to where the small pile of cargo sat on the deck. With an exclamation, the captain swooped down on the brown case. "Why didn't you say you got that one?"

"Didn't get the chance, sir."

The captain turned to Cheynou. "This incident is still a serious blow to our profits, Mister Chan, but with this part of the cargo, we have not lost so much."

"I told their leader that you would be dealing with Lord Giron of Voges, sir."

Jatu mused a moment. "I'll have to think that one over for a bit."

Cheynou did not like to question the captain in public, so he lowered his voice. "You mean, perhaps it really is his cargo, sir?"

The captain nodded to the First Officer to take over and turned towards his cabin. Cheynou motioned the bosun to stow the remaining few bales and followed. Inside, Jatu waved Cheynou to a seat.

"You're an officer on this ship and have a right to know. I'm not exactly sure."

Cheynou felt relief course through him. "You aren't?"

The captain smiled sadly. "That's part of the risk of trading, lad. When the price for something seems to be too good, you always wonder at the hidden costs. I bought this cargo for a very good price from someone I thought was trustworthy, so I did my best to assure that there were no hindrances. I could have missed one."

"But it could also be that they are just trying to steal it."

The captain frowned. "Yes, it could."

"But for their leader to tell me who his master is…"

Jatu shook his head. "Out here, past the frontiers of the Empire, some of the lords are as good as kings. They can do exactly as they like, and they answer to no one."

"But if they engage in banditry, doesn't that hurt their trading possibilities?"

"Yes, but in a case where the cargo was valuable enough, and few enough people were involved, Lord Giron might consider it worth his while. He did make one mistake, perhaps."

"What was that, sir?"

Jatu grinned. "I didn't hear the conversation, but I gather that your Kantoon had you close to convinced that his concern was legitimate. That would seem to indicate that he believed it himself."

"I see, sir. So if it really was just banditry, the leader should have been clearer with his man, because they let us go with half the merchandise on the assumption that it would all get cleared up later."

"I agree. Although how you managed to work it that way, I don't know."

"That was the only interpretation that allowed us any chance. I just kept on as if it were the truth."

"Yes, Cheynou, we have all experienced you when you keep on and on. We will weigh anchor for Voges."

"But, sir, the cargo still sits there on the dock..."

"...and you have some plans? Do you think your warlike friend is going to ride away and leave it, as long as our ship is in the bay?"

"Of course not, sir. I thought perhaps later tonight..."

The captain laughed and rose, clapping Cheynou's shoulder. "I know you hate to leave a battle half-won, lad, but I think we should try diplomacy on this one."

"I think of the battle as half-lost, sir."

"Right you are. However, your half-victory has given me some levers to use when I start the diplomacy to win the rest."

Cheynou did not rise. "You are over-gracious, sir. I still feel I have failed."

Jatu nodded seriously. "Then you will perform better the next time."

Cheynou stood. "I will, sir."

"Good." The captain strode onto the deck, calling orders to weigh anchor and set the sails. Cheynou followed with a lighter heart.

16. Lord Giron

Giron was around the end of a long spit that projected north about a league into the sea, providing protection for a comfortable harbour in its lee. Due to the shifting sand and the unknown waters, the *Courser* gave the point a wide berth and sounded her way into the port, arriving at one bell past noon.

Giving the enemy's man plenty of time to report to his leader, as Cheynou reminded the captain.

"I expected nothing else, Cheynou. We will leave the ship anchored outside the inner harbour, I believe, and I will go ashore with a small party. I gather you spoke this bodyguard's language?"

"Yes, sir. It is not too different from the TradeSpeak you use in this area, with some Eastern LandSpeak thrown in."

"Still, perhaps it is best you come along. Toban, you are in command."

With no further instruction, they lowered the gig and rowed away. Cheynou noticed that the oarsmen had not relinquished their cutlasses.

To no one's surprise, an escort was waiting at the dock.

"Well, my barbarian friend. I see your captain is true to your word."

Cheynou thought he detected a note of relief in the man's voice. "Yes, Ashmet Khrem. This is Captain Jatu. He uses the TradeSpeak of the Inner Sea."

Given this hint, the bodyguard changed his dialect, although he was much less proficient. "My lord will see you now."

They followed the burly figure up through the neatly cobbled streets of a small village to the fortress that loomed over the harbour from atop an outcropping of rock. Two sentries guarded the gate, snapping to attention as their party passed through.

"Lord Giron's men are smartly turned out, Ashmet. Your responsibility?"

The man nodded with satisfaction. "They have not my training, but they do well, nonetheless."

"The crew reflects the officer, as my people say."

The man grinned ruefully. "When I returned with the report that you had escaped with valuable cargo, my lord did not express the same opinion, Cheynou Chan. I was quite happy to see your ship enter the harbour."

Cheynou grinned. "Perhaps you could remind your master that if you are well-informed on your duties, you can perform them better."

The larger man raised his eyebrows. "My lord is not an easy man to correct."

"Then I will undertake to deliver the message for you."

The man laughed aloud. "I will be interested to see that."

Captain Juta glanced at Cheynou. "That was too quick for me. What is the laughter about?"

"I just promised to give Lord Giron some advice on the delegating of information to his subordinates."

The captain shook his head. "Perhaps you will wait until I have finished my bargaining before you start on the etiquette lessons?"

"Of course, sir."

They gained the fortress, and Cheynou exchanged glances with the captain as they were led past the formal hall and into what looked more like a set of merchant's offices. Sitting in a comfortable chair to one side of the largest room was a slight, older man, dressed in simple but costly robes. Khrem stiffened as he entered, signalled them where to stand and then moved to a formal position by his lord's side.

The man rose, a polite smile greeting them. "Welcome, Captain Jatu. I gather we have business to discuss."

The captain shot a glance at Cheynou. "Does he speak our TradeSpeak?"

Understanding the situation, Cheynou took over, quickly determining that Kyabran TradeSpeak was the language best known to all. Lord Giron was more fluent than his bodyguard, but Cheynou offered to assist in translation.

With one further glance at Cheynou, the lord turned his attention to Captain Jatu.

"So. Let us sit and discuss why you have entered my territories and tried to load my cargo into your ship."

The captain sat. Cheynou decided to remain standing at his shoulder as Ashmet did for his lord. "Yes, my Lord. I would like to discuss why your men stopped my crew from loading our cargo."

"From my point of view, I wonder at your attempt to continue your actions, when my representative explained the situation."

"And I would be interested in why your bodyguard would attempt to thwart my legitimate trading."

Cheynou noted the colour rise in the lord's pale face and realized the problem. "Excuse me, my Lord, but I believe my captain uses the word 'thwart' in the sense of 'disappoint,' not in the sense of 'cheat.' Is that not so, Captain Jatu?"

"Of course. I had no intention of accusing Lord Giron of anything."

The stiffness in the lord's shoulders relaxed. "That sounds more acceptable. Thank you for clearing that up, Cheynou Chan." The lord smiled faintly. "And that seems to cover the problem. You say it is your cargo, I say it is mine. You have half, and I have half. Now what do we do?"

The captain nodded. "It is best to understand the difficulty clearly. I agree with your assessment. How do we solve this problem?"

The lord frowned. "Since we seem to have conflicting information, perhaps we should search for the source of that information."

"Ah, yes. In my case, that would be the merchant Ervin, who sold me the whole consignment, intact, for a price we both agreed upon. And yours?"

Lord Giron shrugged. "I need no source of information. The cargo is mine. My agents gathered it together; my teamsters carried it to the dock. I was in the process of looking for a buyer."

The lord raised his head. "It seems we must speak to Ervin the Merchant. Ashmet!"

"Yes, my Lord."

"Bring Ervin to me. Immediately."

Cheynou could see the satisfaction forming on the big man's face. He held out a restraining hand. "My Lord?"

"Yes?"

"I do not wish to interfere, my Lord, but it seems to me that Ashmet Khrem needs to understand that the merchant may not be at fault here, either."

"Young man, do you presume to stand in my hall and tutor me in the instruction of my men?"

"I had hoped you would not see it that way, my Lord. I only observed that when Ashmet Khrem approached us out at the dock, he seemed under the strong impression that we were thieves, stealing the cargo. Because of that impression, he made a very threatening approach. Because of his demeanour, I thought myself justified in assuming that I was dealing with brigands attempting to hijack our cargo. It took the best of my diplomatic skills to straighten out the situation."

"Plus the knowledge that you were severely overmatched."

"Some people seem to feel that a military advantage negates the need for diplomacy, my Lord."

The lord laughed: a dry chuckle. "I did not hire a graduate of the Kantoon for his diplomatic skills, young man."

"No, my Lord, perhaps he does not need them. However, the more information he has, the better he will perform his duties. I see him now, leaving here in some embarrassment, looking to the merchant Ervin as the cause of his misfortune. If there really is still some misunderstanding, his attitude towards the merchant at this moment may not be useful in solving it."

The lord frowned, then shot Cheynou a glance. "It seems that someone here feels he has enough diplomacy for both of you. Perhaps you would like to go along to see that Ervin is treated with the proper respect?"

Cheynou looked to his captain, received a nod. "I...would prefer not to, my Lord. I am sure that Ashmet Khrem, having heard this conversation, is quite capable of performing his duties to the fullest of your expectations. I consider my skills more useful here."

"To keep us from quarreling with each other, perhaps?"

"Oh, no, sir. Simply to make sure that your meaning is always conveyed precisely."

"Right!" The lord's hands slapped his chair arms. "Ashmet, you have heard the conversation. You know as much as any man here. Can you bring Merchant Ervin to us quickly, but not with undignified haste, in order to get his help in solving this misunderstanding?"

"I can do that, my Lord." The soldier saluted, bowed, and with a wondering glance at Cheynou, left the room.

Giron turned to Cheynou as well. "Does that meet with your approval?"

"I'm sure you know best, my Lord."

The lord turned his attention to Captain Jatu. "I am beginning to wonder with whom I am supposed to be negotiating."

The captain grinned and shook his head. "My Lord, I find myself wanting to apologize for the behaviour of my Second Officer, but I cannot put my finger on what he has done that requires apology. How can one take offence at reasonable reasoning, at argument that refuses to argue? If you will take my advice, my Lord, it is usually best to listen carefully, nod knowingly, and continue with whatever you were doing when he started. Further argument only keeps him going."

"Could we not just send him away?"

"I note that you already played that gambit, and here he stands."

"At least you and I can recognize a common adversary. That is usually a good point at which to start any discussion."

"It is, my Lord, and since we cannot deal with the matter at hand, perhaps we could use our time profitably discussing other matters."

The lord nodded. "I imagine we could. I gather you have traded mostly in the Kyabran sphere, but are expanding in this direction?"

"Yes. The competition is stiff closer to home, and I find that my small resources do not match well against those with more ships, more political advantage. For a man of my sort, there are more accessible resources in less-organized areas."

"Spoken by a less honourable man, that could be interpreted as one who wishes to work less within established practices, looking for an area where there is laxer enforcement."

Both men's eyes slid to Cheynou.

"I believe you are each understanding the other, sir. There are two interpretations to my captain's words. Please do not accept the one that suggests piracy and smuggling."

Both nodded and returned to their conversation. Throughout the ensuing discussion, Cheynou listened with his full attention, trying to understand and convey every nuance and possible meaning. As time went on and each seemed to gain knowledge of the other, his services were needed less and less, although he continued to listen, more for his own interest, now.

Finally, there was a noise at the door, and Ashmet entered.

"My Lord, the Merchant Ervin."

"Bring him in."

A stocky, fortyish man with a grey beard entered, going straight to Lord Giron. "My Lord, I am so happy to finally get to see you. I had been..." His gaze noticed the others in the room. "...oh! You have met already. This is excellent!"

"It is excellent, is it, Ervin?"

"Oh, yes, my Lord. The cargo you wanted me to sell. I have sold it, as I suppose you know." His hand indicated the surprised captain.

"No, I did not know. Why was I not informed immediately?"

"I tried, my Lord, but we made the deal in Beaumas, and I came into harbour too late last night to call on you. I knew you would be on your rounds most of the day, so I thought to inform you this afternoon when you returned. I tried to stop your man, here, this morning, so that he could tell you, but he brushed me aside, as he said he was on an urgent mission and could not take the time."

"So you were able to market the cargo faster than you thought, and the captain was able to get here to collect it quicker than the news that it had been sold."

The merchant took a moment to absorb this. "Oh. There...there wasn't any ...difficulty, I hope?"

The lord waved it away. "Nothing that couldn't be solved with a touch of diplomacy, Ervin." His hand suddenly firmed into a pointing finger that skewered Cheynou. "And you, young man, will not say 'I told you so'!"

"I wasn't even thinking it, my Lord."

"Hmph. Don't lay on the diplomacy too heavily, lad. Most people do not enjoy being patronized."

Cheynou let it show that he was keeping a straight face with difficulty. "Thank you, my Lord. I will endeavour to follow your advice."

The lord's attention was already elsewhere. "Well, Ervin, it seems this little hitch in plans may have positive results. Captain Jatu has a great deal of information and many contacts in the Empire and is willing to share them with us."

The merchant obeyed the gesture to sit and looked with new interest at the Kyabran. "That would indeed be interesting, my Lord. We have discussed this before."

"That we have, but now we will discuss it again, with one more of the pieces added to the puzzle. Excuse me for a moment, gentlemen." He turned to his guard. "Ashmet. Go out to the East Dock and inform the guards that the rest of the cargo is to be loaded onto the *Courser* immediately when she returns..." he regarded the captain "...tomorrow? This afternoon?"

"Part of the reason that the price was good has to do with getting the cargo to Rhane in the Torrens Islands as quickly as possible. I could stay here, continue with our conversation, and send the ship around to pick it up immediately."

"There you are, Ashmet. Take four stevedores from the North Dock to help."

Cheynou attracted attention with a polite gesture. "A pilot would be useful as well, my Lord."

"Right. Ashmet, send a pilot out to the *Courser* on your way."

Captain Jatu nodded. "Mister Chan, I'm sure we three grown men can get along without your services and avoid serious misunderstanding. Return to the ship, take the pilot out and tell Toban to go and get the cargo. Moor at the dock when you return. There may be other merchandise by that time. We will stay here overnight, but tell Toban we will leave on the tide at...?" the questioning look was directed towards the merchant.

"Just after sunup, Captain, if you want to get away early."

"...at the first bell. If there's any other cargo, we'll lade tonight."

"Aye, sir." Cheynou turned, bowed to the other two. "My Lord, sir."

As he followed Ashmet from the room, he heard the lord comment, "Glad he's gone. Now I can relax. Hate having to be so damned polite all the time..."

The heavy hand of the guard, slapping his back, distracted him.

"I can't believe it."

"What?"

"You did it. You walked in there and made it all look like his fault. Let me tell you, lad, you got me off a barbed hook."

"That's good, Ashmet. Turned out we were right all along, didn't it?"

"We? Oh, certain. After you bamboozled me into agreeing with you."

"Ah, it was just your common sense giving you a nudge."

The guard paused at the fortress gate. "I'll be thanking my common sense for the nudge, and you for slapping me across the nose with it." The grin disappeared. "And now, you get to your boat and I'll have a pilot to you in no time. See you at the East Dock."

Cheynou raised a hand in farewell, but the man's broad back was all that he could see. He strolled down the dock to where the gig's crew was scrambling into place.

They peered anxiously at him, relaxing when he smiled. "No problem, lads. It was all a misunderstanding. We beat the merchant and the money back to the dock, so they didn't know we had already paid."

The bosun spat into the harbour. "Disadvantage of havin' such a fast ship, sir."

"That it is, Freye. We'll be picking up a pilot and going back for the rest of the cargo. Maybe even get that fearsome soldier to help load it!"

The sailors grinned at that and settled down again to wait.

On the ship, Toban puffed himself up further with the responsibility of command. His orders from the bridge deck were sharp, loud and even more detailed than normal. The crew, inured to his style, handled their duties as smartly as usual.

With the help of the pilot, they were able to round the sand spit faster than their inward voyage, in spite of having to tack upwind. Ashmet was waiting with several muscular men, and the loading of the lighter fairly flew. In double-quick time, the cargo was safely stowed and the ship was back in port, nudging gently up to the dock below the fortress.

When all lines were fast, the First Officer turned to Cheynou. "Are you ready for command, Mister Chan?"

Cheynou grinned. "Since she's moored fast, I suppose I can handle it."

Toban did not respond with levity. "It may not be that simple. You must keep the hands on board. They have been at sea for quite a stretch, and they will be at sea a few days longer. Not one of them is to go ashore for any reason." He nodded meaningfully at the dockside tavern advertising its wares nearby.

"I'll see to it, sir."

Taking leave of the pilot, Toban marched his solitary way up the stone-flagged street and was soon gone. The sailors continued with their tasks, tidying up, battening down and generally making the ship look as spruce as usual. Cheynou wandered among them, making a few suggestions, but mostly leaving it up to the crew to take care of things.

After a while, the activity died away, and Cheynou found himself overlooking twelve pairs of longing eyes lined along the rail, regarding the inn door so near.

"Seems a shame, don't it, sir?"

"It does, Noyes. But the First Officer's orders were quite specific. It's very important that this cargo reaches Rhane at the earliest moment, and we can't have sailors wandering back, hung over, at all times of the morning."

"I can understand that, sir. Still…"

"There's no 'still' about it, sailor, you can't leave the ship, and neither can I." He spied a lad leaving the inn. "But that doesn't say we have to do without a bit of a treat."

At his shrill whistle, the boy sprinted over. "What's the chances of a few mugs of ale delivered across the dock, lad?"

"Do it all the time, sir."

"And what's good for eating in the kitchen?"

"Pork stew and treacle puddin', sir."

"We get plenty of pork stew on board, but the pudding sounds tempting. How much would you charge…" They set to haggling, and by the time a wagonload of cargo rattled down the dock, the sailors were relaxed around the deck, finishing the dregs from their mugs and licking sweet syrup off their moustaches.

"All right, lads, it seems we're back to work. Freye and Noyes, you're below to see to the stowage, please. The rest of you, lay out the plank. This looks like small stuff, and we'll take it personal-like."

They chuckled at his expression and turned to with a will. Soon, a line of men marched up the gangplank laden with sacks and boxes, and another line swung down from the rail farther along. The wagon was almost empty when four stevedores showed up, rather chagrinned to find their work almost complete.

"That's all right, boys. My lads would love a break. You can finish the job."

The longshoremen swung into it with the ease of long practice, and the task was finished quickly and professionally.

The leader of the stevedores approached Cheynou. "How will we divide the charges, sir? Your men did the larger share of the job."

Cheynou shrugged. "We do our own lading all the time, and no one gets any extra. I guess it's all yours."

The man's face lightened. "Then I suppose your men wouldn't refuse a token of our thanks?"

Cheynou calculated quickly. It was a full bell since the men had finished the first ale, and the drink from this tavern didn't seem too strong. A bit of hard work would have sweated a good portion of the alcohol from their bodies. "That would be obliging of you, sir."

Once again, the potboy from the tavern was dispatched with his trays of mugs.

Dusk was approaching when the firm steps of the First Officer could be heard, stamping over the cobbles. Cheynou glanced around to see several sailors drifting over to stand more closely to their proper watch positions. The mugs had long been returned to the tavern, and the ship looked her usual smart self.

Cheynou greeted Toban at the gangplank, as was the Kyabrans' routine.

"Everything in order, Second Officer Chan?"

"Aye, sir. The lading went well. Perhaps you would like to check Noyes' stowage."

"I will do that, Mister Chan." He nodded and disappeared below, Noyes following. They returned on deck some time later with the officer nodding in satisfaction and a small frown on the deckhand's brow.

"All stowed safely, sir?"

"It is now."

"Was there something I should know about for the future, sir?"

"Not really. I simply wished to ensure that the perishables were properly protected. In general, the stowage was satisfactory."

"Thank you, sir."

Toban began his usual round of inspection, and Cheynou, ignoring the sailor's glower, followed. From what he could pick up, Noyes always supervised the stowage and Toban usually found something to make him do over. It was none of Cheynou's business.

When the inspection was done, they returned to the bridge deck. "The men seem pleased with themselves tonight."

Cheynou explained about the stevedores' gesture.

"I suppose that was not out of line, as long as no hard liquor was involved."

"I kept careful watch, sir."

The First Officer gave an actual smile. "It is fine for the men to receive a reward for extra effort. Not often, but often enough that they remember."

"I agree, sir. How are the discussions going up in the fortress?"

"Quite smoothly, it seemed to me. I believe we will be doing business here in the future."

"That was the impression I got, although I left before they got down to details."

The First Officer regarded him quizzically. "But not before you had made some kind of impression on Lord Giron."

"Possibly, sir. I was very careful to listen to their conversations and caught a few errors of translation that could have been misunderstood."

"Was that it? I gathered it was something more personal than that."

Cheynou shrugged. "Giron and I did have some discussion on the uses of diplomacy, sir."

"Diplomacy, was it? That would explain the comments."

No more information was forthcoming, and the two men stood there in the dim evening, content to have performed their duties for the day and possibly made a tidy profit as well.

The captain returned just at midnight, and Cheynou could smell on his breath one reason for the smoothness of the negotiations.

"A day worth the living and the working as well, gentlemen, but the next one starts early. Tide is on the first bell."

"Aye, sir."

The captain laid a hand on Cheynou's shoulder. "You surprised me, lad. I had not thought you one to push the bounds of proper behaviour."

"The court jester can often say things to the king that a greater man would not dare, sir."

The captain nodded. "It is a sharp edge you walk, Cheynou. Be very careful you do not slip."

Cheynou smiled. "There are advantages to being young, small, and a foreigner. One receives much more leeway in the social domain."

Jatu frowned slightly. "And when your little-boy act doesn't work?"

"Then I fight, sir."

"You do?"

"Once diplomacy has failed, there is rarely another option. If necessary, I am not afraid to run."

The captain laughed. "I see you have it all thought out. I hope experience never proves you wrong."

"I hope not as well. Of course, there is always the unexpected. Then you improvise."

"I suspect you are also skilled at that, my young friend."

"I do my best, sir."

"As long as you are 'doing' for the best of the ship, I will be satisfied."

"I always act for the best of the Ship, sir. Always."

The captain's smile disappeared, and his eyes narrowed. "Yes, Cheynou, I believe you do." He nodded thoughtfully, repeating half to himself, "I believe you do."

17. TRAINING

The valuable cargo was unloaded in Rhane on time and without incident, and a further load was being assembled for their return to Voges, so the men finally got an evening ashore. Cheynou made certain that he was on watch, because he felt it would not be good politics with the First Officer to go ashore with the men, and would probably be taken amiss by some of them if he were to refuse.

The following morning, when the rest of the cargo had yet to arrive, he approached the captain.

"I have been thinking about the incident at the dock, back in Voges, sir."

"And what conclusions have you drawn?"

"It all turned out fine in the end, but I'm not so happy with my role. I did think of one problem I could solve, though, in case something like that happened again."

"What problem is that?"

"You know how Freye said he could have taken the Kantoon? I don't know the answer to that argument, and I should."

"It is good to know the skills of your men. What do you suggest?"

"I think we should do some arms training, sir. Times like this, when there is a lull."

"I can see the use in that, although some of the men might not be enthused."

Cheynou shrugged. "I had only planned to work with the crew of the lighter, sir. Those who were on that dock with me will be keen, I think."

"Go ahead, Mister Chan. I'm sure a few of the others will want to join in."

Cheynou nodded and stepped forward. He did not raise his voice much but made sure it carried to several nearby sailors. "Anyone for a little fun?"

Heads came up, questioning glances.

"I'd like to see the crew of the lighter on the maindeck. Please scout them out for me."

A few knowing looks were passed, as well as some smiles. Cheynou strolled down to the main deck and waited. If the other sailors thought they knew what was going to happen next, they would be surprised.

The First Officer followed. "If you want the men to respond smartly to your orders, Mister Chan, you're going to have to give them in a firmer voice than that."

Cheynou shook his head. "I wasn't giving an order, Mister Toban. I was sending an invitation. I'll save my snappy orders for when they are really orders."

It was a very short time before the oarsmen were lined smartly in front of them. In Cheynou's mind, they would have come no faster had the First Officer shouted.

He strolled the line, casually straightening a few minor elements of clothing and position. "All right, men, we ran into a problem a few days ago, and I didn't do my best job of solving it. The reason it was so hard to discourage our dear friend Ashmet Khrem was that I really had no idea, if there was a fight, of how useful any of you would be. Freye, for example, assured me he could have taken the Kantoon by himself..." He paused to let them know they were allowed to chuckle.

"So I suggest we find out."

Glances up and down the line, a slight shifting of balance, shuffling of feet. He knew he had them now.

"So, if you please, each of you find yourself a belaying pin."

There was some confusion at this, but, puzzled as they were, soon each man was facing him with a forearm's length of hard wood in his hand.

"So that we don't hurt each other too much, I thought we should have a chance to practise before we go to the real weapons. Pair up and let's see some easy sparring. Don't push it too far. I wouldn't like anybody too injured to continue, this early in the fun."

They paired off and began awkward and half-hearted bouts. He gave them a short time to practise, then called a halt.

"Well, gentlemen, I must say that was very disappointing."

"We don't usually fight with belaying pins, sir."

"It's quite obvious you should. What happens if you come on deck in the middle of an attack and can't get to the cutlass rack?"

They shrugged and muttered.

"All right." He picked up a pin himself. "Anybody like to try a round with me?"

He gazed at each of them. "Don't be afraid."

Sure enough, Noyes took the bait. He moved forward quickly, but slowed when he saw the grin on Cheynou's face. Cheynou crouched slightly, his legs slipping into the old, familiar stance, the firm wood comfortable in his grip. Having seen these men move, he knew that he was quicker and more skilled, so he settled in to give the best lesson he could. First would be defense.

He made a 'come on' gesture. Noyes was not fast, but he was strong. The wood whistled past Cheynou's ear as he ducked and spun away. Once again, the man attacked, more certain this time, and Cheynou ducked in the other direction.

After five or six fruitless swings, Noyes changed his attack. Now, he moved forward more slowly, his swings shorter and quicker. Cheynou nodded in approval and began to counter with his own weapon. After a rather quick exchange, he spun away again, touching his opponent on the ribs lightly as he did so. A chuckle rose from the crew who had seen the move.

Noyes bored in again, this time to be punished more firmly on the upper arm. The growing ring of sailors began to shout.

"Come on, Noyes. We thought you were good."

"Go get him, man. What are you waiting for?"

Even with the extra motivation, Noyes was still outclassed and knew it well. Soon, Cheynou stopped, motioned the man back. "Bosun?"

"Yes, sir?"

"You have been watching. Would you like to have a try at me?"

"I would, sir."

He nodded, and Freye lifted a belaying pin from a nearby pinrail. Cheynou could see by the man's stance that he knew what he was doing, so he proceeded carefully.

He moved slowly at first to let the bosun warm up. Then he quickened the pace, attacking, then backing off and allowing his opponent to challenge him. He soon had the bosun's level, and he was impressed. This man had used a pin before. The men's cheering quieted as the match progressed and the abilities of the fighters were revealed.

When he thought the demonstration had gone far enough, Cheynou took his opponent down with a simple foot-sweep and forced the man's weapon-hand to the deck with his own pin.

The bosun nodded his defeat, and Cheynou extended his left hand, helping the man up. He bowed, and after a moment's hesitation, the bosun bowed as well. He must have had some formal training somewhere. He was certainly far above the level of his sailors.

Cheynou faced the men. "You see now that a belaying pin can be a real weapon if used correctly. The advantage for training is that you don't tend to cut hunks out of people." He waited out the laughter, then took a serious tone.

"If any of you want to learn some of the moves you saw us do, step up."

There were glances and, finally, one pair edged forward. "We wanta know how you put the bosun, here, to the deck."

"Figure on trying it for yourself some time, Jonis?"

The man nodded. "I noticed that you used your foot. A man could use that anywhere: cutlass, belaying pin, bar fight."

Cheynou stepped forward. "That's right, and it doesn't take much to learn. Come here." He took the man by the arm and pulled him forward. As the sailor stepped, while all his weight was on his left foot, Cheynou reached a toe behind his right heel and guided it ahead and to the side. As the man's weight came down, the foot wasn't there, and only Cheynou's lift on his arm kept him from hitting the deck hard. As it was, he found himself sitting at his opponent's feet, looking surprised.

Cheynou helped him rise. "See what I did?"

"Aye Just when my foot was comin' down, you pulled it out from under me."

"That's the trick. You have to catch the foot while there is no weight on it, but after your opponent has committed his weight forward. If he's still balanced on the back foot, he can just lift the forward foot and step again."

Soon, there were sailors stumbling all over each other having varying degrees of success with the move. Cheynou circulated among them, correcting, encouraging, just as he would have with a class of youngsters back on the Familyship.

Once they all had some kind of skill with the foot-sweep, he moved them into some basic attacks and parries with the belaying pins. In order to keep them interested, he only gave them moves that were adaptable to the cutlass.

He kept them at it until he could see signs of flagging interest, then called a halt.

"When you carry a belaying pin and you are facing a sword, you are only expecting to make one parry. Can you tell me why?"

"Because the second pass he's going to kill you."

"Precisely. When two swordsmen meet, there is an instant agreement. Each wants to fight with a sword, so they have a fencing match. They stay at the correct distance and whale away. You have a belaying pin or a boat hook and you get in a fencing match with a sword, you are going to lose very quickly. If you play fair."

185

He and Freye shared a grin, and a few of the lighter's crew, remembering the Kantoon's reaction to the cargo net, smiled as well.

"So what do we do, sir?"

"What do you think?"

"I think maybe run and hide in the bilge."

Cheynou joined in the laughter, then waited for it to die. "That might work, too, but I suggest the opposite."

"What, sir? Attack?"

"Exactly. The last thing you want to do is stay back where he can get a good cut at you. You want to get in close, where he can't use his cutlass at all."

He could see the light dawning.

"I know what you mean, sir. You get in a fistfight with someone who knows how to punch, your best bet is to get in and wrestle with him. You stand back, he'll just keep hitting you."

"That's it. When you've shown me some skill with the sticks, we'll move to something a bit more dangerous. The next lesson will be some moves with the belaying pin and dagger. In any surprise attack, that's what you're most likely to have handy, and that's what works the best once you're in close."

They snorted and made derogatory comments about toys, but he knew he had their interest. He left the main deck and climbed the companionway to the bridge, where the captain was leaning on the rail, watching.

"They certainly could use some training, sir."

Jatu nodded. "We're running a merchant ship in navy-protected waters. Seamanship beats swordsmanship every time when it comes to hiring a new man."

"Wise, sir. Until we move into less protected waters."

"True, Mister Chan, and that's why I'm not unhappy with the work you did today."

"Thank you, sir."

18. ALBATROSS

Cheynou was always sensitive to the crew's mood, so his ears were open. Some of the men had come back from the tavern earlier than they should the night before and they weren't happy. He didn't have to ask why: a fight with a bad ending.

So, that morning, when the whole crew poured out of the hatches and gathered on the deck, silent and frowning, he positioned himself at the head of the gangplank and allowed them to approach. Noyes was in the lead, as usual. "I don't have to ask where you're going."

"No, you don't, sir. We're goin' over to the *Albatross* to clip a few wings real short."

He waited for the accompanying shouts to die and spoke quietly. "Actually, you aren't."

"Damned well are. You thinkin' of stoppin' us?"

Cheynou gave Noyes a level stare. "You go over to the *Albatross* and step on their deck, they'll have the right to take up weapons and cut you down. You go over there and yap around the gangplank like a pack of curs, they'll laugh at you. Then they'll call the watch, and you'll cool off in a dungeon somewhere. Is that what you had in mind?"

The muttering continued, but the press of men thinned.

"What're we gonna do, sir? They beat Whit up for nothin'!"

Cheynou scratched his cheek thoughtfully. "What's really bothering you? Whit has got himself into fights before, and he doesn't always win."

Noyes shook his head angrily. "That's not it, sir. He picks a fight and loses, that's different. They piled on him, about five of them. He didn't have a chance."

"So, if he could get a chance at one of them, man on man, that would be enough?"

The men turned and muttered among themselves. Finally, Noyes stood forward again. "It don't satisfy us, because it wouldn't make up for him bein' piled on. But it would make him damned happy to get a bit of his own back."

"Right. I'll talk to the captain. You," he pointed to the deck of the *Courser*, "will return to your work." He stared them down, and finally they nodded and turned back. Cheynou headed for the captain's cabin.

"They were what?" The captain was on his feet, hand groping for his cutlass belt.

"It's all right, sir. They're back at their tasks."

Jatu stopped, looking at Cheynou. "The whole crew was set to go over to the *Albatross* and pick a fight and you…sent them back to their work?"

"I told them I would try to solve the problem, sir."

The captain motioned to a chair. "Tell me what their problem is."

Cheynou sat and leaned across the chart table. "You know how Whit has a habit of picking fights when he's had a few. Well, this time he was alone, and about five of the *Albatross* crew jumped him. Our boys are really mad about that."

"That it wasn't a fair fight?"

"Exactly. So I said I'd try to solve the problem."

"What do you have in mind?"

"I go over and ask the *Albatross*'s captain if my man can have satisfaction."

"Satisfaction?"

"Isn't that the right word?"

"It is, if you mean what two young toffs talk about before getting into a duel."

"That's what I mean, then."

"Sailors don't go around slapping people's faces with fancy gloves."

"Perhaps not, sir, but they do have their own rough idea of fairness, and it means a lot to them. Witness their feelings at the moment."

"A captain can't just step on board another ship and say, 'please, sir, one of my men would like to fight one of yours over a matter of honour.' I'd be laughed all the way down the gangplank."

Cheynou shrugged again. "I understand that, sir. I suppose we'll just have to let them solve it sailor-fashion."

The captain was completely still for a moment. "Why don't I like the sound of that?"

Cheynou raised his eyebrows politely.

"All right, what are you planning?"

"What the sailors would do, sir, is wait until they saw the *Albatross* crew go into a bar. Then they'd go in after them."

"Mister Chan, we can't have that! We can't have our crew feuding with another ship!"

"My feelings exactly, sir."

"And your solution is to get the other captain to let Whit have a go at one of his men."

"That is one solution, sir."

"I could also go over and ask that captain to have his men flogged."

"Our men would probably find that quite satisfactory as well, sir, but then the next time they met in a bar..."

"I know. The *Albatross* crew would tie into them."

"What do you suggest, sir?"

"I don't know. I still can't see myself just walking up their gangplank..." Captain Jatu shook his head slowly.

"I could go, sir."

"You?"

"Yes. That way, if they laugh at me, it won't be such a slur on the ship's honour. Also, if the captain has nothing to do with it, it isn't official ship's policy to condone fighting."

The captain regarded him for a moment, and a slight smile formed at the corner of his mouth. "You would rather do it yourself, wouldn't you?"

"Yes, sir. It's sort of becoming my position on the ship, if you know what I mean."

"All right. Let's see how you handle this." The captain's smile broadened. "I'd like to go along, just to see how Baltasra takes it." He waved his hand. "Go ahead. Do it now, before I change my mind."

Cheynou was approaching the gangplank when Noyes, who was working conveniently nearby, looked up. "Where you goin', sir?"

"Over to the *Albatross*. I have some business there."

"Like an escort, sir?"

"Noyes, this is diplomacy. No show of strength needed."

"Good luck, sir."

"Thank you, Noyes." He proceeded down the gangplank and along the dock. He did not have to look back to know that every hand was watching him.

The *Albatross* was another three-masted schooner, a bit smaller and older than the *Courser*. Definitely not so trim. Cheynou stood at the bottom of the gangplank, waiting until a crewman appeared at the top.

"Cheynou Chan, Second Officer of the *Courser*. Permission to board?"

"Just a moment."

Soon, the sailor was replaced by an officer. "Who are you?"

"I told your man who I was, and I'm sure he told you. I have business with your captain."

The officer frowned, then gestured. "Come aboard."

"Thank you."

He strolled up the gangplank and stopped, looking around with interest. Definitely not as trim as the *Courser*, but workmanlike, all the same. As with the *Courser* today, there seemed to be a lot of sailors with work that kept them within sight of the deck.

"This way."

He followed the officer into the captain's cabin, which was slightly smaller than the *Courser*'s, but lighter, owing to larger transom windows. The captain was sitting at a desk, writing. He did not get up. The other officer stood aside, watching intently.

"What can we do for you?"

"I am Cheynou Chan of the *Courser*, sir, and I have a matter to discuss with you."

The captain turned slowly and looked up, seeming surprised. "So this is the famous Cheynou the Barbarian."

"My friends use that as a term of respect, sir."

"Respect, is it?"

"Yes, sir. Many of my friends are quite well mannered. Some aren't."

"Well, Mister Chan, I am Captain Baltasra of the *Albatross*. What can I do for you?"

"It is the matter of a fight yesterday, sir, between one of our men and several of yours."

"Why are you concerning yourself with sailors' brawls?"

"The other alternative was to have my whole crew storm over here looking for the guilty parties, sir. I felt you might not appreciate that."

"Your whole crew?"

"Yes, sir. They felt very strongly about it."

"Your whole crew comes storming down the dock, they're going to get a very stiff reception here, Mister Chan."

"That's what I told them, sir. They agreed to let me come instead."

"They agreed, did they?" The man's eyebrows went up. "How polite of them. And if this is such a serious situation, why didn't Captain Jatu come to deal with it?"

"It's rather my responsibility, sir."

"As what?"

"As the arms-master on the *Courser*, sir."

That brought the other's complete attention. He spun around in his chair to face Cheynou, eyebrows raised. "The *Courser* has an arms-master, and that arms-master is you?"

"That is correct, sir. With our trading outside the Empire, we have been running into more situations where a certain show of force is to our advantage. I found the men in need of training, so I took on the task."

"I see. So you have been training the crew of the *Courser* to fight? What kind of fighting?"

Cheynou shrugged. "Whatever they seemed to learn fastest, sir. Hand-to-hand, cutlass, belaying pin, pike."

"And this mob was set to storm my ship?"

"That's right, sir. Are you beginning to realize that you need to take this situation seriously?"

The man stood, towering over Cheynou in the small cabin. "Look here, boy. I don't need some barbarian to come on my ship and tell me how to handle my crew. You just keep your own men under control, or your ship and your captain will pay for it."

Cheynou looked up at the man calmly, then nodded. "Fine. You keep your men on your ship, and I'll make sure they're safe."

"What?"

"I have already made it clear to my crew that they are to stay away from your ship. I thought you understood that. However, once your men venture into the town, they are out of your protection and mine. I have neither the time nor the inclination to shepherd my men when they are on shore leave to protect the crew of another ship whose captain doesn't seem to be interested in their welfare."

For a long moment, the captain of the *Albatross* just stood there. Gradually, a frown formed. He glanced at his officer, then back to Cheynou. "Are you threatening me?"

"Why would I do that? I have come to you to find a solution to a problem that has occurred between our crews. What good would it do me to threaten? What are we? Pirates? Barbarians?" As the captain glared at him, Cheynou allowed a small grin to appear.

The big man's frown turned thoughtful. "There is something here that I don't understand. What exactly did you come for?"

Cheynou nodded as if a decision had been made. "I came to make sure you knew of the problem, which I gather you already did. I came to make sure you understood that it was serious, which I think you do now. I came to ask you if you had any idea of how to solve it."

Baltasra shrugged. "I didn't see any need, actually. I usually let the sailors solve their own problems."

"I agree, sir, but in this case, it seems that your men have overstepped a boundary that my men think is important."

"Overstepped..." Now the captain seemed truly confused. "Are you telling me that there are rules of etiquette in a bar brawl?"

"Of course there are. How do you think they have so many of them with so few deaths and serious injuries?"

"I never thought of it that way."

"They aren't like the 'sabres at sundown' rules the young bloods have, but the rules they have are serious to them."

"I see. And what rule have my sailors broken?"

"It seems there were about five of them, sir. There was some provocation, but they all set upon him with no warning."

"I see. So your sailors feel this was unfair."

"Exactly, sir."

"So what are you suggesting? Cutlasses at sundown?"

"If you can't think of another solution, I was going to suggest the sailors' version."

"Which would be?"

"I'm not exactly sure, sir, but whatever it turns out to be, we don't want to put our captains in the position of sanctioning such a thing."

"I see. That leaves you."

"I would be willing. Perhaps an officer from your ship, to see that all is correct?"

The captain of the *Albatross* raised a hand. "You know something, Cheynou Chan the Barbarian? I don't think I want to have anything to do with this. Don't tell me any more." He turned to his officer. "Dhama, will you see Mister Chan back to his ship? I would hate for anything to happen to him on the way home from visiting us. He might blame me!"

The captain sat at his desk and pointedly turned his back. Cheynou met the eye of the other officer, who nodded towards the door.

Once down the gangplank and away from the other ship, Cheynou glanced over at the other, a tall, gangly man of about thirty. "What do you think?"

"It has to be off the ships."

"Certainly. And not in a bar."

Dhama nodded. "We'd have to pay the damage."

"This is between us. No spectators, no interference."

"We don't tell the men until it's all arranged."

"It doesn't take much to arrange it."

The other officer looked at him. "It doesn't?"

"We only need to arrange six people."

"Six?"

"My man, his chosen opponent, you, me and one witness from each crew."

"The other men don't get to watch?"

"We aren't providing a spectacle, Mister Dhama. All we want is for my crew to feel that justice has been done, and your crew to realize that they stepped over a line. Another time they won't, and that's better for you. The last thing we want to do is make this any kind of fun for any of them."

"I have to agree with that. This kind of trouble is the last thing you need if you're trying to run a peaceful trading enterprise." His glance shot to Cheynou. "How peaceful is your enterprise, Mister Chan?"

Cheynou smiled. "As peaceful as we can get away with, Mister Dhama."

The other laughed. "Let's take a detour and see what this town offers."

It wasn't difficult. The town was small, and there was a flat area on the outskirts just behind the beach where the fishermen dragged their skiffs above the tideline. The ground was hard-packed sand. At mealtime, there was no one about.

"Tomorrow night?"

"We won't be sailing before then."

"Nor will we."

"I'll have my man describe who he wants."

"Fair enough."

In the end, the fight was inconclusive. The *Courser*'s man, true to his nature, had chosen an *Albatross* sailor who outweighed him seriously. This man had a huge black eye, which gave some indication of why he had been chosen. Through the fight, he tried to clinch with his smaller, more agile opponent, but failed. However, he did manage to land a few hard punches. The *Courser*, in his turn, couldn't get anywhere close to his enemy, and had to content himself with jabs of his fists and feet. He landed a lot, none of which did serious damage. By the time Cheynou and Dhama decided to call a halt, both were exhausted.

"Whit, are you satisfied?"

The man panted a moment, then spoke. "I'm satisfied that this tub of shit knows what he tied into the other day."

Cheynou turned to the other sailor. "Are you satisfied?"

Aye. He's a good fighter. He deserved his chance. Too bad he couldn't make use of it."

Dhama grinned over the man's shoulder at Cheynou. "They just won't give in, will they?"

"Didn't expect them to." He turned to the perspiring fighters. "Are you two going to shake hands on this? Nobody's forcing you to."

They eyed each other and shrugged. Each reached out a calloused paw, clenched briefly, then withdrew. Cheynou looked at Noyes and the *Albatross* witness. "You see that?"

"Aye, sir."

"As far as we are concerned, the *Courser* is satisfied. Right?"

"Aye, sir."

Dhama nodded. "The *Albatross* too?"

"Aye, sir."

He turned to Cheynou, and the officers shook as well. Cheynou made a small gesture to his sailors, and they headed off towards town. The other two followed.

"Any guess where they're going?"

"To the nearest tavern."

"They're thirsty. They deserve it."

"As long as they don't start it all over again."

Cheynou laughed. "If they fight, it will be a fair one. Your men will see to that."

"My men?"

"Oh, yes. They were at a real disadvantage, and they knew it. They broke the rules."

"How do you see that?"

"When these men fight, when any men fight, it's all about supremacy. If you win by cheating, it's an empty victory. It doesn't give you any supremacy, and you get a reputation as a cheater. I've probably done your crew a bigger favour than I've done mine."

"You could be right."

"Want to find a different tavern?"

"No, I have my orders."

"All right, then."

"My orders are to invite you and your captain over to the *Albatross* for a drink."

"Oh. Thank you. I'll ask Captain Jatu."

The *Courser* captain may have been surprised but he didn't show it. Leaving Toban in charge, the three officers strolled to the *Albatross* in the deepening dusk.

In the candlelight, the captain's cabin seemed cosy as they settled down with a good brandy. Baltasra raised his glass.

"Here's to getting along with each other."

They all grinned and sipped.

Baltasra turned to his officer. "So did it all go smoothly?"

"Yes, sir. They had their fight, nobody won, and the witnesses were satisfied, but nobody had a good time, either."

"Best solution, I'd say."

"I think so, sir."

The *Albatross* captain turned to Jatu. "So tell me something, Captain. How long have you been hosting this barbarian?"

"About three months, Captain Baltasra."

"One more question, Captain."

"Yes?"

"Why haven't you thrown him overboard long before this?"

The *Courser* captain raised his glass. "I know what you mean. The temptation has almost overcome my better judgement several times."

"I'll drink to that."

The others raised their glasses, and Cheynou drank with them, hiding his smile.

"You've been making some longer voyages, Captain Jatu."

"That seems to be common knowledge."

"Outside the usual Empire sphere of protection."

"I have a good Navigator."

The *Albatross* captain shot Cheynou a glance. "I see. Had some trouble?"

"Not much. The lords on the fringes of the Empire have more autonomy and are less likely to follow the laws and traditions to the letter."

"Which can be an advantage or a disadvantage."

Captain Jatu took a thoughtful sip of his brandy. "I have had this conversation with one of the lords out there. Cheynou was careful to instruct the man that any inference of piracy or smuggling was inappropriate."

"He was, was he?"

"Yes, they speak an assortment of barbarian dialects out there. I have some knowledge, but Cheynou is more proficient."

"A valuable man."

"I keep finding reasons not to throw him to the sharks."

"I see. Do you ever find cargoes that are too large for one ship?"

"Ah."

The other captain, his message given, waited.

Captain Jatu took a moment of thought. "I have worked in partnership with other independent captains before."

"As have I. It gives advantage, especially when not under the protection of the Imperial Navy."

"I think you have something in mind."

"That I do, Captain Jatu. I have a possible cargo in Chanda, but it is too large and too dangerous for one ship. With two ships, especially one of your calibre, I would be willing to risk it."

"The usual route to Chanda passes near the Gamanpra Archipelago."

The other captain turned to Cheynou. "Yes, it does."

"Have you considered the pirates?"

"Yes. That is part of the problem."

"Why not take Kotadi Passage?"

"That's a hard upwind slog."

"And a lot of short tacks in the passage itself. I think *Courser* could handle it. If we unship the spars on the foremast, clean up the windage."

"Would it be worth it? That slows us down on the reaches."

"If it avoids the pirates…"

"You have a point. Do your maps indicate the shoals on the eastern end?"

Captain Jatu answered. "We have never made that voyage."

The other captain glanced at Cheynou. "If we agree to join, I will show you my charts."

"Thank you."

The talk turned to courses, winds, and journey times. Cheynou spoke seldom, listening carefully. Nothing was concluded, but Captain Jatu strolled back to his ship with a jaunty stride.

"This is going to make us some more money, Mister Chan."

"I think so, sir."

"How did you know so much about the Gamanpra Archipelago?"

"I listen a lot, sir."

The captain paused, looked down at Cheynou. "You listen."

"Of course, sir. When I'm ashore especially. In my home Fleet, it was the Navigator's task ashore to glean whatever information he could. He then reported it to his Craft, and they talked it over, trying to decide what was fact, what was sailor's gossip."

"So you have been making a picture of this area in your head, all these months."

"That's right, sir. And collecting any maps I could."

"I haven't seen them."

"I'm sorry, sir, I didn't really try to hide them. They are available to you at any time. Of course, they aren't very good. Sort of like sailors' gossip, if you know what I mean."

"Yes. Kernels of truth, if you can separate them from the stories and exaggeration."

Toban met them at the gangplank as usual, glaring at Cheynou with undisguised suspicion as the captain bid him a cordial good night. Cheynou gave the First Officer a politely correct greeting, no more. Overdoing his response, either friendly or cool, would make no difference. The only way to mollify the other man was to become useful to him. The element of competition that lay between them would not disappear any other way, if it ever did.

19. Man Overboard!

Unfortunately, as the days passed, the problem worsened. Cheynou had seen it before. If an officer depended on his rank to control his men and discovered his control slipping, he had nothing to fall back on. So he exerted further control, which only made the men angry. Then began a cycle of petty infractions and petty punishments, slowly growing until they became more serious, usually ending in a flogging. According to tales he had heard in this Sea, extreme cases could end in mutiny.

Sarasha had told Cheynou that it takes two mistakes to bring disaster. The situation was ripe for it, because the first mistake had already been made.

The second happened in a brief, sharp squall that took them all by surprise. They had been the subject of these quick storms for the past few days and handled them all with dispatch. There was nothing to indicate that the disturbance bearing down on them was any different from the rest, so when it hit at twice the force of wind, they were considerably over-canvassed. At the sudden change, Cheynou scrambled from his cabin where he had been going over some charts on his off-watch. His eye swept the deck to see if his help was needed.

In the clattering of rigging on the heeled-over ship, the First Officer and Noyes were on the aft cabintop, struggling to reef the mizzen. The mizzen boom was flogging all over, and the sheet tangled. They both bent over the knot of rope, and Toban called for the helmsman to bear off, get some wind in the sail to straighten the mess. The sail filled, and Noyes seemed to have some trouble with the knot. Toban shouted instructions, shouted again, angrily, and finally committed the unforgivable. He shouldered the man aside and started to work on it himself. Noyes straightened and stood back, anger in every line of his body.

That was when the final bad luck hit. A sudden gust of wind from a completely different direction caught the mizzen sail on the lee side, and the weighty boom swung across the cabin top.

Cheynou shouted, but Toban did not look up. Noyes saw the boom coming, looked at the officer, hesitated, then threw himself flat to let the spar pass over his head. Toban, bent over the ropes, had no warning. The heavy wood struck him on the side, lifted him and swept him off the cabintop, over the rail, and into the water.

Cheynou sounded the 'Man Overboard' cry and jumped to the rail, calling up to Noyes, "Keep pointing to him!"

The sailor looked anxiously at the boom, now flogging out to the other side of the ship.

"Point to him!"

Reluctantly, Noyes pointed, his attention half on the boom, half on the man in the water.

On the call, the sailor at the wheel had put the helm up, and the ship pointed into the wind and slid to a halt, sails rattling and banging. The other sailors were handing the jibs, and someone finally got the mizzen boom under control.

The ship was now out of danger, but the man in the water was not. Cheynou, following Noyes's pointing finger, could see that Toban's head had not come up. He was either stunned or unconscious. In the time it took to lower a boat in these choppy seas, he would drown.

Cheynou grabbed a coil of rope, threw a double loop around his chest and tied it tightly. Handing the coil to a nearby sailor, he moved to the rail. "As you love me, sailor, don't let go of that rope!"

He dove cleanly and was several strokes towards the stricken man before he broke the surface. It was a tough swim, glancing back at the stiff figure on the cabintop to orient himself, then ploughing through the choppy water, but finally he made it. The dark bundle ahead of him did not respond to his touch. He lifted the man's head from the water; his face was ashen.

Nothing to do now. He waved to the ship and locked his arms around Toban's chest. Soon, he was surging through the water as strong backs on the deck hauled with a will.

When they approached the ship, he locked his arms around the First Officer. The men yanked them both, scraping and bouncing, up the side of the ship, and many hands dragged them over the rail.

Cheynou lay there, gasping, looking up at the ring of faces over him.

"Sail...the...ship," he finally got out.

Several heads disappeared. "How is he?"

Another head gone. Cheynou rolled over, sat up. The First Officer lay on the deck beside him, limp. There was no sign of life. Weakly, he grabbed the man's shoulder, tried to roll him over. The men, seeing what he was doing, helped, and they put the injured man face down. Cheynou pushed against his back, trying to force the water from his lungs.

A small trickle ran from the man's mouth, but that was all. After a while, Cheynou stopped.

"I think he's dead, sir."

"Yes. His face was under water from the first. Maybe the boom knocked him out."

By this time, the squall was fading, and the boat rode evenly again. Cheynou stared down at the dead officer, a great emptiness in him. He looked up at the men, standing silent, unsure what to do. With an effort of will, he heaved himself to his feet. "Take him below, leave him on his stomach with his head low. There is a chance he will come around on his own."

Three men lifted the inert form and carried it away. Cheynou had heard of men who had seemingly drowned coming back after a while, but he wasn't optimistic.

A blanket was wrapped around him, and a strong arm moved him forward. He looked up to see the captain's profile, staring angrily ahead. He allowed himself to be urged into the captain's cabin, a glass of brandy pushed into his hand.

He sipped slowly, appreciating the glow that spread through him.

"I was forward. I only saw the last part of it. What happened?"

Cheynou explained the tangled sheet, the sudden gust.

"Yes, I felt the boat heel. It was a strange bit of wind, no doubt about it."

"No fault in the man at the wheel, sir."

"I agree. I'll tell him so myself. An unfortunate accident."

"Yes, sir, and the squall took us all by surprise."

The captain shook his head. "The watch officer is not supposed to be taken by surprise, Cheynou. Ever. I know it happens. In this case, it killed him."

Then Jatu shook his head. "If that's all, I'll put it in the log."

He was about to rise when Cheynou's gesture stopped him. "There's something else, sir. Something you might not want to put in the log."

"Oh?"

"Yes. Noyes saw the boom coming. He looked at Toban, said nothing, and ducked. He could have warned him, could have saved him, perhaps, if he had pushed him down. He didn't."

"He could have saved him?"

"He definitely had time, sir, but I couldn't prove it."

"Why would he act like that?"

Cheynou explained the action over the knotted rope.

"Toban actually pushed a man aside and took over the task?"

"He did, sir."

"So Noyes was steaming mad, I imagine."

"I would say so, sir."

"And that's why he let the man die."

"I doubt if he thought he was going to die, sir. A swat with the boom is rarely fatal."

"But the end result is the same. You're right. I can't write that in the log. What are we going to do about it?"

"Nothing I can think of at the moment, sir, but I recommend you put him ashore at the next port."

The captain shot Cheynou a swift glance. "I thought he was a favourite of yours."

"I try not to have favourites, sir. It's bad for the rest. He is a leader and I think I turned his leadership in a positive direction."

"But you still think he should go."

"In the first place, sir, we can never trust him."

"Granted."

"In the second place, he knows it. That makes his position here difficult. Third, he will never know if the rest of the crew saw it. He could become a pariah, sir. Sailors being superstitious, it could get worse than that."

The captain nodded slowly, rose and went to the door. "Send Noyes here, immediately."

The man showed up quickly, as if expecting the summons. He entered and stood facing the captain, turning slightly towards Cheynou as if to ward off an attack from either of them.

Captain Jatu stared up at him for a long time, then sighed. "Why didn't you warn him, Noyes?"

"I didn't have time, sir. It happened all of a sudden-like…"

The captain raised a hand. "You had time, Noyes. You were angry, and on the spur of the moment you decided that he had put himself in that position, and he could take the consequences."

The sailor was silent.

"So."

"I didn't know he was going to die, sir. You can't say I killed him!"

"No, I can't. I can't even say you intended him serious harm."

Noyes relaxed slightly.

"But I can't have you on the ship, either."

"You gonna put me ashore, Captain?"

"I have to, Noyes. You can see that."

"But...!"

"There is no discussion, Noyes. You go ashore at Jadima. Full pay, no penalty, no record. I can't prove it, so I won't write it, and I won't ever mention it."

The man's body deflated. "Yes, sir."

"Until then, you may resume your duties. The rest of the crew will not be informed unless you decide to tell them."

"Thank you, sir."

The captain nodded, and the sailor spun about and left the cabin.

"So you and I will go watch-and-watch until we replace the First Officer."

"Yes, sir."

"Anything else you can think of?"

"I assume you'll do the service, sir?"

"I've done it before, lad. Not many times, but too many."

"Aye, sir." Cheynou, glad to be freed of at least that duty, rose to go.

"That was a brave act, Cheynou."

He looked back, smiled sadly. "Thank you, sir. I'm sorry it wasn't more useful. Might have left you with no officers at all."

"You seem to be a good swimmer. Most sailors aren't."

"I can swim, sir, but not fast enough to catch a ship, even hove to in that sort of wind. But I gave the rope to a man I trust."

"Don't worry; we had a boat ready to go over the side, as well."

"Glad to hear that, sir."

The captain gave his own pale smile, and Cheynou was dismissed.

The service was simple, yet heartfelt. The captain spoke briefly, stating accurately enough that the dead man had been a superlative seaman. He neglected to mention any faults, and the body shot over the side and down, a rock from the ballast assisting.

The men moved somberly about their duties, and the ship sailed on.

A chance comment, overheard by mistake, told Cheynou that the trouble wasn't over. He called Noyes to him. Once again, they talked on deck near the rail.

"I heard what you said to Jonis."

"What was that, sir?"

"You've been going around the crew, trying to figure out who ratted on you. Doesn't sound very smart to me."

"What do you mean, sir?"

"I mean, that if you go around trying to bully people into telling you who told the captain, pretty soon everybody is going to be wondering what the captain was told."

"I see."

"It was me."

"What?"

"I was the one who saw what happened. I told the captain."

"You! But...but...I thought..."

Cheynou shook his head. "You know me better than that, Noyes. You know why I did it. No matter what I think of you, you know I would."

The man sighed. "Aye, sir. For the good of the damned ship."

"I'll thank you not to speak of the ship like that. I'm not superstitious. Not much. But I depend on this ship to keep me alive, and I'll not have her sworn at."

"Sorry, sir."

"Don't apologize to me."

The man looked at him. "You want me to apologize to the ship? Are you sure your head wasn't in the cold water a bit too long?"

Cheynou grinned. "That sounds better. I'm glad you understand. It's too bad, really. If you hadn't been partly responsible, the captain would have probably promoted me to First, put the bosun in as temporary Second, and set you to cover for the bosun."

"Me, sir?"

"You're as good a sailor as any, and the men look to you."

Noyes stared at the planking. "So I really scuppered myself, didn't I?"

"It was a rash act in a moment of anger."

"But you think I'll do it again."

"I think you could do it again. I can't take that chance."

"Come on, sir. You know I was provoked."

"I know what happened. It doesn't matter. As an officer, I have to make decisions sometimes that a crewmember may not like. I can't be worried that he'll take it out on me."

"I wouldn't, sir."

"The problem is, Noyes, that I can't see any way to be sure of that. How can you regain trust once it's lost?"

"I dunno, sir."

The sailor turned to him. "Couldn't you influence the captain to keep me on? I like this ship. I like sailing with the captain, and with you."

"I'm sorry, Noyes. You know how I feel about it."

"I suppose."

"At least now you won't be pushing the crew around. You don't want to get into a position where everybody on board is upset at you. It can have disastrous consequences, as you may have noticed."

"You mean I...he...?"

"That's right, Noyes. What would be the difference?"

"Oh."

"Right. Your best choice is to let it all drop. The sooner they all put it behind them, the better."

"But you won't."

"I didn't say that. I just couldn't pass it over. Not for…"

"…the good of the ship. I know, sir."

Cheynou shrugged, his hands open helplessly. They stood there a while, then the sailor straightened. "I'm on watch soon, sir."

"Me too. We seem to be short an officer for some reason."

"Don't remind me."

"Good idea."

They parted, each to his own duties.

Over the following days, as the ship ploughed her way towards Jadima, Noyes settled back into his old position, but his heart wasn't in it. He seemed to be trying to win Cheynou's approval, but didn't really know how, because that was not his way of doing things. Cheynou, for his part, didn't know how to handle the man, except to treat him exactly as he always had.

The squalls increased in frequency, and the temperature dropped. Cheynou could feel the storm coming, and he looked around to see if anyone else did. Sure enough, the crew was edgy: snapping at each other, slower to respond to orders, but then working harder than usual.

He approached the captain late on the third day. "Big one brewing up."

"You think so?" Jatu scanned the sky. "No sign up there. Too early in the year for a hurricane."

"I can feel it, sir."

"You can?"

"No question, sir. It's building slowly, and the slower it builds, the harder it hits."

"Is that some of your barbarian wisdom, Mister Chan?"

"It is, sir."

"I have not come to harm by following your advice, Cheynou. When?"

"Can't tell, sir, but in the next two days for sure. Of course, it could go right past us."

"If I counted on that kind of luck, I'd be at the bottom long ago. Let's look at some charts."

They studied the map somberly. "If it's a big storm at this time of year, it will be coming down from the tropics. Westerly winds when it hits, then the eye, then easterlies."

"We don't get storms quite like that in the Southern Ocean. More straight in a line, building and building."

"Something to do with the warmth of the ocean, I think."

"So it's a huge circular weather pattern?"

"That's right."

Cheynou's finger traced a curve on the map. "But if it doesn't pass right over us, if we're on one side or the other, then we only get wind in one direction."

"That's right."

"So you can tell where the centre is by the direction of the wind?"

"Yes. The spin is always in the same direction: around to the right. I have heard that in the far north, it spins the other way."

Cheynou considered. "So if we get wind from the east, the eye is approaching us. Wind from the north means it's passing to the west of us, wind from the south means it's passing to the east."

"That's right."

They looked at the map again. "If we get north winds, we could run to Hingol."

"South winds would send us here..."

"...where there is no shelter."

"And east winds would allow us to reach here..."

The captain shook his head. "Those atolls would give us no shelter. There is too much shallow water around, and the breaking waves will run right over them."

"That simplifies things. What about riding it out at sea?"

"We can do that. We are well-ballasted, and she's a tight ship."

"That pretty well makes our decision for us, then, sir?"

"I believe so. First, we make sure we are ready for a blow. We keep our heading for Hingol. If we get north winds, we keep going. Any other winds, and we ride it out."

"Right."

He spun and left the cabin, giving the "All Hands" call. When the crew was assembled, he told them the truth.

"We think it's an early hurricane. No telling how strong, so we'll take all precautions. Bosun, we need to get the upper staysails off. Will you work on that?"

"Aye, sir."

"When you are finished, see to the storm sails. You know what to do. Check them all over carefully, despite the fact that we already did it ten days ago. Jonis, I want you to take three men and double-batten all the hatch covers. Remember that new lashing I taught you."

"Aye, sir."

"Noyes, the cargo is your responsibility as usual, and there's nobody looking over your shoulder now, so do a really good job. I probably don't need to tell you, but if you can get that pig-iron down any closer to the centre line do so, and triple-lash it."

He pointed to the rest. "You two are responsible for securing the boats on deck. Make sure we don't lose them, but that we can get them if we need them. You two, make sure the pumps are well greased and in perfect working order. You'll all be taking your turns down there in the next few days. Cook, you won't be turning out too many hot meals, and you know how to handle that."

He looked around the group. "Any ideas, comments?"

"What about the masts, sir?"

"I don't know, Bosun. The captain and I only discussed the upper staysails. What is your usual procedure?"

"If we thought we were in for the corker of the century and we had a full day, we could unship the square yards, sir. But that's a bugger of a job and it cuts down our sail area if we are trying to run for cover."

"At the moment, there is still a chance of making it to Hingol, so I think we had best keep sailing."

The sailors all saluted and went about their tasks willingly. He could feel the relief in them, being given something to do to take away the worry. Counting on the men to do their jobs, he started at the bow and covered the ship in detail, looking for anything that might cause a problem: chafed lines, splintered wood, rusted metal. Thanks to Toban's incessant pickiness, he found little.

Satisfied with that, he climbed into the rigging, starting with the foremast and moving aft, once again checking all ropes, standing rigging and fittings he could see. As he worked, he kept an eye on the sky, wind and waves. Sure enough, soon he began to feel the lift of the ship change.

He completed his survey as the sweating sailors lowered the last sails to the deck and hustled them below. The captain looked up from the charts as Cheynou entered the cabin. "You're very thorough, Mister Chan."

"It's nice to have time. I don't want to be caught unawares."

"You move well in the rigging."

"Played there as a child, sir. You should see the number of lines aloft on a full square-rigger."

"I imagine. Everything shipshape up there?"

"Credit to Mister Toban, sir, the ship is in good condition."

"No credit to him for not being here when we need him. He was the one who knew this ship the best."

"We'll have to depend on the bosun, sir."

"That we will. How's the deck work going?"

"Last spar lashed down, all the other jobs finished. I'll be helping them lay out the storm sails."

"Right. We won't be in any hurry to reef down. We still might make Hingol."

Cheynou stared at the captain a moment. "No, we won't, sir."

The captain was puzzled as well. "What do you mean?"

"The storm will be passing east of us, sir."

"What? A while ago we agreed we didn't know where it would be coming from."

"That was a while ago, sir. Can't you feel her?"

"Feel her?"

"Yes, sir. There's a new swell building. Coming at us from the northeast. It's running underneath the normal waves at a longer interval. That means bigger waves somewhere off to the northeast. That's where the storm centre will be."

The captain strode out on deck and stood by the helm, staring off into space, his knees flexed. Then he went to the windward rail and looked down at the sea for a long time. Finally, he straightened.

"You could be right. There is a counter-swell of some sort."

"It's there, sir. You'll be feeling it more and more as the night goes by."

"I'm happy to take your word for it, Mister Chan. So, if we have no chance of making it to Hingol, at least that means the eye will be missing us. Should we run off to the west, to try to miss it even more?"

"We could do that, sir."

The captain turned to the helmsman and called out a new course. Soon, the ship was running on a close reach to the west.

"You had better be right, Mister Chan. We seem to be heading exactly the opposite of where we want to go."

"If this hurricane is like you described, sir, we don't want to be there."

"I agree."

Night deepened, and still the weather seemed fair. The clouds scudded before the northwest winds, and a few stars shone. The only evidence something was wrong was the building swell from astern, noticeable now to everyone, especially the helmsman. Soon, the sailors were cheering as the ship picked up speed, running down the face of each wave as it passed under, slowing as the heaving water hoisted her up again.

"Those are big swells."

"They are, sir. I'd say three chains, crest-to-crest."

The captain nodded to himself. "I'm glad to be running from whatever made those."

"Not running fast enough, sir."

"Not in this wind."

As the night progressed, the wind began to veer, first to the north, then farther and farther east. With dawn, they could see a huge bank of cloud to the east, and the breeze began to freshen.

The ship ran swiftly before the wind now, surfing down the growing swells, labouring up the backs. Throughout the day, the gale strengthened, and soon they were running under reefed sails, the mizzen double-reefed to keep the wind from pushing the ship's stern sideways. Now the craft wallowed, rolling back and forth as the smaller waves from the present wind struck her at different angles from the deep swell pushing her from behind.

It was a trying time, knowing there was trouble coming yet unable to do anything but run. Cheynou remembered how it was back on the Familyship, with all normal duties forgiven and everything done to keep the Crew's spirits up. He went to the captain.

"I think we need some entertainment, sir."

The man looked at him as if he had lost his wits.

"Entertainment. The men are tense, and there's nothing they can do. The galley is still working. Could we have a bit extra for supper and a round of grog?"

The captain glanced up at the storm clouds racing overhead, then back at the wave that was just building behind them, level with the deck.

"You want a celebration at a time like this?"

"Yes, sir. We have to laugh now, so we're ready to work later."

The captain shook his head. "Once again, my better judgement falls before your strange, barbarian ideas. Talk to the cook."

It turned out that the cook had several ideas, and supper that night, the final hot meal before the storm, was truly a celebration, with a spicy sauce on the usual salt pork, a treacle pudding for dessert, and a round of grog at the end. The men went on deck with grins and a few derogatory shouts at the waves, whose crests now rushed by at deck level. One of the sailors pulled a pipe from his jacket and began to play, and soon there was a wild dance on the main deck, the whistle of the pipe fighting the whistle of the wind, and the sailors' hard feet beating time.

A particularly large wave from a strange angle brought the ship's head around, and the sailors sent catcalls and jibes to the struggling helmsmen, then went without orders to trim the sails again.

Once more the sails were reefed, with the larger sails removed completely and replaced with heavy storm trisails. Not wishing to be taken by surprise, the captain took the precaution of having the gaffs unbent from the masts and brought down to deck level to reduce windage. This reduction in power did not seem to slow the pace of the ship at all, although it made the helming easier.

All the long night, the *Courser* ran from the storm, shouldering off the rollers that threatened to engulf her. Cheynou snatched a few hours sleep just before dawn and came on deck to see what had been hidden in the darkness.

The water all around them was steely, the tops of the waves being torn off in streams of spume driven downwind across the face of the sea. The sky felt low, with spray from the combers and scudding cloud meeting in a seamless grey that obscured the horizon.

The ship's motion was steady, though, and while the sailors manned the pumps at regular intervals, there seemed nothing to be concerned about.

Cheynou relieved the captain, who went into the chartroom to plot his best guess of their course. There was nothing to navigate by: a universe of grey sea and grey sky.

The sailors went about their tasks carefully on the tipping, slippery decks. Cheynou made his way forward and began another detailed survey of the ship's rigging and spars. This time, several sailors came with him, and he pointed out the problems they missed.

He had just set the last one about some small task when there was a loud snap and the thunder of tearing canvas above him. Looking up, he saw that the main trisail sheet had parted, and the sail was in the process of wrapping itself around the mainmast, tearing at the fittings and projections. In this wind, the sail would be ribbons in moments.

There was no sailor handy. Without a thought, Cheynou sprang to the cabintop and up onto the main boom. Grasping several halyards, he hauled himself up the mast, fighting the flogging sail under lines pulled tight against the wood. By the time he got to the top of the sail, it was under control.

He turned and looked down. "Ease the halyard!" He mimed the action as he called, cursing the lack of mast'ns signs on this ship, resolving to teach the sailors the first chance he got. The sailor below him slackened the line, and he was able to pull the damaged sail loose. As he pulled it down the mast, he rolled it around itself, lashing it with loops of the halyard. When he reached the cabintop, there were two sailors standing there to take the sail from him and bring it safely to the deck.

He made certain they had it under control, then moved back to the helm. To his surprise, the captain was there, waiting for him. To his further shock, Jatu's face was contorted in anger.

"What kind of stunt was that, Mister Chan?"

"Sail was flogging itself into ribbons, sir. There were no sailors available."

The captain looked around the deck, nodded to the bosun. "You're in charge, Freye." He frowned at Cheynou. "Come with me."

Cheynou followed Jatu into his cabin, worried now. The captain whirled as soon as they had closed the door and faced his officer.

"I have rarely in my life been so shocked and disappointed at anyone."

"Pardon, sir?"

The man paused, looked at him for a moment, then shook his head, his face relaxing. "You don't even know?"

"What have I done wrong, sir?"

"You are the officer of the watch. Who was taking care of the ship while you were up there doing crewman's work?"

"The bosun was on the bridge, sir."

"Knew that, did you?"

"Yes, sir."

"When I came on deck, he wasn't."

"He wasn't?"

"Oh, he wasn't so far away but, as it happened, he had his back turned, and he had no idea you were going to pull that stunt."

"Stunt?"

"Yes. Don't you realize, we are in the middle of a serious storm, with worse to come, and you are the only officer I have? You do not risk yourself! Especially doing seaman's work."

"But by the time I found a sailor, the sail would have been ruined, sir!"

"I have other sails, Mister Chan." The captain's finger beat the rhythm of his words on Cheynou's chest. "I. Do. Not. Have. Other. Officers!"

"Oh."

"There was a sailor headed in your direction before you got to the cabintop. He would have been up there two breaths after you. Then you could have stayed on the deck, where an officer should be, to direct the operation, which is what an officer is supposed to do."

"Yes, sir. I didn't think."

"It is the officer's job to think, Mister Chan. Not to act. You give the orders, and the sailors perform the deeds. Do you understand that?"

"I thought I did, sir, but I suppose I didn't, really."

"That's right. You may have been on a ship all your life, but you have never been an officer. Now get out there on deck and act like one."

"Aye, sir."

The captain slapped him on the shoulder as he turned. "Don't worry too much, lad. No harm done."

"Not this time, sir."

"Exactly. Take your good luck and learn the lesson."

The wind tore Cheynou's "Aye, sir" from his lips as he left the lee of the cabin. He surveyed the ship. All seemed to be well. He nodded to the bosun to acknowledge that he was taking command, strode to look at the compass, and swore under his breath. He had missed something else.

"How long since the course change, helmsman?"

"I'm trying not to change course, sir, but the wind seems to be veering again, and it's hard to hold her."

"I can see that. Are you on a good course right now? One you can hold comfortably?"

"Aye, sir."

Cheynou nodded and stuck his head back into the captain's cabin. "Wind's veered another point south, sir."

"The eye has passed, then?"

"Could be, sir. Should we change course?"

"It would be good to make a bit of northing if we don't get too close to those atolls."

Cheynou looked at the course laid out on the chart. "I'd say we were well clear so far, sir."

"Then bring her a point or two north. See where you can balance her the best."

"Aye, sir."

He returned to the tumult of the deck, motioning the bosun to join him at the wheel. "We're going to try to make a bit of northing. Two points if we can. Let's change course, trim the sails, see how she holds."

"Aye, sir, two points north."

The bosun called to the men, and they set about trimming the sails to the new course.

Now that they were not running with the waves but quartering across them, the ship's motion changed. The swoops were longer with less rocking, as the pressure on the sails held her heeled over.

After several waves had gone under her, Cheynou raised his eyebrows to the bosun, who nodded in satisfaction. Once again, he entered the cabin.

"Course change successful, sir. She's riding even easier."

"I can tell. Carry on."

"Aye, sir."

For the rest of the morning, they ran northwestward while the wind continued to veer farther and farther south, and they trimmed their course with it. Finally, at noon, they were sailing due north, with the waves now starting to come from the south as well. The captain came to take over his watch.

"She's gone by."

"Must be, sir. Wind's down."

"Can she handle more sail?"

"I think so, sir. Bosun?"

"Aye, sir."

"Let's get some more sail on her. Just the inner jib and the main, still reefed. That will help her steer."

"Aye, sir."

Under the power of the two larger sails, the motion of the boat evened out more, and they set her course farther east. By sunset, the sky was clearing, and Cheynou was able to take a sighting.

"We're quite a few leagues west of Hingol, but we've made some northing, so if the wind fills in from the northwest as it should, we can run down easily in a couple of days."

"We'll keep adding sail as the breeze drops. You can get some sleep, Mister Chan."

"Thank you, sir."

He went gratefully to his bunk, but he did not sleep right away. He went over his actions again and again, inventing ways he could have done it without making mistakes, but always circling back to the fact that he had made a mistake, and only luck had kept his ship from suffering because of it.

20. BAR FIGHT

Cheynou peered through the warped glass of the bar window but could make out no details. The noise was enough to tell him all he needed. He shoved through the door and regarded the mêlée inside. There seemed to be no pattern, no centre of battle. Simply a group of men, spread evenly about the common room, going at it with serious intent.

Cheynou pursed his lips and whistled. There was a lull in the din, and he pitched his voice to carry. "*Coursers* to me!"

He was quickly surrounded by his men, in various stages of drunkenness and battle damage.

"What's going on, here, Freye?"

"Just a little disagreement, sir."

"Any reason for concern?"

"I don't think so, sir."

"Do we need to clean them out, or are you just having fun?"

"Just a friendly tussle, sir."

"Good. If I might be allowed a bit of peace at the bar, you may carry on."

"We'll see that you're not disturbed, sir."

"Thank you, Freye."

Cheynou strolled to the bar and laid a coin down. Behind him, the fight picked up momentum again, but the impetus was gone. He turned to observe, and only a few individual fights continued. A stranger approached him, fists raised, but he merely held out an admonishing finger. This distracted the poor man long enough for a *Courser* sailor to lay him out with a fist to the side of the head.

Cheynou sipped his drink as the din subsided. As his men finished their individual battles, they moved nearer to him. Once he could be heard clearly, he slapped a larger coin on the bar. "*Courser* stands the house."

There was a hearty cheer at that, and the fight was over. Cheynou gestured to the barkeep. "And here's another for whatever damage was done."

The man grinned. "Thank you, sir. No real problem." He turned back to filling mugs.

Cheynou turned his attention to his men. "Sorry to spoil your fun, lads, but we've had a change of orders."

There was a low grumble.

"No real rush. Finish your drinks. But we sail in three bells, and there's a bit of cargo to load. Hand all right, there, Whit?"

The man shook his hand, winced. "Mighta broke a finger, sir. Guy over there has an awful hard head."

"Well, don't hit him in the head, Whit. What kind of stupidity is that?"

The sailor grinned sheepishly. "I know, sir. You taught me better. He just slipped and turned at the wrong moment."

Cheynou nodded. "That's how it goes. They never stand still like you want them to. Impolite, I call it."

"They learned better manners tonight, sir."

"I'm glad of that, Whit. It is the task of the Empire to bring civilization to these barbarian lands, is it not?"

"If you say so, sir."

"The emperor says so, and I say so."

"It must be true, then, sir."

"It must." He finished off his ale, looked around. "So, if we are done obeying the emperor's edicts, shall we go back to making a living for ourselves?"

There was a chorus of unenthusiastic agreement, and the men set down their mugs. As they approached the door, the traditional cry rang out. "Here's to the *Courser*; thanks for the drinks!" The *Courser* crew left the tavern on a rush of good will.

"What was the fight about, Freye?"

"Not sure, sir. Honour of the Empire, I believe."

"As good a reason as any, I suppose."

"Of course it is, sir."

"Anything else?"

"Maybe, sir."

"Such as?"

"Word's gettin' out, sir."

Cheynou played innocent. "What word is that, Freye?"

"That the *Courser*'s tough, sir. Then they all gotta try us."

"Hmm. What a bore."

The bosun licked a split knuckle. "Oh, I din't find it so boring, sir."

"I mean, it's a bore fighting every time they want a fight, not because you choose to. Perhaps we should move to the next level."

The sailors all leaned in. "What level is that, sir?"

"The level of 'The *Courser* is too tough to mess with.' Next time you're on shore leave, I'll show you, if you don't mind drinking with an officer."

There were several grins. "If it means another good lesson, I guess we can put up with it."

Cheynou had a chance to demonstrate his strategy when they hit Voges. Once again, the men headed into town, but his time he tagged along.

They had only been drinking for a half-bell when Freye groaned. "So much for a quiet evenin's drink."

Cheynou turned to regard the noisy mob that was just shouldering through the door. "Who are they?"

"Crew of the *Harrier*, sir. Always lookin' for a fight. That big fella in the middle, well, take a look at him. He's near as sharp as an anchor fluke, and about as hard in the head. He could handle any three of us, no problem, and then the rest of them have us outnumbered."

"Well, if they bother us, I'll take the big one."

"You will?"

"Aye. Just make sure you finish the others off real quick and come and give me a hand."

"Oh. I see. We can do that, sir."

It wasn't long before the *Harrier* crew, who had settled themselves at the next table, started to make overly loud comments about the 'lackeys of the Empire,' and other such inanities. Cheynou waited until the big man said something, then moved quickly.

"You!"

"Aye?"

"Did I just hear you insult the Emperor of Kyabra?"

"I dunno, did you?"

There was a general scraping of chairs as everyone rose, either to be ready for battle or to get out of the way.

Cheynou looked down at the monster. "All the others have the upbringing to stand when the Emperor's name is mentioned. What's wrong with you? Got no manners?"

There was a snigger from behind him, and the man's face began to redden. Cheynou heard a sudden scuffle and the smack of a fist on flesh. His crew hadn't lost any time. Good. Up close, this man was even more frightening.

His opponent began to rise, and just when he was at the balance point, Cheynou stepped forward and pushed him back down. He hit the chair with a thump and a look of shock that turned to rage.

This time he came up low and hard, and Cheynou had difficulty in ducking a swinging arm. As he twisted away, he kicked a stool into his enemy's feet. That slowed the giant down and gave Cheynou a chance to choose his ground for the next encounter.

Once again, the man lowered his head and charged, big hands grasping. Cheynou slipped to the left, pushing the swinging right arm as he did, and his attacker bulled on past him, spinning

224

quickly to attack again. There was no pause for breath or talking, just the animal desire to cause pain.

Cheynou ducked the same way, this time with a punishing jab to the lower ribs as his opponent swept by him, but it seemed to have no effect; he merely pivoted quickly and came in again. A wild fist connected with the side of Cheynou's head, stunning him, but fortunately pushing him out of the way of the next charge.

Cheynou backed away, buying time for his head to clear. His opponent slowed as well, seeming calmed by the success of his blow, stalking his prey. A quick glance showed that the rest of the *Coursers* were making short work of the other crew. Cheynou sidled around until his back was to the door.

Now his enemy approached slowly, jabbing with one fist. Cheynou parried and ducked, knowing what was coming. A few more jabs, and the big hammer was going to come from the other fist.

Fortunately for Cheynou, two of his men came up behind the big sailor in time. When the punch came, he slipped outside it, pulled sharply on the arm, and ducked behind.

"Out the door!"

The two sailors jumped forward, and the big *Harrier* crewman, propelled by three hearty pushes, burst through the closed door with a splintering of wood, tripped on the step and fell face down on the cobbles outside.

The man lay a moment, stunned, then started to get to his feet, turning as he did. When he saw Cheynou in front of him, he came up with a roar, but Cheynou met him as he rose and drove his knee into the man's face. There was a crunch, and the sailor subsided backward.

Standing over him, the pain in his knee turning his voice hoarse, Cheynou held out a restraining hand. "Don't get up."

The *Harrier* froze on his hands and knees, panting, blood dripping into the street.

"Bring the rest out here."

His crew hustled the defeated *Harriers* out to be presented with the picture of their champion, on his knees before a man half his size.

"We are drinking here tonight, and it seems you can't be trusted to let us have a peaceful evening. Go elsewhere. You may come here tomorrow night, once our ship has sailed."

He turned and strolled back into the bar, trying desperately not to limp, and his men crowded in behind him. The landlord, grateful that the fight had been so short, accepted their coin for the broken door latch and another round of ale, and they returned to their drinking.

Freye put his glass down and wiped a bit of froth from his lip. "Nice move, sir. Where did you learn that?"

"A trick I learned from a mercenary commander named Haskel, back up on the Southern Ocean where I come from. It's a way of evening the odds when the sides aren't to your advantage."

He held up a hand. "I know that shortens the fight, so you maybe don't get so much fun out of it. But sometimes it's nice to just win, you know?"

Appreciative nods, and a chuckle or two.

"What if we didn't get there in time, sir?"

"Oh, I can run like a rabbit."

They all laughed as if he was joking. He wondered if he would be able to walk back to the ship.

21. SUMMONED

Their trading centred on Voges, but Jatu, confident in the strength of his crew, wasn't afraid to push farther and farther west. He picked up a new First Officer who was at loose ends because his heritage on the Western Continent led him to be treated with suspicion. But he proved competent and afforded Cheynou a chance to practise his WesternSpeak. Better still, he had no problem with Cheynou's leadership role in the crew. So the leagues rolled out behind them and their personal credits rose in Captain Jatu's ledgers. And then they pulled in to the dock at the little island of Vallorbe. The captain left the ship, but returned on board too quickly.

Cheynou met him at the gangplank. "Something wrong, sir?"

"I don't know, Mister Chan. Two different people have told me that the Imperial Navy is looking for us."

"The Navy?"

"Yes. I can't think why."

"We haven't done anything wrong." Cheynou stopped, looking at the captain. "Have we?"

Captain Jatu laughed. "No, Cheynou, I have not been smuggling contraband under your nose."

"Sorry, sir. I shouldn't have doubted. What could they want?"

"I have only one thing on board that the Imperial Navy could be interested in."

"What?" Cheynou realized that the captain was waiting for something. He thought, frowning. "Me?"

"What else?"

"The Masterships!"

"That's my guess."

"They must have run into some more of them."

"And they want your help again."

"What do we do?"

Jatu shrugged. "A poor but honest working captain does not question when Admiral Larone calls. He ups anchor and comes in."

"But our trading!"

"Don't worry. We'll just have to find cargoes that are profitable in the right direction. We'll make our way by stages towards the Empire. Sooner or later, we'll run into some official notice. Then we'll have a better idea what to do. I can't see that there's any rush, when all we have to go on is rumour."

Cheynou grinned. "No, sir. Admiral Larone is a big boy, and he has plenty of friends. I'm sure he can manage without me for a little while longer."

The captain winked and returned to the shore. Despite the joking, Cheynou noticed that they left port quickly with a relatively small cargo.

Eight days and three cargoes later, they pulled into Voges. Ashmet Khrem, who met them on the dock, seemed pleased to see them.

"Good day to you, Captain Jatu, and to your officer, Cheynou Chan the Very Important Barbarian. My Lord would see you both at your earliest convenience. The unloading of your ship has been arranged." The burly arm swung towards a group of stevedores waiting nearby.

The captain went back on board to give the bosun his orders, then returned to the dock. "Lead on, Mister Khrem."

"Why the 'Very Important,' Ashmet?"

The Kantoon strode ahead, a superior smile on his face. "Ah, my small barbarian friend. You seem to be not so small in the estimation of someone in authority."

"So the rumours are true. The Masterships are here."

"I say no more. I must maintain my discretion."

They could get no more from him, and had to be satisfied with small talk until they were settled, as usual, in Lord Giron's big office, with drinks in front of them.

228

"I have a lucrative possibility for you."

Captain Jatu leaned forward. "I may not be able to take it up. It seems I must move in the direction of the Empire for the moment."

The lord grinned and slid a package across the table. "Perhaps this will aid your decision. It has been waiting here for you for almost a month."

"You know what is in it?"

"Not specifically. I do know that there have been some serious pirate attacks, mostly on seaside villages in the east of the Empire. What I can't understand is what that has to do with a merchant sailing in the west. I give you credit for a lot, Captain Jatu, but not with having your ship in two places at once."

"It isn't me they're after, Lord Giron."

The lord's eye slid to Cheynou, sitting silently to one side, his translation scarcely needed any more.

"Him? What do they want him to do? Talk the pirates to death?"

"Those pirates are his former people, the ones who drove him ashore."

"Ah. Tactics. So you are about to lose your Second Officer."

"I'm afraid so."

"Too bad. You'll probably have some less-interesting voyages."

"True. And less lucrative as well."

"Perhaps this will help. I assume you will be heading back to the Empire, now?"

The captain slit the package with his dagger. "We'll soon know." He scanned one of the sheets inside.

"Yes, that's it. I'm to take Mister Chan to the nearest naval base. This document," he held out the second paper to Cheynou, "gives him passage on the first available ship to meet the admiral, wherever he is campaigning."

Cheynou winced. "Sorry, sir."

"So am I, but not completely."

The two waited for his explanation. He finished reading the page, then nodded. "I'm to be paid for delivering you. A considerable amount."

Giron nodded, satisfied. "And you'll be taking him to the naval base at Liore."

"Well, Massiv is a bit closer..."

"But if the admiral is in the east, surely Liore would get Mister Chan there faster."

"I suppose."

Cheynou laughed. "Captain, Lord Giron has been trying to tell you something ever since we sat down. Perhaps we could let him say it before he bursts."

"Thank you, young man." The noble turned to the captain. "I have a cargo that needs delivering at Liore, and another to bring back. Does this suit you?"

"I think so, if I can find some new crew. We're already one short, now going to be two."

The lord glanced from one to the other. "A tough voyage."

"Some bad luck."

Giron seemed unconvinced. "It happens. Who are you missing?"

"One common seaman and now one officer."

"I see. I may have a solution. A nephew. Plenty of experience..."

"With due respect to your nephew, my Lord, I would probably rather not."

"Influence?"

"You understand, my Lord."

"I do. You traders are an independent lot."

"It is one of our greatest strengths."

"And one of your weaknesses also."

"Possibly."

"However, we are not going to argue about a fact which is agreed upon beforehand." He turned to Cheynou. "Did I say that right?"

"You did, my Lord. Thank you for making me feel useful."

"It is not necessary to use your talents at all times, young man. Among friends, it is sometimes possible to chat and not to play the games."

Cheynou raised empty hands and eyebrows in innocence. They laughed and sipped at their drinks. Cheynou reminded himself that this lord was a very shrewd man.

"So, my friends, tell me about your voyages. They have been profitable in the financial sense, regardless of what they have cost you in other areas."

Captain Jatu gave his edited version of the past few months' travels and trading. Cheynou listened carefully as usual. This time he was interested, not only in translation, but in what the captain considered free information and what he was concealing, even from a trading partner.

Late the following morning, the *Courser* crested the outward tide, heading back into the Empire. There was a strange nostalgia in hauling out the old, well-worn maps and sailing through the familiar straits, at the same time realizing that these could well be his last days on the old ship. Leaving her would be difficult. He had only ever left one ship before, and it wasn't something he wanted to do again.

He was saved an emotional scene by the efficiency of the Kyabran Imperial Navy. A swift dispatch sloop met them a day out of port, ran up alongside and hailed them. "Is there a Mister Chan aboard?"

"He is."

"I have orders to take him to Admiral Larone immediately."

"Stand by."

The captain turned to Cheynou. "Grab your duffle, lad. When the Kyabran Navy calls, we answer."

"But...the ship..."

"I think we can manage her for one day without you, Mister Chan."

"I suppose you can, sir, it's just that…"

"I think you are keeping said Kyabran Navy waiting, Mister Chan."

"Oh." He gave a guilty glance over the rail, then scooted off below. His duffle was mostly packed, but he searched his cabin frantically to make sure he had left nothing behind. He thought briefly of his charts, and decided to leave them in the Chart Room.

Back on deck, he stood, feeling useless, as the captain hove the ship to while a rowing gig pulled over from the sloop.

Disdaining a ladder, Cheynou tossed a rope over the side, put his duffle strap over his shoulder and, after a brief handclasp with the captain and the bosun and a nod to the crew, skimmed down the rope into the waiting boat.

The crew gave him a cheer as the gig moved off, and then the sails were sheeted in and the *Courser* pulled away. Sitting in the stern of the low rowing boat, he realized how rarely he had seen the *Courser* sailing. She still looked trim.

The officer beside him followed his glance. "A tidy ship, sir."

"Ah…yes, she is. We do…did our best, sir."

"Sir?"

He checked the officer's sleeve. "I am not familiar with your insignia, sir. Nor do I have a specific rank in your navy. So I really don't know how to address you."

The officer laughed. "Nobody told me, either. My name is Fowler. You are Mister Chan. Why don't we solve it that way?"

"Fair enough, Mister Fowler. What is your position on the…?" He peered at the sloop, but her transom was hidden by a wave.

"The *Valiant*, and I'm the First and only officer. Commander Talinen is in charge."

"A sleek hull. Her lines look very fast."

"Oh, she's fast, all right. The navy's dispatch sloops don't waste any time. Deep keel, heavy ballast, long waterline: well over a full chain on deck."

"And so, a huge sail plan."

"Exactly. We'll have you in Veyne in no time."

"Is that where I'm headed?"

"That's where we were headed when we spotted you. Where you're going after that is anyone's guess."

Cheynou nodded and held his peace. He seemed to be back in an environment where information was not freely available to everyone. He amused himself by analyzing the rigging of the sloop, much of which was new to him.

The *Valiant* rode low in the water, so the deck was an easy step up from the gig. He was greeted with some formality by Talinen, a young officer with a large amount of braid and a cheerful smile. The moment the gig was aboard, the sails were run up and the little ship skipped lightly over the waves.

The commander noticed Cheynou's glance. "Twelve knots on a beam reach."

Cheynou nodded in appreciation. Most ships he knew could do seven or eight. A vessel that could do that speed and sail close to the wind would be invaluable for sending messages and delivering people and small cargoes.

The commander was proud of his ship and eager to take a knowledgeable admirer on a full tour, from the anchor locker in the bow to the steering quadrant in the stern.

Throughout the tour, Cheynou listened carefully, but did not say much. There was a lot to absorb in a short time. Once they were back on deck, he started with his own questions: draft, maneuverability, crew, fighting capability.

After a while, Talinen paused. "You seem to need a great deal of information."

Cheynou smiled. "Do you know why I'm here?"

The other responded with a wry grin of his own. "This is the Imperial Navy, Mister Chan."

"I don't think it will hurt anyone if you know this. I gather the Empire is having pirate problems."

"That is true."

"My people are...or were...the pirates. We were driven out of the Raider Fleet because of our beliefs, so I have no problem with aiding the Empire in dealing with them. I have already been helpful to Admiral Larone in their first encounter."

"That huge five-master they captured?"

"That's right."

"Wait a moment. What's your name again? Cheynou Chan?"

"That's right."

"Cheynou the Barbarian! You're the one who took her."

"Yep. All by myself. With a bit of assistance from Admiral Larone and his fleet of ships and marines."

"You were his tactician."

"That's right. So I am trying to learn as much as I can about the capabilities of your ships so that I can help with the tactics as much as I can. How long will I be with you?"

"Five or six days, depending on the wind."

"So, you tell me all you know about your navy, and I will respond with all I can teach you about the pirates. Fair trade?"

The Commander grinned. "I suppose if it turns out you are a pirate spy..."

"Then I have fooled many people very senior to you, and you haven't told me anything that isn't common knowledge. On the other hand, if I am what I say I am, you are one more officer who knows the enemy, and the more you know, the more effective you will be."

"Which might not hurt my career. I'll take the risk."

"Fair enough. So how many crew do you carry, and what are their fighting skills?"

The five days it took them to reach port were a joy. The Commander and his First Officer were young, enthusiastic, and intelligent. Their crew responded with alacrity to their orders, and the ship was truly a pleasure to sail. Cheynou spent many bells at the wheel, enjoying the feel of her slicing through the waves, responding to his lightest touch.

"You are a fine helmsman, Mister Chan."

"Taught since I was strong enough to turn the wheel."

"There's a sort of joke going around, but the sailors aren't too happy with it."

"What's that?"

"Well, it's the cook. When we're in rough seas, he can tell who's helming. He said he'd bake a fancy dessert for supper tonight as long as you'd steer while it's baking. He says you make the boat ride smoother, and there's less chance the cake will fall."

Cheynou shrugged. "Sounds fair to me."

"And can you give my helmsmen a lesson?"

"I don't know. I might be able to give them some hints."

"Once the cake is baked."

Later that day, Cheynou stood at the wheel, a line of six uniformed sailors confronting him.

"It's difficult to know what to say, gentlemen. You are all experienced helmsmen. Maybe you can learn something from me, maybe I can learn from you. Why don't you just watch me for a while and see what you see. Doesn't sound too difficult?" They grinned and nodded.

He concentrated on the ship, feeling her way through the waves, drawing her power from the wind. The sailors stood watching. Finally, after a long, peaceful time, one of the crew spoke up. "You don't move the wheel much."

"I suppose not. I'm sure you know that any pressure of your hand in turning the wheel pushes the rudder sideways against the water. By pushing the rudder one way, you push the hull the opposite way. This creates friction against the rudder and the hull, stops the boat's free movement with the waves and slows it down. When I steer, I just wait for the ship to start to move in the direction I want, then let go of the wheel. The ship turns freely, then I stop the wheel on the new course."

"May I try, sir?"

"Certainly." He stepped aside, and the sailor took over. With his hundreds of watches of experience, it wasn't long before he caught on. Then the others wanted to try, and each had a degree of success. They were all feeling quite proud of themselves until a head in a white hat appeared in the companionway in front of them.

"Huh. I thought so." The head disappeared.

"The cook can still tell, can he?"

"He's a picky bugger, but he's a good cook, so we don't complain. What else can you tell us, sir?"

"All right. I was noticing your stance at the wheel. You're steering with your hands."

Puzzled frowns.

"Your hands. You're planting your feet firmly, locking your knees, and steering with your hands. Don't do that. Bend your knees and steer with your feet."

Even with his demonstration, they found it hard.

"All right. Close your eyes. Feel the boat move under your feet. Try to picture the waves as they come, the wind in the sails. Feel for the pattern."

There was near silence for a while, only the rush of wind and water.

"You have your eyes closed, sir!"

Cheynou looked at the man. "Obviously you don't."

"But you were steering with your eyes closed."

"That's what I told you."

"But how do you do that, sir? You were steering with your eyes closed!" He looked around at his fellows. "He was!"

"Aye. You have to be able to steer by the feel of the ship, as I was trying to tell you, but you weren't listening. You can feel the movement of the ship like she was a part of you. The slightest change in her movement comes to you like the feel of your lover's body, and you react, ever so gently, to bring her back." He opened his eyes again to see their mouths gaping at him.

"I don't think you were listening, men."

"Oh, yes, sir. We were listening. We couldn't miss the part about the lover's body, sir."

He grinned. "But I doubt that's going to help you with concentrating on your helmsmanship."

They laughed, but not for long.

"That's all I can tell you, men. You have to be able to feel it. Next time you're on watch, try it for short periods. I suggest you have a friend standing by with his eyes open, if you don't want to get in trouble with the cook. Or the captain."

"That's all." He looked around for the Commander, who stepped forward and dismissed the sailors, chuckling.

"Thank you, Mister Chan. There will be a different level of helmsmanship on this boat for the next little while." He shook his head. "With your eyes closed!"

"I can't do it for long. My grandfather was going blind and only the family knew for years. He didn't really need more than the deck under his feet, the wheel in his hands and the wind on his cheek. Do you mind if I steer for a while longer?"

"No, go ahead. Enjoy yourself. Just keep your eyes open most of the time, will you? It does wonders for the confidence of the men."

Talinen walked away, laughing at his own joke, and Cheynou settled into some serious communion with this beautiful ship.

Unbidden, into his mind came an image of Kendra's face. A warm glow suffused him, along with a pang of regret. He was back in Kyabran territory. Maybe he would get to see her again. Maybe she had sent him a letter; he didn't know how. He'd have to ask the admiral. He chuckled to himself. He could imagine a letter sent to 'Cheynou the Barbarian, Imperial Fleet'. He wondered if the famous Kyabran efficiency could cope with that.

The sun shone on the crystal blue water, the wind blew warm and fair, the ship slipped nimbly along her graceful path between the waves and the wind and Cheynou, just for a while, allowed himself to dream of what could never be.

It turned out that he was to get plenty of time to practise his helmsmanship. Upon arriving at Veyne, the *Valiant* was immediately ordered to transport him to the flagship, where the fleet was anchored at the mouth of the Panjhali River. They made good time, despite the upwind beat the whole way. It occurred to Cheynou that he was getting very close to Port Tenet. He wondered if he would get a chance to visit. He doubted it. He was in the navy now.

22. Flagship

Late one afternoon, they approached the fleet, row after row of various sizes and sorts of ships, as neatly organized as a tapestry. By now, Cheynou was used to the lack of communications. When they were close enough, they read the signal flags, which ordered *Valiant* to drop her hook in a prime anchorage just inshore of the flagship.

Talinen gave Cheynou a wry smile. "We got here in good time. Let's see how long we wait."

There was no need to answer, so they did exactly that, looking out over the fleet while Cheynou asked questions about the ships and their capabilities.

The next morning, they were on deck again when they spied a gig pulling in their direction from the flagship. Sure enough, it slid smartly alongside, and Cheynou dropped aboard.

There was no climbing of ladders on the Kyabran flagship. A boarding stair ran up the side, and Cheynou scampered up. No sense in seeming to keep an admiral waiting. On deck, he was met by a young ensign who saluted and led him to the admiral's cabin.

Larone was at his desk, writing. He waved the boy away and got up to shake Cheynou's hand in the Kyabran manner. "I didn't expect to see you so soon. Out west somewhere, I gather?"

"I was, but Kyabran shipmasters know who protects them. I came as soon as I could."

"And I thank you. Please sit down."

Cheynou took an embroidered chair across the desk from the admiral. "You have another Mastership, Admiral?"

"Aye, we do, Mister Chan. More than one."

"I see."

"Yes. This last lot was a pair of them with a fleet of five smaller ships. We were about evenly matched, at least in tonnage, so we attacked, using the ideas you gave us."

"I told you nothing about fleet maneuvers."

"No, you didn't. Those rams work amazingly well."

Cheynou winced.

"They also had clean bottoms and full crews. They handle those ships like racing skiffs!"

"I recall mentioning that, sir."

"You have to see it to believe it. They caught one of my ships between the two of them, crushed her like an egg."

"I have seen that myself."

"They use their superior speed well when they have the weather gauge."

"And they use the smaller Familyships to shepherd or lure the opponent into a vulnerable position."

Larone nodded. "Then, wham! The Mastership moves in for the kill, with ram, hull, fire and boarding parties. Those men can fight!"

"I was in the Navigators' Craft, sir, and even I was trained in hand-to-hand fighting to the point where none of the sailors on any of the civilian ships I have met could touch me."

"They seem to have superior communication, as well."

"They have coded masthead flags as you do, and handheld signal flags and mirror flashes as well."

The admiral frowned. "I see. So never attack a fleet on a sunny day?"

"A point to consider, sir."

Larone sat silent for a moment, staring at his fingers, steepled before him.

"Did you manage to take them, sir?"

"Oh yes, finally. Our local knowledge let us run one of them onto a submerged reef that my ships could pass over. Then we used our superior upwind ability to cut individual ships from the fleet and take them."

The older man shook his head. "That was nasty fighting, Cheynou, exactly like you told us: their desperate courage, defending their homes. I had thought you were exaggerating about the women, but it happened several times. Women with babies slung on their backs, fighting to the death, jumping overboard at the end. It was senseless."

"You need to get word to the Familyships, sir."

"What word?"

"The Familyships are the lower classes, in thrall to the Masterships. At least a few of them, if they thought they had a chance, would break away."

"That's something to consider. What about the Masterships?"

"They have always lived by dominance, taking by force: from their own people, from all others. Expect them all to fight to the end."

"Not surprising."

"What was the end, in this case? With the last Mastership?"

"I decided it would be too expensive to try to board her. She had taken on the crew of the wrecked Mastership, and she was crawling with awesome fighters. So we took an idea from the way the wolf packs of the mountains handle deer."

"Harried and bothered and nipped away?"

"That's right. We ran alongside and pushed her, we hooked onto her stays and her bowsprit and anything else we could to keep her from sailing away downwind. She tried to run, but we hassled her and harried her into a lee shore position on some low islands she didn't notice until it was too late.

"She dropped anchor between two islands and sat there. We cordoned off the escape routes and sat outside, waiting."

"They carry a lot of supplies."

"They had two crews on board, and we didn't let them off to fish. Finally, they surrendered. We made them come ashore in groups of fifty and handled them that way.

"There was no amnesty this time, Cheynou. They had burned out several villages, killed a lot of people."

"What did you do with them?"

"We hanged the captain from his own yardarm, as we would any pirate. Before you ask, we're sure we got the right man. Several on the Familyships were happy to point him out.

"Then we divided them up into family groups as much as possible and turned individual families ashore in separate places. Any unconnected males of fighting age were sent to the Kyabran Imperial Army, to be spread among the units so they can't get together and cause trouble. We don't dare take them into the navy, superb sailors as they are, because it looks as though we may be facing more of them."

"Have any been sighted, sir?"

"No, but we are not going to sit around and wait."

"What do you have planned, sir?"

"How do you like the *Valiant*?"

"She's a little beauty, sir. Takes the waves like a dolphin. Twelve knots, sir!"

"Would you like to take a voyage on her?"

"Certainly, sir. Are we going to look for the Masterships?"

"That's right. We can't afford to pull any major ships off patrol duty in case some of the pirates have slipped through, but we must know what's out there."

"And we're heading east, sir?"

"You've just come in from the western rim of the Empire?"

"Much farther, sir. No word of organized pirates there. Just the usual land-based ones with fast sloops and oared galleys to attack and run."

"Then we'll assume that your analysis is correct, and they are coming in from the east."

"You are sending a ship out on a voyage because of my conclusion several months ago, based on one small fact and a lack of information from the other direction?"

"I'm sending a fleet of three ships out on that basis."

Cheynou thought a moment. "What were the names of the Masterships you took?"

"We couldn't read them, but I knew you would ask, so I had them copied exactly." The admiral pushed a piece of paper across the table.

"Eland and Gazelle. Eastern Fleet for sure. These Familyship names: Turtle, Otter, Okkim's Pride? Not so conclusive. I've never heard of a Familyship with a name that wasn't a bird or animal before, so that ship has never been anywhere near the Western Fleet."

The admiral nodded. "So these names, plus the position of the raids, plus your news of the Western Rim, all point towards an eastern incursion. Assuming that the fabled Strait of Kuhak really exists."

Then something clicked. "Wait a moment, wait a moment. I can do better than that!"

"Yes?"

"I have some other information that points us eastward, sir. It isn't really... information, as such. It's more like...history."

"History? I can't ever remember there being pirate incursions from the east before."

"No, longer than that, sir, Before the Empire."

"Before the Empire?"

"Yes. My companion, Kendra of Kirigata, is a historian, and she was telling me about this before I took ship with Captain Jatu. What empire came before the Kyabran one?"

"Before the Kyabran Empire? No one, I shouldn't think."

Cheynou grinned. "I'm about to become disrespectful, sir."

"Oh," the admiral's brow creased, "we can't have that, can we? Before the Kyabrans, you say. Well, there was obviously someone in power, the ones we took over from."

"I think so."

"Yes, now that you mention it, there was a race of people called the Frasians, who had mainly a sea-trading empire, if you want to call it that."

"And let me guess, sir. They traded mainly to the east."

"That's right. How do you know that?"

"Languages, sir."

"Languages? Now I really have no idea where you are going."

"It's this way, sir. There are three main languages in the area of the Great Southern Ocean. SeaSpeak, LandSpeak, and WesternSpeak. Two of them don't matter here, because they come from farther away. SeaSpeak is very interesting, though, because of who use it: Sea People of the Southern Ocean, landsmen along the eastern shore, and — most interesting — the folk of the Inner Provinces. They call it Frasian."

"You mean the people of the eastern part of the empire."

"Exactly. Which means that some time in the past, they came from the same place. Since it's all in the east, I suspect that they are the remnants of an empire, probably a sea-based one, as you say, that lost its power quite a while ago. I don't know how long, because I don't know how long it takes a language to change that much."

"So that would lead us to expect that there is a good sea route somewhere between the Southern Ocean and the Inner Sea, and that it is to the east."

"Another reason to suspect the connection. Look at that term, 'Inner Sea.' Inner means central. It's the same word in Kyabran and SeaSpeak, which means the word predates the Kyabran Empire, which means there was another empire with this body of water at its centre."

The admiral shook his head. "This is fascinating, but I doubt if I'll get too far with my superiors, telling them I sent a squadron chasing the history of a language."

"I suppose. Sorry, sir."

"Oh, no. No, no, that's what you're here for, Mister Chan. New ideas, new ways of thinking. I take them all into account, even the very strange ones."

"Thank you, sir." He had another thought. "What about the logs from the Springbok?"

Larone shrugged. "Everything was encoded, and the maps were too large scale. They were more like daily course plotting."

"Could I take a look at them?"

"I'll have them sent over."

"I can start on them right away. If I find anything else, I'll send word."

"Good enough, but even if they tell us nothing, I think what you have told me is worth three sloops for a month or so."

"Yes, sir."

"Glad you agree. You'll be in charge."

"Me, sir?"

"Almost. We're sending a Senior Captain to be Commodore of your little fleet. *Valiant* will be his flagship, and you'll be second in command, with a rank of Commander, which puts you even with the captains of the three sloops. The commodore will be instructed to follow your lead in any contact with the enemy, and anywhere else it seems useful."

"Where did you find a Senior Captain willing to take over a little bunch of boats like that? With a mere Commander, who is also a barbarian with no experience in the Kyabran Navy, calling the strategy?"

"A Captain whose own ship was recently turned into scrambled egg by the Masterships. Captain Gargia is extremely anxious to be of use in the battle against the pirates, as you might guess."

"What kind of man is he?"

The admiral mused a moment. "How to put it..."

Cheynou grinned. "The kind to get caught between two Masterships?"

Admiral Larone shot him a glance. "There are Captains who might have avoided it. Many would not."

"I see. Do you have any advice for me in dealing with him?"

"He will follow his orders. I have told him to listen to you, so he will."

"When do I meet him?"

"This afternoon. I wanted to brief you first."

"I think the best way is for the three of us to meet together to plan strategy. Once he sees how you and I interact, perhaps he will be more comfortable with the situation."

"How you and I interact?" The admiral raised his eyebrows, lowered his head. "There is a certain latitude allowed one of my rank, especially when dealing with a civilian, in the setting aside of formality."

"Exactly, sir, and I abuse it unmercifully."

"You do."

"So, it would make Captain Gargia more comfortable to see that in action before I begin working it on him."

"I agree. I will endeavour not to encourage him to start anything he can't handle."

"That is considerate of you, sir."

"Considerate for him, I would say."

"It will help me, as well. I won't be starting from the bottom, that way."

"Cheynou, there is something I don't understand. You tell me you were a member of a society with an incredibly strong hierarchy, with religious and secular control over its members. How did a group like that produce a person like you?"

Cheynou shrugged. "I was on a ship that ended up exiled for heresy. My Captain was a wonderful man, who only used his power for the good of the ship. His daughter, Sarasha...well, you really had to meet her. She was adamantly against all misuse of power. She was the one who kept us together when we were driven ashore. I spent a lot of time with her, and some of that would have rubbed off.

"Also, I was the youngest and brightest of the Navigators, so I was allowed some of that latitude you were talking about. I have always been sure never to overstep the boundaries."

"You have?"

"Have you ever heard me impolite, disrespectful?"

The admiral grinned. "By some people's standards, constantly."

"By artificial standards only. In reality, I am always respectful of others, both above and below me."

The admiral nodded. "A good attitude for an officer."

"I hope so, sir. I have not had much command experience, and I have made my own mistakes. I hope not to repeat any of them, because I know there will be others coming."

"A good tenet on which to base your career."

"Since my life may depend on it, I had better choose wisely." He had another thought. "Oh yes. Also, I never argue unless I'm right."

The admiral threw back his head and laughed.

"Why do you find that funny, sir?"

"Because everybody argues when they think they're right. That's the point of arguing, isn't it?"

"No, sir. I respectfully wish to disagree."

"I await your argument with anticipation, Mister Chan."

"People often argue when they think they have to be right. Some people argue only because they want to be right. The actual truth is secondary to them."

The admiral thought about that, his face growing solemn. "Yes, I see what you mean. And how do you determine this 'right' that you will argue for?"

"The good of the Ship."

"You answer very quickly. That's all? The ship?"

"In specific, yes. In general, that extends to the Fleet, and to all people, in the long run."

"So, now that you are an officer in the Kyabran Imperial Navy, you put all your energy into what is best for your ship, the navy, and the Kyabran Empire..."

Larone cocked his head. "Why do I not hear such a quick response?"

"That's a more difficult question, sir. Especially to someone who has had my experience with empires."

"I see."

"So, for the moment, I can guarantee that I will be loyal to my ship. As long as my ship remains loyal to the Navy, I will do my utmost for you. Further than that, well, I'm sorry, sir, but I'll have to wait and see."

The admiral shook his head. "I suppose I can live with that. Thank you for being honest with me. I wouldn't go around the Navy espousing that idea out loud, though."

"And especially to Commodore Gargia."

"I think that would be a wise plan."

"Sir, can you tell me something?"

"What?"

"The Kyabran Empire has ships seaworthy enough to travel anywhere they wish on the Oceans of the World. Why don't they?"

"A good question. I have thought it myself, especially when I was young and adventurous, as you are. I think the reason is that Kyabra is a land-based Empire. The Navy was first created, if I remember my history, to transport troops along the shore. As you go west, the land gets flat and rocky, with scant grass. After five hundred leagues, the shoreline turns south and begins to get dryer as well. I have little knowledge of anything past there, because there is no reason for the Empire to expand that direction on the land, and no merchants for our merchants to trade with on the sea. Superstition says that ships that sail farther south don't return."

"I can understand that."

"Having heard your stories of your people, I can too."

"What about the Western Continent?"

"There are people there, but they are primitive and warlike. Too far away and too little profit for trading. Hence, we don't go there."

"Thank you, sir. I understand. Mostly."

"Ah, I can remember feeling the same way, once."

"But you don't, now?"

"I have enough troubles of my own, now. I suspect it is the same with the Empire. I don't think it disloyal to note that there have been several changes of Emperor in quick succession over the past few years. Political instability does not lead to exploration or expansion, especially into marginal territories where a return on investment may not come for a generation."

"Spoken like a merchant captain, sir."

"The merchant captains are the Navy's main responsibility and best support. I listen when they speak." He glanced at the chronometer on the wall. "And as I think about listening, I am reminded that, fascinating as our meetings are, I have a fleet to administer."

"Yes, sir. Sorry to have kept you."

"I doubt it. Your honesty does not preclude diplomacy."

"If you say so, sir."

"I do, Cheynou Chan. Now, go away before you entice me into any more philosophical debate."

"Aye, sir. I will return after the third bell." He spun on his heel smartly and left the cabin.

His crew was waiting to take him back to the *Valiant*, and they shot away from the flagship at a good pace.

"An interesting chat with the admiral, sir?"

"It was." He glanced at the stroke oarsman "We spoke of the history of languages and the nature of rightness."

"I'm sure you did, sir."

"And I'm sure you would row better if your mind was on your oar."

"Aye, sir. My head can't quite deal with the nature of rightness and rowing at the same time."

"Which is how I get to be an officer, and you don't."

"As it should be, sir."

"And therein lies the nature of rightness. Well done, sailor."

There was a long silence, broken only by the rhythmic splashing of the oars and the ripple of water on wood. Cheynou leaned back against the side of the boat and basked in the warmth of the sunlight.

"But you're not rowing, sir."

"You really are demonstrating intelligence today, sailor. In truth, I am not rowing."

"But you said I wasn't an officer because I couldn't think and row. You aren't, either."

"Hmm. You know, it's a good thing your back is to me and I don't know your name."

"Why is that, sir?"

"I might take it into my mind to promote you out of sheer nastiness."

"Oh, please, sir, couldn't you just have me flogged instead?"

"I suppose it would be kinder."

"Oh, thank you, sir."

"Quite all right, sailor. I'm in a generous mood. At least I was."

"Point taken, sir."

They were approaching the *Valiant*. Further enjoyment of the ride, or of the conversation, was impossible.

Commander Talinen met him at the rail. "A good chat with the admiral, Mister Chan?"

Cheynou frowned slightly. "I have had this conversation before."

"You have?"

"Yes. Who is that sailor? The shorter man, there, with the blond hair."

"Oh, no. Has he got to you already?"

"Most definitely. Who is he?"

The Commander grinned. "Ives is one of my crosses to bear. They sent him to me to keep him out of trouble. Or to keep whatever ship he was on from running into trouble with him, I often think."

"He seems quite bright."

"And completely irreverent."

"I noted that."

"He wasn't disrespectful?" The officer frowned.

"Quite the opposite."

"Good. You have to slap him down every once in a while, or he tends to lose perspective."

"An object lesson for me. I just spent the past three glasses with the admiral, playing the same tricks."

"Did you?"

"Pretty well. As the admiral puts it, he has a certain amount of latitude in the suspension of formalities. Since I am quite non-military, and since I am very careful not to overdo it, he exercises that latitude in private"

"Hmm."

"Aye. Hmm. Have you heard about our assignment?"

"Not officially, but we have been tossing ideas around."

"Well, I gather we will be getting the specifics very soon. Do you know Captain Gargia well?"

"Only by reputation. Why?"

"I'm sure your orders will make that clear."

"Ah. Of course."

"What's his reputation?"

Talinen shrugged. "I don't know. Nothing bad, nothing good. Just a decent sailor who does his duty. Not especially liked or disliked by the men."

"Well, if he's competent and follows orders, I suppose we'll be all right."

"Whose orders? Not yours!"

"No, the admiral's."

"And what orders are those? If I may ask."

Cheynou grinned. "His orders are to follow my orders."

The other officer just stared at him for several beats. "You're serious, aren't you?"

Cheynou shrugged. "It's going to be a weird situation, Talinen, with a commander 'suggesting' a course of action to a commodore. But there isn't any other way."

"A delicate situation, Mister Chan. I don't envy you the task."

"And I don't envy you, either, being right in the middle of it."

"Me? In the middle? Does that mean what I think?"

"As I said, I'm sure your orders will arrive very soon. I'm to return to the Flagship at the third bell to meet the Commodore."

"As it happens, so am I."

* * *

Commodore Gargia stood over the chart laid out on the admiral's meeting table. It was a quick copy Cheynou had roughed out, using what he could decipher from the Springbok's logs to adapt a sketchy, tattered parchment, which was the only information the Navy had on the area.

"We are assuming that these Raiders are coming from the east, most likely from the Great Southern Ocean. This means that they must pass here," Gargia's stubby finger indicated a spot on the map, "between our continent and the Wilderland. Our task will be to patrol that strait and make a count of the sea traffic there. We will only allow direct engagement with the enemy as a last measure. First, because they outman us, and second, because we do not wish them to know what we are about. We will also chart the area as we move. Understood?"

"Aye, sir."

"I gather your sloops can come directly alongside the provisioning ship. *Valiant* will start immediately. I will move onboard at that time. *Peerless* will follow. We will provision, anchor overnight and leave at sunup. Any questions?"

There were none. The admiral merely said, "Good luck, men," and they filed out onto the deck, parting towards their gigs.

Talinen sat with Cheynou in the stern of the gig, steering the boat himself. "You seem to be good luck for me, Mister Chan."

"How so?"

"Half a month ago I was a Commander in charge of a Dispatch Sloop. That's a not-quite-captain, commanding a ship that's not quite big enough to need a real captain. Now, without changing my rank or ship, I'm commanding the flagship of a fleet, small though it is, going out on an important and possibly dangerous mission. The chances for promotion increase."

"As do your chances for death from violence or boredom."

"Picket duty is like that. You wait and wait and hope something happens, and fear it will and you won't be able to handle it."

"That fear triples in this situation. I hope all the captains got the message about no heroics."

"Oh, we got that loud and clear."

"I sort of figured so."

Cheynou had a sudden thought. "By the way, I have a small demonstration I would like to give. Since we're anchoring here overnight, do you think we could have it on the *Valiant*?"

"Of course. What kind of demonstration?"

"I want the other two crews, and their officers, to get an idea of what they're facing."

"A little cutlass play?"

253

"I think so."

"Good idea. We'll clear it with Commodore Gargia as soon as he comes on board and invite the other captains to bring their ship's champions over immediately after supper. Our men will be really happy to see someone else humbled."

"Your men are good fighters."

"Only three of them are in your class at all, and they are at the bottom of the class."

"Rigid military training with a lack of battle experience."

"And you?"

"Desperation training, and an equal lack of real battle experience."

"Lack?"

"I'm a Navigator, remember. I've been in battles at sea, but I've never been on a boarding party or a landing party. Our captain was too smart to let anyone board us. Except for a brief encounter when we took that first Mastership a few months ago, I never had a chance at a real fight."

"Then your training must have been pretty tough."

"You might say that."

"I'll be pleased to see you pass some of that desperation along. I've done all I can to get the men to develop their fighting skills."

"I'll do my best."

The other officer frowned in thought. "If picket duty gets boring..."

"Good idea."

23. Preparation

The commanders and their ship's champions came on board the *Valiant* with enthusiasm and curiosity. Cheynou stood among the sailors in his oldest sailing clothes, watching them with his own interest. These were young officers on their way to higher things, and the admiral had given him the best.

Then Commodore Gargia stepped forward, and there was silence. Cheynou hoped he would play his part well.

"You may be wondering why this group has been gathered together. I wish to provide a demonstration of what we are up against.

"As you have probably deduced, we are going on a reconnaissance mission against the pirates who call themselves Masterships. We have, here, a former member of a Mastership's crew. He has volunteered to show us his skills."

Cheynou stepped forward humbly, as a Familyship Crewman would act on the deck of a Mastership. He kept his blunted cutlass pointing downward.

"Our volunteer will have a friendly — and I emphasize the friendly nature of this engagement — bout with each of your champions. I think you will find the experience educational. Whose champion would like to begin?"

The sailor from the *Audacious* caught his captain's eye, received a nod, and stepped forward. He was not a big man, but he was well muscled, with a longer reach than his height would indicate. Cheynou read him for speed.

The man hefted the blunted cutlass he was handed, making it whistle through the air. Then he strode into the open deck space lined by the grinning sailors of the *Valiant*. They had seen Cheynou in action several times and were looking forward to this.

Cheynou stepped into the circle as well, bowing to his opponent. The man hesitated, then responded with a nod of the head. Cheynou watched him as he moved: his stance, his balance, which foot he led with. An idea was forming to counter a swordsman with the kind of rush he had taught the sailors of the *Courser*, but he never allowed his conscious mind to control him in a fight. Instead, he felt the grit of the deck under his feet, the weight of his sword, the slow movement of his opponent's blade.

Then the man raised his weapon to strike and it all came together. Cheynou lanced forward, the hilt of his sword catching the downward-swinging cutlass of the other before it had a chance to gain speed. His left arm was around the other's waist, and he pushed him to the right. The moment his opponent resisted, he reversed the pressure, pulling him to the left and tripping him at the same time. In less than two heartbeats, the *Audacious* sailor was on the deck, his weapon arm pinned under Cheynou's foot, a sword point at his throat.

Cheynou met his eyes, got the nod of defeat, and reached out, as usual, to help the man to his feet. After a moment of surprise, the sailor accepted the aid and found himself bowing to the applause of the *Valiant*'s crew. With a sheepish smile, he returned to his captain's side.

There was a brief discussion between the next competitor and his officer, and then the man stepped out into the cleared spot. The *Valiant* crewmembers pretended to be impressed, oohing and ahhing in fake appreciation of the musculature of the sailor who stood before them.

Cheynou could almost hear the commander's instructions to his champion: 'He's fast. Don't commit yourself, but hit hard.'

Well enough. Maybe it was time to show that his lightning attack wasn't just luck. A solid defense against such a strong opponent would be impressive.

Now Cheynou stood and allowed his opponent to approach. The cutlass lashed out, a quick jab, and Cheynou parried. Not hard, just enough. Again, the probing single swing, and again a parry. More confident, the sailor tried a beat and cut, but Cheynou's blade was there for both. Emboldened by his opponent's lack of response, the *Peerless* sailor began to rain blows, one after the other. As Cheynou had expected, his opponent got set in a pattern. The next time through, his second cut met empty air, and there was no one in front of him.

The sailor turned, spurred by the hoots of the *Valiant* crew, to see Cheynou pacing the other side of the circle, making a 'come here' gesture.

However, this was a cool fighter. He did not respond to either the crew's jibes or Cheynou's taunting, but obeyed his captain's orders. He stalked slowly towards his opponent, his cutlass swinging freely back and forth. He made a sudden overhand cut, but followed it with an underhand that Cheynou had seldom seen before. While his mind was registering this fact, his hand was reacting. Instead of parrying, he ducked, and as the sword whistled past him, he rang a sharp blow to the back of the blade, up near the hilt, in the direction of the swing.

This sudden push swung the big sailor around and tore the cutlass from his grip. He found himself weaponless, his back to his enemy. The *Valiant* sailors cheered. He spun, and Cheynou pointedly laid his weapon on the deck and stepped forward. The sailor flexed his hands, a grin replacing the shock on his face.

Cheynou played no games, now. This was dangerous. If the big sailor got hands on him, he would be finished. He moved in at an angle, watching for the punch that was sure to come. When it did, he slipped under, grabbing the wrist as it passed over his head, redirecting the force of the blow. Falling to his back, he pulled the sailor forward, placed a foot in his stomach, and threw him headfirst across the deck.

Before the dazed man had a chance to recover, Cheynou had him pinned in a particularly painful arm lock.

"Enough?"

"Enough."

Once again, Cheynou helped his fallen opponent up, bowed to him, and walked to his cabin.

Behind him, he could hear the good-natured calls of the sailors and then the sharp command for silence, instantly obeyed.

Then the voice of Commodore Gargia rose, pointing out the lessons of the demonstration.

Cheynou quickly changed into his new uniform and reappeared on the deck.

"And now, I would like you to meet my second-in-command for this voyage, Commander Cheynou Chan."

The *Valiant* sailors raised a cheer, and Cheynou approached the captains under his command to clasp hands and exchange grins. Then he turned to his two vanquished competitors.

"All right, boys?"

There was a confused "Aye...sir" from both of them.

Cheynou turned to the assembled crew. "You have all seen me fight. You have to believe that I was not particularly renowned on my Familyship for my fighting skills. There were thirty men on that one ship who would not bother to appear in competition with me. Nor would I trouble them with my poor talents. Every ship we meet on this expedition will be crewed by sailors like that. They have been born and raised on their ships and have been trained in sailing and fighting all their lives. Against the Raiders, I put most of you at two to one on a level deck."

Here, he turned to the smaller of his two formal opponents. "Mattos of the *Audacious*. How do you think you would fare, trying to attack me from this deck if I was standing at the rail of the admiral's flagship?" He indicated the height of a three-master's deck, far above them.

"Don't know what I'd do, sir. Die well, I guess."

"The Commodore and I aren't interested in having you die well, sailor, unless it's absolutely necessary to the survival of the ship. We will think very carefully before we put you into such a situation."

He turned to the two other commanders. "I gave this demonstration mainly for your benefit, gentlemen. I wish to impress upon you the futility of a straight-out attack against any of our enemy. If you haven't talked to any of the marines who attacked the Familyships of the last bunch of Raiders, you should."

"I did. Some of the stories seem hard to credit."

Cheynou grinned coldly. "Think about it. Those are tales told by men who won their fights."

Light dawned on their faces, and all the officers nodded.

The Commodore shook his head, once. "Yes, one of our bullyboys who got killed by a little woman with a baby strapped on her back did not return to tell of it."

"Or by a couple of twelve-year-olds with kitchen knives."

That left them thinking for a moment as well.

"However, I do not wish to discourage you. I only want to impress upon you that this is a reconnaissance mission. We have superior speed and upwind ability. If we keep a sharp eye out, we should be able to avoid contact. In fact, the less our enemy knows of our presence, the better."

24. Departure

The commodore asked the other captains to join him in his cabin. For a moment they sat there, the five men who were to lead this expedition, looking at each other, thinking. Then Commodore Gargia spoke.

"All right, gentlemen. We have our orders, and I am sure we all understand them. Within those orders, of course, lies the method by which we will execute them.

"I, for example, have never before been in charge of more than one ship. I have dealt with admirals enough to know that my task is to concentrate on the overall objectives. I will not interfere with the daily running of your ships."

They all nodded, grateful that he was at least aware of that problem. How his attitude worked out on a day-to-day basis was yet to be proven.

"Mister Chan is in a similar position. While equal in rank to you, he is second in command of this fleet. In my absence, his word is the law. This could pose other problems, as Mister Chan has not been trained in our Navy or its protocols. Again, on a daily basis, this will not cause trouble, because he will not have any reason to exert his authority.

"It will be in engagements with the enemy that his knowledge becomes most important, and I suggest you follow his ideas, no matter how strange they seem. So far, he has been able to explain his thoughts. I hope he will continue, as it will make it less stressful for the rest of us."

There were chuckles around the table. Cheynou joined in, with some relief. This captain seemed to be genuinely willing to try to make this unusual command structure work.

"Other than that, I do not see any problems. We are all officers in the Imperial Navy of Kyabra, and we know our chain of command, our duties, and our traditions. I'm sure we will all do our utmost to fulfill the expectations of our admiral and our emperor."

A steward had placed glasses of red wine in front of them, and everyone reached out to lift his glass in what seemed to be a traditional toast. Cheynou, every sense aware, tried to copy the gestures as well as he could.

"Mister Chan."

"Yes, sir?"

"You are not joining in the conversation. Admiral Larone led me to believe you were a talker. Is something wrong?"

Cheynou grinned. "You have to take anything the admiral says about me with a certain amount of skepticism, sir."

"Skepticism? Are you suggesting the admiral might not be completely honest with me?"

"Oh, no, sir. It's just that he isn't quite sure himself why he puts up with me, and so anything he tells you is part of his attempt to understand."

"I see. I think."

"As far as my lack of conversation goes, sir, perhaps he also told you that I listen a great deal in any new situation. I don't start talking until I have it all figured out."

"A practice many of the younger generation could put to better effect."

"You challenge me to defend my generation, sir. I must respectfully point out that it is a practice that does not lose usefulness with age."

"Admiral Larone did suggest that I should be especially wary when you become respectful."

Grins began appearing around the table, but Cheynou affected not to notice. "The admiral seems to have been overly free with his advice. I shall have to adapt my tactics accordingly."

The *Valiant*, Kyabran Imperial Navy,
Fourth Day, Third of Fall.

Dear Kendra,

Since I wrote to you last, things have most certainly changed, as you will note from the delivery of this letter. I hope you received my message in which I told you about being 'loaned' to the Kyabran Navy to help deal with a Mastership that got loose in the Inner Sea. Since that action was so successful, Admiral Larone developed a good opinion of me.

So, when they had another incursion of Masterships, two this time, with some Familyships in attendance, he thought of me. They dealt with that threat without my help, but this has made the admiral nervous. I can't tell you any more than that, but I have been given a commission in the Kyabran Navy as a commander, one step below captain. I could actually command one of their smaller ships!

We are going on a mission but I shouldn't say where, although if I tell you that I am following one of your language paths, I think you will figure it out. The admiral was intrigued by your ideas as well, and it helped make up our minds about this mission.

I hope this letter finds you in good health: you and the baby, if it has arrived. Take good care, and I hope to see you soon. Once this mission is over, if the results are good, I might get some shore leave, or even be allowed to return to civilian life! If so, I would return to Port Tenet, either to find a new ship or to wait for Captain Jatu to return.

Sorry that this letter is so brief, but that's how things go in the Navy!

Love always,

Cheynou

25. MAIL SHIP

"Sail to weather!"

The lookout's call galvanized the crew. It was a wonder the poor vessel didn't capsize with the rush of men to the windward rail, trying to spy the elusive sail of *Indomitable*, the sloop assigned to bring them mail and new provisions.

Cheynou felt a slight stir of excitement in his breast, too. From what the others had told him, there was enough time for his letter to reach Kendra and a response to return. Having heard no word from her for the whole summer, he was anxious for news. Perhaps the baby had come!

As the *Valiant* was on patrol, she was lucky that the *Indomitable* had found her. Otherwise, they would have collected their messages at the temporary office the commodore had set up in the largest village ashore. He was there, himself, at the moment, trying to establish some relations with the natives, to find out what their link with the Masterships was and to keep the two connections as far apart as possible.

On Cheynou's suggestion, the third ship had never appeared at the harbour. Instead, when the sailors on the other two ships were ready for shore leave, *Valiant*'s crew took half the *Peerless* men ashore with them, fostering the idea that there were only two Kyabran ships, with larger crews. A small subterfuge, but any move could be important if the pirates had spies ashore.

Both ships hove to, and a lighter was lowered from the *Indomitable*. This brought a cheer from the off-watch sailors lining the rail. The larger boat meant a load of new supplies: hopefully, some fresh food. Few of the men were literate, so mail was a concern of the officers only.

The mail sack was handled with casual care and the officers waited until the boat had pulled away before they pounced. The contents were soon spilled out on the captain's table, and the three sorted through the meagre harvest without formality.

"Letter from home, Talinen." The First Officer handed over the thick package. He and Cheynou rolled their eyes and made sniffing noises; Talinen's fiancée was generous with her perfume.

Cheynou fingered a single, sealed sheet of parchment. "Orders from the commodore."

"Read that later, Cheynou. Look at this!" Talinen waved a well-wrapped packet.

Cheynou held out his hand, and the captain tossed the letter. It was from Kendra; he recognized her businesslike script. He held it casually, watching with polite interest as the others sorted the rest of the mail.

"Oh, go ahead and open it, Cheynou. Unless you were expecting more?"

"No, I was just waiting for the rest of you to be finished."

"Don't be so polite. We know it's important."

"Thank you." He turned and left the cabin, followed by the disappointed jests of his fellow officers. It was a pleasant day, so he stayed on deck, sitting on a hatch cover while he slit the package open. It was only a few pages, neatly written.

Port Tenet, Twenty-third day, Third of Fall.

Dearest Cheychan,

I am not a happy person! I am huge and ungainly and I cannot sleep in any position for long. There is always something pressing against something, or someone moving, or my legs going numb. At least the cooler weather helps a little.

Whoever this person is inside me, he or she is very restless. Always moving, twisting, twitching. After what he (or she) has put me through, this child is going to have to treat me with dignity and respect for the rest of my life to make up for it!

Come to think of it, why didn't I do the same for my mother? Because I didn't know. Wisdom always seems to come too late.

However, the midwife seems to feel this is all very natural, and tells me that I am 'healthy as a goat', whatever that means. If it means eating everything in sight, she might be right.

You will be happy to know that my cottage is back to normal. I returned most of those books to their owners. It turns out they (the books, not the owners) weren't much use. They all said the same things in different ways. Some facts were different, depending on who was making up the story. I'm sorry, I mean who was recording the history. You know what I mean.

Anyway, I'm long since finished dealing with all the old histories and have found the places where my new ideas can fit. This is where the owners of the books have come in handy. Some of them. When I was able to show them the spots where their histories were weak, I wasn't telling them anything new. The more thoughtful ones were already aware of that.

But when I showed them I could fill in the gaps by using my theories on how language and culture change, they (a few of them at least) were fascinated. Once I told them what I needed, they have been bringing me more information of the right sort, and a very small few are actually beginning to have ideas of their own!

So I now have a following and a delivery system, mostly of greybeard scholars, but useful, since I am not in any condition to get out. I can't walk far, and I couldn't stand to ride for more than half a glass in one of those rattle-wagons they call carriages. As for getting on a horse, if I could, I would fall off laughing at the idea of being there.

I have received three of your letters, numbers one, two, and obviously five, the one that gave me your military address. Imagine, Cheynou Chan, Commander in the Imperial Kyabran Navy! Take care of yourself on that little ship. I don't know much about navies, but on land, the small skirmishers are always the ones that take the most risks.

Captain Jatu came back into port recently. I had the temerity to invite him to visit me, and he came, a bit puzzled, I think. However, once he realized the situation, he took great pleasure in telling me all about your voyages. He has said so many complimentary things about you that I will not repeat them for fear of making you careless.

If you decide to leave the Navy, I am sure there would always be a place for you, or you and your family, on his ship. Or on one of his ships. He has had such a profitable year that he and his backers have decided to build another ship to service the new trade he has found in the west. She will be similar to the *Courser*, but with some new design ideas he has been thinking over. He was particularly anxious that I tell you that he would like to speak to you about the design. He is such a nice man. I can see how he found it possible to put up with you and your habits. Plus the money you made for him.

Notice that I have taken one of your endearing traits and made it my own. If I use it on you, you have only yourself to blame.

More news of home:

Maksa and Miranra came back into town a month ago and were ecstatic at my condition. They have provided well for me, making sure I have the best medical attendants, the finest food of any sort I desire. And I do, believe me. The twins are still the twins, cheerful and serious as usual.

Although the stories tell me that childbirth is not exactly dancing on the lawn, I am quite looking forward to having this all over with. I have dreams in which you come back a year from now and find me lying here, still huge and uncomfortable, doomed to be pregnant forever. And those are only the slightly bad ones.

I am sorry to have spent all this time complaining, but I have so many people depending on me to be cheerful and brave, and you are the only one to whom I can tell the truth. Of course, the truth is probably that I am in a perfectly normal condition, putting up with what every mother has put up with from the beginning of humanity, and, as the woman says, 'healthy as a goat.'

I was about to close the letter with my love when I realized that I must get used to sending 'our' love instead.

So, love to you, dearest Cheychan, from both of us. Please take very good care of yourself and come back to us safe and well.

Kendra the Beached Whale

When he had finished, he immediately read it again. Poor Kendra! She was so used to her freedom of movement. Obviously, her child was already showing its mother's tendencies.

He was grateful to Captain Jatu for spending some time with Kendra and pleased that the captain spoke well of him. The new ship design sounded very interesting. He would look over this sloop with a new eye to see what ideas he could pick up.

So, Kendra's ideas had found a following. Reading between the lines, he suspected that her group of supporters was very small. However, that would be all she needed. Once she started showing results, more would gather round.

He finished, returned to the last two paragraphs, read them again. He had at first assumed that the 'our' meant her and Suta. Read another way, it could mean her and the child. He noted that she had not mentioned Suta by name. Was he reading something into that? How could he?

Now he wished he had prepared another letter to send out, but there had been nothing to say. The secrecy of the military had taken over his thinking, replacing the secrecy of the Trade he had been raised in. He would write a letter for the next mail, now that he had one to answer.

He dearly wished to ask what she had meant, but he must remember his promise. He could only respond and hope something in her next letter made it clearer. Since it was probably clear to anyone but him, he knew it wouldn't happen. He thought of his promise and put it out of his mind.

Then he unfolded the letter and read it one more time.

With a guilty start, he remembered the other document in his hand. Opening it, he read the single line, spun, and sprinted to the wheel.

"Ready about, Helm."

The man looked at him a moment, mouth agape.

"Bosun! Ready to tack?"

"Um...yes. I mean, yessir!"

"Tack over to a close reach when ready, Bosun. I'll have a new course for you once you're around."

"Aye, sir." This standard procedure settled the man down. Cheynou raised his voice. "Ready to tack...! Helm down!"

"Helm alee, sir."

The ship tacked around, and the sailors hustled to trim the sails to the new course Cheynou had set. The action, of course, brought Commander Talinen to the deck.

"What's happening, Mister Chan? Problem?"

"No problem. I just looked at our orders." He passed over the paper.

"I see."

Cheynou grinned sheepishly. "I was a bit too wrapped up in my own mail. Should have read that one first, I guess."

Talinen looked out to the east, where the *Indomitable* was only a dot on the ocean. "Bosun!"

"Aye, sir."

"There's a ship out there, Bosun!"

"Yes, sir, there is."

"Why is she in front of us, Bosun?"

"I don't know, sir. Must be some mistake."

"I'm sure it is, Bosun. Fix it."

"Aye, sir. We'll just do that." The bosun grinned and turned to stare the length of the ship. "Hands to sail trim!"

The sailors, sensing some fun, jumped to the lines, and soon the sloop was a bustle of activity, with sailors trimming lines by minute fragments, changing sails and trying to eke the smallest bit of speed out of the ship that their lore could give them.

Slowly, as the afternoon progressed, the *Valiant* overhauled the other ship, although around the fourth bell it became apparent that the *Indomitable* had joined the race, because her pace increased a fraction as well. It was not enough. Talinen and Cheynou prowled the ship, demanding a change here, a tightening there, urging the sailors to their utmost. Slowly, very slowly, they made up distance.

Talinen paced the bridge deck. "We aren't catching them fast enough, Bosun. These waves are stopping us dead every once in a while."

The bosun turned to Cheynou. "Sir?"

269

"Yes, Bosun?"

"Perhaps you would take the wheel, sir?"

"Me?"

The bosun rolled his eyes.

Cheynou raised his eyebrows to Talinen and received a nod.

A small glow of pride burned up through his chest. He took the wheel gently, feeling the ship beneath his feet, the wind on his face, the pressure on the spokes. After a moment, he spoke softly, as if not to disturb a sleeper. "She's not balanced. She's trying to come up in the gusts. We need to take some pressure off the stern."

"Slack the mizzen sheet?"

"As long as the sail keeps pulling."

Word went out to the sailor at that task.

Cheynou scanned the sails, something nagging at the back of his mind.

"That's better." His eyes roamed the sails, the waves, the ship ahead. Another gust, and the luff of the big mizzen sail fluttered, and the ship heeled over. Then he had it. "We can get more out of her. Rig a block from the mizzen boom to the lee rail. Pull it down."

Out of the corner of his eye, Cheynou could see a puzzled frown. "When you let the sheet out, the boom rises, and the shape of the sail is too full. It flutters and heels us over. You need to vang it down on a close reach like this, flatten it out."

"Oh. Aye, sir. I understand."

Talinen watched the proceedings with interest. Once the mizzen sail was pulling well, he nodded. "What about the others?"

"Let's get this one working first. It's complicated. Bosun?"

"Aye, sir."

"That sail has to be trimmed in and out with every gust. You need a man on the sheet, another on the vang. They have to talk to each other and to me. I'll call the gusts."

270

"Aye, sir."

Cheynou glanced around, raised his voice. "You understand me, men? When she gusts, the sheet goes out, the vang comes in. I'll come up a bit. Once she's on the new course, you both ease a bit as she comes up to the new speed. Then, when the wind drops, I'll bear off a touch, you bring the sheet in, let the vang out, and we start all over again. I want that sail full, but not too full."

"Aye, sir."

"Understood, sir."

"I hope so. Gust coming."

"Easing, sir."

"Vang in, sir."

"Well done. Can you feel her pick up speed?"

"Aye, sir."

"All right, she's up to speed. Gently, now, ease them."

"Easing, sir."

"Now! Feel that?"

"Aye, sir."

"She's hit the groove, sir."

"Right, but now the wind's easing."

"Sheet in, sir?"

"That's right. Don't ask me, don't wait for the command. Just bring it in."

"Aye, sir."

"Commander?"

"Aye…I mean, yes, Mister Chan?"

"We can work the main this way as well, but the communication is more difficult with the sailors farther from the wheel. Jibs are easier, because the sailors know how. Sheet in when it gusts, out in the lulls. The idea is to keep the angle of the sail to the wind the same."

"Bosun, did you catch that?"

"Aye, sir."

"Set it up. Best men on."

"Aye, sir."

"Tell them to take it very easy. A fingerlength either way."

"Aye, sir."

Now the gap between the two ships was closing faster. Soon, the *Valiant's* crew could see the frantic activity on their quarry.

"They're breaking out the big reaching jib, sir."

Cheynou glanced over to *Indomitable.* "Can they hold a reacher on this course?"

The First Officer answered. "Doubtful, sir. They'll have to bear off in the gusts."

Cheynou grinned. "Then shall we keep on as we are and just sail over the top of them?"

Everyone on the bridgedeck grinned.

"As you were, men. Lively now, gust coming." He spoke to Talinen, almost as an afterthought. "It wouldn't hurt to have ours ready, though." Orders snapped. With minimal fuss, a large, light jib was flaked out on the foredeck.

Soon, the crew was working in closer and closer harmony, and information began flowing back to the helm, as well.

"Gust coming, sir. Three shiplengths."

"Thank you. Ready, men. There it is. Ease her into it. There, there! That's it."

"He's got his eyes closed again."

"Pay attention to your line, sailor. Easy, now, it's going...it's...gone. Can you feel that?"

"Aye, sir."

"They've pulled in the reaching jib, sir."

"Too late."

"Flat spot ahead, sir."

"Where away?"

"A point upwind. Five lengths, sir."

Cheynou peered forward. Sure enough, oily smooth water warned of a calm patch. "Prepare to ease all. Softly, now. Reaching jib ready?"

"Ready, sir."

"No hand-over-hand on the halyard. I want three men on the tail. When I call, you run down the deck with it."

Three burly sailors took the line, spitting on their palms for grip.

"Run it up as I bear off. Now!"

Gently, he allowed two spokes to slide past his fingers. Three sets of calloused feet pounded along the planks, and the sail zipped up the inner forestay.

"Sheet her in. Jibs ease. Just a touch." On the new course, the big, loose foresail was able to fill, and he could feel the *Valiant* surge ahead.

A quiet cheer came from the sailors as they ran down towards the other ship. Soon, the call of "Her stern is abeam, sir," came from the bow lookout.

Cheynou searched the sea upwind and ahead.

"Coming up again."

"Reacher ready to drop."

"On my command...now!" The sailors handed the canvas in efficiently, and now the two ships were running side-by-side, a chain between them, with identical sailplans, holding identical courses. "Concentrate, men. Now it's boat-for-boat."

"Gust coming."

"We're headed. Trim in, I'm bearing off."

"Sheeting in, sir," came from several voices.

"I'm on course. Ease."

"Easing, sir."

Cheynou glanced over and caught their opponent changing course a few beats later. Now the *Indomitable* mainmast was opposite his position at the helm. He smiled at Talinen. "That's all we need. If we can beat them to a wind shift twenty times, we'll be ten lengths ahead."

"We do that all day, we'll be a league ahead."

Cheynou glanced at the sails, the sky, the sea, and then at the crowded deck. "Perhaps, but we can't double-watch all day."

Commander Talinen looked around in amazement. Every sailor on the ship had a hand on a line somewhere, eyes intent on sails, the water, the other ship. Even the cook was on deck, passing mugs to men who could not leave their posts.

Fortunately for the captain and crew of the *Indomitable,* the call of "Sail, ho!" rang from the lookout, and soon there were two other ships within sight of the deck, reaching down to them from the west. As they approached, they tacked over, and the little fleet ran in formation towards the rendezvous point, a protected harbour in the lee of an offshore island tall enough to provide a good lookout.

The commodore was rowed over to his flagship with Commander Tuchan. As he reached the deck, he gazed around with some interest. "What's been going on, Commander Talinen?"

"What do you mean, sir?"

"Only that your crew looks like they've been promised a double grog ration, and the *Indomitable* looked definitely unhappy as we rowed by. A little race, perhaps?"

Talinen grinned. "We did give them a good start, sir."

Commodore Gargia nodded. "Healthy competition. Good for morale."

Commander Mendar, captain of the *Indomitable,* was not so calm. He was a lanky man, and his arms waved as he expressed himself loudly. "What in the Lady's name did you do, Talinen? I've never had another sloop sail over the top of me. Not one so similar."

"Secret weapon, Commander."

The other captain frowned, following their glances.

"You haven't met Commander Chan, I gather."

"I haven't had the pleasure." The two exchanged proper bows.

"Now, what's this about a secret weapon? Some new sort of sail?"

"Helmsman, Mendar. You ever heard the expression 'I could beat you with my eyes closed?' Well, Mister Chan can do just that."

The man's disbelieving stare was met with nods all around, even the commodore's.

"You mean he steers with his eyes closed, and this makes your ship go that much faster?"

They nodded again, but Cheynou took pity on the other captain. "It isn't quite like that, Mister Mendar. I do steer by the feel of the ship, but the crew of the *Valiant* was working the sails very closely as well."

"I'll say they must have been."

"To get the very best out of a ship, the orders can't be going only one way."

"You have sailors giving orders?"

The others smiled, but Cheynou stayed serious. "Not orders as such, but the sailors do send information back to the helm. Wind shifts, changes in pressure on their sails, that sort of thing. I also want them to make changes without being told. If they wait for an order, it takes just that much longer to make the change. Also, if they are responsible for the changes, their attention is on their task, not just waiting to be told."

"Sounds like a recipe for chaos, to me."

"I wouldn't try it with any but a superbly trained crew."

The captain shook his head. "I can't argue with success. I've never had another ship sail over me like that." He looked at Cheynou suspiciously. "With your eyes closed, you say?"

"Only sometimes, when I really want to concentrate on the feel of her."

"Ah."

"However," the voice of the commodore broke in, "it is time that Mister Chan earned his reputation with more than helmsmanship."

That brought their attention around. The commodore motioned to the table, and they all sat. He remained standing, a sheaf of papers in his fist. "We have new orders from the admiral. He is not happy with our lack of success." He raised a hand to forestall the protests. "He is not unhappy with us. Just our lack of success. He is unshaken in his suspicions that the pirates are coming from this area. He just wants more information and quicker, before the winter storms make travel in the Southern Ocean too difficult."

"We're going into the Southern Ocean."

"Exactly. Our enemies aren't coming to us, so we will go looking for them." His eyes fixed upon Cheynou. "And this is where you can help us."

"I have been thinking along the same lines, sir. I'm not very familiar with the habits of the Eastern Fleet, but I can give you an idea of their general pattern at this time of the year."

"Good."

"The Southern Ocean is most dangerous in the winter, so they aren't as free to go where they want. In the fall, they try to store as many provisions as possible. Since the farmers have all just brought in their harvests, that means raiding. And since the whales are migrating, that also means whaling."

"Where?"

"It's the oncoming of winter that drives it. In the fall, the whales move from the Far South, where they spent their summer, to the north and east. Nobody ever followed them far enough to find out where they go, but they pass that way. So, the Eastern Fleet will be moving farther east as the fall progresses, whaling and raiding as they go. They raid sporadically, because the whales are far offshore. They'll be moving slowly, because whaling takes time."

"Which means that if they follow their usual pattern, they will be moving away from us."

"Not if they started well to the west of us. They might be moving right past us."

"I see. How can we tell?"

"A couple of ways. We go into the Southern Ocean and head east. We check on the shoreline communities. If they've been raided, we'll know the fleet has already passed. Or we move farther South, straight out into the Ocean, and look for whales. If there are none, then we are too early or too late."

Talinen held up a finger. "And if there are only a few whales, we have to stay long enough to see if the numbers are increasing as at the front of the migration, or getting fewer, as at the tail end."

"Exactly."

"How far south do we need to go to intersect the path of the whales?"

"I'm sorry, sir, but that I can't tell you. Three hundred leagues to the east, where the Eastern Fleet meets them, they come to within a hundred leagues of the shore. Since they are coming in from the Far South, I have to assume they are considerably farther offshore at this point. Perhaps as far as two hundred leagues or more."

"We can sail that in four or five days. Less if the winds are good."

"The winds will be good, sir."

"You can tell?"

"The prevailing winds are from the northwest, sir, and they blow from storm to gale to storm and back again all winter. Right now, they'll be running about twenty knots, steadily, all day, every day, unless a storm blows through. Waves average two fathoms high."

"So if we string out in a line and sail a bit west of south for four days, we'll ride fast and easy and we should see either whales or pirates, or maybe both."

"That's my best guess, sir. Unless we've missed them completely, because this political upheaval has messed up their schedule."

"How likely is that?"

"Not very. Nothing changes the traditions."

"And if it has, is that bad or good?"

Cheynou spread his hands. "It's anybody's guess, sir. When things were stable, there were no raids in the north. So if things settle down, maybe the raids will stop."

"But you don't think so."

"No. There is too much upheaval, too many disaffected ships. Some of those will be breaking away, now that they know there are such ripe pickings in the north."

"And you think they know this?"

"Word will get around, sir."

The commodore mused a moment, regarding the map. "We'll be in a tough position if we do meet them because they'll be upwind and can cut us off from this strait and safety. Once we get around them we can beat back up to the strait, but up to that point, we could be in trouble."

"I'd agree, sir. But perhaps we should bear away east some, so if we have to scramble, we'd be coming upwind, at an advantage."

"It goes against everything I've learned, to stay downwind for safety."

"I know, sir," Cheynou grinned, "that's what I'm here for."

"Sir?"

"Yes, Tuchan?"

The *Peerless* captain leaned over the map. "We've been here for almost a month. There has been no raiding that we have heard of. I don't see that they've gone past."

The commodore's glance passed the question to Cheynou.

"I agree, Mister Tuchan. However, it isn't just navigation, it's politics. If the Priest-Admiral is worried about losing ships who

278

can escape to the north through this strait, he may keep the fleet far offshore until they are well past here."

"Politics!"

"Mixed with religion."

The other officers chuckled, and the commodore slapped his hand on the table. "So, we're set to go. No sense staying near shore if they won't raid here. *Audacious*, you lead off. Pick a comfortable course that makes us good southing and a bit east. The flagship will take the centre. We'll keep you just in sight. *Indomitable*, stay the same distance to the rear.

"Anyone who sees a sail, turn away. The rest of us will follow. We don't want them spotting us if we can avoid it, and especially spotting all of us. They're much bigger so, with any luck, we'll see their topsails first."

"Our lenses give us superiority as well, Commodore. They don't have anything like that."

"I wonder why not?"

"Tradition, sir."

The commodore shrugged. "Our good luck, then. That means a sailor with tubes in the crow's nest at all times."

"Looking for ships and whales."

"Right."

"Have any of your men ever worked whaling vessels?"

There were dubious frowns around the table.

"It really helps to know what to look for. These are sperm whales, and they spout a tall geyser of breath."

"Oh." Mattos grinned. "I thought we were looking down in the water for them."

"No, you can see them quite a distance away. Not as much in waves like we'll be seeing, but quite a way, still."

"We'll have to pass that along to all the lookouts."

"Anything else, Mister Chan? Anyone else?"

There was no response, so the commodore stood. "Well, there we have it, gentlemen. Up anchor as soon as you return to your ship, *Audacious*, and take the middle of the strait. We'll follow at a distance. No sense being seen together by a gossipy shepherd."

They all nodded and filed out of the cabin.

26. Wreckage

They were two days out, running cheerfully along the wavetops in a beam wind, when an alert lookout spotted a ship to windward and ahead. She was hard to see, low in the water and flying only enough sail to keep her steady in the heavy seas. She had once been a three-masted Familyship, but no longer.

"Look at the damage to the bowsprit and the snapped foretopmast. She's made a bad job of a ramming."

Fowler grinned. "Not that bad."

"Why do you say that?"

"She's still afloat."

Cheynou shrugged. "In truth. Commodore, can we get in closer? There is no likely danger, and they have already seen us."

Gargia nodded. "Commander Talinen, if you will, signal the *Peerless* to stand by and the *Audacious* to fall well astern in case she hasn't been spotted yet."

"Aye, sir."

"Do you see any other damage?"

"Let's approach her across the wind, sir. No sense in letting them know our ship's capabilities."

"Good thought, Mister Chan. Sail accordingly, Mister Talinen."

They stared intently as they neared the stricken vessel. "Damage to the hull on the port bow, sir."

Cheynou nodded. "She's taken a ram, herself. They've got a sail pulled tight over the hole. With these waves, they must be pumping like mad to stay afloat. They have her heeled over to keep it dry part of the time on this tack. If they go on the other tack, the break will be under water."

Gargia stared at the ship a moment. "Do you advise we close, Mister Chan?"

"As long as we stay upwind and keep a sharp lookout for other ships, I see no danger. Their boats could not attack us in this sea. As long as we give them no opportunity to board."

"They would try to board us? A well-manned naval vessel?"

"Usually they would have fifty of the best fighters, fifty more of fighting age. Have you heard the reports of what happened when the Imperial Navy boarded the other Masterships?"

There were grim nods.

"Any ship that has taken that much beating has lost some crew, maybe a lot. But they will fight, have no doubt. Let's just get within hailing distance. I always prefer talking."

The commodore nodded, and the course was set. As they came near, Cheynou thought of the last time he had done this maneuver. "Prepare for a flight of arrows."

There was general movement on deck as everyone found a safe spot to stand near. When the *Valiant* came alongside, a chain upwind, Talinen ordered the sails loosened, and the naval vessel slowed to the pace of the larger ship.

"*Kinshala's Hope.* I've never heard a Familyship name like that. They must be from the Eastern Fleet."

"Hail them, and let's find out."

Cheynou jumped up on the railing, one hand on a stay to steady himself. "Cheynou Chan of the *Valiant* hails the Familyship *Kinshala's Hope*. Do you need assistance?"

There was a pause as the group on the bridge deck conferred. Finally, a voice came back, faintly. "The Sea People take no assistance from strangers." Then the shouter seemed to have a thought of his own. "Who are you?"

"We are sailors who see a ship in trouble. We will not attack. I repeat, are you in difficulty?"

He motioned to the helmsman to move his ship in closer.

Soon, the voice came back. "No, we are just enjoying a pleasant sail on a summer afternoon. What do you want?"

Cheynou translated this witticism, and the officers around him raised their eyebrows. He grinned, slanted his head to one side. "Nobody ever said they don't have a sense of humour."

He turned again to the stricken ship. "We want only information. We have planks and shipwrights and portable pumps. What kind of aid would you like?"

The discussion took longer, this time. Finally, a new voice rang across the water. "Will you parley?"

The Kyabrans looked at each other in surprise. This voice was female.

"We will send a party. Five men."

"Three. Unarmed."

"Three, armed. Do you think we're stupid?"

This time the female voice came stridently across the water. "If you stop to help without thought of gain, perhaps you are."

He translated this, then answered. "Three intelligent men, armed."

"Done."

"Who goes, sir?"

Gargia took a moment. "I must go. Mister Chan, of course. Another officer."

Eyes turned to Fowler. "I guess I'm the only choice, sir."

Talinen clouted his First Officer across the shoulders. "You just want to see the owner of that voice."

The commodore's personal gig rowed them across, and a rope ladder was let down the side of the Familyship. Cheynou climbed it first and stood on the rail, scanning the ship. Several armed sailors observed him from a comfortable distance. Closer, a small group stood ready to greet him. Darker skins prevailed, and most had curly black hair. Another anomaly. He looked back to the gig, nodded to the others to ascend, and jumped down to the deck.

It took a while for the commodore to get up the ladder, giving Cheynou time to assess the ship. She had been hard-used and poorly crewed, at least recently. He could spot a handful of seamanship errors without even trying: lines led wrong, cleated loosely, lying uncoiled. There seemed few sailors about, especially with strangers coming aboard. Where was the rest of the crew?

He spoke in Kyabran to pass this information to Gargia as they waited for Fowler to join them. Then they stepped forward.

"This is Commodore Gargia of the Kyabran Imperial Navy. I am Cheynou the Navigator, once of the Familyship *Eagle*. This is Fowler, First officer of the *Valiant*."

The group moved ahead, led by a stocky woman in sailor's garb. "I am Yasola, once Captain's Wife, now Captain of *Kinshala's Hope*. Welcome aboard."

"Not Priest-Captain?"

"I was never a Priest, never wanted to be one."

Cheynou turned to his party. "She was the captain's spouse, and now she has taken over. He must be dead, along with the other officers."

Gargia nodded. "Tell her we are pleased to be of any assistance we can."

He relayed this information, watching her reaction. Pride warring with caution and real need lined her pale face. "What makes you think we need help?"

He shook his head. "We waste time, Captain Yasola. If your men were keeping up with the pumps, your ship would rise so that you could mend the ram damage. If you could turn a point or two to the north, you could reach calmer water and a safe shore. But you cannot, because turning north exposes the damage to the waves, bringing more water in, and the pumps cannot keep up. You are doomed to run downwind across the Ocean until your crew's energy is spent. When they can no longer man the pumps, you will sink."

The woman's shoulders sagged, and a girl behind her reached a supporting hand to her back. "You speak truth to the point of cruelty, young man. We have no one on board with the knowledge to make repairs."

"There are times when pride is a crime. We can send over pumps and strong backs to man them. We have carpenters who can mend your hull, at least temporarily."

The older woman raised her head and regarded him straight on. "What do you ask in return?"

"Information. We wish the location and condition of the Fleet, and any news of the political situation that has caused this. Which we already know about, in any case." His gesture took in the damage, the group of women and oldsters who backed her.

"All right. We can use the pumps and the carpenters. We have planks aplenty. Once repairs have begun, we can talk."

Cheynou gave the gist of the conversation to his superior, who nodded. "I will return to the *Valiant*. You two stay here to coordinate the transfer. We'll have to run a line between us and sling a pump across."

Cheynou relayed the instructions, and two sailors began to lay out a heavy hawser on the deck. The returning gig towed a light line to the other ship, and sailors on deck there used it to haul the hawser aboard. It was then tied to the mainmast of each ship, and when the helmsmen steered slightly away from each other, the rope came taut.

Then began the laborious process of slinging the heavy pump on a carriage that ran below the hawser and hauling it across to the stricken ship. At the same time, a lighter was lowered to row some sailors and carpenters across so repairs could begin.

While this was happening, Cheynou stood beside Captain Yasola aft of the wheel of the *Hope*. The lad steering was working manfully and with some skill to keep the tension on the line, but the waves were defeating him.

"Big one coming."

The lad looked over his shoulder, nodded gratefully, and began to spin the wheel.

"No, wait until our stern lifts. Feel it? Now, gently."

The helmsman did as he was instructed, and the ship wallowed through the comber but the line stayed tight. Cheynou winked at the captain as the boy's face brightened with pride. She found a faint smile in response.

Two new sailors from the *Valiant* clambered over the rail and rushed to ease the pump to the deck. They freed it from the carriage and whisked it down an open hatchway to its duty in the bilges.

Following the sailors came the *Valiant*'s carpenter and his assistant, who reported to Cheynou. "We took a look from the outside, sir, but we can't see through the sailcloth."

"You need to go below."

"Aye, sir."

Cheynou glanced at Yasola, who turned to the girl who had spoken earlier. She looked like a slimmer version of the captain, with the same dark hair and upright stance. "Molele, take them down."

The girl beckoned the men to follow.

"I think I'd better go with them. They are not familiar with the Sea People's ship design."

The captain nodded, and he followed.

Down below, in the flickering lantern light, rancid bilge water lapped over the flooring of the hold. Cheynou stepped into it, trying not to wince from the cold. Fall was approaching, and the currents from the south were already chilling the brief summer's warmth from the surface water.

Splintered timbers at the waterline showed where the ram had slid along the side of the ship, never quite piercing the thick planking, but opening all the seams. Smaller planks floating broken nearby showed where attempted repairs had failed. The carpenter pointed to one of the massive ribs, showing where it was cracked as well, allowing the damaged planking to flex. With every move, water poured in.

"We'll have to support that, but these beams are in the way. What are they for?"

Cheynou rested a hand on the long, crossed supports that ran parallel to the keel. "These longitudinal braces stiffen the hull. She can be made lighter, and she doesn't flex in a storm."

"I don't think we better put any sideways pressure on them, then."

"No, you push them out of line and they'll snap. Then we're in real trouble." He struggled to remember the design of the Familyship. "What's on the other side of this bulkhead?"

The girl pointed into the water. "I think there's more flooring, down lower, laid directly on the keel."

"If we run braces down from the damaged rib to the bottom of the bulkhead, then support the bulkhead on the other side…?"

The carpenter nodded. "We'll need to see what's under there."

Molele led the way up a short ladder, then down again on the opposite side. The water was deeper here, up to her thighs, and her dress swirled as she moved. She seemed impervious to the cold.

The carpenter peered down into the murky water, felt around with his foot. "Yes, there's solid bracing there." He pulled out his measuring line.

"I'll leave you to it, then, and go back and see what's happening with the pumps."

"Aye, sir. We'll need some square timbers for the bracing. Hull planks will do to support the rib on either side."

"The carpenter's storage is further aft, along this side. I'll send someone to help you and show you where our tools are."

"Thank you, ma'am."

Cheynou nodded. "Good enough. Please show me where they put our pumps."

"Sir?"

He turned back to the shipwright. "Yes?"

The man glanced at Molele, then spoke quietly. "Don't be slow, sir. If we get this fixed in decent time, there's no problem.

But there's a lot of pressure on that broken rib. If it fails and hits one of those parallel stringers, this whole section of the hull will collapse. She'll go down in an hour."

He slapped the carpenter's shoulder. "Then let's get it fixed. I'll pass that along to the *Valiant.*"

"Thank you, sir."

Cheynou motioned Molele to go ahead, and she led the way farther aft through the dark interior of the ship to a scene from purgatory. Waist-deep in frigid water, men and women tugged at the seesaw handles of the pumps, lifting them up, pulling them down, over and over, their faces drawn in the weak light of the lanterns. There seemed to be few able-bodied men, and everyone looked too tired to notice who was passing through.

The Kyabran sailors had dropped the intake from their smaller pump into the water and were swinging on its handles with a will, the efficiency of their equipment and their fresh strength sending a pulse of water through the thick hose at every rotation.

Cheynou looked around one more time. "You need help down here."

"We're doing what we can. We've been pumping like this for five days."

He held up his hands in defence. "And you need help. We'll send more sailors."

"Armed ones?" Her lip curled. "I think you'll need to ask the captain."

"I understand the problem." He turned and climbed up towards the main deck. "You don't want armed strangers on board; we don't want our men to go unarmed on a strange ship."

"And we're sinking, so you win." She pushed ahead and strode along the passageway, her hips swinging.

"There's no need to look at it that way."

She glanced back over her shoulder. "There isn't another way."

"Yes, there is. We are helping you, and you have to show some trust."

"I don't like that 'have to' part."

"Have you looked at our ships?"

"Not closely."

"My ship is less than half the length of this one. She will do twelve knots on a beam reach in winds like this. She will sail within four points of straight upwind. Do you see what that means?"

She stopped and faced him. "It means you're blowing wind. No ship can do that."

"It means we have no use for your ship. She's heavy, slow and in very bad condition. We have no reason to take her over."

"I can think of several."

He gestured for her to move on. "I need to talk to the captain about this."

Wordlessly, she led him to the bridge deck, knocked on the captain's door.

"The Helmsman would like to speak to you, Mother."

"Send him in, dear."

Cheynou noted that little exchange, and moved into the captain's chartroom, so spacious after his place on the snug little *Valiant*. "You need more men, ma'am."

"Is your Admiral willing to send them?"

"Molele mentioned weapons, Captain."

"I can understand the caution. We might have a hold full of our own Raiders, waiting to massacre you all, then take over your ship."

"Something like that. Plus you are dealing with military people. That's how they think."

"And you don't?"

"I'm a civilian, borrowed from my usual berth on a trading vessel to help on this mission."

"And what is this mission that you are on?"

"To investigate some pirates that have been appearing in our waters. Huge, five-masted ships, square-rigged, with hordes of fierce Raiders on board. Sound familiar?"

The captain opened her hands. "Well, at the moment, I don't feel a whole lot of loyalty to those who put us here. I feel much more charitable towards those strong backs down there with those wonderful pumps that push out twice the water ours do. Tell your Admiral that I would be pleased to give him all the information I can. Tell him I would be grateful if he could send over some more men, and they can come armed to the teeth for all I care."

"Mother!"

"No, Molele, face the truth. We are doomed. We have no defences, and these men have two shiploads of trained fighters. We will do as the weak always must: throw ourselves on the mercy of the strong and accept what happens."

Cheynou's heart ached for this proud woman, beaten down to this point. "Ma'am, I don't know what to say..."

"You don't have to say anything, lad. Your people are saving our lives. That speaks loud enough for me. Would your officer meet with me here? I would not like to leave my ship."

"I understand. If I can borrow a pen, I will send a message."

"Can you not signal?"

He grinned. "The Sea People have a few things these wonders of the Inner Sea have not thought of."

She raised her eyebrows, smiled slightly and pushed a writing box across the table to him.

As he finished the note and looked up, Molele was regarding him closely.

"What?"

She smiled, a small twist of the lips like her mother had. "I was wondering what brought you to this position."

"Why? Because you may be heading in a similar direction?"

"That's part of it. You seem so comfortable. How long is it since your ship was Beached?"

"Two years and a bit."

"You have done well for yourself, then."

"Better than most of my people, I'm afraid. They have stayed together and supported each other as a Crew should. It sometimes bothers me that I should have prospered so much more by going my own way."

"I will never leave my Ship!"

He smiled. "Bitter experience tells me that you are not in a position to make that choice."

Her shoulders slumped. Behind the flashing eyes and the quirky smile, she was dead tired, too.

"You should get some rest."

"There is too much to do."

"I disagree. Sooner or later, your captain is going to come to the end of her endurance. If she does not get some rest, someone else should, to have the strength when she does not."

"You think that I...?"

"I think that you are much like your mother, and she is a strong woman. When our people were attacked, we were led by a nineteen-year-old. Her father was killed, and she continued the battle."

"She must have been very brave."

He smiled. "She was more than brave. She was...it is a long story."

"Did you love her?"

"She wasn't very lovable. She had a foot crushed in the battle and she was in pain all the time. She had an incisive skill for wielding the truth like a surgeon's scalpel. She cut exactly where she wanted, and as deep as she wanted, never more." He shook his head. "She was as hard on herself as on anyone."

"You did love her!"

He met her eyes, dark and sparkling in the light that streamed in through the transom windows.

"If it makes you feel happy, you can believe that."

She laid a hand over his. "It does make me happy. We haven't had any romance lately. It's good to be reminded that it still exists."

He slipped his hand out, patted hers gently. "You'll get your romance. There's plenty of nice young men in the Kyabran Empire, just dying for a chance at a beautiful barbarian princess."

"I'm not a princess!"

"You're a captain's daughter. That's good enough. They won't know any better."

"And how am I going to get to this Empire?"

He opened the writing box again, drew her a quick sketch. "Once winter sets in at the centre of the continent, there's a wind that blows off the land. It's cold, but it counters the Northwesterlies we are sailing in right now. If you hug the shore, anchor when the winds are against you and sail when they are fair, you can reach this strait. It leads to the Inner Sea, where the Empire is. The *Hope* is a big ship, by their standards. You could make a living hauling bulk cargoes."

"The *Hope* is also heavy, slow, and in very poor condition. You said that."

He waved away her objection in his enthusiasm. "In fact, if you can make it around to here, there's a town called Port Tenet, at the mouth of the River. Ask for Lady Kendra, tell her I sent you. She'll help you."

"Who is Lady Kendra?"

He grinned. "Another barbarian princess."

The girl shrugged. "Thank you for giving me something to dream about, Mister Chan. I doubt if my captain will go for your plans."

"Think about it. The Masterships are moving west. East looks to me like a good direction. And the Inner Sea has a navy protecting it."

At that moment, the captain returned. "Your Admiral is on his way over again. I will answer his questions. I assume you will translate, Mister Chan." She turned to her daughter. "You, Miss Molele, are officially off watch, and I order you to your bunk. Do you have that clearly?"

"Aye, ma'am." Then her head came up. "You're ganging up on me!"

"Pardon me?"

She pointed at Cheynou. "He just said the same thing!"

"Thus proving our combined intelligence. Off with you."

The girl leaned over and gave her mother a quick peck on the cheek. As she turned to go, she flashed Cheynou a glance that held several meanings: part threat, part entreaty, part speculation. He mused on that as he waited for the captain, her two advisors, and Gargia to settle themselves.

"My admiral wants to know what has happened in the Fleet to cause all this upset."

She drew a deep breath. "A great curse has been laid upon the Priest-Admiral and the Fleet."

"A curse? That's not what I'd call it, but please go on."

"There were heretics, and when the Priest-Admiral followed to chastise them and bring them back into the Fleet, they made unholy alliances and used witchcraft and sorcery to destroy him and his Flagship."

Cheynou nodded. "That would be the official explanation for what really happened."

"What do you mean, what really happened?"

"The new Priest-Admiral is hardly going to admit that twelve Masterships and a like number of their support were put to rout by the remnants of eight Beached Familyships."

The woman glanced meaningfully at her companions.

"Nor are they likely to admit that one nineteen-year-old female mast'n could climb the anchor rode of a Mastership at night, set the whole rigging afire, drop a bomb down the main companionway, and burn the ship."

"One woman?"

"That's right. And she was crippled as well. Nothing wrong with her brain, though. Please allow me to translate our conversation for my admiral."

He did so, allowing the Sea People time to murmur among themselves. Then he turned back to them.

"And what specific ill has befallen the *Kinshala's Hope*?"

"Something similar to your ships, I suspect. We got involved in some kind of political wrangle and didn't even know it. We were whaling, with all the boats out, when two Masterships and their escorts attacked us. By the time help came, it was...too late."

Another suspicion confirmed. "So you have few men left. How many crew?"

She shook her head. "More than a full complement. There were two of us. Only the *Hope* got away in sailing shape. We took the survivors off the *Cutlass* before she sank."

"Now you have two Ship's worth of Families but few able-bodied sailors. Can you handle the ship?"

"If we aren't worn out from manning the pumps and if we don't get hit by a storm, yes. If we can find a sheltered harbour, we might even make her seaworthy again."

"Do you know how far you are from shore?"

"A hundred leagues, give or take. We couldn't keep the time, but we know our latitude well enough. With these repairs, we can make it. The problem is, we can't follow the Fleet. Their raiding will close shoreside trade to us. I don't know how we'll survive the winter, because we'll have to stay near shore to avoid the storms."

Cheynou explained about the winter winds and the strait to the Inner Sea.

"You think we could make that much easting?"

"If you choose your sailing days."

"And we'd be welcomed in this Empire of yours?"

"As long as you follow the rules. Raiding is definitely frowned upon. Three Masterships have tried it, and they have all been Beached. Two Priest-Captains hanged."

"I can't say I'm sad about that."

"Can you give us more information about the Fleet? Real facts, not propaganda from the Masterships."

"I know for sure that the Eastern Fleet is in better shape than the Western Fleet. Your friend who killed the Priest-Admiral rammed a big wedge right down the middle of the Fleet. Two different Priest-Captains were vying for the Flagship, and their supporters had a big battle, burned a lot of ships, killed a lot of people. In the end, nobody won, and the Fleet split in two. They're still sniping at each other and trying to prepare for winter at the same time.

"Us Easterners stayed out of that. We decided to wait and see who came out on top before throwing in with either side. However, when nobody won, there was no strong hand at the helm, and little squabbles suddenly became outright battles. That's what happened to us." She gazed around her ship, then shook her head.

"The Fleet is still mainly together, though, except for a few, like the Springbok and the Eland, which just disappeared."

"Those are two of the pirates that showed up in the Inner Sea. The Gazelle also."

"The Gazelle was Beached, and her Priest-Captain hanged?"

"That's right."

"You seem to be the bearer of much good news, Mister Chan. The Gazelle was a nasty ship with a nasty Crew, and Priest-Captain Telroi was the worst of them all."

"He won't be bothering anyone again."

"Good."

"So, the Eastern Fleet hangs together without leadership while the Westerners fight it out for mastery?"

"That sums it up. Plus all the petty rivalries which have simmered for years and are now breaking out."

"Do you see the whole Fleet breaking up and going their separate ways?"

"No. They'll stay together for safety. A solo ship is too easy a victim for those we have preyed upon all these years."

Hearing this translated, Commodore Gargia shook his head. "These are not good people to have wandering around with knives."

"I couldn't agree more, sir, and I was one of them."

The commodore stood. "Well, it is getting on towards dusk. We will send another watch for the pumps at the seventh bell. Mister Chan, you are relieved of your duty here. I'll get Mister Talinen to send his bosun over to supervise."

"If you don't mind, sir, I'd like to stay here for the evening."

Gargia considered that. "Well, the admiral trusts you. If you disappear in the dark with our sailors and our pumps, I'll not take pleasure in telling him he was wrong."

"I hadn't thought of that, sir. Kidnapped by a boatload of women!"

The commodore grinned. "I saw the captain's daughter eyeing you. At least I don't have to worry about you making any social slips. You ought to be aware of the rules, here."

"Don't worry, sir. I'll be a good little sailor."

"That's what I'm afraid of."

Cheynou turned to Captain Yasola. "How are you for supplies? Food, water?"

"We have a decent supply of staples: pork, biscuit. Nothing much fresh: no energy for fishing. Why? You thinking of staying for supper?"

"If I could. It would be nice."

She laughed, a sort of cracked hiccough. "It's been a while since I thought of anything as being 'nice.' It might be 'nice' to entertain for a change."

Gargia turned to the door. "I will send a boat for Mister Chan and the shipwrights at the seventh bell, with a change of watch for the pumps. He will sleep on his own ship tonight. Until the morning, Captain Yasola."

"Until the morning, Commodore. And I have hope for a happier sunrise than the one I was expecting."

Once the commodore had departed, the woman turned to Cheynou. "So why did you stay? Nostalgia?"

"Some. Also, there are things I can do to help."

"What did you have in mind?"

"First, to check on the carpenters. Then we'll see."

"Please proceed. I assume you know your way."

"There are a couple of twists and turns I wasn't expecting. It's strange, because it all seems familiar, and then it isn't."

"I suppose. Well, carry on."

"Aye, ma'am."

He took a lantern and moved down into the bilges, where the two carpenters were doing most of the work, watched and sometimes aided by three young lads, barely into their teens.

"How's it going?"

"It's going fine. Once we get this brace into position, that cracked rib will stop flexing and it should stop about half of the leakage. After that, it's mostly a matter of caulking and bolting some planks on either side of the crack."

"Can you finish the brace in one bell?"

The man's grin was shadowed in the lantern light. "If I don't stand here talking too long."

"How's our little problem?"

"Once I get this done, we're a bit safer. Still a ways to go to finish the job."

"Need any more help?"

"No, it's mostly cutting and fitting, and then taking it out and fitting it closer. The lads there can understand lifting and holding."

"Fine. The commodore is sending a boat for you at seventh."

"Best we get at it, then. They'll sleep easier if the pumps can float her a half-fathom higher."

Cheynou nodded and headed back to the fresh air of the deck. The captain was beside the helm, giving instruction to a young man who looked about ready to drop.

"Could you use another helmsman?"

"Would you?"

"I imagine I can make her ride easier. Let me work on the sails a bit, first. Do you have two sailors on duty?"

She gestured to two older men, one of whom had a stump where his right hand had been. They followed Cheynou the length of the ship, trimming the sails, correcting mistakes. When he felt his helpers were at the end of their ability to work any longer, Cheynou returned to the bridge deck and took over the wheel.

It was different, being back at the helm of a larger ship, and the *Hope* rode sluggishly through the steep seas. However, he began to get the feel of her, and soon had the vessel moving better.

He knew that anything he could do would help. With the extra pumps and men, the ship would begin to float higher and the damaged area would be submerged less often, leading to less water getting in, and thus letting the pumps catch up more. As the water level fell, the carpenters could mend the break faster. If he could keep her riding easily so the hull flexed less, he could aid the healing process.

Half a bell later, he could already feel the difference.

"You have a deft touch on the wheel, Mister Chan."

He startled out of a daydream of children raised on ships, shading his eyes against the setting sun. "I like steering. It soothes me."

"Soothes, is it? You're working pretty hard for soothing."

He smiled. "Only my body, ma'am. My mind is calm."

"Well, the ship is a lot calmer for it."

"She's riding higher. I think we're getting on top of the problem, now."

"Yes, I can feel the difference in her response."

Cheynou thought a moment. "You know, if we were to put on a bit more sail higher up and turn slightly northward across the wind, the extra heel would lift the injury, and less water would come in. Now that she's riding higher, the waves don't matter as much. Do you have someone who can set a couple of gaff topsails?"

"They are already bent on the masts; we can unfurl them."

"Let's start with the mainmast and see how she takes it."

A sailor with a bandaged head moved slowly up into the rigging, and soon a sail blossomed. When it was sheeted in, Cheynou slowly eased the ship's nose around. The ship heeled, raising her injured side above the waves, and Cheynou began to wind between the wavetops, seeking a smoother path through the swells. He nodded to the captain.

"Let's leave it with just the one. I don't see any point in working your crew any more."

"Kind of you."

"I imagine they'd rather do the work up there than down on the pumps." He glanced over his shoulder. "Look."

There was a scramble on the deck of the *Valiant* as they belatedly realized the *Hope*'s change of course and speed.

"They're good enough sailors, but they just don't have the polish. Landbound all their childhood."

She snorted. "As long as they're good carpenters, they can be as rough as they like."

"Heeling the ship will make their task easier."

"Whatever helps them work faster."

A bell rang seven times on the main deck just as the lighter pulled away from the *Valiant*, rowing manfully to keep up to the Familyship.

"We could slow down, I suppose."

"As long as we don't change the angle of heel."

"We could overtrim that topsail. It will pull less and heel us more."

She gave the order, and soon six burly Kyabran sailors were filing down into the hold. The men going off-watch then appeared, followed by the shipwrights.

"The new men are the lucky ones, sir."

"Why is that?"

"We got that brace well set and it really helped the flexing. Were you steering, sir?"

"You could tell?"

The man grinned. "It eased up considerably, and then she heeled over and the water all ran to the other side of the boat, so I said to myself, 'Mister Chan's had somethin' to do with that.' Helped a lot, not havin' to work underwater."

"Good. I guess we're for our bunks now."

The man looked at his hands, wrinkled and white. "I could use a rest."

"What should I tell the captain?"

"Tell her the pumps will be able to catch up and they can stand down half of them in about a bell. If she has anyone who knows caulking, they can start now. Otherwise, we'll finish it tomorrow. Then we can support that crack and she'll be safe." He took Cheynou's arm. "They aren't out of trouble yet. Tell them not to get feisty."

"I'll pass it on."

Upon hearing this report, the captain insisted on clasping the arms of both the shipwrights.

The carpenter blushed. "If you would, sir, tell her it's a pleasure to help them out." He moved closer. "You realize there ain't nothin' but women, kids and oldsters on this ship?"

"Yes, we knew that. I'm sure they're all grateful. If not for your work, she'd be sunk in the next three days."

"True enough, sir."

"Well, the boat's waiting. You load in, and I'll just say good night to the captain."

The carpenter grinned. "Don't forget to say good night to her daughter, too. We'll wait."

Cheynou turned, and sure enough, Molele was at her mother's side. "Did you get some rest?"

The girl nodded. "She's riding better. Is the hull mended?"

"They got that brace in. She needs caulking now. And remember, it isn't finished yet. Don't put any more pressure on those braces than you absolutely need to."

"I'll do the caulking. I'd rather caulk than pump."

"Well, you'll sleep easier tonight, Captain."

"You certainly will, Mother." Molele took the captain's arm firmly. "Canjala can take the watch. It's bed for you. Right now."

The woman smiled wanly at Cheynou. "Don't bully the captain in front of strangers, dear. It isn't seemly."

"Mother..."

"I'm going. I'm sure I'll see you in the morning, Helmsman Chan. Tell your people that they have our undying thanks."

"I will, ma'am. Good night to both. Sweet sailing."

"Sweet sailing to you."

He turned away, but not before he saw the girl reach up and touch a tear away from her mother's cheek. He vaulted to the top of the rail and skimmed down the rope into the waiting boat. "Let's go home, boys."

They responded with a pull that almost overbalanced him, and a chuckle ran through the oarsmen as they pulled away.

27. Sail Ho!

When Cheynou came on deck at the first bell, *Kinshala's Hope* was a different ship. She had put on more sail during the night and changed course even more northerly. Now she was on a beam reach, heeled over more than necessary. The protecting canvas was gone, and two men were standing on a platform slung over the side, driving oakum into the cracks between the planks. As Cheynou watched, a wave dashed against the ship, dousing them, but they toiled on.

At the speed they were now making, the rowing boats could not keep up, so it was necessary for the *Valiant* to pull ahead and drop Cheynou and the shipwrights, who rowed across to the *Hope* as she overtook them.

It was a different scene on deck. There were people everywhere, working or resting. Children played in sheltered nooks, and some of the older ones were taking a lesson on knots on the forecastle. Captain Yasola met them at the rail, wearing a real smile.

"She's riding well this morning."

"We worked on the caulking all night. We're down to one pump now, and she's floating up to her proper lines."

When he translated this for the carpenter, the man nodded. "We'd better finish that support, then. Shame to have her work all that caulking back out again."

They turned towards the companionway, and Cheynou followed.

Down in the forward hold, there was no water sloshing around, and the planking was flexing very little. A sheen of leakage still trickled down the boards, but there seemed to be no bad leaks.

Molele was there, however, looking considerably worse for wear. Her hair had escaped the bandana that was supposed to keep it out of her eyes. Her skirt clung damply to her legs and her blouse was torn. She and a younger girl were in the process of moving a plank along the wall so that she could reach a spot that needed more caulking.

"Had a rough night?"

She turned. "Pretty bad. It's just so damned frustrating! We get it all caulked, and then the water starts coming in somewhere. We fix that, and it comes in somewhere else. I don't know what to do!"

"You might consider stopping."

"I can't. As long as we keep the caulking in, we don't have to pump, and everybody's so tired. We just have to keep going."

He took her by the shoulders, turned her away from her work. "No, you don't. The carpenters have to finish repairing that rib. Then they can support the weaker planks so that they'll stop flexing and spitting your caulking out."

"Oh. That's good, because I'm…just…so…tired."

To his dismay, she burst into sobs, standing there with her hands limp at her sides, the tears running down her already-wet cheeks.

He glanced helplessly at the shipwright, who frowned and made a 'go to her' gesture with his head. Rolling his eyes, Cheynou did so, putting his arms around the girl and holding her head to his chest. The carpenter grinned, clouted his gawking assistant on the arm and went to work.

As the girl's sobs slowly calmed, he released her until he was standing with one hand on her shoulder and the other behind her head. When she looked up at him, he shook her slightly. "Did you work all night?"

"I had to."

"Molele, there are two or three hundred people on this Ship. Some of them presumably know how to do caulking."

"Well, yes, but they were all so tired."

"And you aren't?"

"I am now, I guess."

"Well, your mother has had a good sleep and is looking very chipper this morning. You, on the other hand, would be a disgrace to be seen on deck. Scurry off and clean yourself up, and report to the bridge deck."

"Aye, sir."

"I like you when you're tired. You don't argue so much."

"Don't think of taking advantage of it."

"Me? Take advantage of a poor, tired girl I just rescued from a terrible death? Where do you find these awful ideas?"

Her head lifted. "Just keep your mind fixed on that 'terrible death.' It could be arranged."

She swung past him, a lift to her step, and he followed, shaking his head. This girl must be made of hull planking or something tougher.

They parted at the main companionway, and he went up on deck. The captain was in the Navigator's Chartroom laying out a course on a map. "I have us placed right here."

He looked over her shoulder. "I'd agree. Maybe a bit farther west, actually. I think your time is about half a glass off."

"Can you correct me?"

"Certainly. We have very accurate timepieces on Navy ships." He glanced at the sky, mostly blue, with scattered, wispy clouds. "When I'm back on the *Valiant*, I'll flash you the time."

"Thank you."

He strolled out to the helm and stood a while, watching the sails, the waves and the wind, as the captain herself was doing.

"Molele was down there caulking all night."

Her mother shook her head. "She's stubborn, that one."

He grinned. "It's only stubbornness when you're wrong. If you're right, it's strength of character."

"Whatever it is, she's got more than she needs."

"As do you, ma'am."

"Me? More than I should have?"

"Perhaps just exactly enough, ma'am."

"A wise response."

"Yes, ma'am. I make it a policy not to offend captains before the second bell."

"But after that?"

"Only if they need it."

"And do I?"

"Not that I've noticed."

"That makes me feel so much better."

"What makes you feel so much better, Mother?"

They turned to see the new arrival. With her face washed, her hair brushed back and a fresh dress on, she looked positively sparkling.

"Helmsman Chan was just indicating approval of my Captaincy."

"He'd better if he doesn't want a swim."

"I had enough of that water yesterday in the bilge."

"So did I."

He turned to the captain. "Have you decided on a course, yet?"

The woman smiled wanly. "It seems strange to hear you say that. I've been Captain for six days, and I don't think I've actually made a real decision yet. It's always just been a reaction to what was happening to me."

"Tale of my life."

"Even now, I don't get to decide on a course. I have to get to shelter and I have to avoid the Fleet, so I go as far east as my Ship can manage until I reach the shore. Then we see how much repair we can handle. Then, maybe, I'll get a chance to make a decision."

"If something else doesn't come along and force you to do something else."

She looked at him a moment. "You really do understand."

"I wasn't joking about my life."

"I'm sorry for you, then. Just as I'm sorry for all of us." She brushed hair out of her eyes, surveying her Ship. "But not too sorry at the moment. I was about to suggest that we could give your pumps back. The sailors, too, I suppose."

Cheynou grinned. "Don't worry. You'll find plenty of men if you start sailing the Inner Sea."

Molele smiled archly at him. "Would you like to join us?"

He grinned back. "I'm tempted, but I have other duties, other commitments."

"Is the barbarian princess one of them?"

"You might say that, but you'd probably be wrong."

"That sounds intriguing."

"Don't count on it. Your mind's off course from lack of sleep."

"Probably."

"Why don't you have a nap? You aren't needed swinging those pumps around."

"I'll gratefully accept your suggestion." She turned to her mother. "I'm off to my bunk. Take care of things while I'm gone."

"I'll do my best."

With a final grin over her shoulder, the girl disappeared below.

"How do you want to arrange this, Navigator Chan?"

He shrugged. "Communications are a problem. Let's pull closer and shout."

They did so, and soon a boat was pulling away from the *Valiant* with the line for the hawser. Cheynou went below to pull the sailors off the pumps and put them on dismantling the system for travel.

It was an easier task to move the pumps to the deck of the lower boat, and soon all was complete. Cheynou and Captain Yasola stood at the rail, nodding with satisfaction.

"A good job, Helmsman Chan. We have an even chance, thanks to you."

"The weather looks reasonable. You'll make shore."

"I think so."

"What would you have done if we hadn't shown up?"

She shrugged. "Continued sailing until she foundered. Put as many people on boats as we could and let the rest die."

He shuddered. "How do you decide who goes and who stays?"

She shook her head grimly. "As I mentioned, I don't seem to have made any real decisions since I took over this Ship. I suppose those choices would have been my first."

"Not choices I would like to make."

"No. I would have had to take the most useful members of the crews. The old and the very young would stay, I suppose."

"What about the crew of the *Cutlass*? Wouldn't you leave all of them?"

"No. We are still one people and our chances of survival would be better by taking the strongest of all."

"A good guide for making the choices, but it wouldn't make it any easier."

"And thanks to you, I don't have to make them." She turned, faced him squarely. "My daughter wasn't speaking off the cuff. We have great need of someone like you. Are you sure you won't stay?"

He shook his head. "My answer stands. Much though I like your daughter, much though you have need...."

He was interrupted by a shout from the other ship. At Talinen's gesture, they steered the vessels closer together. Talinen seemed anxious. "Everyone back to the *Valiant*. Commodore's orders!"

"Send a boat."

The *Valiant* piled on sail, pulled ahead and dropped a boat. By the time it reached the *Hope*, Cheynou had the carpenters and their tools waiting by the rail.

"Sail, ho!" The call came down from the crow's nest on the foremast of the Familyship.

"Where away?"

The lookout pointed off to the south. There was nothing to be seen over the white caps of the waves.

Cheynou turned to the captain. "One of the Fleet?"

"Probably."

"Enemies or friends?"

She shrugged. "Who can tell?"

"Would they have sent anyone after you?"

"I doubt it. They wouldn't have been able to find us. This must be a chance meeting."

"What will you do?"

"Keep on sailing. If they are friendly, we might take whatever they offer. If they are neutral, we keep on heading towards land. If they are hostile, we want to run anyway."

"I know what's going on in the commodore's mind."

"Yes. You don't want to be seen."

"And we have no way of helping you. We're probably leaving."

"What do you want us to tell our people, if they ask about you?"

"As little as possible, but the truth is best. It won't help you to hide anything, and it won't hurt them to know there will be trouble if they come north."

Molele appeared at his elbow, her hair mussed, her face creased from sleep. "Helmsman, if you wanted to stay, now would be your chance. If you don't come across, they won't have time to send the boat back."

He smiled down at her sadly. "Much though I'm tempted, I must go."

She reached up, threw her arms around his neck and held him fiercely. He responded for a moment, feeling the taut roundness of her body against his. Then he gently untwined her arms, kissed her cheek and turned away.

Captain Yasola was politely looking away. "I meant what I said about helping you. If you can make it to Port Tenet..."

The captain smiled. "It could happen, Helmsman Chan. If the Gods will it."

"It has a lot more to do with what *you* will, ma'am."

"I would like to agree. Until we meet again."

The two clasped arms, Officer to Officer, and he turned and dashed for the rail. Balanced there, he looked back. "The time! You're 27 minutes slow."

She tipped him a salute, and he slid down the rope.

He looked back from his seat in the lighter, and the *Kinshala's Hope* rode gamely now, her full sails pulling her through the waves at a decent speed. A small figure at the rail raised a hand, and he waved in return. Then the business of boarding his ship took his attention, and by the time he looked again, they were too far away to pick out any details.

"Are we leaving, sir?"

The commodore nodded. "There doesn't seem to be any other option."

"I agree, sir. If that's a Mastership, there's nothing we could do, and it would compromise our mission."

"We have actually accomplished our mission. With the information the captain gave us, we can go back and tell the admiral what he needs to know."

"Nothing definite, I'm afraid."

Gargia grinned. "I think that's a matter of no news being the best there is."

"True, sir." He turned to the rail, staring at the retreating Familyship. "She asked me what she should tell them about us. I told her to tell them as little as possible, but not to put herself in jeopardy by lying."

The commodore nodded, but did not reply.

"We should modify our course, sir."

"Why? Don't we want to get upwind of that ship?"

"Yes, but we don't want them to realize how close to the wind we can point." He thought guiltily of his bragging yesterday to Molele.

"I suppose. Commander Talinen, give the order, please."

"Aye, sir."

"I don't think they ever spotted the *Audacious*, sir. Captain Yasola mentioned our two ships several times."

"Good. Not that I think our petty subterfuges are going to make any difference, but I would hate to give away anything that might help us."

"I agree, sir."

The commodore cocked his head to one side. "Why didn't you stay, Mister Chan? I hear the captain has a daughter who is quite impressed with you. The shipwright says she's an absolute

309

firebrand. If you hadn't been on that lighter, I wouldn't have stayed for you. You could have returned to your own people."

"Thank you, sir, but it wouldn't be right. Too many things to go wrong, too many other plans fouled up. Besides, it feels wrong to jump ship like that. Even if I'm only temporarily in the Kyabran Navy, I have to show loyalty."

Gargia slapped him on the back. "Well said, lad. Now, I have a way for you to show that loyalty some more. The admiral is going to want a complete written report of absolutely everything you saw and heard, along with your comments on what it all means. You spent the most time on that ship, and you're the one to tell the story."

Cheynou exaggerated a sigh. "Reports and more reports. I must be in the Navy, sir."

"You must be."

The *Valiant* chased her cohorts upwind to the northeast, and the *Kinshala's Hope* ploughed bravely northward, a sail on the far horizon now visible following in her wake.

Soon, the two Fleet ships were out of sight, and the Kyabrans sailed alone on the Great Southern Ocean. There was a lightness in the crew, an easiness in their movements, with frequent horseplay and laughter. They knew they were going home. Cheynou allowed himself the thought of seeing Kendra and the baby, but not for too long. That way led him somewhere he didn't want to go.

28. Back to the Fleet

Cheynou laid his pen on the big plotting table and stretched. "It must be nice to be an admiral."

Admiral Larone looked up from the chart he was studying at his desk. "And this comment is apropos of...?"

Cheynou shrugged. "Nothing in particular, sir. I was just thinking."

The admiral smiled. "That it's tough to be a junior officer, where your decisions are hedged about with orders and rules and don't seem to mean much once you make them, because half the time they are messed up by another order that comes down the chain of command."

"Something like that, sir. I know that feeling must be pretty normal, but I've been thinking about that sort of thing for some time now, and being in the Navy hasn't given me any new perspectives."

Larone leaned back, his head to one side. "A deep thinker, aren't you?"

"I guess so. I'm always considering things, you know? The importance of what we do, short term and in the long run. Doesn't seem to do me much good."

"You think being an admiral would be any better?"

"I suppose not. You have political masters to answer to, and your decisions probably get trumped for all sorts of reasons."

"Exactly. It is the way of life. What have you to complain about?"

Cheynou sat down, his fingers laced in front of him. "It's the idea that every time I make a decision it doesn't seem to be a decision. Not a true decision that I get to make, all by myself."

"I would consider you the last person to be bothered by that. Are you seriously suggesting that you have come from a ship on the Great Southern Ocean to sitting in the office of an Admiral of an Empire you had never heard of, discussing philosophy, through no choices of your own?"

"A lot of the cause of that was far beyond my control. The problem is to separate the parts that are mine, where I actually made a choice of my own free will."

"Free will? You are looking for free will?" To Cheynou's surprise, the admiral seemed genuinely amused. "And you think an admiral has any more free will than a commander?"

"I'm not going to argue the point. I believe we covered it already."

A discreet tap on the door interrupted them. "Yes?"

The door opened, and a midshipman poked his head through. "Dispatch from the admiralty, sir."

Larone glanced at Cheynou. "Free will?"

The secretary frowned uncertainly, then held out the package.

"Is there anything else, Midshipman?"

"No, sir."

"That will be all, then."

"Aye, sir."

Cheynou moved towards the closing door. "Should I go, sir?"

"Wait a moment, in case this has something to do with our mutual problem." He slit open the packet, scanned the first sheet.

"No, nothing new. If you have finished writing up that analysis, you might as well rejoin your ship."

"And what do I do then, sir?"

The admiral lowered the paper and regarded Cheynou. "That is not a question most people under my command would consider proper to address to their admiral after they had been dismissed."

"I understand, sir. It's just that if there are no Masterships about to come raiding, then there isn't anything more for me to do, and I would like to go back to my life, sir."

Larone frowned. "You mean you want out of the Navy? After such a short stint?"

"I'm sorry, sir. I thought it was understood. Like last time, you borrowed me from Captain Jatu because you had need of my special knowledge. If there is no more use for my knowledge, then that need is over, and his need becomes more important to me."

The admiral sat back with a calculating look. "More important to you, but not to the empire. If I tell you that once you join the Kyabran Imperial Navy you don't drop out just like that?" He raised a hand. "No, don't bother to answer. The first opportunity, you'd be ashore and back over those mountains with your own people. Quite rightly, too. We had a deal, and you have completed your part."

"If there is ever a problem with the Raiders, sir, I'd be pleased to come back."

"I'll hold you to that, Mister Chan. I don't think we've seen the last of them, and neither do you."

"No, I don't, sir. That ship we saved made contact with a Mastership. No matter what the *Hope* told them, the Priest-Admiral knows your Empire exists. They consider themselves to be masters of all. They have no fear of anyone. It may take years, but they will follow."

"Well, then, I'm sure you and I will see each other again. I'll draft up orders to have you sent back to Port Tenet with the next mail boat."

Cheynou felt a sudden, unexpected sinking in his heart. "Just like that, sir?"

"Of course. Having second thoughts?"

"No, sir...no, not at all."

The admiral smiled. "Do you need a ceremony? A medal for your service?"

"Not really, sir. The completion of the duty is enough." Cheynou laughed. "It surprised me, that's all. I thought I would be happy, but I was disappointed, too. I think I just have a hard time leaving a ship."

"Leaves you adrift, does it?"

"It feels that way, sir. I don't know why. I suppose it's because I always had my Ship to depend on. Since the *Eagle* was Beached, I haven't had that."

The admiral leaned back, hands clasped around one knee. "Everyone needs something to cling to. Something basic they need to believe in. Once you have that figured out, you can go about getting anything else you want."

"If you know what it is."

"A truth. Deciding on your basic belief is probably the most important choice you make in your life."

Cheynou nodded. "Think of the tragic results if you choose wrong. You could spend your whole life chasing a false ideal. Then, even if you achieved it, where would you be?"

"A lot of people do that."

Cheynou shook his head wryly. "It used to be so easy. For the Sea People, it has always been the Ship. Now that I don't have one…" He suddenly pinned the admiral with his gaze. "What is yours, sir? The flagship? The Imperial Navy? Maybe the whole Empire?"

Larone laughed. "Perhaps only the emperor needs the whole Empire. I'll settle for the Navy." He sobered, leaning forward. "I gather that's not enough for you."

Cheynou smiled. "I'd sooner say it's too big for me."

"Then what is it that you need? What is essential for you?"

Cheynou shrugged. "I'm not sure." There was a moment of silence. Then he spoke slowly. "And maybe I do know, but it's something I can't have."

"Can't have? Never? Sounds like you made a poor choice."

"If you truly need it, I guess it's not really a choice, is it?"

"Could be."

"However, I'm not making any progress on it in the Imperial Navy, so I'd like your permission to seek elsewhere."

Larone smiled. "Understood. As I said, I'll release you from duty with a commendation, on one condition. Next time the fleet anchors in Port Tenet, I'll have you on board as a guest. I have some friends there who would like to talk with you."

"About what, sir?"

"Life in general."

"I'd be pleased, sir."

The admiral rose. "You see? There is an example of one of those decisions. I made it for many reasons, but it is now made, and it is to your advantage. If the Masterships show up in hordes next month and you are off in the west trading, I will perhaps rue the fact. But I have chosen."

"Again, I thank you, sir."

The admiral reached out and clasped Cheynou's arm, one hand on his shoulder. Cheynou stepped back, saluted and turned sharply away.

"Tell your gig to wait awhile. I'll have some orders to take back with you."

"Aye, sir." His hand was on the door latch.

"Cheynou?"

He turned back.

"Have you ever considered that there might be no reasons? That there is no overall purpose to our lives? That all the thinking and worrying really has no meaning?"

"Of course, sir. That part doesn't bother me."

"It doesn't?"

"No. If there is no meaning, then I can do what I like. It's only if there is meaning that I have to worry about thinking, so that I get the meaning right."

"I see." The admiral frowned thoughtfully. "I see." With a faint smile and a slight shake of his head, he motioned Cheynou to leave, and returned to his writing.

As Cheynou left the admiral's cabin, a lightness flowed through him. He was going home! It would be hard to leave the *Valiant*, but... he allowed himself a brief lapse of will. To see Kendra and the baby. Surely the baby had come by now. There had been no letter, but he had expected none. A baby would take up all her time. Life would be very different for her. He wondered where he would fit in.

Another choice he had no control over. No sense worrying about it.

As the *Valiant's* gig pulled away from the flagship, he sat in his usual place, a package of messages on his lap, and looked around at the power of the Kyabran Imperial Navy: rank upon rank of ships, anchored in precise rows. He wondered if that force would ever confront the Masterships in a head-on battle. What would happen? What would the tactics be?

That would be something to ponder in the days to come, so that when the call came, he would have ideas for the admiral to use. For the moment, all he could think about was going home.

29. HOMEWARD RUN

Cheynou leaned on the rail of the *Valiant* watching the wavetops run by, his eye automatically tracing the path he would follow if he was steering. Every once in a while, he would glance back at the helmsman to see if the man was paying attention. He grinned to himself. *Not my problem.*

Talinen ranged up beside him. "Like to take the wheel, Mister Chan?"

"I'd be pleased, Mister Talinen. You in a hurry?"

"No, there's no rush. I just thought you might like another chance."

Cheynou nodded to the sailor he was relieving and grasped the spokes gently, willing the ship through the water. They were running across the southeast winds, riding along the troughs, and once in a while a higher crest would slap the side of the ship, sending a spray of foam across the main deck. He made a game of avoiding these taller waves, weaving the sloop effortlessly through them.

"You were on board the flagship for a long time, yesterday."

"I was."

"Whatever did you talk about? Any specific plans?"

"No, we weren't talking Navy."

"No?"

"Philosophy."

The other commander stood looking forward while Cheynou slipped around a particularly steep roller. "You spent the afternoon talking philosophy with the admiral."

"That's right."

"I don't understand."

Cheynou shrugged. "We were talking about making decisions. You know how it is. You wonder whether you're really making any difference in the world. You wonder why you should bother."

"Oh. The kind of thing we talk about around the boardroom table when we've had a glass too many at supper."

"You have the picture. I think the admiral is a bit lonely. He can't let down and chat with anyone around him because of his position. Me, he can chat with."

Talinen grinned. "And you always have interesting things to say. What I can't figure out is how you get the nerve to say them."

Cheynou steered for a while, thinking. "I guess it has a lot to do with my upbringing. I was the apprentice Helmsman to my father and my uncle. I can never remember a time when we weren't a team. Everyone had his strengths and everyone had his weaknesses. Especially me, of course. But everybody did what he could, and the Ship prospered."

"You spent your childhood learning a trade instead of playing."

Cheynou had to acknowledge the accuracy of that observation. "When you're a Helmsman, it's hard to have friends among the other children. You live such different hours. They're put on a watch when they're ten years old, and from then on, their lives are set: when they work, when they eat, when they sleep. Navigators are up all hours and sleep when they can."

Talinen nodded. "So, you were thrown into the company of adults."

"And they never treated me like a child. I got used to treating them as equals. Gave me the habit. I treat everyone that way."

"Including the admiral."

"Why not? If it bothered him, I wouldn't."

"Well, you won't be bothering him anymore."

"Not unless he needs me."

Talinen looked at his friend quizzically. "And who decides that?"

"Both of us, I guess. He needs me, he sends for me; if I can make it, I come."

"And if you're busy with something more interesting?"

Cheynou grinned. "Then I come a little later."

The commander shook his head. "I can't see the admiral liking that very much."

"He's letting me go. What can he do about it?"

"I don't know. He's a man who keeps everything very much under control."

"Not me!" Cheynou looked out to port. "Look at that one!" He called out to the sailors on watch. "Ease the sheets a bit, boys. Let's take a ride."

The huge wave lifted them, and he allowed the wheel to slip through his fingers. The ship accelerated rapidly, sliding down the dark face. As the crest rushed past, Cheynou called for hardening the sheets and turned back onto the old course again, getting another quick rush across the back of the wave. The sailors cheered as the spray flew in sheets from the bow.

"The cook won't appreciate that."

"No, but it sure was fun!"

They continued through the afternoon, shooting the waves, riding the crests, moving ever closer to Cheynou's freedom.

When they reached Liore, they endured the last element of their mission. Each of them was subjected to a serious grilling on their adventures and the possible effects of the situation in the Southern Ocean. The board of senior Captains took an especially long time with Cheynou, and he was exhausted when he returned to the *Valiant*. Talinen was waiting in his cabin, the wine bottle already open, glasses poured.

"Hung you up and drained you dry, did they?"

Cheynou paused to take a hearty draught of his wine. "They did that. Those are some smart men in there."

"They are the senior officers of the squadron."

"Well, they've got as good an idea of what's going on as I have. Better, even. Between us, we laid out the Priest-Admiral's possible moves, how they might affect our ships, and what we might do about it."

He reached into the breast of his jacket. "Only after they finished with me did they give me this."

"Your discharge?"

"Read it."

Talinen scanned the document, whistled, and grinned. "I told you the admiral had something planned."

"He did. On reserve at half-pay."

"Not bad. But it means that if he calls, you better come running."

"But how can I complain? He made me a captain."

"It was the only promotion possible after commander."

"But I'm too young to be a captain! I couldn't command a ship! I've never even been First Officer."

"Well, you're not expected to command a ship. Notice you're not a post captain. Well, you are posted, but not to a ship. You're on the admiral's General Staff."

"I see. I think."

"It's the same thing as going with our squadron. He made you a commander so you would be equal to us. Now he's made you a captain so you have some clout with the others, should it come to a situation where they need to listen to you."

"I see. But won't they still ignore me, because I'm so young?"

"How old are you?"

"I'm seventeen. Eighteen by your people's reckoning."

The other officer frowned. "How does that work?"

"You folk reckon age by birth date. We reckon it by year. I was born in Winter First, so I've been eighteen for more than half a year by your time. Back on the *Eagle*, I'd still be seventeen until the year was over, at the end of Fall."

"Complicated. Well, don't let your age worry you, Admiral Larone was a post captain in his own right commanding his own three-master when he was twenty."

"He was?"

"I told you. He isn't lacking in intelligence, that boy. Also, there was a war going on at the time."

"A sea war?"

"To some extent. It was against the people of the Western Continent, and I think it's one of the reasons we haven't expanded in that direction."

"Did Kyabra lose?"

"Not really. Of course, our histories say we won a glorious victory, but if you read the accounts carefully, it was a war of attrition. In the end, both sides decided they couldn't afford any more, so they withdrew into their own territories."

"What kind of battles were they?"

"Rather strange, actually. The Westerners don't sail much. They have huge rowing galleys, some with as many as three banks of oars. Same huge bow- and sterncastles your ships have, similar rams. Their main technique was to ram a ship then send in a huge boarding party over the bow. Worked pretty well, if they ever caught one of our ships."

"Then the outcome of the battle would depend a lot on the amount of wind."

"Exactly. It was also a strange war because the Westerners never came very far out of their ports. Their ships couldn't support their massive crews for more than a few days. They were pretty much invincible in their own areas, but we were free to sail where we wanted."

"But it didn't do you any good."

"You can see how it ended."

"Yes. And I have some idea where our shipwrights got some of their designs."

"Yes. It sounds like your people discovered a way to make one of those big galleys self-sufficient."

Cheynou shook his head. "Amazing. Sometimes I understand why Kendra is so interested in history."

"Be good to see her again?"

"Oh, yes. She'll have had the baby by now, that's certain. I haven't heard from her. Probably just too busy."

"I gather babies are like that."

"Speaking of womenfolk, why are you sitting here drinking with me when your fragrant sweetheart is languishing ashore?"

Talinen laughed. "One of the disadvantages of dropping in unannounced. She had an engagement she couldn't get out of. A garden party of some sort."

"Why didn't she find you an invitation?"

"I think it's all ladies."

"Sounds like fun."

Talinen stared at Cheynou for a moment. "You really mean that? You'd walk into a room full of women and find it fun?"

Cheynou shrugged. "Sure. I'd get plenty of attention."

Talinen's fist hit the table. "Want a chance to try?"

"What?"

The other slapped Cheynou's orders. "This is as good an excuse as any. I can go to the party if I take along a newly promoted captain. The ladies will be impressed. Especially one so young, handsome, and romantically barbaric as you!"

"I'm sure they'll be disappointed on the last part."

"That won't matter. Throw on your dress coat and let's go."

"I don't know. That's a pretty strong wine we've been drinking. We don't want to embarrass your fiancée."

The other officer winked. "Why not? Give them something interesting in their little lives."

Shaking his head, Cheynou followed Talinen out the door.

30. A New Beginning

She stood there in her doorway, a bundle in her arms. His pace increased, and she moved slowly to meet him.

It was awkward, trying to hug with the baby between, but they managed somehow. He held the two of them awhile, then pulled back to look at the baby.

"She looks...looks..."

She laughed. "I know. She looks like a baby."

"Hmm. I'm glad she does, since that's what she is. She's a she then."

"Hmm."

"Yes."

"Didn't get my letter, then?"

"Not that letter. I only got the whale one. How is she?"

"Fine. Doesn't sleep much, so neither do I, but she eats well and she's growing. Just the restless type, I guess."

"How are you?"

"I'm great! Tired, but great. I like being a mother." She made a wry face. "It's so much better than being pregnant."

She took his arm with her free hand and steered him into the house. "How was the voyage?"

"Not too boring."

"That's good."

"Had one brush with the Sea People."

"I thought you might. Successful?"

"You could say so. The Fleet's pretty broken up, but still hanging together. Sarasha and Leide shattered the Priest-Admiral's power."

"With a little help from you."

"We all did our share."

"What happened to the ships the Navy took?"

"The crews are Beached."

She grinned up at him. "Die like the *Eagle*?"

"Nothing so romantic. The Navy has the hulls: picking them apart for ideas."

She gestured, and they sat together on the couch as usual. But not quite as usual. "What's her name?"

"Erlena. For my mother."

"That's a nice name. It flows."

"Glad you like it. I told everybody she was yours."

He closed his eyes, took a deep breath, and shook his head. "You always try that on me."

"I know. It's fun."

"And once you've had your fun, then you usually explain."

"Do you remember what I told you about women and their choice? The only important one?"

"I could hardly forget that."

"I told everybody that Erlena is yours. You're her father."

"Why did you do that?"

"She needs a father. I made my choice. I want it to be you."

"But she already has a father."

"No, I told him the same."

"You told Suta that he wasn't the father of his baby."

"That's right. She's my baby. I didn't want him to be her father."

"I'm not sure I'm happy about that."

Her languid poise slipped, and some of the sharp, old Kendra slid into her voice. "Cheynou, somewhere in this world there may be a realm where a woman can choose to do what she wants. That realm is neither here nor now, and a woman must do whatever is required. Happy or unhappy doesn't come into it. So I told him she was your baby."

"Why mine?"

A slight smile. "I think we covered that."

324

"So where is he?"

"He died."

"Oh."

"Yes. Long after he left, though. I broke off with him because I was pregnant with your baby. He understood. He was a soldier, after all. He was leading an expedition against somebody-or-other out to the west and was killed in a skirmish a few months ago."

"I'm sorry. He was a good man. I liked him."

"I did too."

"That wraps it up neatly."

"Yes, but it wouldn't have mattered, Cheynou. She was always yours. Yours and mine."

He peered into the blanket that wrapped the baby. "Don't you think people will notice, sooner or later, that I'm not her father?"

She shrugged. "You're darker than most Sea People. I'm light-skinned. She can be any colour she likes."

"So, what does this all mean?"

"It means what it sounds like."

"You mean, you…that you and I…"

That slight smile again, tinged with triumph.

"But, Kendra, you're older than I am. You're…taller than I am…"

"And I love you."

"You do?"

"Well, I hope so. I've decided that you're going to be the father of my children. You know what that means."

"When did you figure this all out?"

She reached over and laid a hand against his cheek. "I believe the usual response is 'I love you, too.' Or words to that effect."

He pushed her hand away. "No, no. You can't get out of it that easily. You've known that I loved you since that day at the pool on the prairie. When did you figure out the other part?"

She forced his hand down, kept it trapped firmly in hers. "Cheynou Chan, that was not love. That was lust."

"At first, perhaps. What about you?"

"I've loved you for a long time, Cheychan. I was just too afraid of you to let it happen."

"Afraid of me?" He surged to his feet, shaking his head, and turned to stare down at her. "You started this whole trip with me because you thought I was no threat!"

"Yes, I thought it would be fun to travel with you. I never had a little brother, you know?"

"Travelling with me isn't fun?"

"Sometimes. More often wonderful and meaningful." She jiggled the baby to a more comfortable position. "I admit to few mistakes in my life, and no big ones. Except that one." She smiled up at him. "Rather a happy mistake, as it turns out."

"So now I'm a mistake. It sounds like our life together is back on its usual footing."

"That's good, because it's going to stay that way for a long, long time and I have to feed the baby. Look how she's rooting around."

He watched in fascination as Erlena, still half asleep, nuzzled at her mother, her mouth seeking. Then she found the nipple and started sucking happily. Something inside his chest began to ache.

"She's beautiful."

"So will you take her for your daughter?"

"Does that mean I have to put up with her mother?"

"For the rest of our lives."

A thought struck him. "Do I get to make a choice anywhere here? Even a little one?"

"I don't think so."

"Hmm."

"Um-hm."

"I guess I can handle it, if you can."

He slid in beside her, his arms around both of them. They sat for a long, contented time staring out at the fine, crystal blue of the Inner Sea.

"You had this figured out before I left."

"Um-hm."

"Why did you let me go?"

"Kendra's first rule of how to lose a Helmsman. Tie him down with a child when he's just been given his first ship."

"What are the other rules?"

"I'm making them up as I go along."

Erlena burped softly, then went back to feeding. His eyes lingered on the soft hair at the crown of her head, slid to the swell of her mother's breast. He pictured a slim girl stepping over the rocks to a clear mountain pool.

He spoke, as if to himself. "No, it was love. From that moment. Maybe even before."

"It's a prettier story that way." Their eyes met, and they both smiled.

"How soon will she be able to travel?"

"We're pretty well self-contained. Washing diaper-cloths will be a problem. Water or land?"

"Does it matter?"

"Not much."

"Babies sleep well on ships."

"Do they?"

"I think so."

"Well, that's settled, then."

"Did I see a map on the table?"

"A few places I'd like to look into."

"New books, too?"

"Ship design."

"Captain Jatu?"

"Yes. He's anxious to know what you think."

"You seem to have us all organized."

"I wanted to have everything you would need."

There was a long, contented silence. He ran a finger down her cheek, dropped it to caress the softer cheek below. "I have everything I really need, right here."

His gaze slid outward, through the window to the sea beyond. "Now I can try for what I want."

Epilogue — The End of an Empire

"We are in deep shit, sir."

The Thousand-Prime glanced at his subordinate. "Not a correct military term, Espirdo, but accurate." He turned to observe the long line of Warlanders filing out of the rocks, their bright, enamelled armour glistening in the sun, their huge, long-limbed horses prancing.

The officer regarded his three small squares of determined soldiers, their shields locked, their faces blank. He shook his head. "Do we have someone who can talk to these people?"

The younger officer almost shrugged. "I'm not sure what language they speak."

"Then it's up to me, I suppose." Sheathing his sword, he stepped forward to stand alone before his troops.

A Warlander on a sleek black stallion pushed ahead of the ranks and, to the surprise of the Kyabran, dismounted and removed the helm with the fierce visage painted on it. Underneath was a bearded face: handsome, wide browed and calm.

"I am Cabanillas, Prime of a Thousand, of the Emperor's Fourth Legion. To whom do I have the honour of speaking?"

There was no response, so he repeated himself in Frasian, the only other language he knew. To his gratification, the Warlander answered in an accented but understandable version of the same tongue.

"I am Orrik Bren, Fourth of that name to lead the Petrels."

"What is your intention here, Orrik Bren of the Petrels?"

The sturdy man before him settled into the pose of a narrator and began to speak. "One hundred years ago, my people were forced off our ships and onto the Great Prairie on the Roof of the World. It was a difficult life, but we have prospered. From Raiders of the Ocean, we have become Riders of the Prairie.

"But the Great Prairie is not a fertile place. We grow, and the land will not support us. We seek other, more useful earth."

"The ground in this area, arable or not, belongs to the Empire of Kyabra."

"At the moment."

"The Kyabran Empire is a mighty force, not to be toyed with."

"I have little knowledge of your Empire, Thousand-Prime Cabanillas. But I know that in this area, you have no more power than what I see in front of me."

"You seem sure of your facts."

"Sure enough to act on them."

"If I withdraw my men, how will you treat those who live here?"

The burly Warrior shrugged. "We are not a cruel folk. We have endured tyranny and would see no other suffer it. But we take what we need. If your people wish to stay on the land that was yours, they may. If there is no fighting, there will be no reprisal."

"But..."

"They will simply work the land under new masters."

The soldier shrugged. "If I accept, will you allow my soldiers to withdraw?"

The Warlander considered. "In three squads. Each group will follow one of your candles in time after the other. You may gather your people together for ten days. They may take with them what they choose. We have no need of your fabrics and your jewels. We need space to live. We will establish ourselves here."

The soldier's hand swept towards the surrounding mountains. "You are welcome to it. My Empire found it a hard land to tame. We made little profit in these valleys. That is why you have this small resistance to your invasion."

The big man grinned. "Along with the political wrangling back in Kyabraen, where they need your troops to keep the peace."

The Kyabran looked at the Petrellan with new respect. "I do not deny it. Still, you will find this a harsh land."

A deep chuckle. "Compared to the Great Prairies or the Southern Ocean, this is a paradise. Here, we will stay."

The End

Now ends the first trilogy of the Petrellan Saga. For the next events, we must jump four hundred years into the future, to discover the crops that have grown from the seeds planted here.

ABOUT THE AUTHOR

Brought up in a logging camp with no electricity, Gordon Long learned his storytelling in the traditional way: at his father's knee. He now spends his time editing, publishing, travelling, blogging and writing fantasy and social commentary, although sometimes the boundaries blur.

Gordon lives in Tsawwassen, British Columbia, with his wife, Linda, and their Nova Scotia Duck Tolling Retriever, Josh. When he is not writing and publishing, he works on projects with the Surrey Seniors' Planning Table, and is a staff writer for <indiesunlimited.com>

www.ingramcontent.com/pod-product-compliance
Lightning Source LLC
Chambersburg PA
CBHW070626260626
47161CB00007B/2597